KITTY NEALE

Abandoned Child

AVON

AVON
A division of HarperCollins*Publishers*
77–85 Fulham Palace Road,
London W6 8JB

www.harpercollins.co.uk

This Paperback Edition 2013
1

A catalogue record for this book is
available from the British Library

ISBN-13: 978-1-84756-245-6

Typeset in Minion by Palimpsest Book Production Ltd,
Falkirk, Stirlingshire

MIX
Paper from
responsible sources
FSC˚ C007454

I'd like to dedicate this book to Geoffrey and Margaret Hanson, with my love and congratulations on the occasion of their 60th wedding anniversary, which falls on 24th December 2013.

A diamond wedding for a diamond couple who are loved by all their family and friends.

PART ONE

Chapter One

'Look, Mummy, look.'

'Not now, Penny,' Ruth said impatiently. 'For goodness' sake, Carmela, she's supposed to have an upset tummy. Why isn't she in bed?'

'She feeling better, Senora Smeeth, and she want show you her painting.'

Ruth grimaced at her Spanish nanny-cum-housekeeper's pronunciation. Smeeth was almost as bad as Smith and she rebuked her. 'Not Smeeth, Carmel. It's Smyth.'

'Si, Senora,' the short, tubby, dark-haired middle-aged woman said.

Ruth wondered why she bothered. She had been correcting Carmela's pronunciation since the day she had hired her, but it was a complete waste of time. Penelope had picked up the Spanish pronunciation of some letters of the alphabet too, which made the child sound like she had a lisp. This was something else that irritated Ruth, and she was sick of correcting her to the point where she had just about given up.

'Look, Mummy, it's a doggy.'

1

It had been Penny's birthday at the beginning of the month and she was now six years old. Ruth gave the painting a cursory glance and then said brusquely, 'Yes, very nice. Now off you go.'

'Come, Penelope. You Mamma is busy.'

Now that she'd been interrupted, Ruth had lost track of her calculations and, unwilling to go back to the tedious task, she pushed the paperwork to one side. The temperature was rising and the sun blazed down from a clear blue sky on that Monday morning in mid-July. It would be hot outside, but with the blinds drawn and ceiling fans on full, it was relatively cool in her lounge. Ruth's eyes closed, and her mind drifted.

She had been living in Spain for seven years now, leading a totally different life to the one she had left behind in London. Once known as Adrianna, an exotic dancer, she had fled to Spain in 1970 to get away from the notorious and violent nightclub owner, Vincent Chase.

Ruth shuddered, shying away from those memories, and instead recalled her journey to Spain. She had met Laurence Hamilton-Smyth, a well-bred and -preserved older man, whom she decided would be useful to her until she found her feet in a foreign country. Laurence had been smitten with her, offered to put her up in his villa on the Costa Blanca and soon after, when she'd found that she was pregnant, Laurence had married her.

Six months after they married, seventy-three-year-old Laurence had a stroke and died. With no other family, Laurence had left her fairly comfortably off and she enjoyed a luxurious lifestyle, but now Ruth frowned worriedly as she roused herself to once again look at her bank statements. Even if she pulled her horns in, cut down on expenses, she reckoned there was only enough money to live on for another year. Maybe she could get rid of Carmela, but Ruth baulked at the thought of taking on the housework and cooking herself. Anyway, what Carmela earned was hardly going to make a difference. Ruth knew that if she wanted to maintain her present standard of living, she had to find a way to make money, and plenty of it.

When there was a knock on the door, Ruth heard Carmela going to see who it was. There was the sound of voices and this was followed by the clatter of heels across marble tiles as her neighbour and friend, Lorna Johnson, walked in, looking cool though plump in a white cotton dress, her brown hair tied back in her usual unflattering style. Lorna had another woman with her who was slender, wearing pink, flared cotton trousers, a flowery top and a low-brimmed sun hat.

Lorna smiled and her brown eyes were warm as she said, 'Hello, Ruth. This is Maureen Day, my cousin, and she's here on holiday. I've popped round to see if you'd like to join us for lunch.'

Maureen pulled off her hat, revealing a mass of short, curly red hair, her eyes widening as she gasped, 'Adrianna?'

Ruth's stomach turned a somersault. She had never expected to see any of the girls from Vincent Chase's club again, but facing one of them now she managed to hide her feelings behind a tight smile as she said, 'Hello, Lola.'

'How do you know my cousin's stage name?' Lorna asked, looking puzzled. 'And why did she call you Adrianna?'

It was Maureen who jumped in with the answer, 'We once performed at the same club in Soho and that's what she called herself then. Isn't that right, Adrianna?'

Lorna's voice was high as she said, 'A stripper! But you told me you used to be a model, Ruth.'

'I wasn't a stripper. I was an exotic dancer.'

Maureen snorted. 'Still on your high horse I see. You always acted as if you were a cut above the rest of us, but call it what you like, you were still a stripper. It was only thanks to having Vincent Chase as your sugar daddy that you got the top spots.'

'You don't know what you're talking about. I hated Vince and he owned me, kept me isolated, a virtual prisoner in his house until I managed to get away,' Ruth protested, but then wished she had kept her mouth shut as Maureen's eyes narrowed.

'Vince was badly burned when someone set fire to his house, and at the same time you disappeared. The police were looking for you, journalists too, but nobody had a clue where you'd gone.'

All Ruth's composure cracked. 'I don't know anything about a fire,' she lied. 'It must have happened after I left. Please, Lola, when you go back to England, don't tell anyone that you've seen me.'

'I doubt anyone would be interested. Vince died in prison a couple of years ago and he's old news now.'

Ruth found the breath leaving her body in a rush. It took a moment before she could take it in. Vincent Chase was dead. Suddenly it hit her: she felt as though she was free at last – free of him, and free of her fears.

Despite finding out that Ruth had lied to her, Lorna was very fond of her friend. They were as different as chalk and cheese, both in looks and personalities, yet got on well together.

'I really did think you were a model,' Lorna said, yet looking at Ruth it was easy to see why she'd been taken in. Tall and lithe, well spoken, with a haughty manner, Ruth had bearing and poise. She was also a beautiful woman, with long, dark hair, and green, almond-shaped eyes that gave her an exotic appearance.

'Lorna, I'm sorry I lied to you,' Ruth said, 'but you know what the ex-pat community is like. If anyone had known the truth I'd have been ostracised.'

'Who are they to talk or pass judgement? I think a lot of them have reinvented themselves and their pasts too, making themselves out to be something they're not.'

'I know, but imagine the gossip – and I have my daughter to think about.'

As though on cue Penny ran into the room and threw her arms around Lorna's legs. 'Aunty, Aunty, look at my dolly.'

'Hello, darling,' Lorna said gently as she crouched down to hug the pretty little girl with dark hair like her mother, though she had rounded, brown eyes.

Once Penny got over her initial shyness she chatted happily to Maureen who seemed enchanted with her. The chilly atmosphere had lightened, but after five minutes Ruth told Carmela to take the child away.

Penny waved prettily at them as she was led out, and smiling, Maureen said, 'Adrianna, she's gorgeous.'

'I use my real name now so please, call me Ruth.'

'Yeah, all right, and you can drop the Lola,' Maureen said as her eyes swept the room. 'Looking at this place, you've done all right for yourself. Have you found yourself another sugar daddy?'

Lorna gasped in shock. 'Maureen! That's a terrible

thing to say. Ruth's a widow and has been for many years.'

'Blimey, trust me to put my foot in it. I'm sorry, Ruth.'

'That's all right. You weren't to know.'

There was a moment of awkward silence which Lorna filled by saying, 'Let's start again. I don't know about you two, but I'm starving, so would you like to join us for lunch, Ruth?'

'I'm not sure.'

'Come on, Ruth,' urged Maureen. 'As Lorna said, let's start again.'

'All right then. I'll just put some shoes on and then we can go.'

Soon, after walking down to the nearby seafront, they were sitting on the terrace of a small bar eating a selection of tapas. Lorna was glad that she was wearing huge sunglasses as they concealed the tears that had suddenly flooded her eyes. In an endeavour to fight them she tried to concentrate on what Maureen was saying to Ruth.

'I generally don't tell anyone outside of the business what I do for a living so I can understand why you felt you had to keep it quiet, Adria— sorry, I mean Ruth.'

'Don't worry, I find it hard to think of you as Maureen too,' Ruth replied.

Lorna's stomach twisted. She had kept something quiet too – something she should have told Richard when he'd asked her to marry him, yet for as long as she could remember her mother had insisted that it remain a secret. It had even been concealed from the rest of the family, her grandparents, aunts, uncles and cousins, so fearing that she would lose him, Lorna had hidden it from Richard too. He was ambitious, and just before they got married a property developer had offered Richard an engineering job in Spain.

When they married, loving Richard so much, the closeness of the sexual act had been enough for Lorna. With a wonderful career ahead of him, Lorna had hoped that the other ramifications wouldn't matter. For the first two years, they hadn't. They had been happy, with Richard so busy that the subject was rarely mentioned, and if it was she had been dismissive, saying there was plenty of time. Gradually though, when nothing happened, Richard spoke of it more often and Lorna continued the deception by pretending to be disappointed. But she knew that no matter what she did she would never be able to bear the children they both so desperately wanted.

'Are you all right, Lorna? You're very quiet,' Ruth asked.

Startled back to the present, Lorna quickly said, 'Yes, I'm fine. This is lovely wine.'

'Yeah, it ain't bad,' Maureen agreed. 'Here, Ruth, do you remember Yvette?'

Ruth frowned in thought. 'Was she a hostess?'

'Yeah, and when Vince's place closed she tried for a job at the Playboy Club in Mayfair. She fancied being a Bunny Girl.'

'Did she get taken on?'

'You must be joking. With all the rich and famous people that frequent the Playboy Club they only want the best. Yvette didn't pass muster.'

'Where is she working now?'

'In "Kats", and I'm performing there too.'

It all sounded like another world to Lorna. She could remember the shockwaves that had gone through the family when it came out that Maureen was a stripper, but she was fond of her cousin and refused, like some of them, to ostracise her.

'Lorna, all this must sound dreadful to you,' said Ruth.

'Not dreadful, just strange,' she answered, forcing a smile.

'You're lucky to have Lorna for a friend,' Maureen told Ruth, 'she's got a good heart and never judges anyone. How long have you known each other?'

'We met three years ago, soon after Lorna and Richard moved here.'

At the mention of her husband's name, Lorna's stomach churned again. Things had come to a head when Richard said he was worried that it was his fault, and he'd been so concerned for her feelings that she just couldn't lie to him any longer. She had broken down, at last telling him the truth.

It had been the beginning of the end. Richard had looked at her differently, worked longer hours, buried himself in his career, and stayed away from home more and more. Then, three months ago, having met someone else, Richard left her for good.

Tears welled again, and this time as they rolled down her cheeks, Lorna had to take off her sunglasses to wipe them away. 'I . . . I'm sorry.'

'What's wrong?' Maureen asked her worriedly.

Lorna knew that she couldn't keep it to herself any longer and said, 'It . . . it's Richard. I know I told you he's away on business, but the truth is, he's left me.'

'Oh, Lorna, why didn't you tell me?' Maureen said.

'I . . . I thought he might change his mind,' she stammered, 'but he's found someone else and wants a divorce.'

'The bastard,' Maureen spat. 'If I get my hands on him I'll have his guts for garters.'

'No, no, you can't blame Richard. We . . . we've been having problems for a long time, and it's my fault.'

Ruth probed, 'What sort of problems?'

'I . . . I don't want to talk about it, but it means our house will be sold and I'll have to go back to England.'

'Surely you'd rather stay here?' Ruth said.

'I would, but once the mortgage is paid off there'll be little equity to split between us. I'll hardly have enough to live on so I'll have to find work.'

'Aren't there any jobs here?' Maureen asked.

'Yes, but as I can't speak Spanish I'd be limited.'

'Lorna,' said Ruth, 'with business opportunities opening up now that Franco is no longer in power, more and more Brits are moving to this area. I'm sure you'll be able to find some sort of work.'

'I'd probably be able to get a job in an English-owned bar, or restaurant, but the pay is terrible and wouldn't be enough to cover the rent on a flat. I was a secretary in England so if I go back I should be able to get a job with a decent salary.'

'Well, love, I know you ain't keen on your stepdad, so if you come home and need a place to stay until you find your feet, you'd be welcome at my place. I've only got one bedroom but you can kip on my couch,' Maureen offered.

'Bless you, and I'll keep it in mind,' Lorna said, and not wanting to spoil any more of Maureen's holiday she forced lightness into her tone. 'I feel better now that I've told you . . . a trouble shared as the saying goes, so how about we let our hair down and order another bottle of wine?'

'You're on,' Maureen said.

The wine was drunk, and then another bottle ordered, the conversation ranging from Maureen telling them about the Queen's Silver Jubilee that had been celebrated earlier in June with street parties all over the country, then on to the latest punk fashion that they all hated and music, with Abba a firm favourite.

At four o'clock, arms linked, all three young women somewhat unsteadily walked home.

Ruth's head was thumping from the effects of the sun and alcohol. She wasn't that bothered that Lorna might be returning to England. Ruth had never had any deep feelings for anyone, only herself, but it was something she'd learned to hide from a young age. She copied others, pretended to care when it was expected of her, feigning affection, and at times, if necessary, sympathy.

Impatiently she told Carmela to keep Penelope quiet and went to lie down for an hour, the blinds down to shut out any light. The overhead fan cooled her naked body until she eventually dozed off.

On waking, Ruth took a tepid, refreshing shower, her mind clearing, only to settle on her problems again. She had to find a way to make money, and within a year.

When she had fled to Spain, Ruth's dream had been to open her own nightclub. Only this time, instead of being a performer she would be the boss, with everyone dancing to her tune. That plan had been shelved when she'd found herself pregnant, and since her marriage, followed by becoming a widow, Ruth had been able to lead the life of a respectable woman of means.

However, with the coffers growing low, maybe it was time to resurrect those plans – yet as this thought crossed her mind, Ruth knew it wouldn't be possible. Even if she sold the villa, it wouldn't give her enough capital, and though Spain was more liberal now, it would be some time before any bank would lend a lone woman the money to set up a decent-sized club. That left her one choice. To return to England, something she could do now that Vincent Chase was dead. If that was what it would take to own her own business, then that's what she would do.

'I'm sorry, Senora, I have to leave now,' Carmela said as she led Penny into the room.

Ruth glanced at the clock. It was six o'clock, and she reluctantly said, 'Yes, all right. I'll see you tomorrow.'

As Carmela left and Ruth took charge of her daughter, her mind was still on the future. Thinking about it a little more, she realised that even if it was possible, the thought of setting up a nightclub left her cold. Ruth enjoyed her status, her standing in the community and having left that sleazy world behind, she didn't want to return to it. There had to be something else she could do, something that wouldn't cost a fortune to start up, but a lot depended on how much she'd get from the sale of the villa.

She'd have to get an agent round to value it, but since inheriting the place Ruth had developed an interest in the property market and had a fair idea of what it would sell for. That train of thought sparked an idea and she felt a frisson of excitement. She lacked experience, but surely it wouldn't be that hard to learn and not only that, it should be relatively easy to set up.

Yes, her idea could work, Ruth decided, and as long as she employed experienced staff, her own lack of knowledge wouldn't be a drawback. Of course, as she spoke very little Spanish, it made more sense to open the business in England. There was no fear in that thought now, and as long as she kept well away from the Soho area of London, it was unlikely that anyone would ever recognise her.

In fact, she had no need to live in London. She could choose anywhere in England to run a respectable business – safe then in the knowledge that she had left her tawdry past behind.

Chapter Two

Maureen woke late the following morning. She had a quick shower and then threw on a thin cotton dress before going to look for Lorna. She wasn't in the house, but Maureen saw her sitting outside on the terrace. Lorna looked so sad, and though she had said it was her fault, Maureen still cursed Richard for leaving her cousin.

In an attempt to cheer Lorna up, Maureen threw open the glass doors and danced her way outside, loudly singing last year's Abba hit, 'Dancing Queen'. Lorna's expression immediately lifted and she joined in, waving her arms in the air as she sang along. When they finished the chorus, Maureen joined her cousin under the huge parasol that shaded the garden table where she saw a basket of fresh bread, and a selection of jams.

As Lorna poured her a glass of fresh orange juice, she said, 'I hope this is all right. I don't usually have a cooked breakfast.'

'It's fine, thanks. Perfect,' Maureen assured her and tucked in while looking across the terrace to the small garden beyond. It was a nice little house, but nothing compared to Ruth's stunning villa with its large swimming pool. She felt a twinge of envy, a resurfacing of the jealousy she'd always felt when it came to the woman she'd known as Adrianna. Yet it wasn't just jealousy. There was something about Adrianna that had repelled her and still did – something in her eyes that was cold and calculating. She was a mother now, yet it was still lurking there beneath the surface and contradicted her friendly smiles.

'What would you like to do today?' Lorna asked. 'We could go down to the front and take a dip in the sea.'

'I can't swim, but I'll be happy to paddle and sunbathe,' Maureen said. So far, there had been no mention of Richard, but if Lorna wanted to confide in her, she'd listen. If not, rather than upset her cousin, Maureen decided not to probe.

'After that, we'll come back here to change and I'll show you a bit more of the area. Perhaps have lunch further along the coast?'

'That sounds good to me,' Maureen said.

Thankfully Lorna hadn't suggested asking Ruth to join them, and that suited Maureen just fine. Lorna seemed fond of Ruth, so for her cousin's sake Maureen had put her feelings to one side, and though it looked like they were getting on well together, deep down she didn't like Ruth, and never would.

Ruth was eating a solitary breakfast. She was deep in thought, planning her business venture, yet the more she went over it, the more daunting it became. Maybe she should just forget it – think of another way to replenish her coffers, but nothing suggested itself. The thought of working for someone else didn't appeal, and anyway, other than exotic dancing she lacked any skills. Ruth's memories drifted back to the clubs again; to her

14

performances, the men ogling her, and she shuddered, determined that no matter what, she'd never return to that life.

What she needed, Ruth finally decided, was to talk to someone with business experience – someone who could advise her. Her late husband's friend, Charles Pentlemore, came to mind. He'd run a successful wholesale business in London before retiring to Spain and though what Ruth had in mind was different, he still might be able to provide some of the answers she needed.

Ruth had bumped into Charles socially on many occasions since Laurence had died, but hadn't seen him recently. He sounded a bit surprised to hear from her when she rang him, but agreed to meet her for lunch.

That left Ruth the rest of the morning clear, so after a leisurely swim she was in a good mood and allowed Penny to join her in the pool. Her daughter had learned to swim almost before she could walk and was like a fish in water, ducking and diving, frolicking like a seal until Ruth grew impatient at being splashed and climbed out.

'Mummy, watch me,' Penny called.

Ruth towelled herself while looking at her daughter's exuberant antics, but then called Carmela to take over her supervision. She would shower now, and then dress to impress before going to meet Charles Pentlemore.

'It's lovely here,' Maureen said as they left the beach to walk along the wide promenade. It had been too hot to sunbathe for long, but she'd been reluctant to go, as a good-looking bloke had been giving her the eye. Deep down she dreamed of meeting a nice man, of settling down and having a couple of kids, but nice men didn't want to date strippers. The ones who ogled her in the club only wanted her for one thing, but she wasn't going to oblige, well, not unless they had very deep pockets, Maureen thought with a chuckle.

'Hello ladies.'

Maureen turned and was chuffed to see it was the bloke from the beach, a friend with him. 'Hello to you too,' she said flirtatiously.

'Would you like to join us for a drink?'

'No we wouldn't! Go away!' Lorna said sharply.

His eyebrows shot up at her tone, but then he shrugged, 'Fine, please yourself. Come on Barry, let's go.'

Disappointed, Maureen watched as they walked away and said, 'That's a shame. I rather liked the look of them.'

'You can go for a drink with them if you want to,' Lorna said, a touch churlishly, 'but I'm too upset about Richard to even think about other men.'

'Of course you are,' Maureen said, ashamed of her insensitivity.

'Oh, Maureen, I'm sorry for being such a misery. You're on holiday and I'm spoiling it for you.'

'Don't be daft. I haven't seen you for ages and I'd rather spend my time with you,' Maureen assured her cousin.

Lorna gave a smile, albeit a small one, and soon they were back at her house having a cold drink before they changed to go out to lunch.

Maureen wore a blue mini dress and, mindful of the sun this time, she picked up her large-brimmed cotton hat. Lorna appeared in a below-the-knee flowery yellow dress that was cinched in at the waist and did nothing for her plump figure. As usual she wasn't wearing a trace of make-up which was a shame, Maureen thought. Lorna was so negligent about her appearance, but with the right clothes and a decent hairstyle, she would look really attractive.

'Are you ready to go?' Lorna asked.

Maureen nodded, glad that there was still no mention of Ruth joining them. The less she saw of her, the happier she'd be.

Unaware of Maureen's feelings, Ruth was on her way to her lunch appointment dressed in a cool, cream linen dress, the thin brown belt around her slim waist matching her sandals and handbag. She had brushed her hair back to fasten it at the nape of her neck, and her make-up was carefully applied to emphasise her slanted, green eyes.

At twenty-nine years old, Ruth knew from the attention she drew that she looked good. With her chin slightly raised, she walked haughtily into the restaurant, where she saw Charles at a table set for two.

'Ruth, it's lovely to see you,' he said as he rose to his feet to kiss her on both cheeks. 'How are you?'

'I'm fine,' she said, taking the chair that Charles pulled out for her.

'You look wonderful, my dear. I've already ordered a bottle of white wine, but if you'd prefer something else . . . ?'

'A chilled wine will be lovely.'

'Well, this is nice, Ruth. I haven't seen you since that do at Joyce Mapleton's place. You were with a young chap from the British Consulate; Rupert wasn't it, or Roger?'

'Rupert.'

'Yes, of course. How is he?'

'I have no idea. It wasn't a serious relationship and he was posted elsewhere months ago, the Far East I think.'

The waiter arrived with the wine and after he had opened it they ordered their food, both choosing just a salad. While they waited, Ruth didn't bother with any more social chat and instead outlined her plans. 'So you see, I don't know if the sale of my villa will provide sufficient capital to set up the business. I'm hoping you'll be able to advise me.'

'You would probably be able to lease premises, though of course it depends on size and location, but before we look at staff costs and other outgoings, tell me why you want to do this, Ruth?'

'Financially I have no choice. It's a question of needs must.'

'I assumed that Laurence had left you comfortably off?'

'I thought he had too, but I'm afraid I only have sufficient funds to last me for about another year. After that . . .' Ruth trailed off.

'I see,' Charles mused, his gaze somehow speculative as he looked at her. 'So that's why you've come up with the idea of opening a property agency.'

'Yes, and as I've seen the rising trends, both here and in England,' Ruth enthused, 'I think there's money to be made in that area. I could manage lettings.'

Charles reached out and laid his hand over hers. 'Ruth, commerce is a man's world and a beautiful woman like you shouldn't have to worry about business matters.'

The salad arrived and Ruth was glad of the diversion as it gave her an excuse to pull her hand away. From the way Charles was looking at her she was becoming uncomfortably aware that he was flirting with her. He was in his mid-seventies, with white hair above a tanned face that was lined with age. After being one old man's trophy, she wasn't going to be another's. She grew tense now as she looked down at her meal without appetite.

'Ruth, I could help,' Charles said as he picked up his cutlery.

'That's very kind of you, but I'm not looking for a partner. I just need advice on setting up the business.'

'You misunderstand me, my dear. I wasn't offering a business partnership. I'm a wealthy man and I'm offering to look after you. I'd see that you'd want for nothing.'

Ruth managed to stay calm, but only just, her tone hard as she asked, 'And just what would you want in return? No, don't tell me, I can guess.'

With a sickly smile, Charles said, 'I'm glad we understand each other.'

Ruth removed her napkin from her lap and threw it on the table as she reared to her feet. 'I came to you for advice, that's all. I may have financial problems, but I'm not for sale and never will be!'

'Ruth . . .'

She ignored his call and marched out of the restaurant. Ruth had wanted advice, but instead she'd been propositioned. It sickened her, but she had also learned a valuable lesson. By showing her financial insecurity, she had made herself look vulnerable. It had been a mistake, but one that she would never make again.

Chapter Three

Maureen had flown home that morning, leaving Lorna feeling down in the dumps. Her cousin's exuberant presence had helped to keep the agonising thoughts of Richard with another woman at bay, but now the house felt empty again and a sense of loneliness washed over her. There was really only one person she could confide in, one who would understand why Richard had left her, yet Lorna doubted her mother would be sympathetic. Despite that, for a moment Lorna was tempted to ring her, but fearing her mother's reaction, she decided against it. She had always felt that her mother was ashamed of her and she would probably just berate her for telling Richard the truth, something she now decided to hide from her.

Lorna could barely remember her father. She'd been just four years old when he died in a tragic accident, and then, just before her thirteenth birthday, her mother had married again. From the day he had moved into their home, Lorna had felt that Ted Redman resented her presence and she had never been able to think of him as her stepfather. She had felt in the way as her mother's life began to revolve around Ted, and even now when she went to visit them, he made her feel so unwelcome that Lorna was glad to return to Spain.

Lorna felt lost, alone, with no one to turn to as she faced an uncertain future and was almost on the point of tears when there was a knock on her door. Glad of the distraction, she hurried to answer it.

'Hello,' Ruth said brightly. 'I've called to see if you and Maureen would like to come round to my place for lunch and a dip in the pool.'

'That sounds lovely, but Maureen left this morning.'

'Did she? Well that explains why you look a bit down. I assumed she was here for a fortnight.'

'No, just a week and I miss her already.'

'Come swim with me, Aunty,' Penny urged.

Lorna was used to this routine. Carmela didn't work weekends and if Ruth knew that Richard was away she was fond of inviting her round to keep her daughter amused. Not that Lorna minded. She enjoyed being with Ruth and Penny, but her heart was heavy at the thought that this time Richard wouldn't be coming back.

As Penny tugged at her skirts and looked up at her appealingly, Lorna forced a smile and said, 'All right, darling, I'd love to swim with you.'

'And you'll stay for lunch?' Ruth asked.

'Yes, and thanks. I'll just get my swimsuit,' she said, thinking that a dip in her friend's pool and then lunch might take her mind off Richard and her financial worries for a while.

They walked to Ruth's villa, where on the back terrace sun loungers were set around the kidney-shaped pool, with parasols to offer shade. They were soon making the most of the water, Penny frolicking and Lorna happy to play with her while Ruth, after a short dip, settled on a lounger.

It was Lorna who saw to Penny when they both climbed out of the pool, and when the child was absorbed with her dolls, shaded by the fronds of a palm tree, Ruth suddenly sat up and said, 'I'm going to sell my villa and return to England.'

Lorna hadn't seen a sale board outside and surprised, she gasped, 'But why?'

'If you must know I'm bored with my life here. I'm still only twenty-nine and want to achieve something for myself. With that in mind I intend to set up my own business.'

It seemed a bit odd to Lorna. Ruth was wealthy and had never shown any signs of boredom, her life a constant round of social activities and shopping for lovely outfits, along with hair and beauty treatments. 'What have you got in mind?' she asked. 'Are you going to open a hair-dressing salon, or something like that?'

'No, and you'll probably think I'm mad, but I'd like to go into the property business.'

'I used to work in an estate agency so I certainly don't think you're mad.'

'Did you? I had no idea,' Ruth said, looking suddenly animated as she perched on the edge of a lounger. 'I thought you were a secretary.'

'Yes, I was, for the owner of an agency. I handled his paperwork, and also did typing for the sales team.'

'Lorna, this is wonderful. I'll be able to pick your brain.'

'Mummy, I'm hungry.'

Ruth rose to her feet and said impatiently, 'It's impossible to talk with these constant interruptions. I'll make us some lunch and then Penny can have her afternoon siesta.'

Lorna called Penny over and hugged her, thinking that Ruth didn't realise how lucky she was to have such a lovely daughter. Tears welled in her eyes. She felt empty, lost and alone again, made worse by the knowledge that for the rest of her life she would be longing for something that she could never have.

Ruth had been busy since her encounter with Charles. She had spoken to an agent about selling the villa and it had been interesting to see how he worked. Photographs of the property had been taken, a board would go up shortly, and now he would market the villa, none of which seemed overly difficult to Ruth for the amount of commission he charged. She felt the procedure used would be virtually the same in England, but finding out that Lorna had worked for an estate agent was a stroke of luck.

'Please, sit down,' Ruth said, after placing a bowl of pasta salad on the dining room table, along with some cold cuts of meat and cheeses. 'I'll just get the bread.'

When she returned, Ruth saw that Lorna had put a selection of food on a plate for Penny and had cut it up for her, the child eating happily. Hopefully, after her antics in the pool and a full tummy she'd be tired, her siesta a long one. When she saw that her daughter's plate was empty, Ruth rose to her feet and said, 'Come on, time for your nap.'

Penny obeyed immediately, which was no more than Ruth expected. The child knew better than to play her up and Ruth ushered her to bed, abruptly telling her to go to sleep before closing the door.

'She's such a good little girl,' Lorna said when Ruth returned to find her clearing the table.

Impatient to gain information, Ruth said, 'Leave that. I'll do it later. You carry our drinks onto the terrace and I'll get a pad and paper to take notes.'

'Ruth, I don't think I'll be of much help to you,' Lorna said when they sat down. 'I was just a secretary.'

'I'm sure your job was very valuable and you must have seen the workings of the agency.'

'Well . . . a little I suppose . . . but . . .'

'There's no need to look so worried,' Ruth interrupted. 'All I want to do is to run my ideas by you to see what you think. I don't expect you to give me expert advice.'

'Oh, that's all right then.'

'To start with, I want to set up in an area that offers potential for lettings and therefore property management too. With that in mind I've been considering somewhere on the coast where I could get in on the holiday rental market. What do you think?'

'I somehow thought you'd want to go back to London.'

Ruth shook her head. 'I have no desire to live there again.'

'In that case the coast sounds like a good idea.'

'I'll shortly be getting in touch with some commercial agents to get an idea of the costs involved in leasing premises, ideally ones with living accommodation above. As I have no experience myself, I'll have to employ at least one negotiator, maybe two. What sort of salary will they expect, Lorna?'

'I have no idea. I didn't handle the wages, though I could tell you what sort of office equipment you'll need if that would help.'

'Thank you. Perhaps you could write me a list,' Ruth said, while thinking that it would be of little use to her.

'If you handled the accounts, perhaps you could give me some idea of what profit margins to expect.'

'I'm afraid I can't help you again. My boss used a qualified accountant.'

This was a waste of time, Ruth thought. Lorna wasn't going to be much help. Not that it really mattered. Most of what she needed to know she'd be able to find out easily enough once back in England. Her biggest problem was Penny. It would be impossible to set up and run a business with a child in tow so she'd have to find a replacement for Carmela. However, this time, as she'd be working on Saturdays, ideally Ruth wanted someone who could live in.

With a sigh, Ruth knew that it was unlikely she'd be able to find the right person until she was back in England so for now she put the problem to one side and said, 'Would you like another cup of coffee, Lorna?'

'Yes please, I'd love one, and if you don't mind me asking, when are you putting this place on the market?'

'I already have and hope it won't be too long before I get a sale.'

'I think I'll have to return to England too, but I'm a bit worried as my office skills are rusty. I'll have to stay with my mother until I find a decent job, but I'm not looking forward to it.'

It was then that Ruth was struck by an idea that felt heaven-sent, and if Lorna agreed, it could solve both of their problems. She leaned forward eagerly. 'Lorna, I might be able to help you. How would you like to work for me?' she said, going on to explain what she had in mind.

* * *

Lorna went home, her mind reeling. She hadn't really wanted to leave Spain, a country she had come to love, yet without Richard her mood was so grey that the blue sky and sunshine felt a mockery. The thought of seeing him with this other woman was unbearable too, yet probably unavoidable if she remained in Spain. That alone was enough to drive Lorna away and she had almost decided to go back to London. The only thing that held her back was the thought of staying with her mother and Ted until she found her feet. Even Maureen's kind offer of a couch was preferable to that, though it would mean living in Soho.

Now though, Lorna had been given another opportunity, and it was one she had told Ruth she would seriously consider. She flopped on the sofa, deep in thought. Despite what she'd put Richard through, he'd been generous in telling her to draw out what money there was in their joint bank account. It wasn't a huge amount and she'd been worried sick about her finances, but now she'd been offered a job.

As a former secretary, Lorna wasn't sure she'd be any good as a nanny, but Ruth had also said she could work part time in the agency when Penny was at school. With the possibility of accommodation included, along with the decent pay on offer, it was tempting, and as her office skills were rusty it would give her the chance to catch up on her shorthand and typing speeds.

There wasn't really much to think about, Lorna decided. She adored Penny, and as they'd spend so much time together she would be a sort of surrogate mother. With that thought, Lorna made up her mind. She jumped to her feet and rang Ruth to say that she'd accept the job.

26

Chapter Four

Richard was working on a development further along the coast and rang a few days later to say he had spoken to a solicitor about a divorce. He also said that he wanted to put the house on the market.

Since he'd left her in April, Lorna had been expecting this – yet had hoped as time passed that he might have changed his mind. That proved a forlorn hope now and when he asked her if she'd agree to the sale she choked, 'Yes, all right.'

'I'm snowed under with work, but I'll see about contacting a few agents.'

'I . . . I could do that; find a good local one.'

'As you'll be there to show him around, and any prospective buyers, I suppose it makes sense, but I want to be consulted regarding the price it goes on for.'

'I won't do anything without your agreement.'

'When you know which agent we'll be using, ring me with his number and I'll get in touch with him.'

Lorna said she would and then Richard abruptly ended the call. He had sounded so distant, so formal, but Lorna knew it was no more than she deserved. They had once been so happy, so in love, but her deception had ruined any chance they had of a future together. Richard had someone else now – someone who could give him what he wanted, but the pain was still so raw that Lorna's body began to shake with sobs.

It was some time before she was able to pull herself together, but eventually her tears dried and Lorna splashed cold water over her face. She had to accept it. Her marriage was well and truly over, and she only had herself to blame.

Unhappily, Lorna ambled into the kitchen and began to work her way through a packet of biscuits; as always, when upset, finding a measure of comfort in food. A half hour later, feeling marginally better, Lorna knew that somehow she had to move on, and at least she had taken the first step in accepting Ruth's offer of a job.

It was time now to take the second step. She had to get the house on the market and as Ruth had already found an agent Lorna decided to go round to see her. It was close to August now, the sun beating down from a cloudless sky when Lorna stepped outside, and though it was only a short distance to Ruth's, her face was moist with perspiration when she arrived.

'You look hot,' Ruth said. 'Sit down and I'll tell Carmela to bring you a cold drink. What would you like?'

'Just water with lots of ice would be nice. I've just popped round to ask who you're using to sell your villa?'

'John Manning.'

'What do you think of him?'

'It's too early to say, but he sounded competent enough and seems to think he can get me a sale at the price I'm looking for.'

'In that case, as I'm putting our house on the market too, can you give me his telephone number?'

'Of course,' Ruth said as Carmela came in with her drink.

'Gracias,' Lorna said, wondering how the Spanish woman would feel about the impending loss of her job. Carmela had been with Ruth for a long time, and as she'd cared for Penny since she was a baby, she was obviously very fond of her. 'Does Carmela know that you're returning to England?'

'Yes, I told her before the "Se Vende" board went up outside. I'm just hoping she won't look for another job until we're ready to leave.'

'I suppose it depends on how long the properties take to sell, but let's hope we get buyers at around the same time.'

'It would certainly make things simpler,' Ruth said as she rose to her feet to riffle through a book by the telephone. 'Ah, here's the number. I'll just write it down for you.'

Lorna took the proffered piece of paper, and shortly after returned home to ring the agent. It was another step towards her new life, one in which she hoped she'd eventually be able to find happiness again.

Over the following four weeks, though many businesses in Spain closed down during August, the agent Ruth had chosen continued to work. He brought several people round to view the villa, but with no sign of a sale Ruth decided to listen in when he showed it to a British couple. They were about to retire and appeared to like the villa, but the woman seemed hesitant and asked the agent if there were many other Brits in the area.

'Yes, quite a few,' he said offhandedly, leading them outside to see the terrace and pool. 'As you can see, beyond this area there is a landscaped garden with orange and lemon trees.'

They wandered down to look, while his wife remained and asked Ruth, 'What are the neighbours like?'

'They're very nice. An English woman lives on one side and a very pleasant Spanish family on the other,' Ruth said, and picking up on the woman's concerns she added, 'We have very good health facilities in this area, and it's easy to make new friends as the British social club is close by. They hold regular dinner dances along with bridge and whist evenings. If you play there's a tennis club too, and golf is very popular, with two courses within easy reach.'

The woman smiled and said, 'Thank you, that's very reassuring. I think your villa is lovely, but we have several more properties to see before we come to a decision.'

When they left Ruth decided that if they didn't buy the villa, she would have a word with the agent about improving his sales pitch. When it came to English buyers he not only had to sell the property, he had to sell the area too. It had seemed so obvious to her, Ruth thought, and smiled as she realised that once she got to grips with valuations in England, she might have the makings of a really good negotiator.

Lorna had viewings too, and a few days later, during the first week in September, she took a call from the agent. An offer had been made for the property and at almost the full asking price, for a quick sale with the furniture included. She rang Richard at his office to ask him if he was happy to accept.

He was, and said he'd ring the agent as well as arranging for someone to handle the legal side of the sale. 'Lorna, as the property is in joint names, we'll both have to go before the notary.'

'Yes, I know, and Richard, as I'm going back to England soon, will you split the equity with me before I leave?'

'I'll have to speak to my solicitor about that, but I can't see it being a problem.'

'I won't be making any further financial demands.'

'He'll probably want that in writing, and if the divorce papers aren't drawn up before you leave, he'll need an address for you in England.'

'I don't know where I'll be living yet, but any correspondence can be sent to me care of my mother's.'

'Very well. My solicitor will be in touch. Goodbye, Lorna.'

Before Lorna could say another word she found herself listening to the dialling tone. Richard's voice had once been caressing, soft, as he had whispered words of love, but now he sounded so cold. Tears threatened again, but Lorna blinked to keep them at bay. She had cried so much that she felt emotionally drained, and needing a distraction she hurried round to Ruth's to pass on the news about the sale.

'I'm pleased for you,' Ruth said, unaware of the inner turmoil that Lorna was fighting. 'So far I haven't had any luck. Viewings are few and far between at my price range, but I'm loath to lower the price.'

Unlike Ruth, Lorna knew she wouldn't gain much from the sale of their house and realised that if her friend didn't soon sell her villa it could cause problems. 'The couple buying our place want a quick sale and that means

I'll probably have to move out by the end of September. It'll make things a bit difficult.'

'Difficult? Why?' Ruth asked.

'I'll have nowhere to live, but I suppose I could move back to England and stay with either Maureen or my mother until you sell this place.'

'Don't be silly, there's no need for that,' Ruth said. 'You can move in here until I find a buyer and then we'll return to England together.'

'Are you sure? I don't like to impose.'

'If it will make you feel better, Carmela has just told me that she's leaving. You'll be able to take over from her, so it solves both our problems.'

'In that case, I'd love to move in,' Lorna said, relieved and realising that maybe the quick sale was fortunate after all. She didn't want to make a mistake – to find out after returning to England that she couldn't live under the same roof as Ruth. Now she would find out in advance and if it didn't work out, it wouldn't be too late to change her mind about taking the job.

Unbeknown to Lorna, Ruth was thinking along the same lines. It wasn't going to be easy to find accommodation above commercial premises large enough for them all, but she really did want a live-in nanny as it would make her life so much easier. A lot depended on how well she and Lorna got on, and though unused to considering other people's feelings, Ruth knew she would have to make the effort to be amenable or she would lose her friend.

For now though, she couldn't move on with her plans until the villa was sold. 'I think I might try another agent. I'm not impressed with John Manning.'

'Oh, I found him very good.'

'He's found you a buyer, so you would say that.'

'Perhaps you're asking too much and he'd have a better chance of selling this place if you lower your price?'

'Unlike you, I know the market,' Ruth snapped, 'so maybe you should refrain from making uninformed suggestions.'

'I . . . I'm sorry. I was only trying to help.'

Ruth could see she'd upset Lorna and said, 'I know you were and I should be the one apologising. I've got an awful headache and it's making me a bit grumpy. If you don't mind, I think I'll go and lie down for a while.'

'Of course I don't mind, but can I get you anything before I go?'

'No, I'll be fine. Carmela is here if I need anything,' Ruth said, relieved when her friend left. She didn't have a headache, but had used it as an excuse to get rid of Lorna.

Scowling, Ruth poured herself a gin and tonic. She'd hated having to mollify Lorna, yet knew that this was an example of what was to come. She'd have to watch her tongue, to appear gracious and amenable, but would she be able to keep it up? It was doubtful, but she'd have to try, and of course if she made a success of her business it wouldn't have to last for ever.

Ruth perked up at that thought. In a couple of years, if she could afford the fees, she would send Penny to a boarding school. She wouldn't need a nanny then and she'd be able to live the life she wanted, free of her daughter's encumbrance.

Chapter Five

Lorna moved in at the end of September and as though this brought her luck, Ruth at last had an offer for the villa, which she accepted.

It would be many weeks before the sale was finalised, but in the meantime she made preparations for their return to England. While looking for her commercial premises on the south coast, she knew they would need somewhere to stay. To save on hotel costs Ruth got in touch with an agency to rent a furnished flat, unseen, and just hoped it lived up to the agent's description.

Lorna had been marvellous in tackling most of the packing and so far, other than her being morose at times, Ruth had no regrets that she'd employed her. Of course she was still upset about Richard, so Ruth made allowances for her, and had even pretended to be sympathetic when his solicitor had sent papers for Lorna to sign regarding her settlement.

There had been no further communication from the man since then and it was the end of November when they arrived back in England, finding it cold, the sky grey and a fine drizzle falling. They still had a long onward journey and finally arrived in Margate during the late afternoon. It was raining heavily when they got out of the train, lugging large suitcases onto the platform, and with no idea of which direction to take, Ruth hailed a taxi to take them to the agency to pick up the key.

Adam Mortimer, the man she had dealt with by telephone, wasn't there, but a chit of a girl wearing the latest punk fashion that Ruth found unfeminine and ugly handed them over. It was then a short drive to Harpers Road, where Ruth's already low spirits fell even more when she saw the small, cramped flat they would have to live in.

If she hadn't been so tired, Ruth would have turned tail and marched out again, but it would have meant finding a hotel and she just didn't have the energy. She had settled on Margate because it was a very popular seaside resort. However, from what she'd seen on this dismal day it made her wonder if she'd made the right decision.

Lorna was putting on a cheerful front as usual and said, 'I think what we need is a nice cup of tea. I'll pop along to that shop we saw on the corner to get some basic provisions.'

'Light the gas fire first. It's freezing in here.'

Ruth saw Lorna's lips tighten and even she, who was usually insensitive to others' feelings, could see the strain in her eyes. 'No, it's all right, Lorna. I'll do it,' she quickly said. 'Here's some money for the shopping.'

'Penny looks exhausted and I need to get her out of those damp clothes first.'

'I'll see to her too,' Ruth offered, noticing that her daughter had flopped onto a sofa.

Lorna nodded, took the proffered notes and then

hurried out. After lighting the fire, Ruth sat down beside her daughter. She took in the room: the ugly wallpaper, cheap furniture, and the huge damp patch on the ceiling. Her jaws ground in anger. This was nothing like the agent's description, and while urging Penny out of her coat Ruth knew that she couldn't bear to stay in this dump for more than one night.

After an uncomfortable night in damp and lumpy beds, Ruth told Lorna that she was going to see Adam Mortimer. 'If he can't offer us a better place than this I'm going to demand my money back and we'll move into a hotel.'

Lorna could see that Ruth was in a foul mood and if she hadn't also been disgusted with the flat, she might have felt sorry for the agent. Ruth could be formidable, yet looked stunning in another of her designer outfits, her black coat purchased for an English winter along with long, high-heeled boots. 'We could come with you. I need a bit of fresh air and I think Penny does too.'

'I'm in a hurry and Penny always dawdles. Take her out for a walk, but don't go far because when I get back we'll be moving again,' Ruth said assuredly while pulling on her leather gloves.

As soon as she left, Lorna urged Penny into her coat, scarf, woolly hat and mittens. She was a beautiful child and looked so cute that Lorna hugged her before she put on her own coat. Penny was easy to look after, rarely naughty, a girly girl who loved dolls and all things pink.

When they left the flat, Lorna turned left to head for the sea. Harpers Road was deceptively long, but they eventually came to an intersection and, unsure of which way to go, she asked a middle-aged woman for directions.

'You just need to turn left and then first right into King Street. You'll see the sea in front of you and a nice parade to walk along. Mind you, it's a bit nippy today.'

'Yes, it is,' Lorna agreed, and after thanking the woman she followed her route.

Shortly they were there, looking at a rough, grey sea and immediately to her right Lorna could see the harbour. It couldn't compare to the turquoise sea and sunny coast of Spain that they had left behind, yet as Lorna saw a long sandy beach in the distance, she felt this would be a lovely area in the summer.

Despite the dismal weather, there was something about Margate that drew Lorna – a historic charm, from the cobbled streets she had seen in the Old Town, to the Victorian architecture. A strange, shivery feeling suddenly washed over her. She was a Londoner, yet Lorna somehow felt that she had come home.

From the moment the woman walked into his agency, Adam Mortimer couldn't take his eyes off her: she was stunning, and obviously classy. From behind his desk he immediately rose to his feet. With a practised, charming smile, he said, 'Good morning. How can I help you?'

'Are you Adam Mortimer?'

'Yes, that's me. Please, sit down,' he offered.

As they both sat the woman said brusquely, 'You can help by finding me something far superior to the flat in Harpers Road. I refuse to stay in that hovel for another night.'

'Harpers Road? Oh, you must be Mrs Hamilton-Smyth. You rang me from Spain?'

'Yes, that's right, and you offered me what you

described as a lovely, spacious flat. It isn't lovely. It's a dump!'

Seeing her face to face, Adam wasn't surprised that she didn't like the flat. The double-barrelled name should have given him a clue. Ruth Hamilton-Smyth looked like she belonged in the Ritz but he recalled their conversation and, wondering if she had fallen on hard times, he said, 'For the rent you wanted to pay, I'm afraid it was the best I could do.'

Her lips tightened as she argued, 'I could have offered more rent, but as your description of the flat made it sound perfectly acceptable, there was no need.'

'I'm sorry if you feel I misled you,' Adam placated her, thinking now that she might be well off. He was rarely this patient towards troublesome tenants, but this woman was different and he found her intriguing. 'If you're happy to pay more I can show you another couple of flats that you could move into straight away. One has sea views, while the other is in Upper Dane Road which is next to Dane Park,' he said, finding the details for her to look at along with the rental costs. 'However, with the seafront property you'd have to sign an agreement to rent the flat for a minimum of six months.'

'No, I only want to rent on a monthly basis while I look for commercial premises.'

'Maybe I can help. What sort of premises are you looking for?'

Her eyes swept the office. 'Something similar to these would be ideal, especially with living accommodation above.'

'There is a large flat upstairs, but it's rented out as I prefer not to live on top of my business.'

'Have you got any like this on your books?'

'I'm afraid I don't handle commercial property, but as I know agents in the area I'll put out some feelers for you,' Adam offered.

'Thank you,' she said, smiling for the first time.

'What sort of business will you be starting up?'

'A property agency.'

'I see. So, you'll be going into competition with me.'

'Hardly,' she said; her expression distasteful as she looked around his untidy office.

Adam found her superior attitude a bit annoying, but managed to mask his feelings behind an ingratiating smile as he said, 'As you want to rent a flat on a monthly basis, that only leaves the one in Upper Dane Road.'

'It might be suitable,' she said, looking at the details, 'but I can't see any mention of a second reception room? I employ a nanny to look after my daughter and ideally I would like one for her use.'

'There isn't one, but there is a separate dining room.'

'I suppose that could work. Could you show me the flat now?'

'Yes, of course,' Adam agreed, impressed that she employed a nanny. It smacked of class again, but why rent a flat if she had money to buy a property? It was a bit of a mystery and he wanted to find out a few more things about Ruth Hamilton-Smyth, mainly if there was a man in her life.

Adam hoped not. If the woman had money she could be of use to him – and from what he'd heard so far, in more ways than one.

After locking his office, Adam Mortimer led Ruth to his car. He was tall, very good looking, with blond hair and grey eyes, and Ruth had already noted his expensive suit, silk shirt and tie. He reeked of money, from his expensive cologne to his snazzy Jaguar, but Ruth's mind was on other things as he drove her to Upper Dane Road.

If she could lease premises set on a corner, just like Adam Mortimer's, they would be ideal. She liked the large windows facing out onto two streets which would be perfect for showcasing properties, and once settled into another flat she'd go to see every agent she could find in her search for something similar.

It wasn't long before Adam lifted his hand from the steering wheel to point ahead. 'There's Dane Park. It looks a bit bleak now, but it's very nice in the summer.'

'Yes, I'm sure it is,' Ruth murmured unenthusiastically.

Adam Mortimer must have picked up on her tone and said, 'Margate comes alive in the spring and summer. The Dreamland amusement park attracts thousands of visitors, and there are other attractions too. It's my busiest time, as I handle a great deal of holiday lets.'

Ruth liked the sound of that, and her mood lightened.

'The flat I'm showing you is on the ground floor and I think you'll like it,' Adam said as they drew up outside an obviously well-maintained, redbrick, end-of-terrace house.

When they went inside, the first room they entered was at the front with light streaming in from the bay window. It looked freshly decorated and that pleased Ruth, along with the furniture. It wasn't anything special, but the green sofa and chairs with wooden arms looked fairly new. They moved on to the rest of the rooms, and though the kitchen wasn't huge, there was enough room for a small table and chairs which meant that Lorna could have the dining room.

Adam Mortimer opened the back door to show her a small, low-maintenance garden, but as Ruth didn't expect to be there for long she only gave it a cursory glance. On the whole she liked the place. It was more expensive to rent than Harpers Road, but still worked out a lot cheaper than staying in a hotel.

'Would you like to make an appointment for your husband to see the flat?'

'I'm a widow so that won't be necessary. The flat is fine and I'll take it.'

Adam Mortimer drove her back to the office to sign the paperwork. Ruth had expected an argument over the refund of her deposit, but there was none as the man just transferred it to the new agreement. She was warming to him now, more so when he offered to drive her back to Harpers Road.

'Thank you. That's most kind,' she said.

'It gives me an excuse to spend a little more time with you,' Adam Mortimer said as they walked back to his car. 'In fact, if I'm not treading on anyone else's toes, I'd like to ask you out to dinner on Saturday night.'

Ruth quickly thought about her reply. Adam had already proved useful in offering to get in touch with commercial agents, and she might be able to use him to her advantage to find out about the holiday rental market. Smiling, she said, 'Thank you, I'd like that.'

'Great, how about I collect you at seven-thirty?'

'That's fine,' she agreed, thinking as they drove to

Harpers Road that things were really looking up. All Ruth needed now was to find the perfect commercial premises, and then she could get her agency up and running.

Chapter Six

Lorna had rung her mother to tell her that she was back in England, and that there might be post arriving for her, but so far she still hadn't received the divorce papers from Richard's solicitor.

Ruth was so busy that Lorna hadn't liked to ask for any time off, but hoped that in the New Year she'd be able to take a short trip to London to see her mother. The closeness they'd once shared had dwindled when her mother remarried and Lorna had to admit her part in that. She had been a sullen and stroppy teenager who had resisted Ted Redman's intrusion into their lives. Ted in turn was an impatient man who demanded her mother's attention, and to placate him, Lorna was often sent to her room. She had felt hurt, neglected and had put up a wall, an emotional barrier that separated her from her mother and to some extent, it still remained.

Though it wasn't quite the same, it hadn't taken Lorna long to realise that Ruth too had little time for her daughter, rarely showing Penny any love or affection. Lorna had no idea why, but as it wasn't to do with a man, she wondered if it had something to do with Ruth's childhood. Perhaps her own mother had been cold and unloving, but Lorna was loath to pry. Ruth didn't like talking about her past, so to make up for her mother's lack of affection, Lorna smothered Penny with lots of hugs and kisses.

They had become very close, Penny like the child she would never have, and soon after moving into the flat, Lorna had found a local infant school for her. However, as it was near to the end of term she wouldn't be attending until after the Christmas holidays.

Ruth had purchased a car and was out most of the day looking at commercial premises, while as Christmas drew closer Lorna had kept Penny amused making festive decorations. They were now hanging up in the lounge, along with a small tree festooned with baubles and fairy lights that Lorna had found in Woolworths.

It was now the Friday before Christmas Day which would fall on Sunday and that afternoon Lorna was making mince pies. Penny was helping, but Lorna had to giggle at the sight of the little girl covered in flour, and there were bits of pastry stuck in her hair. Lorna put the pies into the oven and then lifted Penny down from the stool. 'Come on, let's get you cleaned up before Mummy comes home.'

She had barely got Penny into the bathroom when the front door slammed, then Ruth appeared in the doorway. 'That was another waste of time,' she said huffily. 'The premises were far too small and the price they wanted for the lease was ludicrous.'

'Never mind, something is sure to turn up soon,' Lorna soothed. 'I'll just give Penny a wash and then I'll make you a nice cup of tea.'

'Look at the state of her! What on earth have you been doing?'

'We made minth pies, Mummy.'

'Don't lisp!' Ruth snapped. 'It's mince . . . not minth.'

Lorna saw Penny's eyes welling up with tears and said, 'Penny was with Carmela for a long time and has picked up her Spanish pronunciations.'

'I'm well aware of that, but we're not living in Spain now.'

'Give her time and I'm sure she'll grow out of it.'

'See that she does,' Ruth ordered.

Annoyed and unable to hold it back, Lorna said crisply, 'Yes, madam, certainly, madam.'

There was a moment of silence and Lorna expected Ruth's temper to erupt, but instead she laughed, saying, 'Goodness, Lorna, for a moment I thought you were going to stand to attention and salute me too.'

'It's a wonder I didn't. Sometimes you make me feel that I'm in military service.'

'Oh, Lorna, I'm sorry,' Ruth said, looking contrite. 'I don't know why you put up with me. I've come home in a rotten mood but I shouldn't have taken it out on you.'

'You've upset Penny too.'

'I know, and I'm sorry, darling,' Ruth said, giving her daughter a very rare hug. 'I can't wait to taste one of your mince pies.'

'Aunty Lorna said I should leave one out for Father Chrithmas. Will he be here thoon? I want to ask him for a thister or a brother for Chrithmas.'

'You can forget that. He only brings toys, and you won't get any unless you learn to speak properly. *Soon*, not thoon. Now you try.'

'Shoon.'

Ruth's lips tightened, but before she could open her mouth again, Lorna jumped in. 'Clever girl, that was

45

'nearly right,' she enthused. 'Now close your eyes and I'll wash your face.'

'I'll leave you to it,' Ruth said. 'My feet are killing me and I'm going to get these boots off.'

Penny didn't complain when Lorna washed her face and hands, nor when she brushed the pastry out of her hair, though she wanted to know why she couldn't have a brother or sister. Lorna did her best to placate her, saying that as an only child she was very special, and at last her incessant questions ceased. She was such a good little girl, so easy to love, and it would help when she was at school with other children to play with.

When they returned to the kitchen, Ruth didn't even spare her daughter a glance. It was a surprise though to see her making a cup of tea, and as she spooned tea leaves into the pot, she said, 'I'm seeing Adam again this evening.'

'Will you want something to eat before you go out?' Lorna asked as she went to check on the mince pies. Ruth had gone out to dinner with Adam Mortimer soon after they had moved into this flat, and she now saw him several times a week.

'No thanks. Adam is taking me to a fish restaurant.'

'That's nice,' Lorna said politely and seeing that the pies were ready she lifted them out of the oven. The sweet, spicy aroma assailed her nostrils and suddenly evoked memories that made her stomach knot. Richard had loved her mince pies, but she had lost him and though the pain was no longer so raw, her heart still ached. Tears threatened and she blinked rapidly.

'What's the matter, Aunty Lorna?'

'It's nothing, darling. Just something in my eye,' Lorna said as she hid her feelings by delving in the cupboards

46

to find a wire rack to cool the pies on. She wanted to grab one, to stuff it in her mouth, but knew she would have to wait. Once Ruth had gone out and Penny was in bed, she'd be able to eat as many as she liked, drawing comfort from the feeling of a full stomach crammed with food.

Adam sat opposite Ruth, noting that as always she was dressed immaculately, drawing looks from almost everyone in the restaurant.

'I've tried every agent now and not one of them could show me any decent leasehold premises,' she complained.

'I've talked to my contacts too, but unfortunately there isn't much on offer at the moment,' Adam replied, pretending sympathy. Of course in reality he was happy that Ruth hadn't found what she wanted. It would have ruined everything if she had.

Ruth studied the menu, and when the waiter arrived she ordered soup to start with, followed by halibut in a mustard and dill sauce. Adam frowned at the prices, but had to keep up the facade of being comfortably off as he too went for the soup, and then the lemon sole. In reality, financially he was in a fix, a big one, and this continuous fine dining in expensive restaurants wasn't helping his overdraft. Adam knew that he'd been an idiot, living beyond his means, but he'd wanted it all, an expensive car, Savile Row suits, and though he had liked what he'd seen, there had been no need for him to take on such large premises. Now he was up to his eyeballs in debt and if he couldn't persuade Ruth to fall in with his plans, he stood to lose everything.

'I'm going to have to consider other areas,' Ruth said,

returning to the subject of property, 'perhaps Broadstairs or Ramsgate.'

Adam inwardly cursed that he hadn't considered the possibility of this happening. He'd wanted to gain Ruth's trust before making his move, but now couldn't risk waiting. He had to get Ruth to agree. If she didn't he could lose everything: his premises, his business, and his car.

However, despite desperately needing an injection of cash and having had to let the young girl who worked part time for him go, Adam knew he'd have to tread carefully. Ruth had to think he was doing her a favour so, reaching out, he placed his hand over hers, saying with false sincerity, 'Ruth, I've already checked with my contacts in those resorts, but unfortunately none of them have anything on their books with the square footage and accommodation you're looking for.'

'It was good of you to try and thanks,' Ruth said. 'I'll make a few enquiries myself, but it doesn't sound promising.'

'I'm afraid that premises like mine, especially on a corner plot in a good location, are at a premium and rarely come on the market.'

'Yes, I realise that now, and though loath to do it, I suppose I'm going to have to settle for one of the smaller places I've been shown here in Margate. It will mean continuing to rent the flat which isn't ideal, but it seems I have little choice.'

Their soup arrived and for a minute or two neither of them spoke as they tucked in, but then Adam made his move as he said, 'Ruth, I've just had an idea that could help you, though I'll have to give it some thought.'

Ruth waited, saying nothing for a while as he continued

to eat, but then obviously growing impatient, she spoke. 'Come on, Adam, what's this idea of yours?'

'I'm wondering whether I should offer to share my premises with you. I think there's room enough.'

Ruth shook her head. 'It's kind of you, Adam, but no thanks. I'm not looking for a partner.'

'Neither am I, Ruth. I'm just trying to do you a favour by suggesting that we share my premises. Our businesses would remain separate.'

'In that case I must admit it sounds interesting,' Ruth said, smiling now. 'But how much would this so-called *favour* cost me?'

'Well, Ruth, as a businessman, I can't offer you something for nothing.'

'I don't expect you to.'

'Right then, how do you feel about a lump-sum contribution towards the original lease and a fifty-fifty split of the bills? That would make it equally beneficial to both of us.'

'That sounds fair financially, Adam, though when I think about it, in other areas I don't think it could work. We would be in competition when it comes to lettings.'

Adam had already thought of that and was ready with his answer. 'Ruth, as I'm already in competition with existing agents in the area, one more, and a fledgling one at that, won't make much difference. I'm very well established, so much so that there are times during the summer season when I'm so busy that I can't take on any more clients. When that happens, instead of mentioning my contacts in other agencies, I'd be happy to pass them on to you.'

The waiter arrived to clear away their soup bowls, and

Ruth said nothing until he had moved away again. 'Adam, thank you, but I still don't think it would work. I've got so many plans for how I want my agency to look, the décor, the furnishings and though your premises are in an ideal location they're in a bit of . . .'

'A mess,' Adam finished for her. 'Yes, I know, Ruth, but I'd be happy for you to take the place in hand.'

'How would we divide the space?'

Adam cocked his head to one side and chewed on his lower lip as he pretended to give it some consideration. 'When I think about it, I don't really need a lot of room and I suppose I could use the back office while you have the whole of the front.'

'Really? That would be marvellous,' Ruth said, her eyes lighting up.

'Hold on, Ruth. It would have to come at a cost. To make it fair I'd want you to pay two-thirds of the bills.'

'I'd be willing to do that.'

'Do we have a deal then?' Adam asked.

'I think so, but what about the upstairs flat? If it's big enough, I'd like to live in it.'

'As I once told you, it's rented out, but you're in luck because their tenancy agreement runs out at the end of January.'

'In that case, you've got a deal,' Ruth said, holding out a hand for him to shake. Adam took it, hiding his relief behind a smile. He had got what he wanted and soon a nice chunk of Ruth's money would be going into his bank to clear his overdraft. Little did she know it, but that was just a start. One day Adam intended to gain a lot more. Both the woman – and her bank balance.

Chapter Seven

The new year heralded changes. Penny settled happily into her new school, leaving Lorna free hours to help Ruth as much as she could in setting up the agency. It was such a frantically busy time that Lorna still didn't feel she could ask for any time off; a situation that continued into the first week in February when they moved into the flat above the office. In the short time they had been back in England this was their third move, and Lorna had begun to feel like a gypsy as once again she had packed and unpacked their things.

Now that they were both living and working together in such close proximity, Lorna learned more about Ruth. She could be impatient, demanding and snappy at times, but as she was under so much pressure to get the agency up and running, Lorna found it understandable.

Now though, on this Thursday afternoon towards the end of February, they were at last close to opening for business. Ruth was going to target the area with a leaflet drop setting out their services, and she had interviewed a young but experienced negotiator who would start work when they opened the agency on Monday.

The sign writer stuck his head inside and said, 'If you'd

like to come and look at it, I've finished and just need your approval before I pack up.'

Lorna followed Ruth outside to look up at the elegant, royal blue copperplate script, edged with gold on a cream background which read, *Hamilton-Smyth & Mortimer, Property Sales and Services.* She smiled wryly. The name had been the subject of many arguments between Ruth and Adam. They were equally stubborn. Adam had said that as the original sign, along with all his stationery and business cards, read, *Adam Mortimer Property Sales, Lettings and Management Services,* it should remain unchanged.

Ruth though argued that as she was paying more than him, her name should be displayed, and first. It had taken days to come to an agreement, but Ruth was obviously happy now as she peered up at the sign, saying with approval, 'Yes, it's fine. I like it.'

Lorna did too and the colour matched the theme that Ruth had chosen when it came to décor and furnishings for the agency. Lorna had expected her to go for an ultra-modern interior, but instead Ruth had chosen mahogany half-panelling and desks, with a rich blue and gold colour scheme. When Lorna had asked her why, Ruth had said that she wanted the decor to give the impression of permanence, of old, solid, trustworthy and reliable class.

It certainly smacked of that, Lorna thought as they went back inside, but she soon had to go out again to pick Penny up from school.

Penny came skipping out holding a drawing, but when they arrived at the agency Ruth was so busy that she hardly spared her daughter a glance. Lorna took Penny upstairs. Though it had taken them a while to settle into the flat, this one was by far the nicest. The living room was large, with high ceilings, picture rails and cornices, along with a large fireplace. The carpet was threadbare in places, but deep red, as were the velvet curtains, and the brown leather furniture, though cracked and old-fashioned, was comfortable.

Ruth had said that as soon as she had more time she would refurnish every room, but for now they would have to make do. The rest of the rooms were of good proportions too and after settling Penny in front of the television to watch a cartoon, Lorna went through to the spacious kitchen to make a start on preparing their dinner.

They ate at five, but it was six-thirty before Ruth came upstairs. While she went to freshen up, Lorna reheated her dinner and asked Ruth when she sat at the table, 'Did Adam like the sign?'

'Yes, he's happy with it,' Ruth replied as the telephone rang.

Lorna answered it and her stomach lurched when she heard her stepfather's voice. 'Lorna, is that you?'

'Yes, Ted. What is it? What's wrong?'

'Your mother asked me to ring you. She isn't well and she wants to see you.'

'What's wrong with her?'

'It's some sort of tummy problem.'

'Has she seen the doctor?'

'Yes, but whatever he prescribed isn't making her feel any better and as I said, she wants to see you.'

'All right, tell her I'll be there tomorrow,' Lorna said worriedly, as she said goodbye and replaced the receiver.

'From what I heard, I take it someone is ill,' Ruth said.

'Yes, my mother and I said I'd go to see her.'

'Yes, I gathered that too,' Ruth said, looking less than pleased. 'I suppose you'll have to go, but how long will you be away?'

'I don't know. It depends on how I find her, but hopefully it isn't anything serious and will only be for a day or two.'

'This really couldn't have come at a worse time. I still have a lot to do and the last thing I need is to be lumbered with Penny.'

'I'll be back as soon as I can.'

'See that you are,' Ruth snapped.

Lorna was usually slow to anger, but concerned about her mother she retorted, 'You seem to forget that I haven't had a single day off in five months.'

For a moment Ruth's eyes seemed to spark with anger, but then she suddenly changed, her manner contrite as she said, 'Lorna, I'm being insensitive and I'm sorry. It's just that I've got so much on my mind and with the agency opening on Monday I don't know how I'm going to cope with Penny if you aren't back by then.'

'I'll do my best, but I can't offer any guarantees.'

'Thanks,' Ruth acknowledged, quiet for a while as she picked at her food. 'If the worst comes to the worst I suppose I could ask Adam to take Penny to school and then pick her up again. I doubt he'd mind. He's sorted out his office now and as it's off season he doesn't appear overly busy at the moment.'

Lorna wasn't so sure. From what she'd seen Adam largely ignored Penny and only acknowledged her existence when he had to. She began to worry about what would happen to the little girl while she was away. There'd be no hugs and kisses, no bedtime stories, things Lorna knew she would have to make up for when she returned.

She just hoped that her mother's illness was minor and that she wouldn't be away for too long.

On Friday morning, Myra Redman looked at the clock yet again. It was nearly ten-thirty and she'd expected her daughter to arrive earlier than this.

At last, nearly half an hour later, there was a knock on the door and Myra went to answer it. 'So, you've arrived at last.'

'It was a bit of a trek to get here from Margate,' Lorna said as they walked down the passage to the kitchen. 'How are you, Mum?'

'I feel a bit better now, but it comes to something when I've got to be ill before you bother to come and see me.'

'I haven't been able to take any time off, but I'm here now.'

'I expect you'll want a cup of tea.'

'Yes, but you sit down and I'll make it,' Lorna said as she took off her coat.

Myra frowned as she looked at her daughter. 'You've put on a lot of weight.'

'I know, but I'm going on a diet,' Lorna said as she hung her coat on a hook behind the door and then filled the kettle with water.

'This came for you yesterday morning,' Myra said, holding out a brown envelope.

Lorna placed the kettle onto a gas ring before reaching out to take the letter. She opened it, her teeth biting into her lower lip as she read the contents. When she looked up, her eyes were awash with tears. 'It . . . it's the divorce papers from Richard's solicitor.'

'There's no point in getting upset. From what you told me on the telephone you knew this was coming, and as Richard left you for another woman I hope you take him for every penny he's got.'

'No, I won't be doing that,' Lorna cried, adding with a small sob as she fled the room, 'I don't blame him for finding someone else. It's no more than I deserve.'

Myra froze. She heard Lorna running upstairs, then the bathroom door slammed, but her mind was reeling. No, no! Surely Lorna hadn't told Richard the truth!

Chapter Eight

Adam looked around his small office, thinking it a come-down, yet knew he only had himself to blame. He'd been so desperate for money that he'd suggested this arrangement, and now his business had been assigned to the side entrance. It wasn't ideal, but he was hoping to make the best of it.

When Ruth called out that she was back, a scowl marred Adam's handsome features. She had got everything she wanted, the bulk of the premises along with her name appearing first over the main part of the building, but Adam was damned if he was going to let her emasculate him any further. When she'd asked him to take her kid to school that morning it had been the final straw. As he'd told Ruth, there was no way he was going to do that. He was a businessman, not a flaming babysitter.

Adam took a seat behind his desk to ring Denis Young, the chap he used for maintenance and repairs to the properties he managed. There had been a complaint from one of the tenants about a broken pipe and as he was telling Denis to fix it, Ruth walked into his office.

She perched on the side of his desk, listening to the call and said as he replaced the receiver, 'Do you invoice your clients for the maintenance costs to their properties?'

Adam gave little away as he said, 'Of course.'

'I assumed that your work just entailed finding tenants for the properties you handle and collecting the rent, but it seems far more complicated than that.'

'It isn't something you can jump into without experience, especially when it comes to the legalities, tenancy agreements, evictions and such.'

'Yes, I realise that now,' Ruth said, a little worriedly.

Adam felt happier as he hid a small smile, willing to bide his time and to let Ruth find out the hard way that it would be a long while before she showed a profit when it came to property management. She was going to blunder into a business she knew nothing about, and when things went wrong, which of course they would, Adam would be there and ready to make his next move.

Lorna had spent a long time in her mother's bathroom before she was able to pull herself together. She had been expecting to hear from Richard's solicitor, but as such a long time had passed without a word, she had again dared to hope that he'd changed his mind.

What an idiot she'd been. Of course he hadn't, and seeing the divorce petition in black and white was like a blow to her stomach. Richard had cited grounds of unreasonable behaviour as the cause of their marriage irretrievably breaking down, but thankfully not the true reason for his wanting a divorce. He'd been kind, which was more than she deserved, and for that Lorna would be forever grateful.

She was now facing her mother, who was almost hysterical, and though she was trying to calm her down, it was difficult to get a word in. 'Mum . . . please, I had to tell him.'

'No you didn't. Lots of women have difficulty conceiving and you could have come up with some sort of excuse!'

'I tried that, but I couldn't stand the guilt and deceit any longer.'

'But don't you realise what you've done? Richard is sure to tell his family why he left you. They live close by and they won't keep their mouths shut! God, it'll all come out and we'll never live it down!'

'I can't help the way I was born, but all you seem to care about is that people might find out. You act like I'm some sort of freak that you're ashamed of!'

'That isn't true. All I've ever done is to try to protect you.'

Lorna was too emotionally drained to argue any more and just said, 'If you say so, Mum, but I don't think you need to worry. Richard left me in April last year and if he'd told anyone the true reason why, I'm sure you'd have heard about it by now.'

'Yes, that's true,' Myra said, looking a little placated.

'I . . . I'll finish making the tea,' Lorna said and to change the subject she turned the conversation to her mother's health. 'You said you feel better, but what's been wrong with you? Ted said something about an upset tummy.'

'It's been playing me up and I've been worried that I was going the same way as my mother. It's why I asked Ted to ring you, but thankfully the stuff the doctor gave me seems to have worked at last. He must be right and it's just acid indigestion.'

'That's a relief,' Lorna said.

'I expect you think I've dragged you here for nothing.'

'No, Mum, I'm just glad you're all right.'

59

'Now that you're here, how long will you be staying?'

'I'll get a train back to Margate this evening.'

'Lorna, it's been ages since I've seen you and at least you could stay overnight.'

'If you needed me I'd have stayed as long as necessary, but you seem fine and Ruth is rushed off her feet at the moment. Once things have calmed down and the agency is running smoothly, I'll be able to take some time off. I'll come to see you again then and promise to stay for at least a few days.'

'Very well, I suppose I'll have to be content with that, but don't leave it for too long. I hardly saw you when you lived in Spain and hoped things would be different now that you're back in England.'

'Margate isn't exactly round the corner, Mum, but I will try to see you more often.'

'I should hope so too,' she said, and at last, as they shared a pot of tea, things seemed a little easier between them.

Lorna looked around the kitchen, seeing that little had changed. Her mother had lived in Battersea all her life, and in this house for nearly thirty years. It wasn't large, with a front lounge, this kitchen-cum-dining room, and a handkerchief-sized back garden. Upstairs there were two bedrooms and the bathroom. It was council property, identical to every other redbrick terraced house in Birch Street, but her mother had never shown any ambition to move. Her life was one of routine, socially too, with bingo every Tuesday and Thursday nights while Ted went to the pub. She was only fifty-one, but having lived such a narrow and unadventurous life, she seemed so much older. 'Mum, it's a shame you didn't come to Spain for a holiday. I think you would have enjoyed it.'

'As I told you when you invited us, Ted doesn't like travelling. It takes weeks of nagging before he'll agree to a holiday in Brighton, so you can imagine his reaction when I suggested Spain.'

Lorna wanted to tell her mother that she could have come on her own, but knew it would be pointless. She waited on Ted hand and foot and would never leave him to fend for himself. Instead she asked, 'Have you ever been to Margate?'

'Yes, but it was a long time ago. You were just a toddler then and we went on a coach trip organised by your dad's firm. They were good employers and laid on an outing for their workers and families every year.'

Lorna knew her father had worked in a paper mill, but it had closed many years ago. All she had left of him was a framed, treasured, black and white photograph that she would never part with, along with distant memories of his laughing face. With a sigh she said, 'I like Margate and feel at home there. Maybe it's because I can remember being there with Dad.'

'I doubt that. You were only about two years old at the time and even I can barely remember the place.'

Lorna felt that her mother was probably right, yet there was no getting away from the feeling of déjà vu she experienced in Margate – that every road or street she walked along for the first time felt familiar, as if she had trodden the same route before.

Margate felt like home to Lorna now and as soon as she could decently leave her mother's house, she would get the train back to where she belonged.

Chapter Nine

Relieved that Lorna's mother didn't seem to need her daughter back for more than a flying visit, Ruth threw herself into launching her business with even more energy. She extended her leaflet drop and made a point of contacting anyone local who might be useful. She visited the big hotels and restaurants and the smaller guesthouses and cafés, reckoning that you never knew when a passing comment would lead to something. Word-of-mouth recommendations would be slow to build up but she had to start somewhere.

Meanwhile her new employee was left to answer the phones and deal with any postal enquiries, although there were very few to begin with. Robert Harrison had plenty of experience in property management from his years in London, but he had grown tired of the pace of life there. Even though he was barely into his thirties he wanted something steadier, a place where he could breathe fresh air and didn't have to get the grime off his collar every time he took off his shirt after a long commute home. He had family in the Margate area, and he had recently inherited a small but elegant flat from a great-aunt. He had saved his salary for years and invested it carefully.

Had he wanted to, he could have bought himself a much more impressive property. But he saw no need to. He would wait to see how things went – he wasn't one to rush into things. He also saw no need to discuss any of this with his new colleagues.

The office door slammed. 'So, any new leads today?' demanded his boss, shrugging out of her long black coat. She glanced over to his desk. 'Is that all the post there is?'

'Two bills,' Robert answered calmly, pushing the brown envelopes towards her. 'And a letter from the manager of one of the seafront hotels, saying you'd spoken to him earlier in the week. One of his guests is thinking of staying on for a couple of months and might prefer a short-term rental to a huge hotel bill, so if you'd like to contact him . . .'

'Give me that!' exclaimed Ruth, reaching for the third envelope, pushing her long hair out of her eyes and scanning the letter. She reached for the phone and dialled. 'Mr Beasley please.'

Robert couldn't help thinking he would have wanted to know how much the bills were for first, but evidently that was not his new boss's style.

'Oh, Mr Beasley,' she was saying, 'how nice of you to have remembered me . . .'

Goodness, thought Robert. She was actually purring into the phone. But it seemed to do the trick.

'I'll certainly do that,' she went on. 'Why don't we make it tomorrow? Yes, that would be ideal. I will see you then.' Beaming, she put down the receiver. 'Right,' Ruth said, turning to him. 'Now it looks as if there might be a bit of money coming in, you can show me those bloody bills.'

Feeling more like a secretary than a negotiator, Robert did as he was asked, making sure his emotions didn't show on his face.

The door slammed again.

'Sorry,' said the woman who came through it. 'The wind's really blustery today.' She smiled uncertainly at Robert and then turned to Ruth. 'The school just rang to say there's a concert and all parents are invited. It's short notice but Penny will be in it. Would you like to go? I said I'd let them know as their hall is quite small.'

Ruth glanced up, irritated. 'When is it exactly?'

'Six o'clock tomorrow evening,' said Lorna.

'Oh, I couldn't possibly do that, I've just made what could be a very important appointment. You'll have to go instead.'

'Oh, I was going to anyway,' Lorna assured her. 'Can't have Penny dancing in her first concert with no one to see her. I'd love to go.'

'That's fine all round, then,' said Ruth dismissively. 'Right, I'll see you later. I have to go out again – can't go back to the hotel wearing the same things as last time. Invest for success, as they say.' She picked up her coat and bag and dashed out of the office, the door slamming behind her.

Lorna was left standing in the middle of the office, uncertain of what to do. Finally she composed herself. 'Hello, I'm Lorna,' she said, holding out her hand. 'You must be Robert. Pleased to meet you.'

'Pleased to meet you too,' said Robert, shaking her hand and grinning. 'Would you like a cup of tea? You must be frozen if you've been out in that gale.'

'That would be lovely,' said Lorna, meaning it. 'I still

haven't got used to the English weather. And,' she hesitated, knowing it would sound disloyal, 'I've been to this office lots of times now and it's always been me who made the tea. Isn't that an awful thing to say? So I'd love some.'

'Tea it shall be,' said Robert, his eyes twinkling, thinking he might as well do something useful – because he certainly wasn't putting his professional skills to any good use yet.

Later that morning in the other part of the office, Adam was trying to get through to Denis, his usually reliable maintenance man, for the third time. He was lucky. The man finally picked up the phone.

'Denis!' said Adam, falsely cheerful. 'Been trying to reach you, old man. Been off on your skiing holiday, have you?'

'You've got to be joking,' said Denis. 'This time of the year? One bit of wind and everyone's houses fall apart. That's when a bit of cold hasn't frozen their pipes or their boilers break down. I can't keep up with the work.'

'Oh, that's a shame,' said Adam. 'I was going to ask you about that flat on the second floor, you know the one, with the unusual kitchen.'

'The bad conversion, you mean,' groaned Denis. 'You don't have to dress it up with estate agent speak to me, mate. I've seen the state of the place, remember.'

'Yes indeed,' smiled Adam, inwardly cursing. 'Well, I was hoping to persuade you to take another look at the, er, unique features of its waste pipes.'

'Blocked again, have they?' asked Denis. 'Not surprised one bit. Well, I can't help. But I've got my nephew down from Croydon who's very handy. Shall I send him round?'

'Any recommendation from you is good enough for me,' Adam assured him, deeply relieved. He certainly didn't want to go anywhere near those pipes himself. 'Have him pop into the office to pick up the keys. I'll be delighted to make his acquaintance.'

'If you say so,' replied Denis. 'Name of Joe. Chip off the old block, he is.' And he put the phone down.

Turning to his paperwork, Adam struck out one item on his to-do list and flicked through his diary. A potential client was due at any minute. Straightening his tie and brushing down his lapels, Adam hastily summoned up what he knew about the man, so that he could make the best possible impression.

Right on time, the door opened.

'Mr Casson!' exclaimed Adam, rising to his feet and going to meet the man. 'Dreadful weather, isn't it? Let me take your coat. Yes, do sit there. And how is your wife? Still enjoying the amateur operatics?'

The middle-aged man in the slightly faded but still sharp suit grinned ruefully. 'Oh yes, very much so.' He sighed. 'Anyway, it's about the garden flat I believe we spoke about a while ago. I had private tenants but they're leaving and I'd rather let it through an agency this time. It would be a weight off my mind, especially as Miriam is far too busy treading the boards to help out.'

'That's exactly what we're here for,' beamed Adam, reaching for a folder. 'Now, let me show you our terms and conditions, and I can assure you that your peace of mind is my top priority.'

There was a burst of conversation from the front half

of the office and Ruth appeared around the filing cabinets. 'Adam, I was wondering . . .' She stopped. 'Oh, I do apologise, I didn't realise you were in a meeting.'

'Hello, my dear,' said Mr Casson, suddenly animated. 'I don't believe we've met.' He rose to shake her hand.

'Ruth Hamilton-Smyth,' said Ruth, trying not to wince as the man held her hand just a fraction too long. 'I am the owner of the agency in the front office. We offer a property management service with a major emphasis on quality.' She held the man's eyes. 'I'm sure a gentleman like you would understand the importance of that.'

'Absolutely,' agreed Mr Casson, drawing himself up to his full height, losing all interest in the document Adam had shown him. 'And what exactly do you mean by that?'

Maybe he wasn't as daft as he looked, thought Ruth. She smoothed her hair back with a practised gesture. 'Well, we start from the premise that discerning landlords deserve nothing less than discerning tenants,' she began.

Adam cleared his throat.

Ruth raised her eyebrows at him. 'I'll detain you no further,' she purred. 'I need to prepare for an urgent client presentation.' She turned to go back to her desk, but threw a glance over her shoulder. 'So nice to have met you.'

'Well, that's a wonderful new asset to the business you have there,' said Mr Casson, slowly picking up the folder once more. 'She sounds as if she knows exactly what she's doing.'

'Oh yes, she most definitely does,' Adam agreed, thinking that he'd kill her if she made another blatant attempt to poach one of his customers. 'However, someone such as yourself really needs the reassurance of being in the most experienced hands possible and that's where I can offer you the very best care.'

'That does sound right, I admit,' conceded Mr Casson, signing the paper Adam put in front of him. 'There, that should do it. Would you like to come round to see the condition of the place and pick up the keys?'

'I always make a point of personally visiting every property I represent.' Adam rose to escort the man out of the office. Once he had gone on his way, Adam stepped outside after him. Despite the howling wind, he needed a moment of fresh air to collect his thoughts. It was dangerous having Ruth anywhere near his clients – or at least any male ones. But most landlords were men, and therefore vulnerable to her charms. He was far from immune to them himself. But she couldn't be allowed to damage his business. He needed to keep her sweet so that he could make his next move when the time was right, but he also had to protect his financial interests. He'd have to think of something, and fast.

Chapter Ten

A couple of mornings later, Lorna was heading for the shops after dropping off Penny at her school. The wind was still gusting hard and although she'd tried to tie back her hair into its usual unflattering style, some of it had come loose and was blowing across her face, blocking her vision.

'Oh, excuse me!' someone exclaimed, and she realised she had nearly walked straight into a man. Looking up, she saw a face she recognised.

'Sorry about that!' she said, tugging her hair away from her eyes. 'You must think I'm a complete idiot.'

'Not a bit,' said Robert. 'No harm done.' He smiled in sympathy at her embarrassment. 'Are you walking to the seafront? Shall we go together?'

'I've run out of milk,' she confessed. 'Normally I'm much more organised but what with Penny's concert, it totally slipped my mind.'

'That was last night, wasn't it?' said Robert. 'How did it go?'

She was pleased that he had remembered. 'She's not even seven yet so it's probably too soon to tell but I think she's got real talent. She keeps to the beat so well, and you can see she's enjoying every moment of it. Even though she was one of the youngest she remembered everything perfectly.' She stopped suddenly. 'Oh dear, I'm gushing, aren't I? But it makes me so happy to see her. She's had such an unsettling few months and it's lovely to watch her doing something she's good at.' Nervously Lorna pulled her woollen scarf tighter around her neck.

'Of course,' said Robert. 'She must be a very special little girl.'

'Oh, she is, she is.' Lorna nodded vigorously, at which her hair sprang loose from its clip once more. 'Well, you know I'm only her nanny, not a member of the family, but I've watched her grow up and it makes me proud to see her do well.' She sighed, tempted to say that the child got no support from her mother, but that would be going too far.

'Look, I realise you're in a hurry,' said Robert, 'but would you like to stop for a tea, or a coffee? I'm early and there's no need for me to be at my desk until the post arrives.' Or really at all, he thought. But he could see there was something troubling this woman, and he suspected she might not have too many people to confide in, especially with a boss like theirs.

'In that case, I'd love to,' smiled Lorna. 'That café over there is quite good. I've been there several times.' She nodded to a small but cosy-looking establishment on the corner, and they made their way towards it.

Settling themselves into the seats closest to the window, Lorna took her scarf off and realised her eyes were watering from the gale. 'Such a relief to be inside,' she said.

Robert noticed her eyes were warm and bright, and her face was flushed with the warmth of the café. 'I know,' he agreed. 'So, how long have you known this little girl?'

'Since she was about three,' she said. 'She's Penelope but we all call her Penny. Her mother . . . her mother has always been so busy that I'm almost like an aunt to her. At least,' Lorna paused, not wanting to sound boastful, 'that's how I think of it.'

'I'm sure she's very fond of you,' Robert replied. He couldn't fail to notice how her face lit up when she spoke of the child, that air of worry falling away. 'So you're the live-in nanny? What about your own family?'

Damn, he'd said the wrong thing. That anxious look came back.

'None really to speak of,' she said. Then, when he didn't answer at once, she added, 'My mother and stepfather live in London but I don't see much of them.'

'I used to work in London,' he said. 'Couldn't wait to leave the place. I much prefer it down here, even on a day like this.'

'Oh, I agree!' said Lorna. 'At least you know what the weather's like. In London you're either inside or on a bus or tube. Never need to notice the seasons at all. Whereas I love it in Margate. Even though we've only been here a few months I just know it's my home now. People talk to you and aren't afraid to pass the time of day. I bet if we'd bumped into each other in London we'd have never done this.'

'Well, we won't ever know, will we?' grinned Robert, thinking he would have noticed her smile even on Oxford Street in the rush hour. 'So just as well we both ended up here.'

Lorna looked at him and relaxed once more, feeling safe in his presence. There was something about him that made her feel she could tell him anything and before she knew it she'd said the one thing that had been preying on her thoughts. 'I probably will have to go back to London more often though. My mother's ill.'

'That's a shame,' Robert said immediately.

'I'm not sure what to do for the best,' she admitted. 'She says she's all right, that it's just indigestion, but my stepfather would never have rung me if they really thought that. He can usually hardly bear to speak to me.' No, Lorna knew she mustn't get started on that. She collected herself and went on: 'It's not as if I can just casually drop by – they know it's too far for that. But to take time off to see them properly causes problems for Ruth, and I don't want to inconvenience her when the business is just beginning to take off. And I can't bear to think of Penny upset.'

Aha, that was the nub of it, thought Robert. No doubt she loves her mother, but it's Penny who is at the centre of it all. 'I can see you're in a bit of a dilemma,' he said carefully.

She nodded, now not meeting his eyes but staring gloomily at the chequered tablecloth.

'I wonder if I could help,' Robert continued. 'Look, you can say no if you'd rather. But I have friends in London that I promised to visit. I'll be driving up now and again, and that's much faster than the train. Do you drive?'

'I don't have a car at the moment,' Lorna admitted, not adding that on the wages Ruth paid it was unlikely that she'd get one anytime soon.

'So how about if I drove you up when I go?' suggested Robert. 'It's lonely making the journey on my own. You'd be doing me a favour.'

'Really?' She couldn't quite believe it, but turned her gaze from the tomato-shaped ketchup holder to his friendly eyes. 'I . . . I suppose that would be much quicker. But where in London are your friends? It's a big place.'

'Wandsworth,' said Robert. 'They like being near the common. Do you know it?'

'Yes, yes I do,' said Lorna. 'Actually that's quite good. My mother lives in Battersea, and it's not far from there.'

'There you are, then,' said Robert, his eyes sparkling. 'Next time I go, I'll take you along. Or, if you need to go beforehand, just let me know, as they'll be happy to see me any time. How about that? Do we have a deal?'

'If you're sure,' Lorna said, scarcely able to believe her luck. But she wasn't at all surprised that this seemingly quiet man had such good friends. She couldn't imagine anyone being that glad to see her. But Robert would get a warm welcome, she was certain. 'Yes,' she said, more definitely now, as their plates of toast arrived. 'Yes, I'd like that very much indeed.'

'How did your client meeting go last night, Ruth?' Adam asked, keeping his voice light and friendly. He was keen to know the details but even keener that she didn't pick up on the urgency behind his question.

'Very successful,' said Ruth, pleased with herself and not afraid to show it. 'He's got one definite visitor for me, who's keen to stay for even longer than I thought. And there's another distinct possibility. He also says he'll be sure to put any other custom my way.'

'You certainly have a way with the older gentlemen,' Adam commented, memories of Mr Casson flaring in his mind.

'Not so old, as it happens,' said Ruth, raising an eyebrow. 'Do you have a problem with that? You use the talents you're given, that's what I've always been taught. And it pays the bills, which, if you happen to have forgotten, is what you wanted me to do. So, if it's all right with you, I'm off to view some flats for these new customers. Where's that Robert? He's usually in by now.'

'No idea,' snapped Adam, his irritation surfacing. 'I'm not his boss. But I dare say he'll be in shortly. Strikes me as very conscientious, does our Robert. Even boring, one could say.'

'Don't be ridiculous, Adam,' Ruth shot back. Then she remembered that she had to keep on the right side of him and forced her temper down. 'I'm not interested in how exciting he is, just how good he is at managing properties. So I'd better go and get him some to manage.' She flashed her brilliant smile and was gone.

God, that woman was too much, seethed Adam. How long was he going to put up with this? She thought all she had to do was flirt with a few lonely hotel owners and the world would fall at her feet.

He was so engrossed in his thoughts that he didn't notice someone enter the office, and almost jumped when the young man said, 'Mr Mortimer?'

'Yes?' Adam managed to gasp, while taking in the figure before him – not the classy sort of customer Ruth would want on her books, that was for sure.

'Joe Young,' said the young man, keeping both hands in the pockets of his stained donkey jacket. He tried again. 'Denis Young's nephew. He said you wanted to see me. Denis Young? Does building and plumbing?'

'Of course, of course.' Adam got to his feet. 'Yes, Denis

is a great help to us. Splendid guy. Couldn't manage without him.'

'Right,' said Joe, looking around at the new mahogany panelling and immaculate furnishings. 'Nice place you got here. Uncle Denis didn't say what it was like so I didn't know.'

'We offer only the best,' said Adam breezily, thinking that a compliment from this young man was hardly worth acknowledging. 'Now, your uncle told me you were a useful man to have around. What are your particular skills?'

'I do plumbing, if that's what you're after,' said Joe shortly. 'And other bits and bobs. Replace glass, fix a ceiling, put up a shelf.' He narrowed his eyes. 'Is that what you want?'

'Plumbing, most certainly,' said Adam. He thought for a moment. 'And did your uncle say you came from Croydon? Is that where you used to work?'

'I can get you references from there, if my uncle's word isn't good enough,' said Joe casually, though there was a steeliness to his expression that suggested he wouldn't think much of the idea. 'Croydon and all over South London, as it happens.'

'No, no, I trust Denis completely,' Adam assured him. 'Good to have someone so versatile on board. Is there anything else you used to do . . . all over South London?'

'I've done a bit of this and a bit of that,' the young man said. He had a definite air of somebody who could take care of himself in any situation. 'Security, for one. And . . . what you might call insurance.'

'Security,' Adam echoed. 'And . . . insurance. An unusual combination, Joe. You don't mind if I call you Joe?'

'It's my name,' said Joe blandly. 'And as for unusual, it's not everyone who can do it. Not everyone who has the head for it, if you get my meaning. Not everyone who has . . . the particular skills.'

Adam looked around, trying to see if Robert was in yet. But there was no coat or scarf on the hat-stand, no noise from the other part of the office or the kitchenette they shared. He smiled slowly. 'I think I get your meaning, Joe,' he said. The possibilities opened up before him as the young man's implication became clear. 'Yes, I like the sound of that very much. Plumbing to start with – we have a case of blocked pipes. But after that I might have cause to make use of your . . . particular skills.'

Chapter Eleven

Robert was as good as his word, and the next time he went to visit his friends in Wandsworth he asked Lorna along. Even Ruth was amenable to the idea, as she knew Lorna wouldn't be away too long. Fortunately a school-friend had asked Penny round to play and to stay for tea, so there would be no interruptions to the business. 'Just as well,' Ruth told Lorna as she was checking her handbag. 'I've got to meet some woman who likes the look of one of the flats. She sounds like a right old whingebag but money is money.'

'Nothing wrong about being careful where you live,' Lorna smiled. At least she had no worries on that score now; she loved her room and was happier by the day as she got to know Margate better. She slung her bag over her shoulder. 'See you this evening. Good luck with the flat.'

'Yes, right, thanks,' said Ruth absently, already thinking about something else as her friend made her way down-stairs.

'I'll pick you up at five,' said Robert as he dropped Lorna at her mother's house in Battersea.

Lorna turned to wave as he drove off. The journey had flown by, as Robert was so easy to talk to. She'd been worried that once they were in the car alone there would be nothing to say, but the opposite had been true. Although he came across as quiet, once you got to know him he was a very interesting man, and the best listener she'd ever met. Sighing, Lorna wondered what would be in store for her once she stepped inside her mother's door.

'So, you made it here at a decent hour of the day this time,' Myra greeted her. 'Better come in, I suppose.'

'Good to see you, Mum,' Lorna said, although she wasn't sure that was strictly true. 'I'll put the kettle on, you just sit down.' She busied herself around the kitchen, watching her mother out of the corner of her eye.

'Started that diet yet?' Myra asked. 'You really ought to try harder. No wonder Richard left you, you've really let yourself go.' She shifted self-righteously on her wooden chair.

'Thanks a lot, Mum!' Lorna was seething. 'Well, you certainly don't need to diet. Are you sure you're eating enough? Let's have some biscuits with our tea. I brought some with me, they're your favourites.' She reached into her bag and brought out a packet.

'You have one, if you must,' said her mother. 'I'm right off biscuits. Never did like them as much as you, and these days they just taste like sawdust.'

'I don't like the sound of that,' Lorna said, anxious now. 'Have you seen the doctor again?' She popped a biscuit into her mouth, hoping that her mother would follow her example.

'Ted made me go last week,' Myra admitted. 'Not sure it did any good. He's given me some new pills, painkillers, they are. Appetite killers, more like. Ted says they make me sleep funny too. I wake up all fuzzy in the head, and that's not like me.'

'I should think not!' Her mother had always been sharp-witted – too sharp for comfort most of the time. And it was most unlike her to repeat such a personal comment from Ted. 'Have you been able to go out much?'

'I haven't felt much like going to bingo,' confessed Myra. Lorna's eyebrows rose in alarm. 'Don't take on so, I've still done the shopping and the housework. I'm not at death's door yet, you know.'

'Well now I'm here I can do some of that for you,' Lorna said firmly, draining her cup. 'You might have been overdoing it. It takes a while to adjust to new pills. How about I put a wash on and then go to the shops? Have you got a list?'

Lorna looked around the familiar kitchen, with its small dining table pushed up against the window. It had always felt rather cramped but it was usually immaculate, every cup and saucer in place, all the Formica surfaces gleaming. Now there was a dullness to it, and plates and pans were piled around at random.

'It's over there,' said Myra, pointing to a scrap of paper covered in tea stains. God, thought Lorna, this was awful. How had her mother slipped so far so quickly?

But she couldn't show how worried she was. With a cheerful air she picked up her handbag once more and reached behind the door to where she knew her mother hung her shopping bag. It wasn't there.

Looking around, she noticed its bright orange handle

poking out from a drawer. 'Changed where you keep it, have you?' she asked lightly.

'Oh, Ted must have put it there,' said her mother. 'He popped to the corner shop for me a few times.'

That was it. There was definitely something very wrong – her mother would never, ever have let Ted do something like that in the normal run of things, and Ted wouldn't have been seen dead doing women's work – which included everything to do with the house. Wondering what she should do about this worrying development, Lorna made her way down the road, as she had done every day for all those years until she'd married Richard. There, she'd said his name to herself. She'd tried so hard not to react to her mother's cruel comment, but deep down the wounds were still smarting, even though she knew that putting on a few pounds wasn't the reason he'd left. It had been much, much worse than that.

Although her childhood home hadn't changed for many years, the same could not be said of the neighbouring streets. Where was the old butcher's? Or the ironmonger's? They appeared to have changed hands and become a newsagent's and a clothes shop – not the sort of things she'd wear, by the looks of it. Maybe she would be better off going a little further and heading for the market. There always used to be a bargain to be had there.

'Oh hello, Lorna!'

Lorna stopped abruptly, brought out of her anxious thoughts by the sight of one of her mother's neighbours. What on earth was her name? Mrs Jackson . . . no, Mrs Jameson, that was it.

'Hello, Mrs Jameson,' she said, relieved to have remembered it right. 'How are you?'

'Not bad at all,' beamed the woman. 'Haven't seen you around these parts for a while. Back from Spain, I hear?'

'That's right,' Lorna replied, her smile fixed. 'Couldn't take the heat after all.'

'I see,' said the woman, re-buttoning what Lorna thought was a horrible coat. And was that a knowing gleam in her eye? 'I saw your Richard's aunty the other day down the market, and she didn't say anything about the weather. Or should I say your *ex*, Richard?'

'That's right,' said Lorna, her face rigid now. God, what had Richard told his family?

'And I understand your mother's not been well,' the woman went on mercilessly. 'Saw her the other day too – shadow of her former self, she is. I always used to say, if you want something sorted out, go to Myra, but the other day she wasn't making much sense at all. Almost rambling, she was. It's a shame when people go downhill like that.' Mrs Jameson stopped, finally aware of the effect her words were having. 'Oh, I'm sorry to go on, love. Didn't mean to worry you. Give my best to your mother, won't you?'

Lorna nodded briefly, too stunned to speak. What on earth had her mother let slip? It must be those painkillers – she didn't seem to be able to keep quiet about anything any more. All the pain of losing Richard came flooding back, now with the added anxiety that either he or her mother had revealed her shameful secret. 'Please, please don't let anyone else find out,' she muttered despairingly. Tears were threatening, and she couldn't face the market now. What if they all knew? What if they were all nudging each other behind her back, whispering that she was a freak? It was unbearable.

Maybe that new newsagent's would have some basic groceries. That would have to do. Grasping the orange handle of her mother's bag, Lorna hurried across the street, all the happiness of this morning's car journey utterly gone.

'I just don't believe it!' Ruth threw her gorgeous black coat onto her desk in furious frustration. God, what a morning she'd had.

'Something wrong?' asked Adam suavely, appearing around the cabinets that semi-divided their office. 'Clients can be such a nuisance, can't they?'

Ruth was tempted to turn on him for making such a stupid remark but just managed to stop herself. Still, she might as well vent her temper on someone.

'Not only was that woman the most nit-picking old bag, but there was something wrong with the lock of the flat. So when we got there we couldn't get in. I don't get it. It was fine yesterday when I inspected the place. But today, I could not get the key to work.'

'Really?' Adam looked concerned. 'What did you do?'

'Had to call out a bloody emergency locksmith, that's what,' Ruth snarled. 'Do you know how much they cost? It's almost more than that property is worth! It's outrageous! How am I ever meant to turn a profit when this goes on?'

'That can be a problem, yes,' Adam soothed. 'Of course, if you've built up local tradesman contacts, it's a different kettle of fish. But all that takes time.'

'Thanks a lot,' growled Ruth. 'Bit late now. And even worse, when he got there, he said that the lock could have been tampered with. Since yesterday! Who'd have done such a thing? It's only a one-bedroom flat, for God's sake!'

'That does sound unlikely, I agree,' he said cautiously. 'Margate isn't really like that. London, yes. But not round here.'

'Seems like we've got our very own homegrown vandals.' Ruth was not impressed. She'd come here to avoid all the trouble that always went on in the capital, and now it was following her.

'That's too bad.' Adam decided to push things further. 'So did the old woman walk off in disgust? I wouldn't blame her – it isn't nice to move into a property that's been targeted like that. Still, it sounds as if she'd have been a difficult tenant and who needs them, eh?'

'Well, we do, obviously,' snapped Ruth. 'Difficult or not, as long as they pay the rent, I don't care. Anyway, I talked her round. I persuaded her that the locksmith was only saying that to cover the fact he couldn't mend it quickly and was obviously incompetent. I reassured her we'd use somebody else in the future and that she'd be perfectly safe there. Indeed, now that the flat has a brand new up-to-date lock on it, it'll be the safest place in Margate. She liked that idea very much. So she agreed to take it.' Her eyes flashed in triumph.

Adam took a breath. Maybe he'd underestimated Ruth's ability to think clearly in a crisis. 'That's excellent,' he managed. 'Well done, reacting like that under pressure. Not everyone could have done that.'

Ruth sighed, collapsing into her chair and stretching her long boot-clad legs along her desk. 'Well, it seemed like the obvious thing to say,' she replied. 'And, who knows, it might have even been true.' She gave him one of her radiant smiles. 'Anyway, it's good to know you have the local contacts. So next time, if there is such a thing, I can call your tame locksmith and get things sorted out faster and cheaper.' She paused and turned up the smile another notch. 'Can't I?'

'Of course,' beamed Adam, cursing his own big mouth. Now he'd have to come up with something else. Still, Joe Young seemed to be a man of many and varied abilities, and he was sure they could find another way of exposing Ruth's inexperience. 'Yes, anything you need, you only have to ask.'

Chapter Twelve

The high winds blew themselves out and the rain fell less often as spring began to arrive. Overcast days gave way to sunshine, scudding white clouds against the blue sky. The sea changed from slate grey to turquoise and the first buds appeared on the trees.

It was hard to be unhappy on such days, thought Lorna, but she seemed to be managing it all the same. Even though nobody else had said anything on her latest trips to Battersea, she couldn't shake off the fear that her secret was about to be revealed. Her mother seemed no better, although not actually any worse. She was still too thin, and liable to let slip the most private information at any moment, but maybe the pills were at least stabilising her. Ted appeared to be coping, and Lorna now steeled herself to go to the big supermarket whenever she visited. That way she knew there was food in the house, even if her mother didn't want to eat much of it.

The added agony of Richard's relatives being nearby made things even more painful, making it harder for Lorna to forget him and the terrible end to a marriage she had been certain was for ever. Now the shock of it had worn off and she had settled in Margate, she was left to face the fact that it was well and truly over and the divorce was going through. Even when she had seen the papers for the first time, some inner part of her had held on to the hope that he would change his mind. Now she knew that would not happen.

Robert's presence was an increasing comfort to her, not to mention the useful lifts to London, but she could not allow herself to think of it as anything more. True, her instincts told her he might be interested in her. But it was impossible to believe it. Myra's comment had hit home; she ate too much, didn't make enough of an effort with herself, and worst of all was her painful, shameful secret. So Lorna ruthlessly stopped herself from hoping for a new relationship. Robert was so kind. He'd never mentioned a girlfriend, past or present, but she was sure he wouldn't be single for long. Those understanding eyes and his gentle manner would attract women in droves, so he would soon find somebody more glamorous, more outgoing than her – somebody who was normal.

It came as a surprise to find a letter on the doormat addressed to her. It didn't look as if it was from the solicitors or the bank – and they were the only people who ever wrote to her, she thought grimly. Collapsing on a kitchen chair after taking Penny to school, she reached for a biscuit and opened the envelope. The handwriting looked familiar.

Dear Lorna,

So, where have you been hiding yourself? You've no idea how difficult it was to get your address out of Aunt Myra. For a start she won't speak to me no more on account of my profession – not that she has a leg to stand on, stuck in that house with that miserable old git of a husband, though I shouldn't say it. So I got our cousin Pete, who does talk to me but only when the others don't know about it, to go round and finally he wheedled it out of her. Said she wasn't looking too good. So that's partly why I'm writing, to see how you are.

The other is to say you lucky sod, living by the sea. Don't suppose you fancy a visitor? I'd love to come and see you. Here's my phone number – but don't ring too early as no one will thank you for it.

Love, Maureen

Lorna threw back her head and laughed for the first time in what felt like ages. Her cousin wrote exactly like she spoke, and she could hardly wait to talk to her in person. Hurriedly she checked her watch. No, definitely still too early. Well, she'd give it another hour and then ring her. If anyone could chase the blues away, Maureen could.

Joe pushed open the swinging door leading to the public bar of the pub nearest to his uncle's house. So, it was a bit early for a lunchtime pint, but he felt he'd earned it. He'd just have the one before Denis turned up. He didn't make a habit of it but he needed to think about what he was going to say, and the chances of getting a bit of peace and quiet anywhere else were slim. Gratefully he sipped his bitter, watching the sun's reflection through the lead-paned windows. This was a grand little spot – he'd hate to have to move on too soon.

'All right, Joe?' Denis slid into the seat beside his nephew. 'Bit warm for this, isn't it?' He nodded towards Joe's old donkey jacket, slung over the back of the chair.

'Warm one today, all right,' agreed Joe. 'Glad you could get away for an hour. He works you hard, that Adam Mortimer.'

'It's good regular work though,' Denis replied, licking the froth from the beer on his upper lip. 'I wouldn't knock it. He don't have a clue about that side of things so I get first refusal on the lot. Only too glad to put some of it your way, mind.' He smiled at his nephew. 'How are you finding him?'

Joe tried not to squirm. He could keep a poker face in most situations but not in front of his uncle, who knew him too well. 'He seems okay,' he began. 'Bit posh, of course. Or trying to be,' he added perceptively. 'Doesn't ask awkward questions, usually just lets me get on with things.' He paused. 'It's the things he lets me get on with, though. Some of the jobs have been a bit odd. Do you ever get that?'

Denis looked up from his pint in surprise. 'Odd? How d'you mean? Tricky piping? Got to expect that in these places – old properties, or ones what have been divided so someone can make a bit extra. You wouldn't want to live in a lot of them yourself, but I never came across one I couldn't fix in the end.'

'No, that's not it.' Joe sipped some more beer. 'It's like some things he doesn't want fixed. The opposite, in fact.'

'What, he wants you to break stuff?' asked Denis in amazement. 'Don't talk daft. That'll lose him money, and if there's one thing he doesn't like it's paying for anything he doesn't have to.'

'Not quite,' said Joe. Then he changed his mind. 'Sort of. It's like he's out to cause trouble somewhere. It doesn't make sense, but that's what he's after. Never says as much, but it's like, make that lock stiffer, not easier, fix that tap just enough so it'll last for a day or two but will start to leak after that.' And that was just the start of it, he thought. But if his uncle didn't know anything about it, he'd keep the other stuff to himself.

'No, you must have got that all wrong,' insisted Denis. 'He'd only have to call you, or me, back to do it right. You must have misunderstood.'

'Suppose so,' said Joe. 'Well, you know him better than me. So, have you heard the latest about Aunty Mary? She's only gone and dyed her hair like them punk rockers . . .'

The two men passed the rest of their lunch break speculating about what had driven Denis's youngest sister to throw aside years of respectability, putting it down first to boredom, then losing her mind, then finally to a man. 'Ah well, you should have seen her years ago,' laughed Denis. 'She was a bit wild then. Looks as if she's reverted to type.' He set down his glass. 'Right, got to go. See you later.' And he headed for the door.

Joe stayed where he was, thinking hard. He didn't really care what Aunty Mary did. He was more interested in the fact that Denis genuinely thought Adam Mortimer was on the level, something he himself knew not to be true. So he was the only one who knew about the extra requests. He knew his uncle would say nothing – what went on between family stayed within family. But if he were to share the information with others . . . He'd come to Margate desperate to earn enough to pay off debts he'd built up across South London, and one particularly unpleasant character was becoming increasingly keen to get his money back. But maybe he could be paid with information? Or, Joe could use that information to get the money to pay off the debt, and a little more besides? Which would work best? Now that was a very interesting dilemma to have. He'd be sad to leave Margate, especially as it looked as if the weather was on the turn – it would be great to be here in the summer. But life didn't give you a chance like this very often and he'd be a fool not to make the most of it.

'And what did you do today?' Lorna asked Penny as the little girl rushed to hug her at the school gates. 'Did you sit next to Debbie again? She'll have to come round to play some time to make up for the times you've been to her house.'

'Really?' Penny's eyes lit up. 'Yes please. We did lots of colouring, and we drew birds.' She pointed at a seagull swooping low over the playground. 'Birds like that. With yellow mouths.'

'Beaks, darling, birds have beaks,' Lorna told her gently. 'But that sounds very good indeed. I bet yours was the best in the class.'

'I didn't finish it,' Penny said solemnly. 'I can show you when it's all done.'

Lorna nodded happily, and then decided to share her news with the girl. 'We might have a visitor soon,' she said. 'Would you like that?'

Penny nodded, then had a thought. 'Who is it? Uncle Richard?'

A shadow passed over Lorna's face. 'No, he's still in

Spain,' she said, amazed that the child could remember him. Hastily she banished the familiar pain she felt when anyone mentioned his name. It wasn't the girl's fault. 'But that's very clever of you to know his name. I wonder if you can remember anyone else from Spain? Like the time a lady with red hair came to stay with me?'

Instantly the girl gave a huge smile. 'The one with the lovely clothes? She had a big shirt with flowers on it. Really big flowers.'

Lorna had to laugh. 'That's right. She did. She always has lovely clothes. Well, she's coming to stay in Margate.'

'But where will she sleep?' Penny looked worried. 'Will she have to share my room?'

'No, no,' Lorna reassured her. 'She's going to a hotel.'

'Like Mummy does?'

'Sort of,' said Lorna, making sure her disapproval didn't show on her face. She knew that Ruth was getting lots of business from hotel owners who recommended the agency to their guests, and therefore had to spend lots of time meeting them, getting to know them better and ensuring she made the right impression. She just hadn't realised how much of this Penny had noticed. Still, it probably didn't matter. 'She'll just sleep there and then she'll spend the day with us. Will you like that?'

'She could take me shopping,' Penny suggested.

'Maybe she will,' grinned Lorna. 'Maybe she will.'

Chapter Thirteen

Ruth paced around the living room, wondering how a flat that had at first seemed spacious now felt cramped and confined. In her hand was the letter that had arrived at the office earlier. Thank God she'd seen it first, not Robert. He'd probably have wrinkled his nose in disapproval, wondering how she'd landed in this mess.

She couldn't believe that she'd had such a run of bad luck with her properties – it was non-stop, what with wiring and roofing and furniture. But this was the first time anyone had threatened to sue. She wasn't sure what to do, and she hated that. Once she'd got Denis's name from Adam, that had solved most of the maintenance issues, but this was in a different league.

She briefly thought about consulting Robert – he'd most likely have come across this sort of thing before. But that would mean admitting he knew more than she did. Maybe she could dress it up and pretend it was happening to a friend, or something like that? No, he'd see through it – he was that sort of man, Ruth thought with annoyance; he didn't seem taken with her charms.

So who else could she turn to? Lorna would be useless. She'd only done the typing when she'd worked for an agency before and had been completely unable to remember anything relevant from that. This needed someone who knew the details of contract law. Again she cursed herself for not checking the paperwork. How could she have left out a whole clause?

That only left one person, she thought grimly. Adam. That would mean admitting her vulnerability and woeful ignorance of this side of the business, and she was unwilling to do so. She recalled that she had vowed never to reveal financial weakness to a man ever again. What choice did she have, though? Better to get it sorted sooner rather than later, Ruth thought grimly. The question was, what would be the best way of asking him?

Ruth was more than aware of the effect she had on Adam, and didn't deny that she found him good-looking. When he'd taken her out for meals they had had a good time together, and if she was honest with herself she missed those evenings, which had come to a halt as the business took off. She was just too busy, networking in the circles she so desperately needed to be accepted by to be a success in the town. She came to a decision. She would apologise for her lack of avail-ability, assuming with total confidence that he had found no one else to take her place, and suggest that they resume their meals out together. After all, she mused, it would be no bad thing to be seen out and about at the right restaurants. It would give a certain impression, now that enough local people knew her to recognise her, and that sort of thing was invaluable in the long run. All she needed was the name of a decent lawyer, one who wouldn't charge the earth, without revealing the dangerous state of her own finances. She was sure Adam had never had to worry about such things.

'I'm very sorry,' said Robert when Lorna dropped by the office. Both Ruth and Adam were out, and he'd been alone at his desk when the call had come. 'I won't be able to go to London this weekend after all. My friends won't be there – they've been called up north for a funeral.'

'Oh, poor them,' said Lorna, instantly feeling guilty as relief at not having to cope with her mother washed over her. 'You mustn't worry about me. It's a shame you won't get your break though.'

'It's a shame I won't have your company there and back,' he said, then coughed in an attempt to hide his embarrassment at having said such a rash thing.

'Robert, you are funny,' laughed Lorna. 'I'm just glad I'm not a burden to you. You know I love our conversations. It's made such a difference being able to go by car.'

'Maybe a fortnight after?' he asked, quietly hoping that she would agree. He didn't like to admit to himself that he lived for those drives when he had Lorna to himself. Everyone thought that Ruth was so magnetically attractive but she paled into insignificance compared to her friend. Lorna didn't seem to realise just how lovely she was. He longed to tell her how he felt but knew she had a lot to cope with at present, so resolved to wait for the right moment.

'Well, actually, I can't make that,' she said now, and Robert nodded, gamely hiding his rush of disappointment. Maybe she'd found someone else? He knew that she was getting divorced – she'd mentioned that on one of their earliest trips to London, while adding that she didn't want to go into details. It was one reason why he had been determined not to rush things as he didn't want to push her too far too fast. But now . . .

'That's when my cousin is coming down,' she was saying. 'I haven't seen her since last summer, and she's really good fun. She'll love Margate. I'll have to introduce you both.'

'I'll look forward to that,' Robert assured her. 'Maybe all three of us can do something together. Or will Ruth be joining you?'

Lorna blushed, and looked away. 'Well, the thing is, I haven't told her about Maureen's visit,' she confessed. 'They used to know each other quite well and they don't really get on. In fact, would you mind not mentioning it? I don't want to put you in an awkward position but . . .'

'Think nothing of it,' said Robert at once. But he was intrigued. Lorna wasn't one to make up something like that, but it made him wonder what was behind her request. What could Ruth have done in the past?

Well, that was a turn-up for the books, thought Adam. Fancy Ruth suggesting that they go out together again. True, she'd made it sound like a business tactic: everyone would assume that their firms were doing nicely if they were seen to patronise the local top spots. Confidence equals success, she'd purred. She'd also promised to foot half the bill, so what had he got to lose? He'd be seen in the company of the most attractive and eligible woman in town.

He'd missed their evenings out. Ruth in the office was like a whirling dervish, never still for a moment, always on the phone, doing deals, making speculative calls, following leads, often foul-tempered, impossible to talk to most of the time. Despite himself, he had to admire the way she tackled all the problems he'd caused her. It remained to be seen how she'd cope with the latest one. But he had to find a way of discovering what sort of reserves she had.

Now, as he carefully adjusted his favourite silk tie in the hotel lobby mirror, he reminded himself that he was here to combine business with pleasure. He was not, under any circumstances, to forget that.

'There you are!' Ruth swept in, the long black coat swinging open to reveal a figure-hugging black dress with a tiny flash of diamanté across its almost modest neckline. 'Hope you weren't waiting for long.'

Before he could answer, they were led to their table, one set just in front of a large window overlooking the sea. Good, thought Adam. If we're here to be seen, they'll notice us from inside and out. He made a point of taking the wine list. He didn't care how good-looking or astute a woman was – it was the man's job to choose the wine.

'I'd love a gin and tonic to start,' Ruth said at once.

'Good idea, and I'll join you,' Adam replied immediately, 'as it's so much better to decide on the wine once we know what we'll be eating, don't you think?'

Ruth raised her eyebrows in acknowledgement.

Adam smiled to himself. It seemed they couldn't sit at the same table for thirty seconds without some kind of power game but it definitely added a frisson to the evening. Steady on, he told himself. Business. And that meant small talk first and then, after the plates had been cleared, finding out what this was really about.

But as the evening went on, with more delicious white-bait followed by even better lemon sole, all accompanied by a dry white wine he was rather pleased with himself for selecting, Adam found himself enjoying himself more and more. God, Ruth could turn on the charm when she wanted to, and he was more than happy for her to turn it on full beam for him. Everything about her spoke of class, from the understated earrings that sparkled like the beading on her dress to the clever make-up she'd used on her astonishing catlike eyes. Even if this *was* business, tonight he felt like a lucky man.

'So, Adam,' she was saying. 'It was so kind of you to introduce me to Denis. He's been invaluable.'

Adam nodded, waiting for what came next.

'I wonder if you had any other useful contacts, in other areas of the business?' she went on. 'Say, for example, someone who's really on top of property law?'

Bingo, he thought. His plan had worked. When Ruth had found her first clients, he'd shown her a template for a standard contract but he'd deliberately removed a key clause, meaning she'd be liable for damage when usually it would be the landlord's responsibility. Now it looked as if that might be paying off.

'Law?' he echoed. 'Tricky, as that depends on how much you've got to spend. No such thing as a cheap lawyer.'

Ruth fiddled with her left earring and looked downcast. 'I realise that, and I don't want bargain basement, I want competence. However, as you know, the business is in its early stages and I don't think it can fund someone out of the Yellow Pages. It would be so useful to have a personal recommendation.' She flashed her brilliant eyes at him. 'Always good to keep it personal, isn't it? And I know any personal contact you can suggest will be worth it.' She kept her gaze steadily on his face and moistened her lips just a little. 'Although I suppose I can draw upon my savings if really necessary.'

Bingo again, Adam silently crowed, forcing himself to look away from those glossy lips. She had savings. Although she hadn't said how much, he reckoned she didn't really look that worried about paying for a lawyer, so it must be a sizeable amount. He'd found out what he needed to know and so now he could afford to be generous.

'I have just the person you need,' he assured her. 'I'll give you the details tomorrow.' He lowered his voice. 'And it's definitely better to keep things personal.'

Another flash of those eyes. 'As personal as possible, I'd say.' Ruth sipped her wine, then finished the rest of the glass. 'Wouldn't you agree?'

Was she saying what he thought she was saying?

'Maybe you'd like a coffee?' he asked carefully. 'Or . . . something stronger? There are some very fine liqueurs here . . .'

'Mmm, maybe a brandy,' Ruth breathed, her expression unreadable. 'To remind me of Spain. A brandy on a warm night – nothing to beat it. You should try it some time – the cooling air against your hot skin. After all, there's no hurry, is there?'

'I'm certainly in no hurry,' he said, liking the way things were going more and more. Then a devilish urge prompted him to add, 'But don't you need to get back to your daughter?' He was pretty sure what the answer would be, as it was obvious Ruth cared far more for her career than her child.

'God, no,' she said, tossing her hair, exposing her collar-bones and smooth shoulders. 'Lorna can see to her. She'll look after her for as long as we like.' She gave him a direct look. 'All night, if necessary.'

'And do you think it might be necessary?' asked Adam, hardly daring to believe his ears. 'Do you think we should explore the world of personal contact in more depth?'

Ruth pushed her wine glass forward so that her fingers brushed against his. A few drops of condensation fell from the stem onto his wrist, but he hardly noticed. 'I've always wondered what the rest of this hotel was like,' she said softly. 'So it would be good research to find out, don't you think? I really feel that would be very necessary indeed.'

Adam had to stop himself from gasping. So Ruth could be as decisive in her private life as in business. This was going far faster than he'd imagined or, deep down, ever dared to hope. He stroked her fingers, her palm.

'Then let's go,' he said. 'We can order brandy later. Or anything you like. But let's go at once. Ruth, I want you and I want you now.'

Chapter Fourteen

'It's so good to see you!' cried Lorna, hugging her cousin as the train pulled away from the platform at Margate Station. 'You look great, fitter than ever.'

'It's all the dancing,' Maureen said, pulling her little leather jacket tight against the early summer sea breeze. 'I'm trying something new. Got to face it, you have a shelf life as a stripper, and I'm not going to be one of those washed-out has-beens forced to work the pubs with sticky floors. I'm diversifying. I'm learning burlesque.'

'Really?' said Lorna.

'You haven't got a clue what that is, have you?' demanded Maureen. 'Don't look so horrified. It's an art form. An entertainment. It's much classier than stripping. You don't really show much but you've got to be good at using these great big fans. It's dead hard but once I've got the knack nothing will stop me, just you see.'

'Oh, okay,' said Lorna, not really any the wiser. The sun caught her hair, which, because she'd been outside so much as spring began to turn into summer, was more dark blonde than boring mousey brown. Her cousin, sharp-eyed as ever, noticed.

'And look at you!' Maureen exclaimed. 'Lorna, this place suits you. Your hair is different, and you've lost weight. You've still got to do something about them clothes but I can help you there. But you've definitely changed for the better.' Her expression grew sharp. 'Is there a man on the scene?'

'It's all the haring round after Penny,' Lorna protested. 'She runs me ragged – not that I mind. You remember her, don't you?'

'Yeah, of course. Cute kid, big eyes, dark hair,' said Maureen instantly, but she was not to be put off. 'Come on, Lorna. Spill the beans. I know the signs.'

'Don't be silly!' Her cousin was too much sometimes. 'You know how upset I was when Richard left. I couldn't imagine anyone else wanting me. And I'm still not over the divorce.'

'Lorna Johnson, look at me,' Maureen insisted, coming to a stop on the busy pavement. 'You are a very attractive woman. Any man would be a fool not to see it. So don't give me that. And if I'm not very much mistaken someone has seen it and you damn well know it.'

Lorna couldn't meet her cousin's eyes, and turned to start walking along towards the seafront. Should she put into words what she'd only been dreaming about? It looked as if she wasn't going to get much choice.

'Right,' she said slowly. 'There *is* someone who's really nice. He's been giving me lifts up to see Mum and he's been brilliant about it, he really has. You know what she's like and . . . and he just listens to me. Doesn't judge what I say, but listens. I've never known anything like it. There's nothing more to it.'

'Not yet, you mean,' said Maureen perceptively. 'But you'd like there to be.'

'Yes,' confessed Lorna. 'I keep trying to pretend otherwise, but . . . I really like him. A lot.' Suddenly it was all too much and her emotions overwhelmed her. Desperately she reached for her sunglasses to hide the tears. 'It's hopeless, I know it is. What if he does like me as much as I like him, and then we start talking about the future – I'll have to tell him there isn't one.'

'But why?' asked Maureen. 'Come on, let's sit over there on that bench. Can't have you wandering around in a state. What's the problem? Wish I had a problem like yours – nice kind man doing me favours.'

'You don't understand,' sniffed Lorna, trying in vain to stem the flood. 'I'll have to tell him I'm a freak, and then he won't want to know me.'

'A freak?' repeated Maureen. 'You aren't a freak, and I should know, I've seen a lot. You're the least freaky person I know.'

With difficulty, Lorna managed to calm herself. 'Right,' she said. 'I've never told a soul this, apart from Richard. And of course Mum knows. But no one else. So you have to swear to keep it absolutely secret.'

'Of course,' said Maureen, worried now. 'What the hell is the matter?'

'It's me,' Lorna said, steadily now that she had made up her mind to tell the shameful truth. 'I'm not normal. I'm not a proper woman. Not inside. So I can never, ever have children, and that rips me apart, I can't tell you how much. I don't have a womb, you see.'

'What?' gasped Maureen, shocked. 'How can that be? How can you not have a womb?'

'You see! You see!' Lorna cried, tears flowing again. 'Even you think it's terrible. Everyone will laugh at me if they know. I hate myself, I hate it, I hate it.'

'No, no, no,' said Maureen, almost crying herself now. 'You're not terrible. This . . . this . . . condition, that's what's terrible. Oh, you poor thing. And you've been hiding that away for all this time.' She reached out for Lorna's hand – the one that wasn't wiping away the tears.

'Since I was a teenager,' she gulped. 'Mum took me to the doctor's, wondered why my periods hadn't started. That's how they found out. Told me I'd never have them, because I didn't have a womb. Born without one. It can happen, just not very often. But it happened to me.'

'No periods, well, that's a consolation,' said Maureen, trying to make light of it.

'No,' she said. 'Not much of one. Because I really, really wanted children. Every time I see a baby it reminds me that I can never have my own.'

'And you'd be a brilliant mother,' sighed Maureen. 'Look at how you are with that kid – sorry, Penny. Anyone can see how good you are. Oh Lorna, that is so unfair.'

'Yes,' said Lorna. 'Yes it is. And I hate to speak ill of my friend, who's also my boss, but she doesn't give a fig about her daughter. She doesn't deserve her. Why could she have a baby and not me? It's just not right.' She stopped, exhausted.

Maureen gave a rueful laugh. 'You don't have to apologise to me over her. I know exactly what she's like and you're too good to be working for her. She won't ever give a stuff for anyone but herself. So it's just as well that Penny does have you or she wouldn't get no love at all.'

'You're probably right,' admitted Lorna. 'But it doesn't

103

solve this mess. I don't know what to do. Mum always insisted I should never tell anybody, and turns out she was right, because when I told Richard he left me.'

Maureen thought about that for a moment. 'Okay,' she said finally. 'Okay, but you'd been married for a while, right? You didn't tell him before? So what really hurt him was the deception.'

Lorna nodded, keeping her gaze on the scuffed ground at their feet.

'So, if this is going to get serious with . . . with . . .'

'Robert.'

'Robert. If he's as lovely as you say he is, then you can't let him go. God knows good men are hard to find. If you want a future with this Robert, then you got no choice.' Maureen waited until her cousin met her eyes. 'Lorna, you've got to tell him.'

Ruth stared at the ceiling, watching the patterns made by the curtains blowing in the slight breeze. She was loath to get up. Despite the fact that she had plenty to do in the office, she decided she deserved to relish the rare chance of a lie-in. Although this wouldn't be the first time recently that she'd woken up in a plush hotel.

Who'd have thought it, she mused, even as part of her mind noted the décor and sleek modern lines of the furniture – most likely Habitat. Even the curtains were delicate cream panels, not common old nets. Who'd have thought she and Adam would get along so well in bed? She'd planned to play it cool that first night but had got drawn into the sparring over the dinner table, and then against all odds had realised that she was really enjoying herself and that there was a genuine spark between them.

What had been a spark in the dining room became a blistering blaze once they'd reached the bedroom. They'd barely made it through the door before tearing each other's clothes off, both desperate to feel the other's skin. They'd made love on the carpet, in the bed, in the shower. They'd hardly slept. It had been incredible and her body had known nothing like it. When dawn had broken and they ceased at last she had collapsed, exhausted but completely exhilarated.

Since then they had repeated the experience several times a week, always trying a new hotel. Mostly they had stayed in town but on a couple of occasions they'd gone as far as a country house, away from it all, when they had to drop any pretence that they were only meeting up to impress the movers and shakers of Margate. That had been purely for themselves, to explore this wonderful new element in their lives, to revel in the other's body and to give in entirely to pleasure.

Ruth shook her head, happily amazed at what had happened to her. To think that she'd endured all those revolting slobbery advances from Vincent Chase, that possessive bully. Then Kevin Dolby – at least he had been good-looking, but what a let-down he had been. Laurence, her late husband, had been mercifully undemanding, thanks to the difference in their ages. As long as she'd looked good, he had basically been happy. And that's what she'd been doing ever since, looking her impressive best, trading her appearance for her own advantage.

Now Ruth's perspective had shifted. She wouldn't call it love – no, that was reserved strictly for herself and her all-consuming ambitions. But she loved what Adam did to her and it seemed he loved what she did to him right back. It was a powerful combination and she had the sense that it would take them far.

A good-looking man with his own business, who was prepared to help her build her own – could life get any better? If only she were truly free to do this more often. Lorna had begun to ask questions and Penny had been making comments about people staying in hotels. Ruth didn't know where the girl had got this from but it only made her more irritated with her daughter. Things would be so much simpler if she simply weren't around. Just a little longer and with a few more clients, maybe she would have enough to send the child away to school. Or, better still, if she could combine her income with the assets Adam must have . . .

She heard the shower being turned off and the bathroom door swung open, revealing Adam wrapped in a small white towel.

'That's not big enough to cover anything,' she purred, throwing back the covers. 'So you might as well take it off and come right back here.'

Adam didn't need to be told twice.

Joe was sweating as he put down the phone. He'd deliberately gone to a pub where no one would know him, busy enough so there was a background hum of noise to cover his conversation but not so packed that he'd have to stand close to anyone to make the call. It wasn't something he wanted people to overhear.

He'd put off doing anything with the information he had on Adam Mortimer for as long as he could, wanting to enjoy Margate while it lasted. But now he was under a lot of pressure to repay his debts and the time had come to act. He'd just managed to persuade his most frightening creditor that he had a failsafe way of getting the money but only by promising it by the end of the week. God, he deserved a drink for that. It had been the most terrifying conversation of his life.

Gulping down half of the welcome pint in one go, Joe pondered his next move. Should it be by phone, by letter or in person? The latter, he decided. It wasn't as if he was going to hide his identity. And he didn't think Mortimer had it in him to be physically violent, and even if he did, he was confident that he could beat him. He had to hit him hard where he was most vulnerable and that was easy to spot. His reputation.

Joe had astutely guessed that Mortimer was nothing like as solidly respectable as he liked to make out. From his few visits to the office he could see how busy the man was – not very. That agency must be on very shaky ground, he thought, and one rumour about Mortimer's reliability could well ruin him. He'd never risk it. He might be all cheerful and hearty but Joe was willing to bet he was a coward underneath.

So it was a question of when would be the best time to pay a call. It would have to be when he was the only one in the office. Joe knew another agency occupied the other part of the premises, as he'd often seen a quiet-looking man behind a desk there. Uncle Denis said it was run by a very glamorous woman, but he'd never seen her, much less done any work for her – that was his uncle's territory. But they had both better be out when he went round. Thinking about it, maybe that was who Mortimer was out to sabotage – they'd be direct rivals in the property management side of his business. But would he really be so stupid as to try to ruin someone he shared an office with? Yes, decided Joe, he probably would.

Joe vaguely remembered there was another pub nearly opposite the side entrance to the agency office, which would serve his purpose very well. Better not have any more to drink though, he chided himself. Don't want to blow it. Afterwards would be a different story, but for now he needed a clear head. Reluctantly he pushed away his glass, leaving some beer still unfinished. There would be time enough for all that later.

'Can I have a dress like yours?' Penny demanded, fascinated by Maureen's brightly coloured smock.

'Not sure that they do them in your size, pet,' said Maureen, grinning at the cheeky little girl, 'but if we see one you can try it on. How's that?'

'All right,' said Penny, who wasn't one to complain about things she couldn't change. She was having a great day, showing Lorna's cousin around all her favourite places. 'Look, that's the best ice cream van. Shall we have some? They do flakes and everything.'

'I see what you mean about being run ragged,' Maureen said as she allowed herself to be dragged along. 'And talk about emptying your purse! How do you do it?'

'Well, you don't have to say yes to everything she asks you for,' Lorna pointed out. She found it highly entertaining to see her tough-as-nails cousin having rings run round her by a child. 'She's right, though, those ice creams are the best in town.'

'Better have some to check then,' said Maureen, reaching for her handbag. 'Ninety-nines all round, is it?'

'Yes please,' said Penny. 'Sometimes we come here with Robert and he lets me have one of those too. He says there's nothing to beat them, not even in London.'

'Does he indeed?' said Maureen archly, passing the ice creams around. 'Not likely . . . oh, no, I take it back.' She beamed in delight. 'These are bloody lovely, whoops, don't repeat that, Penny. This Robert must be a man of taste.' She pulled a face at Lorna, who didn't rise to the bait.

'Don't you have proper ice creams in London, then?' asked Penny, fascinated. 'What do you eat there? Can I come and stay with you and find out?'

'Steady on, Penny,' said Lorna. 'Maureen has to work all day and can't be looking after you all the time.'

The girl's face fell.

'Not yet, anyway,' Maureen added hastily, not wanting to upset the child. 'Tell you what, you come when you're bigger. By then I'll have a flat with enough room for you to stay. Do we have a deal?'

Lorna shook her head at Maureen's indulgence but Penny nodded, her expression totally serious. 'Deal,' she said.

Chapter Fifteen

Adam sat at his desk with his head in his hands, unable to believe what had just happened. How had a day that had started so spectacularly well ended up like this? Where had he gone wrong?

Groaning, he looked up and realised he was still shaking. To have been threatened like that by someone he'd trusted had shocked him deeply. Should he have resisted more strongly? It was humiliating enough that he'd been so open to attack, worse to think he'd had no real means of fighting back. Yes, he could always go to the police but the damage would rebound on him. He'd put so much effort into creating the image of a successful estate agent who inspired trust – one well-placed bad word could bring it crashing down. Why hadn't he seen it coming?

Slowly, Adam levered himself out of his chair. Joe hadn't laid a hand on him – he hadn't had to, not after he'd explained what he wanted and why. But the rush of terror had made his legs turn to jelly and he could barely walk. Step by tentative step he made his way to the kitchenette and filled the kettle, which seemed extraordinarily heavy to lift. Searching for a clean mug he managed to knock over two plates, which shattered on the linoleum. The sound echoed painfully in his ears but he was too drained even to jump.

Clutching his mug of black coffee, he returned to his desk, pulled open the bottom drawer and delved into the back of it until he found what he was after. Adam had kept a bottle of single malt in there and barely touched it, thinking it would be for emergencies only – but he hadn't imagined an occasion such as this. He sloshed some into the bitter coffee, reflecting that his lack of sleep hadn't helped. He hadn't exactly been at his most alert when Joe had found him alone in the office.

God, what a mess. What was he going to do? Part of him wanted to run to Ruth for comfort. But realistically, the relationship they'd embarked upon didn't include comfort. Excitement, brutal passion, satisfaction, yes. But they were too competitive and driven to find much time for comfort.

What if she found out? Did Denis know, for instance, and would he be likely to say anything? No, Adam reasoned, Denis was decent to the core and had been loyal to him, even when offered lucrative work elsewhere. He'd always found time to sort out any problems, although that of course was where the whole thing had begun, when he'd offered to send his nephew Adam's way.

He managed to avoid thinking about the next logical step: that if he hadn't decided to sabotage Ruth's properties, then none of this would have happened. Joe would have had no ammunition. Adam was more worried about how he was going to prevent her discovering the whole sorry mess. If anything he now needed her, and her savings, even more. And he would be bitterly disappointed if their nights together were to come to an end, as they surely would if she learnt he'd been trying to wreck her business. While he couldn't say he loved Ruth, he found her completely addictive and couldn't imagine going back to how they were before. He could cope with her foul temper in the office, as long as he had her where he wanted her in his bed.

Morosely, Adam stared at the bottom of the coffee mug. All that money, gone just like that. He felt like one of those cartoon characters running off the edge of a cliff, legs still powering away but with nothing but air beneath. How was he going to survive now?

He couldn't summon the energy to move when he heard the door opening.

Ruth rushed in, gorgeous as always, briefcase in one hand and files in the other, in full professional mode. She came to an abrupt halt when she saw the look on his face.

'What . . .' she began.

'Don't ask,' he said. Then he came to a decision. 'I've made a really stupid mistake.'

As he walked across the park, Robert felt as if he was bunking off school – or imagined that was what it would have felt like if he'd ever tried it, which he hadn't. But the sun was out, the immediate daily tasks were done and Ruth was due back at any moment, so he was free to take an extended late lunch break. God knows he'd covered her back enough over the past couple of weeks when she'd arrived late, left early or simply not appeared at all.

As he'd guessed, there was the woman he wanted to see, with the child, and somebody else who was impossible to miss as she was wearing very bright colours. Even in Margate, where holidaymakers loved to dress brightly, she stood out.

There was a cry of delight and the little girl broke away from the group, yelling, 'It's Robert, it's Robert,' at the top of her voice. She then barrelled straight into him, nearly knocking him flying.

'Hello, Penny,' he said, trying not to wince. 'Still practising the rugby tackles?'

'What's them?' asked Penny, mouth all covered in chocolate. 'Come over here, Aunty Lorna's got someone with her, and she said the ice creams were bloody lovely.'

'Did she?' said Robert, wondering who was going to get into trouble for that one. He could see the woman in the gaudy colours more clearly now. She had bright red hair and was slimmer than her cousin – too thin, he thought, like she runs off nervous energy all the time. Still, that might be no bad thing when it came to dealing with Penny. Grimly he noticed a patch of chocolate on his trousers where she'd collided with him. Oh well, it would come off. Probably.

Lorna was beaming at him. 'What good luck you're here,' she said. 'This is my cousin, Maureen. Maureen, Robert – Robert, Maureen.'

'Pleased to meet you, I'm sure,' said Maureen with a saucy grin. 'Heard all about you, I have.'

'Delighted,' said Robert, shaking her hand, which was covered in big bright rings. 'Lorna's been looking forward to seeing you.'

'I love it here!' Maureen exclaimed. 'And doesn't it suit her? You should have seen her before, all down in the dumps she was, with a face like a wet weekend.'

'Oh stop it,' said Lorna, but he could tell it was all

113

done with affection. 'You do exaggerate. You always did.'

Penny had clearly had enough of grown-ups talking and grabbed Maureen's hand. 'This way,' she insisted, 'I need to show you the lake.'

'Looks as if your cousin is a hit,' Robert smiled, turning to Lorna, secretly pleased he had her to himself.

'Absolutely,' agreed Lorna. 'Penny loves her. It's partly the clothes. Pity about the swearing but I'll deal with that later.' They wandered slowly in the direction of the lake, in no hurry to catch the others up.

'Can't see Ruth being happy about the bad language,' Robert replied, 'even if she uses far worse herself.'

'Well, that's Ruth for you,' said Lorna. She turned her face up to the sun, and he noticed that she had a new smattering of freckles across her nose. They suited her, he thought. Come to think of it, there was a glow about her. Must be the change in the weather. Then she looked serious, and turned back to him.

'Actually, Robert,' she said, all trace of fun gone from her voice, 'I'm glad you're here, for a different reason.'

Oh no, he thought, what was it now? Was her mother worse, or was it something closer to home? Lorna seemed to be steeling herself to speak again.

'Well, you know you can tell me anything,' he said lightly, hoping he'd misunderstood.

'Yes,' she said, 'I really feel I can. And that's just as well. You see, I've got a confession to make. You might think I'm crazy and jumping the gun but I don't want us to get off on the wrong foot. So . . . I have something to say to you.'

Ruth sat back in her chair, trying to make sense of what she'd just heard. She didn't know whether to believe it or not. She realised that she had made a huge assumption about Adam: that he knew what he was doing. Well, she'd been wrong on that count, for a start.

He'd told her how he had been blackmailed – and by Denis's nephew, of all people. Ruth hadn't met the lad but Denis had gone on and on about him, what a good workman he was, even if he'd got into a bit of trouble when he was younger, which was why he'd wanted to give him a leg up. God, Ruth had thought, what I would have given for someone like Denis to help me when I was that age. That boy doesn't know how lucky he is. Then she'd shaken herself. It wasn't the time to revisit her horrible childhood – there were decisions to be made, and quickly.

Apparently Adam had been unwise enough to get Joe to tamper with a few properties on the edge of town that were for sale through a rival estate agency. Nothing too obvious but enough to put off any prospective buyers, and that in turn would annoy the sellers, who'd then look for another agent to sell through. It wasn't as if anyone had got hurt – but it had certainly threatened Adam's bank balance, and his confidence.

So, he'd overreached himself and now didn't know how to deal with the consequences. Part of Ruth wanted to let him sort it out, serve him right for thinking he'd get away with being so stupid. Yet she couldn't pretend she felt nothing for him now that they'd shared such passionate nights together. Besides, the lad had been clever, threatening to undermine the agency's reputation. There was no way that could be pinned on him. Even though they ran two separate businesses, mud would stick and she risked being damaged too. That would not do. She'd have to act, to save both of them.

115

She cast her mind back to anything Denis had said about his nephew. He'd worked in Croydon – but also across South London. Alarm bells had rung even when he'd said it, but she'd told herself not to be stupid. Vincent Chase was dead, and there would be none of his henchmen left who could threaten her. Still, it would be best to be cautious. She pushed herself up and stalked back around the cabinets to where Adam was still slumped.

'Listen,' she said. 'Did you ever mention my name to Joe? Or do you think he's ever seen me?'

'What?' said Adam, confused. 'Not that I know of. He only came here when I was alone.' He had the grace to look ashamed. 'Obviously I wouldn't want you or Robert to hear what we talked about. But he'll know your name – it's on the sign outside, for a start.'

Hmm, thought Ruth, that should be okay. Nobody from her past life knew her as Mrs Hamilton-Smyth, and hardly anyone even knew she was called Ruth. She'd just have to assume it would be fine.

'Right,' she said. 'What do we know about Joe Young?'

'Well, he's a very good plumber . . .'

'No, no,' Ruth said impatiently, 'what are his weak spots? You've got to think like him, Adam. He saw your weak spot at once.' Or one of them, she growled to herself. Really, she should have watched him more closely and not been blinded by his good looks. But she'd have to put that to one side for the moment. 'What does he do in his spare time? What did he say about his past? What has Denis ever said about him?'

'Hell, it's really hard to say,' Adam groaned. 'I can't seem to think straight.'

'It's just as well I'm here then,' Ruth snapped. Now was not the time for sympathy. 'We know he was in trouble before. That's why he's in Margate. What sort of thing might it have been? Women? Gambling? Anything worse?'

'He must have been involved with a heavy crowd,' Adam sighed. 'I think he's no stranger to violence.'

'Unlikely to hit me, though,' said Ruth confidently. She'd had more than enough experience of judging who was going to beat her and who wasn't, though she didn't intend to explain that right now. 'One thing comes back to me. Denis always mentioned meeting him in a pub. I wouldn't be surprised if he was a drinker.'

Adam's eyes lit up. 'Although he never smelt of it when he came here, he would say he was off to the pub after-wards . . . actually he said that quite a lot.'

'So, drinkers need money,' she said, piecing it together, 'but not that much. Denis is helping him out – do we think he's got debts?'

'Now you say it, I did get that impression,' said Adam, more alert now. 'Debts, from someone in this heavy South London crowd. That was one reason he was so keen to work odd hours – he wanted the extra cash.'

'And as Denis is putting him up and he's working all hours, he's got nothing left to spend it on but booze,' guessed Ruth. 'Let's start from there. I'll try the nearest pubs.'

Adam made to rise from his desk.

'Oh no you don't,' she said at once. Then she relented a little, giving him a slow smile. 'Leave this to me. A little feminine persuasion is called for here.'

'So you see,' said Lorna, hanging back so that she was in the shade of the park fence, 'that's why I'll understand

117

if you don't want to know me any more.' She swallowed hard, bracing herself for Robert's reaction, hoping against desperate hope that he wouldn't simply back off and run. She turned away from him, dully noticing that the clematis was about to bloom.

Robert seemed to be at a loss for words. Finally, he cleared his throat.

'Oh my dear girl,' he said. 'Oh you poor thing. What a cruel thing to happen. I can't begin to imagine . . . to want the one thing so badly and to know you can never have it. That's just dreadful. How brave of you to tell me.'

Lorna had been so prepared for his disgust that it took her a moment to understand what he was saying. Gradually it dawned on her that he was still there. Somewhere deep inside of her, there was the tiniest burst of hope.

'Really?' she asked, her eyes searching his face now.

'Really,' he said.

'You don't think I'm a freak?' she went on. 'Or that . . . that I'm not a proper woman?'

'Not a proper woman?' he repeated. 'Oh Lorna, you are every bit a woman. I can't begin to tell you how wonderful a woman you are. Everything about you . . . there's nobody like you, you are the most beautiful woman I have ever seen.'

She was stunned. 'Me? No, that can't be right!' She couldn't stop the pleasure from showing on her face. 'I wouldn't call me beautiful. That's Ruth, that's Maureen. But thank you, thank you.' She realised she must be blushing as pink as the flowers budding on the fence.

'I'm not interested in Ruth or Maureen,' said Robert seriously. 'They can't hold a candle to you. And I'm, well,

I'm flattered you told me. I hope that means you trust me, because you can, Lorna. You can trust me with anything. I would never let you down.' He reached out and held her hand. 'You do believe me, don't you?'

She didn't hesitate. 'Yes, I do,' she said. 'I can't think of anyone I'd trust more. And I know this must be a strange thing to be discussing, but I didn't want . . . didn't want . . . to deceive you. I wanted to be honest, right from the beginning.'

'The beginning?' he repeated, smiling now. 'Are we beginning something? Is that what you'd like?'

'Yes, I think so,' she said, suddenly filled with confidence. 'Yes, that's exactly what I would like.'

'That's good,' Robert said, 'because it's exactly what I'd like too.'

Sounds of voices approaching made her jump but before Penny and Maureen could reach them, Lorna plucked up her courage, leaned towards him and very quickly kissed his cheek.

'To beginnings,' she said.

Ruth scanned the public bar for anyone of the right age in a donkey jacket, which Adam had assured her Joe always wore. Several older men had them on, despite the sun, and they all looked up to observe the newcomer. God, she thought, men were so predictable. At least she didn't have to try to please any of this lot.

Over in the corner, almost facing away from the door, was a likely contender. Ruth sized him up. Young, messy hair, the hideous donkey jacket. And now that she could see a little more of his face, he looked rather like Denis. Time for action.

She swept across the room and sat on the red velvet stool opposite him. 'Joe Young?' she said, eyebrow raised, as she took in the half-finished pint and the chaser – whisky, if she wasn't mistaken.

'Who wants to know?' asked the young man, taken completely by surprise.

'Right,' she said, not answering his question – he'd figure it out soon enough. 'This needn't take long.'

'What do you mean?' he spluttered.

'Look,' said Ruth, summoning all the haughtiness she'd used when on stage to intimidate her audience. 'We both know what you did this afternoon and I'm here to point out a few things to you. One, when you cross Mr Mortimer, you cross me, and, believe me, you really, really don't want to do that. Two, I am more connected than you could begin to imagine and whatever sad excuses for tough guys you think you're involved with will seem like puppy dogs compared to the people I know. Three, you are drunk.' She paused to judge the effect her words had had. Good, they seemed to have hit home.

'What do you want?' the man asked, slightly slurring his words.

'Let's see,' said Ruth, sizing him up. No, he wasn't in any state to cause trouble, but seemed just about sober enough to remember what she was going to tell him. 'Obviously, the money. Looks as if you've spent some of it already, but I'll have the rest back now, thank you. And,' she forced herself to bring her face closer to his, despite the smell of sour beer, 'if I ever hear any rumour doubting Mr Mortimer's reliability, I'll know where it came from. And I will find you. Don't even think I won't.

120

And when I do you will be very, very sorry.' She paused. 'Do I make myself clear?'

The young man seemed completely gobsmacked. 'How did you know I was here?' he gasped.

'Because I always know where to find you, of course,' she snapped. Good, he hadn't even questioned who she was. She held out her hand. 'The money. Now.'

He slumped over his pint, apparently defeated. Then he fumbled for his jacket, searching the pockets until he found an envelope. 'Here,' he mumbled. 'Take it. Then leave me alone.'

'Many thanks,' said Ruth imperiously, snatching the envelope and thrusting it into her bag. 'I won't say it was nice doing business with you because that would be a lie. Goodbye. You'd better hope our paths don't cross again.'

With that, she rose once more and pushed her way out of the bar, noticing with distaste its grubby carpets and yellowed paintwork. Stepping out into daylight, she took a deep breath. She hadn't enjoyed that – but at least she hadn't forgotten Vincent Chase's old methods. It was quite satisfying to use them against someone, rather than having them used against her.

'Who's yer lady friend?' came the catcalls back in the bar. Joe Young glared at the wall, ignoring them all. He was just glad he'd had the forethought to divide the money he owed his creditor from the extra he'd got out of Mortimer and planned to spend on himself. At least he'd kept what he needed to. Sadly, Joe realised that his time in sunny Margate was well and truly over.

Chapter Sixteen

May 1979

'This is a day that will go down in history!' Ruth dashed into the living room and switched on the television for the evening news. She turned to her daughter. 'Come and look at this, Penny. It's important.'

'Who's that?' asked Penny, chewing the last of her eggy soldiers.

'Her name is Margaret Thatcher and she's our new Prime Minister,' Ruth told her. Then, seeing the child's look, she explained. 'She's going to run the country. It's the first time a woman will do it.'

'That's good!' Penny exclaimed. 'Women are better than men anyway.'

'My, my, you have been picking up some ideas.' Ruth looked at the girl with approval. 'Why do you say that?'

'Because all the boys in my class are stupid,' said Penny, as if it was obvious.

'I won't argue with that,' said Ruth. 'Look, she's going to make a speech. Turn up the volume.' She noticed that the little girl seemed interested. Good, maybe she'd make something of her life. It wasn't often that Ruth considered the child's future, and she knew if she was honest that most people would be delighted to have a daughter like hers. It wasn't that she disliked her; she just struggled to feel anything for her, and occasionally this caused her a pang of regret. Her own childhood had been totally devoid of affection, her parents too preoccupied with avoiding the bailiffs, with one moonlight flit following another. It wasn't the best way to learn how to love.

'Where there is discord, may we bring harmony . . .' said the figure on the screen.

Penny looked blank.

'Oh Ruth, you're back,' said Lorna, coming into the room with a couple of bowls of bananas and cream. 'Sorry, I didn't make you anything.'

'Doesn't matter,' said Ruth dismissively. As if she wanted any of that nursery food. 'I'm going out with Adam later for dinner at the Belmont. We're going to try their new bistro and I think this is a day to celebrate. Not sure he'll agree though.' She laughed, as Adam sometimes had very old-fashioned notions about what women were meant to do.

'I don't think Robert will be very happy either,' Lorna predicted. 'He says Mrs Thatcher's policies will be bad for the country.'

'Well, he would,' said Ruth shortly. She was rather fed up with Robert. He had proved himself to be a more than competent negotiator but he was a stickler for keeping to the letter of the law and always played it safe, which she found very irritating. 'I think she'll be good for business and she'll make it easier for women to succeed in whatever they do. So that's good enough for me.' She turned to her friend. 'What do you think?'

123

'Oh, I don't know much about politics,' protested Lorna, setting the bowls on the table. 'Penny, come and have some of this.'

Really, thought Ruth, the woman was too much sometimes. How could she not take an interest in what went on around her? Was that the sort of thing Penny should hear?

Her daughter had other ideas. 'I'm going to do that one day,' she announced, pointing to the television. 'But my coat will be better.' She scooped up a big spoonful of fruit. 'I'm going to be in charge.'

'Yes, you don't want to end up dressing like that,' muttered Ruth, pushing back her chair. 'I've got to get ready. Don't stay up too late, even if you've got to learn how to be in charge.'

Adam was waiting in the bar area of the smart new bistro. He was surrounded by young professionals like himself, celebrating the end of the working week, drinking wine and talking loudly. Hmm, he thought, they obviously weren't estate agents, having to work the next day. At least there was nobody he knew here to interrupt him. A few weeks ago he had almost left a hotel bar to avoid a troublesome acquaintance and he didn't want a repeat of that to spoil the moment.

For the hundredth time he rehearsed what he was going to say when Ruth arrived. He'd watched and waited, observing how her trade had increased over the first year, listening for clues and deducing that her cashflow must be very healthy indeed. He wasn't to know that even though the money was coming into Ruth's agency, it was leaving again almost as fast and her profits were marginal.

He was sure he was making the right move, and told himself there was no reason to be nervous. He had nothing to lose by this, and a lot to gain. It made total sense, whichever way he looked at it. He'd have to present it in the right way – he didn't want to give her an excuse for one of her terrible rages, he'd seen enough of those. He wanted her complete agreement to everything he suggested, and she might even be grateful. He smiled to himself, imagining what form that gratitude might take.

There she was now, striding along the street, causing all the men to turn to look at her. That was one of the things he got great pleasure from – Adam could just see all those men wondering who she was going to meet, and he basked in their envy when they realised it was him. He sensed the women were watching too. They usually did when he was on his own, wondering if they had a chance to make their move. Adam was very aware of his looks and saw no point in false modesty.

Now he looked up as Ruth came into the bar, grinning in what he knew was his most appealing way. He leant forward to kiss her, nothing too obvious, but enough to demonstrate to anyone watching that she was his. 'You look stunning, darling,' he said. 'More gorgeous than ever.'

Good, that was the right way to kick things off. She gave him her dazzling smile. 'Well, I like to make an effort,' she said, smoothing down a dress he hadn't seen before, in striking royal blue. 'No point in meeting the best-looking man in town and letting him down. Do you like this? I bought it in honour of the occasion.'

'The occasion?' God, had she guessed what he planned to say?

'Yes, of course.' She paused. 'What happened today. In Downing Street.'

Oh for God's sake, thought Adam. That bloody uppity woman. 'I'm afraid I missed the news,' he said smoothly. 'Too busy making sure I looked good enough for you. I didn't see the grand arrival. I take it you did?'

'Too bloody right,' said Ruth with great enthusiasm. 'I wouldn't have missed that for anything. The sky's the limit now. We women can do anything!' She took the glass of cold wine he offered her and chinked it against his. 'Including running the most dynamic property agency in Kent! And why stop there? In the south-east! In the country!'

She was on fire tonight, Adam thought. So much the better. That would serve his purpose in more ways than one. But he had to keep a cool head – never easy when she was like this, and so close to him.

'Let's go to our table,' he suggested, gently steering her away from the admiring groups of office workers. 'I'm glad you feel that way. In fact I wanted to talk to you about how to improve the agency, but was going to wait until later.'

'Oh Adam, don't be so conventional,' laughed Ruth, slipping into her seat. 'If you can't say something in front of me when you get an idea, then who can you say it to? You know there's nothing between us.' She smiled seductively.

'Absolutely,' he agreed. Nothing that she knew about anyway, and he intended to keep it that way. 'No, I've been thinking. We work so well together. Our two agencies have run in parallel very successfully and they complement each other. *We* complement each other. You

126

know we're totally right together, in every possible way.' He smiled back at her, and shooed away the waiter who had been hovering. 'Don't you think it's time to move up to the next stage? On its own, each agency is too small to make that leap. But if we combined them . . .'

'We could really expand!' exclaimed Ruth. Her eyes narrowed. 'If we did that then we could go well beyond Margate. The market's limited here and so much of the stock is in bad condition it'll never command a premium. I want to get into the upmarket areas. Canterbury, Tunbridge Wells . . .'

'What about as far as London?' he asked. 'Let's see what plans for development your Mrs Thatcher has.'

'No need to be sarky,' Ruth said reprovingly, but her face was alight. 'She'll be exactly what we need, you wait and see. We have to be in the right shape to take advantage of whatever opportunities she opens up. And I know how you appreciate the right shape, darling.'

Couldn't have put it better myself, thought Adam in delight. She was going for it. No, she was more than going for it, she was taking his idea and making it much, much bigger. How could he resist?

'Darling,' he breathed. 'That's wonderful. It's really exciting.' He felt in his jacket pocket. 'Look, I know we shouldn't confuse business with pleasure . . .'

'Don't be ridiculous,' she laughed. 'That's what we do all the time, Adam. That's what we're about. That's when we have the most fun. That's what makes us, us.'

'In that case,' he said, suddenly very serious, 'shall we do it properly?' He swallowed, as if to emphasise the importance of his next words. 'Ruth – darling – would you do me the honour of being my wife?'

He brought out a small navy box and gave it to her to open. Inside was a ring – one he had got cheap from a house clearance, but she needn't know that, and it was after all the real thing. He felt he'd better not try anything less, as she was sure to know the difference between real and fake stones.

'My God, Adam,' she said, taking out the ring and holding it up to the light. 'This is lovely. What can I say, except . . . yes, yes, yes!'

Lorna had almost dozed off in front of the television when the phone rang. She shook herself awake, puzzled by who could be calling at this time of night. Now the late-evening news was on – more Mrs Thatcher, still promising to bring harmony.

Hurriedly she reached for the receiver before the noise could disturb Penny. 'Hello, who's there?'

'Lorna, that you?' said a male voice, and she realised with a sinking feeling it was Ted. That must mean something serious was going on.

'Whatever's the matter?' she said quickly.

'It's your mum,' he replied. 'She's been took very bad and is on her way to hospital right now. They said I'd better ring you to get here as soon as you can.'

'It's that bad?' she asked, with the faint hope he'd got it wrong.

'It is,' he said bluntly. 'Better get up here right away.'

'I'll try,' she said, thinking frantically. Of course Ruth wasn't back yet, and Lorna had no idea when she would be, if at all. What could she do about the child? 'I'll have to try and get a babysitter or something. I can't really bring Penny with me, unless someone can look after her that end.'

'Don't know about that,' said Ted. No, thought Lorna, don't suppose you would. You never did like children – I should know.

'I could ask Maureen . . .' she began, but then wished she hadn't.

'Don't you go bringing that tart in my house,' Ted exclaimed. 'She don't belong round here no more and I won't have her through my door. Surprised you could even think of letting her near a kid. She's bad through and through and you don't want nothing to do with her if you've got any sense.'

So much for that idea, then. Lorna didn't have time to feel hurt on her cousin's behalf, though Maureen had come down to visit plenty of times over the last year and she and Penny got on like a house on fire. Anyway, she'd most likely be at work at this time of the evening, so it would be no good anyway.

'I'll think of something,' Lorna promised, with no idea what that might be. 'Which hospital?'

Ted gave her directions and rang off abruptly. Lorna stood holding the receiver in shock. While she'd known her mother hadn't been at all well she hadn't seemed to be getting any worse. Now it looked as if things were going downhill fast.

There was only one person to turn to.

'Robert, you've got to help me,' she burst out as soon as he'd picked up. Quickly she explained what had happened and the dilemma she was in. 'Can you think of anything?'

'You can't rely on Ruth coming home,' he said firmly. 'Put that out of your mind. I'll drive over at once. I can take you up to Battersea and Penny can sleep on the back seat – it's Friday, she hasn't got school tomorrow, and she'll think it's an adventure. Then I can leave you at the hospital and return right away.'

'Oh Robert, would you?' Lorna nearly collapsed with gratitude. 'I'll go and wake Penny and explain. It'll give me something to do too,' she added, knowing that she couldn't break down in front of the little girl. 'We'll see you in a minute.'

Hastily she ran to her room and threw a change of clothes and a toothbrush into a bag, and then went to wake Penny. There really was no time to be sad, sorry, or anything.

Another hotel room, thought Ruth, gazing up at an elaborate spotlight. This was definitely the best yet, beautifully designed to be up-to-date and yet classy and timeless. One day she'd have a room like this. And now she was a step closer to her dream.

Her scheme had worked. Adam had finally found her so irresistible he'd offered to merge their businesses and make her his wife. Realistically she knew she was the more adventurous one when it came to making deals, spotting chances and taking advantage of whatever came along, but it would be wonderful to have his backing. And of course his premises. He would lend her the respectability she so needed and she would drive the agency where he would not dare take it on his own. Just in time, too. Her savings had dwindled almost to nothing, but now she would have unlimited access to the lifestyle she so craved. Sighing, she kicked back the Egyptian cotton sheet.

'Adam,' she breathed, 'why don't you put down that

nightcap? You can have that later. I think we need to celebrate properly . . .'

'Mum, it's me,' said Lorna, reaching forward to take the frail hand. 'Can you hear me? Do you know who I am?'

Her mother's eyes flickered and she seemed to be struggling to speak. 'Lorna,' she whispered.

'That's right, Mum, I'm here. You're going to be all right. There's no need to worry.'

On the other side of the room, the doctor shook his head gently. They all knew the end was near.

'Lorna,' her mother said again, pulling on her hand a little. She leant in more closely. 'Make sure you never tell anyone else. You know what I mean. It's for the best.'

'Oh, Mum.' Lorna wasn't sure what to say. She'd never introduced Robert to her mother and Ted, and had spoken of him only as a friend who gave her a regular lift because he was passing that way. Which had been true to begin with.

'Promise me,' hissed her mother.

'Don't worry, Mum,' Lorna replied. 'Look, I know this'll seem strange, but I'd like you to know I've met someone. He's the most wonderful man and I'm the luckiest woman in the world. And, Mum, he knows.'

Her mother's eyes opened a fraction and Lorna could see it was a look of horror.

'Honestly, Mum, it's fine. He doesn't mind. He loves me anyway. It's all fine.'

'Really?' whispered her mother.

'Really,' she said. 'It's the best thing that's ever happened to me. Maybe you'll meet him soon.'

'Don't think so,' said her mother, struggling to swallow.

131

'No time for that now.' She stopped to take a painful breath. 'But I'm glad. I only ever wanted the best for you, you know.'

'I know, Mum.' Lorna squeezed her hand again, but this time there was no response. She looked up at the doctor, who approached the bed.

'You'll have to leave her now,' he said gently. 'All this talking is exhausting her. She can't take much more. You might like to say your farewells.'

Lorna looked at the wasted figure in the bed, who'd done so much to hurt her. And yet she had loved her too. A swirl of emotions hit her, but she couldn't say anything now. It was time to put all that aside. Softly, she stroked her mother's hand for the last time.

'Bye, Mum,' she said.

Pulling into a lucky parking space outside the office, Robert glanced up at the windows of the flat above. Lorna had left the upstairs light on, but there were no others lit, and it didn't look as if Ruth had returned. He wasn't surprised. He knew she and Adam were living it up on every possible occasion and had gone somewhere special this evening. They weren't to know Lorna would be called away. But his heart went out to the little girl on the back seat, who was plainly such an inconvenience to her mother. By the orange light of the streetlamp, he could see she was beginning to stir.

'Where am I?' she mumbled groggily.

'It's okay,' he soothed. 'We've just got back. Come on, I'll take you upstairs.' He'd had a key to the flat for a while – it made sense as it was above the agency, even if he hadn't been so close to Lorna. But he hated using it, never wanting to intrude on his temperamental boss. Now though, he had no choice. Shutting the car doors as quietly as he could, he let them both inside and followed Penny up the stairs.

Once inside he made sure she cleaned her teeth and then tucked her up. She was asleep in moments. Well, he couldn't leave her here alone. He settled himself in Lorna's small living room, and looked around for something to read. Yesterday's newspaper headlines screamed up at him, all about Mrs Thatcher's victory. Somehow he didn't fancy reading that.

Absently he ran his eyes around the room. Lorna had added many tasteful touches to make it comfortable and feel like home: cushions, pictures, a vase of flowers. Her style was nothing like Ruth's. He'd seen how his boss liked to decorate a place – many times when she'd been preparing to show a property to customers she'd flung a scheme together. It was always stunning, even on a tight budget, but never made him feel he'd want to live there. Whereas here, he felt he could stay for ever. The vital difference was, this had been done with warmth.

Robert forced himself to face some awkward questions. Did he really mind that Lorna could never have children? Most men he knew talked about having a son one day, to further their line, or simply to play football with. Did he, deep down, feel like that? Would he come to resent her?

But he knew the answer at once. She was all he wanted. If they couldn't have children then he would be satisfied without. It was Lorna he worried about, who would forever feel that something was missing from her life without a baby. He couldn't bear to see her unhappy, but there was nothing he or anyone could do about it. That

133

was the hand fate had dealt her. All he could do was to try to make up for it in every other way.

Slowly the sun rose and dawn broke over the rooftops of Margate. Robert watched through the partly drawn curtains and came to a decision. As soon as she was back, he'd speak to her properly. He was tired of pussy-footing around, watching her try to please Ruth, ignoring Adam's barely concealed contempt, all the time caring for Penny every bit as dearly as if she were her own. They could do better than this. They could take Penny with them if that was how Lorna wanted it – he'd be more than happy. He'd bet Ruth would be relieved. But something had to change – he and Lorna had been taken advantage of, and it had to stop.

Chapter Seventeen

'No, no, come on up,' Ruth giggled. God, was she still drunk? She'd lost count of how much champagne they'd had, ordering room service in the middle of the night. She could swear, though, that she was high on adrenaline, the success of her ultimate plan to snare Adam and his assets. 'They probably won't be up and we can just ignore them if they are.'

Adam rarely went to the flat – it depressed him, but this morning was different. Soon they'd be away from the dreary place. He'd already earmarked in his mind a lovely penthouse he'd seen for sale with superb sea views. Would Ruth's savings stretch to a deposit on that, he wondered. Or maybe they would be enough to buy it outright? That would be even better.

As they opened the front door they were greeted by sounds of someone crying. Stepping into the living room, they found a distraught Lorna in Robert's arms. Her face was blotchy and he was rubbing her back, and it looked as if they'd been standing like that for some time.

'What's happened?' demanded Ruth. 'We've got some great news that will cheer you up! Adam and I are getting married! What do you say about that?'

If she'd been expecting congratulations, there were none. Lorna made a strange gulping sound and turned to face her. 'Oh,' she said. 'That's nice for you. But Mum has just died, so I'm a bit upset right now.'

Ruth vaguely remembered that the woman had been sick and that was why Penny had had to go to her friend's so often on a Saturday. 'I'm very sorry to hear that,' she said. 'That's very sad.' She managed to inject sympathy into her voice, although it went against her nature to do so. But she knew her friend had mentioned her mother in Battersea and this must have been a heavy blow for her. 'But guess what? We're getting married! As soon as possible! Isn't that exciting?'

'Very exciting,' said Robert, shaking his head. 'You must be very pleased.'

'Oh, we are, aren't we, darling?' crowed Ruth, nudging Adam. 'Say something, Adam.'

'Er, sorry for your loss,' he managed. 'Thing is, we'll be getting married almost immediately . . .'

'Actually, we have some news too,' said Lorna, as her sobbing gradually stopped. 'I know I don't look it right now, but I'm also extremely happy. Yes, Mum's died and that's terrible. But Robert just asked me to marry him and I said yes. I want to wait until the divorce is well behind me so it won't be at once, but we're going to get married as well.'

All four of them fell silent, realising that this was the moment of no return.

'There's more,' said Robert. 'Ruth, it's been an education working with you. But the time has come for me to strike out, and with Lorna beside me I'm sure it's the right thing to do. So I'm resigning.'

If Ruth was dismayed she hid it well. 'I see,' she said. 'In fact that is good timing. Not only am I going to marry Adam, but our two firms are merging. So there will be changes all round.'

Another silence fell.

Finally, Lorna spoke. 'And what will that mean for Penny?' she asked. 'How will you look after her? She can come to live with us if she wants to. I'd be more than happy . . .'

'No, no, that won't be necessary,' said Ruth at once. 'It's time she got a proper education. She won't get that at that dump down the road, and look at who she mixes with. No, I've had my eye on a good school for a long time. She can go to St Martha's.'

'But that's the other side of the county!' gasped Lorna. 'It's closer to Brighton than here! When will we see her?'

'She can stay with you in the holidays,' said Ruth dismissively. Really, these two were the limit. With all the bombshells that had just gone off, they had to concentrate on that blessed child. What was wrong with them?

'Oh no,' cried Lorna. 'That's no time at all. Ruth, please think again. She's not even nine yet. She can come with us, honestly, it's no bother. Imagine how lonely she'll be away from us all.'

'Lorna, be sensible,' snapped Ruth. 'What would it look like if I gave my daughter away to be looked after by someone else? And I can't have her under my feet just when things are really starting to take off at work. Really, it will be the best place for her. She'll love it.'

Lorna began to cry again, even harder this time. The sorrow of the night had exhausted her and she'd barely managed a wink of sleep on the way back, but this was too much. Rage coursed through her, combined with heartbreak at the thought of losing Penny and what the little girl would have to go through. 'I can't believe you're saying that. You don't love her. You never have. You should never have had her.'

'Don't give me that, you miserable old cow,' shouted Ruth, all restraint now gone. 'What'll you do with her? Smother her? Teach her to stay at home and look after a man? Make cakes?'

'She needs to be with people she loves and who love her!' Lorna exclaimed. 'Isn't it obvious? How can you think differently? Who cares what it looks like? This is Penny we're talking about, not some stupid business deal. You pour all your love into that agency and never show anything for your child. What do you think *that* looks like, if that's all you care about? If it wasn't for her I'd have left long ago, but that little girl needs love! She needs me!'

'Well, she's not going to stay around here now I can afford to send her to St Martha's,' Ruth retaliated. 'She'll be too busy there to miss anybody, and that includes you. Both of you.'

'Come on, Lorna, let's go,' said Robert, appalled at the turn events had taken. 'We can come back later for your things. You're coming home with me. You don't have to listen to this.' He wrapped her coat around her and guided her to the door and down the stairs, leaving Ruth and Adam to glare down at them as they left.

None of them saw a small, horrified face gazing down from the upper landing.

'Well, that was a hell of a start to the morning,' said Ruth as she filled the kettle. 'Who'd have guessed she'd be so

138

angry with me? Must be the shock of her mother's death. Still, maybe it's for the best. I have to say I was getting tired of coming home to that long face. Robert's welcome to her. Here, have some coffee – we probably need it.' She grinned suggestively up at Adam as she handed him a mug.

'Yes, two of a kind, made for each other,' Adam agreed. 'He's good at his job, I'll give him that, but he's not exactly fun to have around, is he? You're better off without him. We can take our time and find people that suit us properly.' He sniffed his drink and sighed. 'We can have a big kitchen with a real coffee maker. No more instant granules. How'd you like that?'

'Mmm,' said Ruth. 'Something to get you going in the mornings.'

'Oh, I think we both know what gets me going in the mornings.'

'Stop it!' said Ruth playfully.

'I was impressed with the way you came back about that school so quickly,' he said. 'I know of that place, it's got a great reputation, but it doesn't come cheap. Am I going to be married to an heiress?' He put his arms around her waist and pretended to waltz her round the kitchen.

'No, silly,' said Ruth, almost letting herself be carried away with the moment. 'I didn't think you'd mind. I know you won't want her under our feet. It'll surely be a drop in the ocean for you.'

Adam came to a halt. 'Drop in the ocean?' he echoed. 'Drop in what ocean?'

'Well, your ocean, of course,' she said. 'Your ocean of limitless wealth.'

'Now you're joking,' he said. 'You *are* joking, surely?'

'No,' she said, suddenly sober. 'Why would I joke about a thing like that? Look at you, your own firm, these fabulous premises – and don't forget I know exactly what they're worth. God knows I tried to find some like it for ages, if you remember. You're sitting on a goldmine. *We're* sitting on a goldmine.'

'Ah, there might have been some misunderstanding there,' Adam said, trying to make light of it. 'Anyway, with your savings, it won't matter, will it?'

'Savings?' she repeated. 'What savings? Oh, I had savings once. But they're nearly all gone. Do you think I can dress like this with the tiny profits from the business? I hardly think so.'

They stood stock still, staring at each other. The silence lasted a very long time, as the penny dropped for both of them: the other had no money. They were each as bad as each other.

'Tell me about this misunderstanding,' Ruth eventually said, very slowly.

'These premises came bargain-basement cheap,' Adam admitted, 'and you know that can only happen for a very small number of reasons. In this case it was because it was on a ridiculously short leasehold. I don't own this flat outright – in a few months I'll have no right to it at all. Same goes for the office.'

'So let me get this straight,' said Ruth, unable to believe that she would come out of this with nothing. 'You have no private income, no secret stash of cash, no lovely corner premises with accommodation above.'

He nodded.

'And I have no savings, no property at all, except for

the contents of my wardrobe,' she went on. 'Shit. Shit, shit, shit. I do not believe it. What do we do now? I thought we had something there. I thought we had something really good going.'

'We do, we do,' insisted Adam. 'We are great together. You know that. We'll be huge. We just need some backing.'

Ruth ran her hands through her hair and gazed at the anaglypta ceiling, furiously thinking. 'Okay,' she said. 'We don't have to pay Robert any more – that's the school fees sorted. I don't have to pay Lorna. We can live on the savings from that. But what about the premises? Can we extend the lease?'

'I've tried,' Adam admitted. 'The greasy old sod won't have it. Says he has plans to develop this building. Makes my blood boil when I know we could do it so much better.'

Ruth shook her head. 'There's always a way. Remember what you learnt from Joe Young. You find the weakness – then exploit it. What's his weakness?'

Adam groaned, but then he remembered the hotel from a few weeks ago. 'It's girls,' he said. 'Not just any, but young ones. He's married to someone his own age and her family are big in local politics. He won't want a scandal. And I suspect some of them might be underage.'

'There you are, then,' said Ruth. 'You want to give this one a go? Or are you happy to leave it to me?'

'Ruth Hamilton-Smyth,' he said in admiration. 'Are you suggesting we start our new business venture on the basis of blackmail?'

'How I hate that word!' she exclaimed. 'I much prefer to call it the pursuit of truth. Righting wrongs and all that. You just have to have confidence. If he's done it,

141

and he doesn't want the whole town to know, then he'll give in. Do you doubt me?'

'Never,' said Adam. 'No, I'll never doubt you. I have the utmost confidence that whatever you want you'll get.'

'Good,' she said. 'I'm glad we've got that sorted out.' She looked at him mischievously. 'Well, I know one thing I want very much. Or rather, someone.' And she reached out to kiss him, hard.

PART TWO

Chapter Eighteen

1987

Penny groaned, as she tried to stay awake and focus on the huge textbook in front of her. She couldn't see the point of all the complicated sums she had to get her head around for the forthcoming mock O-levels, as she never intended to use any of them in real life. Still, Lorna and Robert had insisted she try harder when she'd stayed with them for Christmas. 'You'll be glad later on,' Robert had assured her.

But Penny wasn't convinced. She knew they only wanted the best for her but holidays in Margate with them had felt increasingly suffocating. Her classmates would return with tales of outrageous exploits: drinking, sneaking out to nightclubs, riding in fast cars with older men, being asked if they were models. Penny wasn't sure how much of it was true but it sounded more interesting than watching telly or helping in the garden if the weather was fine enough.

It wasn't that she was ungrateful. Lorna and Robert had provided the only home she had, as her mother and Adam were far too busy to have her come to stay in their penthouse, if they even knew when term ended. They were riding high on the property boom, with Ruth taking the market towns of Kent by storm, while Adam expanded into an area of London called Docklands. Penny had no idea what any of this meant, but Robert informed her they were doing exceptionally well and had a real eye for opportunities. Maybe when they'd established themselves they'd have time to see more of her.

Penny knew he was saying it to make her feel better but she was under no illusions these days. Her mother had never had time for her, even when she'd had nothing to do in Spain but sunbathe and socialise. Penny didn't feel that she really missed her, and anyway Lorna was always there with her love and support. Ruth had scarcely bothered to write to her daughter. Once a term or so a short note would arrive, usually telling her to work harder, and making extravagant promises that Penny was fairly sure were only there to impress whichever teacher had the job of checking the letters. It was a strict school and everything was monitored. In fact Penny received far more letters from Maureen, who'd taken a real shine to her, although these were mostly heavily censored by the time they got to her. It only added to the glamour of how she imagined Maureen's life in Soho, with everything so exciting and scandalous that she wasn't allowed to know the details.

Giving up with the revision for the evening, Penny stood and stretched. She'd grown tall, easily as tall as her mother, and she had passed Lorna a couple of years ago. Not bad, she thought, checking her reflection in the mirror. She had her mother's dark hair – at least she'd done that much for her. She didn't know if she resembled her father or not; the only photos of Laurence Hamilton-Smyth had been taken when he was in his seventies, which made it hard to tell. It didn't bother her, as she wasn't given to worrying about something she'd never had. If she wanted fatherly advice, which she usually didn't, she turned to Robert.

Penny realised she was hungry. The food at St Martha's was mostly terrible, but it had been a long time since she'd last eaten and she decided to head downstairs to see if there was anything for supper. She dimly remembered the food from her childhood in Spain – the tortillas, the spicy meatballs, the fruit that tasted of fruit. Everything here was bland by comparison. One day, she thought, making her way down the draughty corridor, one day I'll go back there and see if it's all as wonderful as I remember it. And I'll never have to do maths again.

Ruth was enjoying the feel of her new sports car, which she'd had for just over a week. Adam had teased her about it, especially when she had demanded a red one, but she loved it. There weren't that many roads she could really open up on between Tunbridge Wells and Margate, but sometimes she'd have an excuse to go on the motorway and then she'd really let it roar. There was nothing to beat the feeling of taking charge of such a powerful vehicle, spiced up by the knowledge that she'd done this all herself. She'd earned her car; more than earned it.

Finally, life was good. They'd had to struggle to start with, waiting to see if their daring gambit with the freeholder had worked. But her instinct had been right – he was too terrified of being unmasked to make trouble, and had agreed with all their demands in the end. That had bought them some time and they'd been able to expand, just as the market was ripe. Now Adam was pulling in big clients from the City, looking to relocate to Docklands. Ruth was happy to let him. She still didn't want anything to do with London, even though Vincent Chase had been dead and buried for years now. She was delighted to be wined and dined by the City types as Adam's wife and business partner, but that was quite enough.

Funny, thought Ruth, the lights of the cars coming towards her were behaving strangely. Maybe she was tired? She turned up the expensive stereo she'd insisted on, blasting out George Michael's latest number one. That usually made her feel better. No, the lights were still weaving peculiar patterns.

She realised she had a headache coming on, a really bad one. Now and again they attacked her, but she dismissed them as hazards of the job, which was always stressful. Shit, this was affecting her ability to drive. She'd better pull over and find some painkillers. This was harder than she'd thought as the road seemed to be distorted, bucking and twisting like a snake, even though she knew this part of her journey was completely flat. With relief, Ruth saw a layby up ahead and managed to steer into it, parking at a weird angle. Can't have a headache, she thought, got far too much to do tomorrow, and we're being taken to The Ivy.

Bloody typical, thought Adam. Early start tomorrow, which would surely be followed by a late night, and they could really have done with eating on time this evening.

But there was no sign of Ruth. Probably got carried away playing with that new toy of hers. It wasn't that Adam was jealous of the car; he could easily have afforded one for himself, but he suspected she was taking time off to drive around and test it on every possible route. All very well, but he had a thousand things to discuss with her. Irritated, he made himself some supper, grabbing whatever Waitrose goodies he could find and piling them on a plate.

Adam was just finishing it when the intercom went. Marvellous, not only was she late but she'd forgotten her keys. Clearly he wasn't going to be allowed to digest his hasty meal in peace. Muttering, he went to the front door. 'About time . . .' he began and fell silent at the sight of two police officers.

'Mr Adam Mortimer?'

'Well, yes, what's all this about?' Adam quickly racked his brains to check if he'd done anything recently that might attract the police.

'Your wife is Ruth Mortimer? Also known as Ruth Hamilton-Smyth?'

'Yes, she keeps her name for professional purposes,' Adam bristled, still unable to make out what could have brought on this visit.

'And she drives a red sports car?'

Gradually, it began to dawn on Adam what this might be about. 'She does. What's happened? Has there been an accident?'

'Not exactly, sir,' said the older of the two. 'Maybe you'd better sit down. Through here, is it?'

Confused, and now beginning to fill with dread, Adam allowed them to escort him to his own plush living room.

It had been furnished by Ruth, who'd designed every last detail, from the black leather sofas to the chrome light switches. God, that woman had taste. What were these officers about to tell him?

'I'm very sorry, sir,' the policeman went on. 'Your wife was found in a layby just outside Tunbridge Wells. It would seem that she had collapsed.'

'Collapsed?' Adam repeated, feeling stupid. 'Not an accident, then? Is she all right?'

'Someone called an ambulance and she was taken to hospital,' the other officer said.

'Which one?' Adam was impatient now. 'Obviously I must go to her at once. Is the car all right? No damage? She'll be furious if there is. She loves that car.'

The two officers looked at each other and the older one sighed. 'We can certainly take you to the hospital,' he said. 'But I must inform you, sir, that your wife was pronounced dead upon arrival.'

Lorna was washing the dishes when the phone rang. 'Robert, can you get it?' Hastily she dried her hands. Very few people called them this late in the evening.

'Right, right,' Robert was saying from the hall. 'That's terrible . . . I'm so sorry. Of course. No, absolutely not. We wouldn't want anyone else to do it. Can you tell me any more? . . . No, I quite understand. Please let us know if you need anything else. We'll do it right away.'

He put down the receiver and let out a long sigh. Lorna was seriously worried – that was his equivalent of most people's shouting and swearing. 'Whatever is the matter?' she cried, hurrying to him.

'Come with me,' Robert said, putting his arm around

150

Lorna's shoulder and steering her towards the living room. It was large and yet cosy, as Lorna had kept many of the furnishings from the old flat and had added to them over the years. Now they both sat on the sofa, surrounded by cushions. 'Lorna, you've got to be brave. That was bad news.' He met her gaze, and she thought how gentle his face was, even though it was beginning to show signs of age. 'That was Adam. It's Ruth.'

She shook her head. 'Ruth? What, is she in trouble? What can she have done?'

'No, nothing like that,' he said. 'I'm afraid she's dead.'

'Dead?' Lorna stared at him as if he'd gone mad. 'She can't be. She's my age. There's been a mistake.'

'I'm so sorry,' he said. 'There's been no mistake. She was found in her car. They took her to hospital but it was too late. She was already dead. They'll have to do a post-mortem but they think it could have been a brain haemorrhage. Did you hear me, Lorna? Do you under-stand?'

Slowly she shook her head again, unable to believe what he was saying. How could Ruth be dead – dynamic, deci-sive Ruth? All right, they'd fallen out and had stopped being friends after that last dreadful row in the flat, but because of Penny, they had been part of each other's lives for years and it didn't seem possible that the woman was dead.

'Really?' she asked. 'That's awful, that's ...' She couldn't find the words.

'It is,' said Robert. 'But you've got to pull yourself together. We haven't got time to fall apart. You can grieve for her later. But right now, we have something to do.' He paused. 'Adam wants us to tell Penny.'

* * *

Just over an hour later, they pulled up at the gates of St Martha's. Lorna shuddered. She hated this place, although she had tried very hard to hide the fact from Penny. No doubt it was an excellent school but she had never been able to forgive Ruth for sending her daughter there. Now Ruth was no longer around to forgive. Lorna hesitated before opening the car door, not sure what to feel – anger that Ruth had been so selfish and stubborn, sorry that she'd died so young and, most of all, dread at how Penny would react.

A glow appeared as someone opened the main door. Lorna recognised the figure of the school secretary, huddled in a thick cardigan. 'Come in, come in,' said the woman, ushering them into a side office. 'I'm very sorry to hear about your friend. The housemistress has gone to fetch Penelope.'

Lorna smiled weakly at the formal name, which nobody else used. 'Thank you,' she murmured as the woman passed her a cup of tea. It looked weak in its china cup. Robert smiled at her encouragingly and she tried to sit up straight, to prepare for the ordeal.

The minutes ticked by and the silence seemed endless before there was a knock on the door, and a middle-aged woman led Penny inside. 'Here are your visitors,' she said briefly, and withdrew, followed by the secretary.

Penny looked at them and half-smiled. 'I don't suppose this is good news, is it?' she said. 'I was almost ready to go to bed and Miss Carter came to warn me not to, but not why.' She sat down on a hard plastic office chair. Its legs squeaked on the parquet floor.

'You're right, I'm afraid,' began Robert. 'There's no easy way to put this, Penny. We're here to tell you . . . to tell you . . .' He swallowed and started again. 'Your mother is dead. She was taken ill on her way home from work and rushed to hospital but it was no good. They're doing tests to find out exactly what it was but it's too late to save her. Penny, we are so sorry.'

Lorna looked up and held out her arms but Penny jerked her head away. She backed away into the door and then fled, her footsteps echoing as she made for the main entrance and ran out into the darkness. Taken aback, Lorna stayed where she was for a moment and then she was off, haring after the girl as if the devil himself was at her heels.

'Penny!' she shouted, as she raced across the front lawn, beautifully trimmed even though it was winter. 'Where are you? Penny!'

From behind the sheds came a strange sound; part scream, part shout. Cautiously Lorna made her way around the corner, to where the moonlight was illuminating the yard behind the sheds. Someone was hitting the wooden wall of the furthest one, making the dreadful noise all the while.

'Penny,' she called. 'I'm here. Stop it, you'll hurt yourself. Come here.'

The girl didn't even look up, much less stop what she was doing.

Gradually Lorna edged closer, until she could make out what the noise was.

'Bitch!' Penny screamed. 'Bloody bitch!'

'No, no,' Lorna said gently, reaching out, afraid Penny would hurt herself on the splintering wood. 'Stop it now, Penny, this isn't helping. Come back inside with me.'

'Bitch!' Penny screamed again, punching the wall. 'I

hate her, I hate her, I hate her, she's a bloody bastard bitch and I hate her.'

Lorna felt like screaming too but forced herself to hold it in. Instead she waited until, slowly, Penny stopped screaming and finally came to a standstill. Then she held out her arms and the girl fell into them.

'It's okay,' soothed Lorna, stroking her back. 'It will be all right.'

'It won't,' said Penny, and looked up with a frighteningly adult expression on her face. 'You can stop saying that to me now. I know it wasn't all right before and it won't be all right now. She hated me, I hated her, and now it won't change.'

'She didn't hate you,' protested Lorna, hoping the girl wouldn't hear the hesitation in her voice. 'She just didn't know how to show love, that's all. Some people don't.'

'If that's what you want to believe, then fine,' said Penny bitterly. 'I know she didn't want me and she didn't hide it. I don't know why she had me.' She burst into tears once more.

'Come back inside,' said Lorna. 'It's freezing out here. I want to get warm, even if you don't.' She tried to smile. 'And Robert's waiting. He'll always be there when you need him, you do know that, don't you? Like me. We'll never let you down.'

'I know,' said Penny, sagging exhausted onto Lorna's shoulder. 'I do know that and I'm glad you're here. But I still hate that bloody bastard bitch of an excuse for a mother.'

Chapter Nineteen

'God, I hate funerals,' Maureen complained, tightening her belt as the fierce wind threatened to blow open her coat. 'Don't know why you dragged me along. You know I never liked Adrianna, sorry, Ruth.'

'You know exactly why,' snapped Lorna. Her usual patience had been severely tested over the last couple of weeks and she was in no mood for her cousin's dramatics. 'Because I need you and Penny needs you. Is that good enough? Can you think of two better reasons?'

Maureen looked contrite. 'No, you're right, of course,' she said. 'That poor girl needs all the help she can get and it's not fair that you and Robert have to do it all. Don't suppose *he's* any help.' She nodded to where Adam was standing outside the church, immaculate in a beautiful formal black suit and cashmere coat. 'He never was when the tart was alive, so don't imagine he'd bother to start now. Anyway.' Maureen stroked the fur collar on her coat. 'Gives me a chance to wear this. It's too sober for Soho, there's no call for it there.' She flashed her eyes, then remembered she was at a funeral.

'Give it a rest,' said Lorna, but she didn't mean it. It was a great relief to have her cousin there, joking, keeping their spirits up. Even if her skirt was far too short for the occasion and her blouse open just one button too far.

'Where's Penny now?' asked Maureen, looking round as her hair blew across her face. 'Can't believe how tall she's got in the couple of months since I seen her last. She's going to turn some heads before long, no doubt about it.'

'Well, don't tell her that,' said Lorna firmly. 'She's got her exams soon and she needs to concentrate on getting those. She should do well, especially in Spanish. Seems as if she picked up far more than her mother or I ever did and now her teachers say she could be really good.' For a moment Lorna forgot where she was, full of pride in Penny's achievements. Then she groaned. 'That's if she picks herself up after all this. It's hit her really hard. Not surprising though.' She shook her head. 'She's with Robert, over there.'

Maureen looked across to where she was pointing. 'And who's that other bloke? The one who looks like a crow?'

'Hmm, see what you mean,' agreed Lorna, catching sight of the man's beaky face. He had dark hair and, like many of the others, wore a long black coat. 'He's Adam and Ruth's solicitor – well, suppose he's just Adam's solicitor now. Looks like most of the people here are business acquaintances. Don't think Ruth had any family – or she never talked of any – and now it seems as if she didn't have many friends either.'

'Are you surprised?' asked Maureen bluntly. 'Wasn't exactly a friend in need, was she? Not known for her kindness?'

'She gave me somewhere to live and a job when I needed it,' Lorna replied, remembering how close she'd come to giving up and moving back in with her mother. 'I'll always be grateful for that, even if it ended badly.'

'Exploited you for her own ends, more like,' Maureen pointed out. 'Got a cheap housekeeper and babysitter, all in one go. All right, all right, I won't go on, but just so's you don't go thinking she was a saint just because she's dead. She wasn't.'

Lorna turned away. She hated speaking ill of the dead. 'Look, Robert's waving us over, we'd better go.'

The two women made their way across to where Robert was standing with Penny and the crow-like solicitor. 'This is Kenneth Morris, Adam's lawyer. He's asked to have a word with Penny, so I said we'd stop by his office on the way back to the house.'

Lorna had generously asked everyone round after the service, guessing correctly that nobody else would offer. 'Well, yes, you do that,' she said. 'Just don't be too long, as I'll need someone to help me with the corkscrew.'

'Don't you worry, I can handle that,' said Maureen, just as Robert assured them that of course he wouldn't let them down.

'I can't believe it. That takes the biscuit, even for her.' The guests had gone and Lorna was free to give vent to her anger, all thoughts of not speaking ill of the dead blown away by the information Robert had learnt from the solicitor. 'How could she?'

'Come on, it's exactly what you would have expected,' blazed Maureen. 'When did she ever think about anyone other than herself?'

'Look, she had no way of knowing she would die young,' said Robert reasonably. 'I don't think we can blame her for that. Who of her age makes a will?'

'Not me,' admitted Maureen, 'but then I've not got nothing to leave so it don't really count.'

'Well, I've made one,' said Lorna, turning to her husband, 'and so have you. And one of the reasons we did it was so that Penny wouldn't be left with nothing if we were both to die suddenly. But that never entered her head. So Adam gets the lot and she has to rely on him doing the decent thing.'

'Don't hold your breath there,' Maureen said instantly. 'Him and Ruth was birds of a feather, both as bad as the other. Looking out for number one. End of. Which leaves Penny in a right pickle.' She sank down on the sofa. 'Is that some red left? Don't mind if I do.'

'Steady on,' said Lorna, even though she was longing for a drink herself. 'You had a few earlier, remember.'

'So?' Maureen tossed her hair. 'Might as well enjoy meself somehow. Ain't going to happen remembering the dear departed, is it?' She knocked back half the glass in one go and made to top herself up.

'Fair point,' agreed Lorna, giving in. 'I'll join you. I've been on my feet all day, waiting hand and foot on those . . . those . . . bloody people.'

'Lorna!' cried Maureen. 'You swore! Oh you are cross!'

'Yes, those bloody people.' One sip had broken down Lorna's reserve. 'Those parasites, those vultures with their Savile Row suits and fake accents. Didn't offer to pass anything round, didn't bring anything, just stood there, exchanging business cards, like it was a bloody conference or something. Probably hardly knew Ruth.'

158

'Well, the Ruth we knew was very different to the Ruth they knew.' Maureen banged down her glass for emphasis.

'God, you're loud,' said Penny, coming into the room. 'Is it safe here now? Have they all gone?'

'Too bleedin' right they have,' Maureen half-shouted. 'Come on in here, Penny my lovely, and sit with your Aunty Maureen.' She patted the cushions beside her.

Despite the occasion, Penny had to smile. 'Is that what you are now officially?' she grinned. 'And what did you mean about the Ruth you knew being different?'

Robert cleared his throat ominously but Maureen was in full flow and there was no stopping her. 'Because we went back a long way, your mum and me,' she said, waving her now-empty glass. 'Way back before Spain, way back before Lorna knew her. Oh yes. Mrs High-and-mighty Hamilton-Smyth didn't always have the posh clothes and lovely penthouse, though I grant you she always looked down her nose at everyone else like they was a piece of shit on her shoe, even back then. No, when I first knew your mum she was a stripper called Adrianna.'

After that bombshell, going back to school seemed pretty tame to Penny. Robert had carefully checked that her fees had been paid and that she wouldn't have to go cap in hand to Adam, but it seemed that Ruth had at least settled the amount until the end of the school year.

'I wouldn't mind not going,' said Penny hopefully, knowing that she could never expect any of her shel-tered classmates to understand what had just gone on. But Robert and Lorna insisted that she take her exams. So it was back for another term of mind-numbing lessons and revising and then the O-levels. Penny had no idea how she'd done but didn't really care. The only subject she really liked was Spanish, and that was because it came easily. She quite liked Geography, or at least the parts of it that let her imagine living in different places around the world. If dancing had been an exam she'd have loved that, but other than appearing in school plays there was little opportunity. She knew some of the older girls crept out to go to Brighton on Friday and Saturday nights but she'd never been asked along and besides, despite now being taller than most of her friends, she wasn't convinced she'd pass as old enough.

Still it was a shock to be called to the headmistress's office to be informed that after the summer there would be no more St Martha's.

'It seems your stepfather feels the expenditure is not worth the rewards,' said the stern woman.

'What?' said Penny, confused.

'He's not going to pay your fees,' said the headmistress. 'That's sad, but it happens. Many families feel it is time to move on when a pupil reaches sixteen. And in a few weeks' time that will be you.'

Families, thought Penny, what a joke. Adam might be her stepfather according to the letter of the law but he'd never shown the slightest interest in her, let alone any affection. She didn't know how she felt about the situation. She didn't particularly like her school, but her mother had insisted she go there. While Penny knew that was mostly a matter of convenience, combined with the status of having a daughter at a prestigious school, very occasionally Ruth had implied she thought getting girls educated was important. Clearly Adam didn't agree.

Penny didn't know what to do. Finally she phoned Lorna and Robert.

Lorna managed not to exclaim what she thought of Adam but wasn't really surprised. In some ways he was totally tight-fisted and he'd rather spend more on his beloved penthouse than on his stepdaughter.

'Do you want me to ring him?' she asked. 'See if he'll change his mind? Or if he wants you to go to stay with him?'

'Are you kidding?' snorted Penny. 'He won't change his mind now he's written to the head. He doesn't want anything to do with me and I'm glad. I don't want to live in that horrible place, either. It's all full of gadgets and he doesn't know how to use any of them. Doesn't even know how to switch on the cooker. Can't I live with you?'

'Of course you can!' cried Lorna. 'We'd love you to. Your room is ready and waiting, whenever you want it. But I thought I'd better ask.'

'Thanks but no thanks,' sighed Penny. 'I've already told them here that I'll be at yours and they'll send on the exam results. I don't want anything to do with Adam. I'd rather be with you.'

Lorna couldn't keep the pleasure from her voice. 'We'd be so happy to have you back, love, and you know it. Shall we start looking for a local sixth form? Wouldn't you like to carry on studying? There are some good ones around here, and there are colleges too.'

For a moment Penny was tempted, imagining two more years of Spanish and Geography, no more Maths, just the subjects that would take her to a different part of the world. Then she came back to earth. Who was she fooling?

'No, it's all right,' she said. 'I've had enough of all that. I'll get a job.'

Chapter Twenty

Penny had had hopes of finding something interesting to do in Margate but she was doomed to disappointment. The clothes shops had enough assistants and anyway, she didn't have any experience. The bars wouldn't take her – she was too young. 'More than my life's worth to have you on the premises,' groaned one landlord, who ran the pub closest to Lorna and Robert's house. 'You'd be a hit with some of the punters, and no mistake. But I could lose my licence.'

'Never mind, maybe in a couple of years,' smiled Penny, hiding her growing alarm. Although, from what she could see of the punters, she wasn't too keen on being a hit with them. They were old enough to be her grandfather.

That left some of the smaller corner shops, which she'd hardly been into over the years except on the very rare occasions when Lorna hadn't been organised to get in the bread or milk. The most exciting thing they sold was a series of postcards featuring the lido and the donkeys on the front. But at least they didn't demand that she was over eighteen or had years of experience.

Mrs Manning had run her shop three streets away for almost forty years, taking it over from her parents just after the war, and very little in it had changed since then. She'd made a nod to progress and bought a new till, and she even had a device on which you could swipe bank cards onto little transparent paper slips, but she didn't like to use it and most of her customers preferred to pay cash.

'No credit, mind,' she said to Penny, eyeing her dubiously and wondering if she could be trusted. Still, she was the niece or some such thing of that nice Mr Harrison, and besides, her last assistant had left in a hurry, no doubt because of a very dodgy boyfriend. This girl seemed nice enough, if a bit young, and she wasn't totally sure about how she dressed. But teenagers were different to in her day.

'No, of course not,' said Penny, wondering what she'd got herself into. She'd dressed carefully for the interview, although when given the choice she tried to copy her heroine, Madonna. She'd kept on her wristbands and pendants but deliberately toned down everything else and hadn't used eyeliner at all, so she felt almost naked.

'You got to be here to help me open up at half seven,' the woman went on. 'Folks round here like to pop in to get a pint of milk for their breakfast or a morning paper. Not a slugabed, are you? Nice early riser?'

'Oh yes,' Penny lied. This was getting worse and worse. Still, it wasn't as if she had anything else to do, and she was determined not to be a burden on Lorna and Robert. They couldn't have been more welcoming, but she was growing more aware of the fact they weren't really family. The way Adam had treated her had hit her hard, despite what she said. There was no way she was going to be more dependent on them than she could help.

'Good,' said Mrs Manning, almost smiling at her new assistant's enthusiasm. 'I'll see you tomorrow, bright and early, then.'

Which is how Penny came to find herself behind the counter of the cramped shop, staring through the open door and longing for a bit of breeze, as Mrs Manning didn't hold with fans because they disturbed the magazines. Her boss had stepped out for a 'bit of a break', which Penny assumed was to have a cigarette. There was a radio on the shelf behind her and so she turned it on, fiddling with the knob until she found Radio One. The Pet Shop Boys rang out with 'It's a Sin', and suddenly she felt better. There was no one around, so Penny edged out from behind the counter and began to dance, swaying to the electronic beat and shaking her hair in rhythm. She could just about see herself in the curved security mirror and thought she looked pretty good. 'It's a, it's a . . .' she sang, not bothering to keep the volume down as she had the place to herself.

'What the bloody hell's going on?' a voice shouted.

Penny whirled around to come face to face with her boss. 'Didn't hear you come in, Mrs Manning!'

'Not surprised, with a racket like that going full blast,' Mrs Manning growled. 'For Gawd's sake turn it off, it'll put off the customers.'

What customers? thought Penny, but did as she was told.

'We can't be having that muck on in here,' her boss went on. 'This is a respectable establishment. And you can't even tell if that's a boy or a girl singing.'

'It's a man,' Penny said.

'I don't bleedin' care,' hissed Mrs Manning, 'you are

165

not having that rubbish on in here and as for dancing around like that, you should be ashamed of yourself. Consider this a warning. I only took you on on account of your uncle being such a pillar of the community. It's a disgrace, you letting him down like that.'

Bit strong for one bit of dancing, thought Penny, but she forced herself to look sorry. She needed the money, after all. 'It won't happen again,' she said.

'I should think not.' Mrs Manning straightened her nylon overall. 'Call that music? Makes me sick. In my day we had proper tunes, and you knew what proper men sounded like.'

So that was that. Penny could see the days stretching ahead, no radio for company, only an angry old woman who didn't trust her. Less than a mile away, holidaymakers would be soaking up the sun, swimming, paddling, arranging their deckchairs and making the most of the summer, but she'd be stuck in here in an overheated box, selling crap that nobody wanted. Thanks, Mum, she thought. Thanks a bloody lot.

A month or so later and things were no better. Penny now had to wear an identical nylon overall to Mrs Manning, which was so hot that she thought she might faint. The one concession from Mrs Manning was that they could sometimes have Radio Two on, as long as there wasn't too much talking, which might put off the precious customers.

Penny was restacking a pile of tins of butterbeans, which Mrs Manning insisted everyone liked in summer, but given the amount of dust on them was probably not true. It brought back memories of school dinners, spoonfuls of things almost cold with no sauce or dressing, enough to make her retch. Was she imagining it or did they serve them better in Spain? Don't torment yourself, she thought, wiping the top of each tin and positioning it slightly differently to try to make it look as if some had sold. She was so bored she barely heard the door go.

'So this is where you've been hiding yourself!' cried the new arrival.

'Maureen!' Penny shouted in delight, spinning round and dropping her duster. 'What brought you here?'

'Come to find you of course,' said Maureen. 'Come to show off me new jewellery. D'you like this?' She pointed to a necklace of huge, brightly coloured beads that nobody could possibly miss. 'Gift from a gentleman friend,' she winked, and adjusted it around the collar of her white linen jacket, which had enormous shoulder pads.

'Lovely,' grinned Penny. 'What did you do to your hair?'

'Oh, got to have big hair these days,' said Maureen. 'Bigger the better, 'specially when you're blessed with being a natural redhead.' She winked. 'Some days it's more natural than others. What you doing in that horrible housecoat? Can't see your lovely pendants.'

'Oh it's uniform,' Penny said hurriedly. 'Come and meet my boss. Mrs Manning, this is . . . this is my Aunty Maureen.'

'Pleased to meet you, I'm sure,' Mrs Manning said doubtfully. She didn't know what to make of this young woman, who after all was a potential customer, but who looked extraordinary. Still, probably not short of a bob if she dressed like that, so not worth offending. 'Related to Mr Harrison, are you?'

Maureen turned on the charm. 'Actually I'm related to his wife,' she explained. 'So Penny's more like a cousin, but we say aunty. I wondered if she might be free for lunch. Fancy that, do you, Penny?'

Mrs Manning looked meaningfully at her employee.

'Sorry, Maureen,' she said. 'I've already had my lunch break. I start so early that I take it at twelve on the dot.'

'Early start? You of all people?' laughed Maureen, then controlled herself. 'Never mind, I'll see you back at the house later. Or do you have to work late too?'

'No, I'll be back normal time,' Penny assured her, hastening her to the door before she could say anything more. Then she picked up her duster and returned to the tins of beans, carefully wiping each one and restacking it. Somehow it didn't seem quite so boring with the prospect of a night with Maureen to come.

'So, you definitely not going back to school, then?' asked Maureen, as they drank tea in the guest bedroom while Lorna cooked in the kitchen.

Penny shook her head gloomily. 'What's the point? I don't want to go to university or become a teacher or anything like that. I'd rather earn my own keep.' She fiddled with her favourite pendant.

'What, in that dump?' said Maureen. 'Hot as hell and wearing nylon, no one to chat to all day but that dried-up old hag? Drive me mad, that would.'

'It's not for ever,' Penny protested. 'It'll do for now. At least I'm not cooped up with a bunch of toffee-nosed cows talking about their ponies.' She tried to laugh it off but Maureen knew her too well.

'Got to cheer you up a bit,' she observed. 'You're too young to be miserable. What did you used to like doing best of all?'

Penny thought for a moment. 'At school? Not much, you were always being watched. Every now and again they'd hold a disco in the hall, and that was fun. Or I liked being on stage in the end-of-term plays.' She grinned faintly. 'Dressing up and showing off, I suppose.'

'Bit like me then,' laughed Maureen. 'I know everyone looks down on what I did but I loved my days on stage, even if it was the opposite of dressing up. But it was the challenge, of getting them to look at you and yet keep their distance. It was a balance. Your mother, to give her her due, was brilliant at it. The audience couldn't look away and yet they were terrified of her, she was so arrogant.'

'Glad she was good at something,' muttered Penny. 'Better than mothering, for instance.'

'True, she was pretty crap at that,' sighed Maureen, seeing little point in lying. 'But what I do now is even better. It's an art form. It's real entertainment. It's classy. I love it.'

'Are you on stage still?' asked Penny. 'Didn't you give it up?'

'I did,' said Maureen, a little sadly, 'but I love the teaching bit. And burlesque is different, it's not sleazy. It's all about the moves, the illusion. I wish I'd come to it younger. You don't have to take off all your clothes if you don't want to, you just got to make them believe they might see something they shouldn't. It's a game; you know it, they know it. Trouble is, if you do show a bit of flesh – and I got to be honest, you do usually have to show 'em a bit – they like it to be firm. Now I keep myself in shape – teaching the moves, you have to – but I'm not what I was. And under the spotlights there's nowhere to hide. So I'm realistic.'

'Is it really difficult?' asked Penny, more interested now.

'Depends what you call difficult,' said Maureen. 'Depends if you have a natural talent. You got to have rhythm, you can't just stomp around up there and bat your eyelashes. It's a show. Like revue. You ever seen *Cabaret*?'

'Think so,' said Penny, trying to remember. '"Money Makes the World Go Round", that one? And Liza Minnelli in those tiny black shorts.'

'That's the one,' said Maureen. 'Stand up a mo.' She assessed Penny. 'You could carry off them shorts, and that little black halterneck number she wears as well. Not everyone could. You got the legs for it.'

'And the make-up!' Penny was getting the idea. 'I can do my eyes really well, only you haven't seen it as I don't put it on when I'm at work.'

'You got to be able to dance in heels,' Maureen said. 'See these?' She waved her feet in their impressive stilettos. 'These are nothing to what you'd have to move around in. Do you have any like this or higher?'

Penny looked at her. 'After a school like mine? You are joking.'

'Okay, okay, we'll work on it,' Maureen said, undaunted. 'Try these. Fit you okay? Right, now walk up and down. Very good. You got balance and strong ankles, all that hockey must have done you some good after all. Now we need music. What've you got?'

'Lots of Madonna,' said Penny. 'I love her. And Wham.

And Bananarama. Jimmy Somerville and The Communards . . .'

'No, no, that's all too dancy.' Maureen turned to the shelves where Lorna and Robert had left stacks of cassettes they hardly ever listened to. 'Blimey, here's that old Abba album we used to play when we was in Spain. Takes me back, that does. But it's not what I'm after.' She ran her fingers along the spines, dislodging a little puff of dust. 'Well, what do you know. Wonder who got this? It's *Cabaret*. We'll give it a go.'

Maureen turned to the cassette player on the chest of drawers and found the volume. 'Right, here we go. You copy what I do, you keep them shoes on.'

Hesitantly at first, Penny swayed and strutted, trying not to fall while keeping the beat as Liza Minnelli's voice belted out that money made the world go round. She tried not to look at her feet.

'That's it, that's it,' said Maureen. 'Very good, you got to meet their eyes. It's all about the eyes. Make them think you've noticed them and they're special. If you can do it to this fast tune then you've got promise. Now backwards . . . now side . . . wave your arms like Liza did . . . good.'

From below they could hear Lorna calling. 'Five minutes and it's ready.'

'Better give me those shoes back,' said Maureen. 'Seriously, you aren't half bad, Penny. Not sure I'd recommend showing everything you got till you fill out a bit – no, I'm only saying it like it is,' she added as Penny's jaw dropped. 'But you know how to dance.'

'Thought you said they liked firm flesh?' asked Penny. 'You saying I'm flabby before I even start? Wouldn't I be good enough?' She wasn't used to such personal comments. The girls in the changing rooms at school had been bad enough but this coming from Maureen was deeply hurtful.

'It's not a matter of being good enough,' said Maureen patiently. 'You got great looks, Penny, don't get me wrong. And you can't learn to move your body like that. You can learn new moves but if you ain't got what it takes to begin with then there's no chance, so you got a big head start. You just got to fill out a bit. Like I said, you don't have to show everything, that's part of the fun. You go on stage in them little shorts and halterneck and the punters'll go wild.'

Penny calmed down and was slightly relieved. She remembered the punters in the nearby pub and decided it was maybe no bad thing to maintain some distance from them. 'Do you think I could, really?' she asked. Suddenly it began to feel like a possibility. It would beat stacking beans, that was for sure.

'Hmm, not sure Lorna will like it,' Maureen warned her. 'Maybe leave that to me.'

'She'll have heard the songs,' Penny pointed out. ''Specially when you began to join in. So we might as well say something.'

'Perhaps,' Maureen said, not wishing to inflict her own fate on the girl. Hardly any of her family spoke to her even now, after she'd given up performing. 'Come on.' And they headed downstairs to face the music.

Chapter Twenty-One

Penny lay on her bed in her room, as the sound of the television rumbled from the living room. She didn't want to go downstairs and watch it with Lorna and Robert. Ever since Maureen's visit the atmosphere had been terrible. They couldn't understand why she wanted to leave, let alone follow in Maureen's footsteps. Or worse, in her mother's.

'But I can't stay in that shop!' she had pleaded. 'It's driving me mad, same thing every day, and that old woman on at me all the time.'

'You could go back and take your A-levels, or do another sort of course if you wanted to,' Robert pointed out. 'It's not the shop or nothing; you don't have to go off to London.'

'And you know what people will say about you if you do that job,' Lorna had added. 'Once you lose your respectability, that's it. Look at Maureen.'

Penny had protested that it wasn't the same as stripping and anyway she didn't care about being respectable, which hadn't gone down well. By the time Maureen left nothing had been settled but Penny knew she had to do something. There was a life out there and she wanted to live it to the full, not sit around suffocating in Margate. Lorna and Robert didn't understand – they talked about London as if anyone would have to be crazy to want to go there, but this wasn't fair as they'd both lived there and made the choice to leave. She wanted her own chance to find out.

Groaning, Penny dragged herself through her bedroom door and forced herself to go down to watch the television with them. It was the weather forecast. Michael Fish was saying that someone had asked if a hurricane was on the way. 'Don't worry, there isn't,' he reassured them from the small screen.

She thought that at least that would make a change from the daily routine of shop, home, shop, home, but reckoned she had better say nothing, as Lorna looked alarmed.

'I don't like the sound of that,' she said.

'Well, it's hardly likely,' Robert replied, putting down the paper. 'We simply don't get that kind of weather here. Just as well – people don't want to buy or rent houses without roofs.' He tried to raise a smile. 'Put it out of your head, there's nothing to be concerned about.'

So that was that, thought Penny, not even a bit of wind to liven things up.

Penny slept badly, imagining trees crashing down and houses losing their roofs, all the while mixed up with Michael Fish saying 'don't worry' and Robert telling her there was nothing to be concerned about. She tossed and turned, certain that she could hear loud noises and the screech of high winds, but waking just enough to tell herself not to be so stupid. Finally as dawn broke she woke up properly and ran to the window, just to reassure herself that it had all been a nightmare.

It hadn't.

Where the shed should have stood was an empty space. Some of its contents had fallen into the flowerbeds, which were also strewn with branches and tiles.

Neighbouring houses had broken windows. Penny wondered what else was wrong and realised there was no streetlight. She turned to switch on her bedside lamp but nothing happened. So there must be a power cut.

From below came a wail and she hurried downstairs to find Lorna pointing at the window of the back door, or where the window had been. It was a Victorian house and the back door had had a lovely coloured glass panel in it of which Lorna was very proud. Now most of it lay shattered on the hall floor, along with half a roof tile.

'My lovely window!' Lorna was repeating.

Robert appeared from the kitchen and gave her a hug. 'We'll get it replaced,' he soothed her. 'Least of our worries. And we'll sort the garden out, it won't be too bad. But right now what we need is a cup of tea and the kettle isn't working.'

'What about the camping stove?' suggested Penny. 'Won't that do? Or was it in the shed?'

'Oh no,' Lorna began again, but Robert shook his head.

'Good idea, and we'd moved it to the basement. I'll grab a torch and find it.' He shortly after reappeared with the stove and the spare gas canister. 'We can find some-thing to cook on this, can't we?'

'Yes, yes,' said Lorna, beginning to revive. 'We'll have baked beans and cans of soup until the power is back on.'

'We could build a bonfire with all those branches and cook on that,' Penny said, staring out at the devastation. 'It'd help clear the place up.'

'Maybe,' said Lorna, smiling faintly as she went to the kitchen to find the tea bags. She switched on the small transistor radio which ran from a battery, and gradually they pieced together the extent of the damage the high winds had done, bringing down trees across the south of the country, causing accidents, destroying property. People had died. The local station warned that nobody should venture out unless in dire emergency, and Penny perked up – opening the corner shop definitely wasn't one of those and she had no wish to serve the grumpy customers by candlelight.

Robert was less cheerful. 'I was meant to be going to Maidstone and Canterbury today but I can't see how I'd get there if so many roads are blocked.'

'Don't you even think about trying it,' Lorna warned him. 'We should leave the roads clear so the police and fire service can use them. I know you think every meeting is crucial and you'll be letting people down if you don't turn up but they won't want to come out either. And even if you do, you can't rely on the offices having light when you get there, and we don't know how many phone lines are down. You stay where you are.'

So the three of them drank their tea, ate cold cereal, and eventually decided to go out to see what had happened in the immediate area. They soon found they were lucky; a broken window, lost shed and wrecked garden counted for nothing against a poor couple who had lost the side of their house. Further along, the park had had many of its old trees uprooted and they lay fallen like dominoes, their vast trunks having been thrown into the air as if they were matchsticks. Penny was lost for words. This was terrible – and yet it sent a shiver of excitement through her. To think that something so unexpected could happen, so powerful, again made her feel as if she wanted to take on the world. And if life could be snuffed out so quickly by a random falling tree, it was stupid not to seize the day and live each moment to the full.

When things were slowly getting back to normal, Robert began to discover just how much of his business had been damaged. Property across Kent had been chewed up and spat out by the storm, old houses losing roof tiles, new developments brought to a standstill. Houses he was trying to sell or let would need weeks, if not months of repairs, and just finding anyone to do the work was proving impossible. In desperation he rang Denis, who had long since retired, who said he didn't want to get back into the swing of things full time but he could give him three days a week. 'Just temporary, mind,' Denis said. 'Seeing as it's you. I got very fond memories of your old boss so I'll help where I can but don't expect me to go up no high ladders no more.'

Robert sighed and put down the phone. He was fully insured and was fairly sure everything would be all right in the end but it would be touch and go for a while. The bank would expect to be paid, hurricane or no hurricane, and somehow he'd have to find a way. He knew of several rival firms who were happily putting homeless families into substandard properties and charging them a fortune, but he didn't feel inclined to join them. Making a killing out of other people's desperation was not his way. He'd have to talk to Lorna.

Later that evening, when Penny could be heard playing her endless Madonna records and dancing around to them, Robert forced himself to raise the subject. He couldn't bear to worry Lorna but she had a right to know and if they had to tighten their belts, then they'd do it together. He tried to keep it simple and short and not to exaggerate, but Lorna could see at once how anxious he was. She'd been in and around the business for long enough to learn exactly how it worked and knew that he would never have spoken unless it was serious. She took a deep breath and asked him to go through the figures, so that she could see for herself what the future might be like. People always dismissed her as only the wife, she thought grimly, but she was no fool. She just wanted to know the facts and then she could make up her own mind. Her job was to look after Robert and Penny and she was damned if she was going to let a bit of freak weather take away everything they'd worked for all these years.

Slowly they went through every detail, Lorna asking questions and making notes as she went, as she had done back when she'd been a secretary, before she'd ever been to Spain. She didn't want to jump the gun but it occurred to her that Robert was being too cautious. He hadn't really looked at using savings to fend off the bank. She knew he was extremely averse to risk and had spread his investments carefully, so even when the stock market had fallen badly after the hurricane he hadn't been hit hard. They had enough, they would be fine. And if she had to wait to fix her precious window and flowerbeds, then she would. But before she could reassure him, the living room door crashed open.

Penny stood there, visibly upset.

'You didn't say the hurricane would ruin you!' she cried.

'It won't!' Lorna gasped, standing up and trying to hug the girl. But Penny fended her off.

'Look, I've made up my mind,' she said. 'I won't be a burden on you any longer. You don't have to look after me like this. It's not fair on you and now you've got all this to sort out on top of everything. You should have said something before. I'll be fine. Really I will.'

'Penny, please,' Lorna said, wanting to keep calm, 'you mustn't rush into anything. And never, ever think that you are a burden. We love you and we love having you here. We're not going to be ruined, as I was about to explain to Robert. We'll all be fine.'

'No, I'm going to go,' Penny insisted. 'I know you don't like it but I want to go to Maureen and earn my living with her. I wanted to go anyway and now this has happened I can't stay, I'll hate myself.' Penny had been terrified when she'd overheard their conversation after the record had stopped, all the more so because they sounded so reasonable. It had brought back all the times she'd caught her mother poring over endless calculations, muttering about good times coming to an end, and she remembered all too well leaving Spain, the night in the horrible damp flat, the hurried move to another place and then to above the offices. All the despair of her mother's betrayal and Adam's casual cruelty came rushing back. There was no way she was hanging around any longer waiting for someone else to make a decision. How could she let Robert and Lorna go short when she wasn't even theirs? They would be better off without her.

Robert sighed. He'd glanced at Lorna's notes and could see she was right; he had overreacted out of overwhelming concern for her and the girl. Now it looked as if that concern had frightened Penny into a hasty decision.

'Lorna's right, as ever,' he said. 'You don't want to believe everything we were talking about. We were only looking at a worst-case scenario. In fact, we are all right. More than all right. Don't go running away to London thinking we're going to starve. It's a dangerous world up there, and we want you to be safe. We'd never forgive ourselves if something happened to you. So please just forget all you heard this evening.'

Penny shook her head.

'It's no good,' she said. 'I mean, I'm glad you won't be starving and I know you want me to be safe. But I can't stay here. I've got to try to make it. Maureen will look after me, she's got room now, and I'm old enough to take care of myself.'

'Penny, have you any idea of what you'd be getting into?' asked Lorna. 'I know you call it different but it's a glorified strip club. It'll be filthy old men trying to grab you, ogling you. What's so good about that? And there'll be no escape, as Maureen lives so close to the club. What if they follow you? What if they . . .' She couldn't bring herself to say the words but her mind was flooded with images of Penny being stalked on her way home and attacked, raped, even killed.

'I'm old enough to take care of myself,' Penny insisted. 'I know what you're thinking, but you must reckon I'm daft. I know they ogle you. You think I don't get ogled just walking down the street? At least if I'm on stage I get some protection. They can't just grab me. And it *is* different, Maureen says so. This is classy entertainment. She told you all that.'

'Penny, you've got no idea what men are like,' Robert said soberly. 'This isn't a game. We're trying to warn you for your own good. We love you too much to put you in danger.'

'It's not danger, it's dancing!' shouted Penny. 'And I can't stay here! There's nothing happening here, the place is full of old people, it's like dying slowly on your feet. I have to get away, live for myself, try to make it. If you don't let me go to Maureen then I'll try somewhere else, I'll just run off and you won't know where I am.' Even as she said it she knew it sounded childish, the very opposite of what she wanted, but she couldn't stop herself.

'Oh God,' groaned Lorna. She knew the girl was serious. They couldn't keep her under lock and key. They weren't even her legal guardians. If she was determined to go then her cousin was the best of a bad set of options. 'Look, let me ring Maureen tomorrow, all right? I don't want you just turning up on her doorstep. If she can look after you properly we'll talk again, okay? But please don't run away, not off into the middle of nowhere.' It'd kill me, Lorna wanted to say, but knew she couldn't.

'All right,' Penny said reluctantly. 'But I really am going to go. I can't stay here any longer.'

Chapter Twenty-Two

Penny could see her huge brown eyes reflected in the window as the train pulled into Victoria Station. As she was desperate not to stand out, she began to copy the other passengers who were all buttoning coats, putting on scarves, reaching for their luggage. She'd heard about what happened to lone young girls who didn't know what was what. That's not going to happen to me, she thought. I'm perfectly capable of looking after myself. I relied on myself in that school with no help from Mum – now's my chance to get on with real life.

Guiltily Penny pushed away the image of Lorna waving her off at Margate, lines of worry etched on her kind face. Lorna would be fine. Lorna had Robert.

The train shuddered to a stop and she lifted down her rucksack, which seemed far too small to contain everything she'd need for her new life. At least she could hoist it onto her shoulder without knocking into people. Just getting out of the carriage took ages, as everyone was carrying briefcases, bags, bulky cases. And there were so many people. Come on, Penny thought. Don't pretend you've never seen a crowd before. You can do this. Just get on with it.

As she was swept along on the platform she gazed around, trying to work out where to go. Maureen had written her a letter with instructions, but it was in her back pocket and she couldn't easily reach it with the rucksack on her shoulder. But Lorna had repeated her cousin's directions just before they'd said their goodbyes.

'Remember, all you have to do is take the Victoria Line to Oxford Circus,' she'd said. 'Then you can walk. You don't mind a bit of a walk, do you? So much easier than trying to change trains at rush hour.'

But Penny had obviously arrived right in the middle of it, and now wished she'd timed it better. Out on the station concourse the crowds were even worse. And they weren't like the crowds who filled the parade at Margate during the summer holidays. Those were relaxed, happy, colourful. Here, nobody made eye contact but each person stared straight ahead. With a sigh of relief she noticed the sign for the entrance to the Underground and allowed herself to be buoyed along in that direction.

Not understanding the automatic machines, she had to queue behind a line of tourists to get the right ticket.

'Oxford Circus, please,' she said.

'Just arrived, have you, love?' said the man at the counter. 'On a bit of a break? We get a lot of you back-packers around here, you know.'

'I live here,' Penny assured him, feeling a little tingle of joy. 'I'm going to study dance.' She couldn't quite believe she'd said it.

'Right you are, love,' said the man, counting out her change. 'Well, you look after yourself and watch that bag of yours.'

She smiled back as she carefully put the coins into her

purse, which she'd had the forethought to keep in her handbag, worn across her body. Nobody's getting their hands on this, she thought, holding on to it tightly as she made her way through the barrier and down the escalator. As if the crowds weren't bad enough, a few people were smoking, making her cough in the heavy atmosphere.

A northbound train had just pulled in and she had little choice but to be caught up in the swell of passengers fighting to find a space on it. She found herself tightly wedged in the middle of the carriage, scarcely able to move one arm to grab a pole to steady herself. No need to worry, she was heading in the right direction and all she had to do was stay upright until the stop. But this wasn't as easy as she'd assumed. Passengers kept moving, shoving and manoeuvring for position, all the while never speaking or meeting each other's eye. A few tutted at her rucksack. Others were pressing against her – was that man doing it deliberately? Unwilling to make a fuss but determined not to be taken advantage of, she tried to catch the look on his face. But it was impossible. Craning her neck, she wondered if she could see his reflection. But she couldn't do that either. 'Filthy old sod,' she muttered. 'Don't even think of trying it.'

Damn, now she had lost count of the stops. Everyone was always saying how London was such a big place – one of the very reasons Lorna hadn't wanted her to come.

The creepy man had got off and Penny was finally able to stand next to the doors. As they opened at the next station she gasped. She'd come too far – this was King's Cross. Taking a split-second decision she jumped off and onto the platform, hefting her rucksack with one hand

and clutching her precious bag with the other. Once again she was swept along as she scanned the signs for one that would send her back the way she'd come. But something didn't feel right – and it was nothing to do with getting off at the wrong stop. It was the atmosphere, the crowd. Then she smelt it. Smoke.

Back in Margate, Lorna was busying herself around the house, desperately trying not to think about how Penny was getting on. She and Robert had eaten their evening meal and drunk their coffee. He'd even suggested she have a little extra something with it, to steady her nerves, but she'd said no. She knew she wouldn't calm down until Maureen rang to say the girl had arrived safely. Or, better still, if she could speak to Penny herself. If she hadn't heard in an hour or two, she'd ring anyway just to be on the safe side.

Even though the girl was sixteen now, that still seemed terribly young to Lorna. There was a lump in her throat as she remembered how vulnerable Penny had looked, bundled in her one good coat, struggling with that horrible rucksack. If only she'd allowed her to buy a sensible, smart case. But Penny had wanted to do everything for herself, and reluctantly Lorna had agreed, taking comfort from the thought that Maureen would see that no harm came her way. Although, said a little voice in her head, Maureen wasn't the nurturing kind. Fun, yes. Never a dull moment. But not what you'd call the motherly type.

Still, Lorna thought, stacking plates and tidying them away, Penny's actual mother had been about as far from the motherly type as you could imagine, and yet the girl

185

seemed to have managed so far. She'd got through years at that school – Lorna almost sobbed aloud at the memory of the day the child had been sent there, so small in her stiff uniform, her lip wobbling but with no other trace of her emotions. She'd been good at concealing them, when she had to.

Plates stacked, glasses polished, Lorna had run out of things to put away, and so she turned on the radio, hoping to catch an absorbing drama, or, even better, a comedy to drive away the dark fears. But it was the news headlines. Clutching the nearest chair, Lorna felt herself go freezing cold all over at the words: 'Reports are reaching us of a fire at King's Cross Station . . .'

Smoke. Smoke, and heat.

There was no denying it. Penny had been trying to tell herself that this was just another thing to get used to now she was a Londoner. But now everyone was beginning to panic, turning around, twisting to see what was happening, pushing, heading for the way out. She realised it must be really bad when passengers actually started to speak to each other. Screwing up her courage she asked a woman next to her, 'What's going on?'

'Dunno,' said the woman, her voice shaky. 'Never seen anything like it. Never smelt anything like it either,' she added, trying to inject humour into the situation.

'Where's the way out?' Penny gasped. 'Are we going the right way? I've never been here before.' Her voice caught on her final words.

'Not really sure,' admitted the woman. 'Silly, isn't it? I come this way all the time but now I can't think straight.'

'Oh,' said Penny, thinking that didn't sound good. But

then the woman was swept away from her and, though they'd only exchanged a few sentences, she felt suddenly even more alone.

Someone behind her started to cry. Somebody else murmured, 'I don't want to die. Not here, not now.'

Die? It had never occurred to Penny that she might die. Now she glanced about and the terrifying thought struck her that this might be it. A wave of utter panic hit her and she very nearly fell, her legs turning to jelly, her blood running cold even as her forehead was bathed in sweat. She remembered Lorna's face as she said goodbye and an overwhelming feeling of regret filled her, for things she'd never said, all the gratitude and love and overwhelming longing to see her again.

Then something else took hold of Penny – a fierce determination that this would not be the end. 'Get a grip,' she growled silently. 'Don't start giving up. There's a world out there and you're going to take it by storm, not abandon hope and choke in some stinking underground tunnel.' Fuelled by a new energy, she grabbed the arm of the crying woman. 'Save your breath,' she hissed, as she made out a dull illuminated sign through the smoke-filled air. 'We're going towards that light. See it?'

The woman made a noise which might have been a 'yes', and took hold of one of the rucksack straps, making it ten times heavier and more awkward than ever. All the while the heat increased.

Driven with an urgency she had never known before, Penny kept moving forwards, gasping, coughing, her eyes streaming from the smuts and fumes.

* * *

'Maureen,' gulped Lorna, her clammy hand barely able to grasp the receiver, 'is that you? Maureen, can you hear me?'

'Good God, Lorna, whatever's the matter?' came the familiar voice. 'Sounds like you're in a right state.'

'Can I speak to Penny? Is she there yet?'

'Blimey, you've only been apart for a couple of hours,' groaned Maureen. 'You're not going to be like this all the time, are you? Give the girl a chance. And no, she's not here yet.'

'But she should be, she should be!' cried Lorna. 'Something's happened. She wouldn't be anywhere near King's Cross, would she?'

'Wouldn't have thought so,' said Maureen, keen to placate her cousin, but slightly irritated none the less. 'Look, I've got to pop to the show to make sure one of my new girls does her routine right. She's having dreadful problems with her fan.'

'What about Penny?'

'I'm sticking the key under the mat and a note on the door. She can read, can't she? She is a grown-up now, right?'

'No, no, you don't understand,' Lorna moaned. 'The news said there is a major fire at King's Cross. She might have got lost – she won't know where she is. It's my fault, it's all my fault, I should have given her the fare for a taxi, but she wanted to do it by herself. Maureen, go and find her. Please? I won't bother you all the time, I promise, but go and find her. Find my little girl.' She could say no more.

'Hold your horses,' sighed Maureen, thinking, not for the first time, that her cousin was extremely overprotective. 'I suppose the show will go on without me and if the fan gets dropped then they all get more than they paid for. I'll ask Mark to wait in the flat – he does the costumes and will only be hanging around because he doesn't have anything better to take his sorry self off to. Then if the phone goes while I'm out, he can take a message. Okay? That good enough for you?'

'Thank you, thank you,' cried Lorna. 'I'll never forget this. Just go and bring her home safe.'

Shrugging into her impractical but glamorous leopard-print jacket, Maureen headed out of her flat, wondering if she'd done the right thing by agreeing to let Penny come to stay.

Smoke, heat, more smoke, and now noise. A dreadful, crackling, fierce noise, echoing down the corridors and stairwells, combining with the thunderous footsteps of hundreds of tightly packed passengers and their high-pitched cries and shouts.

Penny did her best to ignore it all, grimly focusing on finding the exit. She'd made it past the first Way Out sign, and was now staggering up what must be an escalator, which was no longer working, though it was hard to make out anything in the gloom. Dully she noticed how the treads were just too far apart to make it easy to climb. If she got out of here, she'd always take the stairs . . . no, not if. When. Her shoulders were aching from the added weight of the weeping woman, who seemed unable to support herself, and her lungs felt as if they might explode any minute. 'Worry about that later,' she told herself. 'One step, then the next, that's all you have to think about.'

Then, the most welcome sight in the world, she could

189

just about distinguish an orange glow above her and a delicious draught of cold air brushed her skin. They were nearly at street level. 'Come on,' she growled, every cell of her body desperate to manage the final few steps. 'We can do it. We're there.'

With a final push there they were, being dragged by rescuing arms out onto the pavement. Streetlamps were blazing, sirens blaring, a crowd of people staring. The woman at her side collapsed, making feeble little moans of terror. Penny gazed around, feeling nothing but a sense of unreality as she gulped blessed fresh air into her sore lungs.

And then, miracle of miracles, she could see a figure waving – a figure with bright red hair. Maureen. Penny didn't have the energy left to question why she was there. All she knew was, Maureen was there and she was safe.

Chapter Twenty-Three

'Right, here we are,' said Maureen, leading an exhausted Penny up a final steep flight of rickety stairs and through a doorway. 'You're in here – sorry it's a bit small but it'll be easier to heat, look on the bright side. You might want to go in there first, that's the bathroom.'

'What? Why?' asked Penny, now totally disorientated. So that would be her room – much, much smaller than in Margate but not so different to the cell-like one she'd had at school.

'I don't want to cast aspersions or frighten you,' said Maureen, 'but you look a right sight. You could do with washing your face at least.'

Penny pushed open the bathroom door, caught sight of herself in the mirror and screamed. 'What's happened to me? Oh my God, I'm covered in something! Ugh, it's all over me. What is it?'

'Reckon it's smuts, lovey,' said Maureen, reaching for the light pull. 'There you are, see more clearly now, can't you? You must have been pretty close to that fire, and you got stuff from it on your face and coat. Here, take this flannel and give your face a wash and I'll get the hot water on so you can have a proper bath in a bit. You come through here when you're done and we'll have a drop of tea.'

Penny did as she was told, brushing her coat as best she could and then splashing water over her face before giving it a good scrub. It was more difficult than she thought as the marks stuck to her, minute flecks of soot on every visible part of her skin. It began to dawn on her just how narrow an escape she'd had, and the combination of that and the strangeness of finally being in London was almost too much for her. To distract herself she looked around the poky bathroom. It had a bare bulb hanging from the ceiling but there were many more lights around the big mirror, which was surrounded by glass shelves covered in pots and tubes. Clearly Maureen was a serious collector of cosmetics. Penny was irresistibly drawn to the eyeliners and mascaras, arranged according to colour, and for a moment she considered trying some on. But then she remembered she would have a bath once the water was hot, and her new landlady would be waiting.

As she opened the door she could hear Maureen on the phone.

'Of course she is. She's just a bit shocked, that's all. We'll get her tucked up soon as we can and then how about you have a good long chat tomorrow? . . . Are you bleedin' joking? Stop frightening yourself by watching the news. She's fine, I'm telling you. No, we are not going to the hospital just in case. She got out, end of. Now I don't want to be rude but I got to get the kettle on for my guest. Think she deserves a cuppa after all that . . . Yes, I was going to anyway. Speak to you then.'

Penny almost laughed. Nobody else ever talked to

Lorna like that, but she was glad Maureen hadn't passed her the receiver. Hearing Lorna would have tipped Penny over the edge. At least by tomorrow she'd be feeling better, less tired, less strange.

Following Maureen's voice Penny found herself in a small living room with a kitchen squeezed off to one side, where she was faced with a stranger.

'There you are,' said Maureen, turning round, 'and you're looking better already. Isn't she, Mark?'

The stranger stood up. He was very skinny, with dyed hair that flopped over one eye, while the sides of his head were closely shaven. He had on a fantastically flamboyant shirt, and Penny wondered at the back of her mind if that's what had brought these two people together – a love of outrageous clothes.

'I wouldn't know, darling, would I?' he said. 'I didn't see her before. Hello, pleased to meet you, Maureen's told me all about you. I'm Mark, and I work at the Paradise Club too. Costume design. So if you need any help in that department, I'm the one to call.' He glanced at Maureen. 'Or for help in any kind of department, such as flat sitting, tea making, generally keeping the train on the tracks.' He stopped. 'Sorry, that wasn't the best thing to say. Are you all right? What a way to arrive. Take a seat, have some tea.'

'Thanks,' said Penny, almost tearing up again. 'That'd be nice.'

'Don't you mind him,' fussed Maureen. 'Always putting his foot in it, he is. But give him his due, he didn't hesitate to come over here and wait while I was out looking for you, in case you was to arrive before I got back. Give him a proper haircut and he'd be the ideal housekeeper.'

'Never you mind my hair,' said Mark, sweeping it back from his forehead. 'I'll have you know it cost a fortune and you're only saying that because you're jealous. Now, when Penny here is ready, I shall take her to the top hairdresser and demand a stunning cut for the best new dancer in town.' His eyes twinkled. 'That's what you're going to be, isn't it? We'll give you a few days to recover and settle in, then I shall whisk you off.'

'I'd like that,' admitted Penny, though she wasn't sure about the costing a fortune bit.

'That's settled, then,' beamed Mark. 'And don't you worry, they'll do it for me as a favour. Owed many favours by all sorts, I am.' He stood up. 'Now I've made your acquaintance I shall take my leave. Don't let Maureen lead you astray.'

'Blimey,' said Penny when he'd gone. 'Is he always like that?' She sipped her tea, which seemed like the only familiar thing in the room. She wasn't at all sure what to make of the young man.

'Most of the time,' Maureen replied. 'He has a heart of gold, but sometimes you got to dig hard to find it. Took a shine to you, though.'

Penny sniffed, and realised that her clothes smelt of the fire. 'Oh no, here am I stinking of smoke and you introduce me to your friend. What must he think?'

'He'll think nothing of it,' Maureen assured her. 'He'll be as glad as the rest of us that you got out of that inferno. Seriously, are you all right? That was Lorna on the phone before, checking you was okay. I haven't seen the news but she said it was a huge fire, so for once she's right to be worried sick. Told her you'd speak to her tomorrow and the cheeky mare told me I'd better not forget. As if

I would. That water'll be hot now so shall I run your bath?'

'Please,' said Penny. Now that she'd had some tea to revive her, she was desperate to get out of the stinking clothes and to wash her hair. 'Do you think everything in my rucksack will smell as well? What'll I do?'

'To be honest, yes, it's out there in the corridor ponging the place out,' said Maureen. 'But we'll sort it out tomorrow. I might not have all Lorna's mod cons but I do know about looking after clothes. You can have one of my shirts to sleep in and we'll worry about the rest when we wake up. Which, don't know about you, won't be very early. So sleep in as long as you like.'

She swept out and there came the sound of running water and a strong smell of flower-scented bubble bath noticeable even over the smoke, before she dashed back in with an armful of silky underwear Penny had earlier noticed hanging over the bathtub. 'Might as well pamper yourself,' said Maureen. 'Use my hair stuff, it don't matter that it says it's for redheads, henna will be good for you. I'll leave a shirt on your bed. See you in the morning, okay?'

Sinking gratefully into the scented bubbles, Penny let her mind go blank. It was all too much to take in. She'd think about it tomorrow.

In the morning, Penny could hardly remember where she was. Then it all came back to her. Her throat was dry, her eyes stung, and her shoulders ached from carrying the rucksack along with the weight of the struggling woman, but otherwise she seemed to be all right. Her hair smelled of the henna shampoo, which she liked. Slowly, she took stock of her surroundings.

Light was coming through the gaps around the thick red velvet curtain across the window, and she could make out framed posters for musicals and West End shows. Crammed along one wall were a wardrobe, a dressing table with mirror, and a battered-looking chair with a wicker seat. Someone had hung a dressing gown on a hook on the back of the door.

There was no sign of the rucksack so she got up and wrapped herself in the dressing gown, which felt wonderfully soft. It was nothing like the practical towelling ones Lorna had bought for her over the years, none of which had a tasselled belt at the waist. She pushed back the curtain some more and posed in front of the mirror, pouting and twirling the cord, but stopped when she heard a voice from the corridor.

'You done me proud,' Maureen was saying. 'I won't forget this, I owe you big time.' A door shut.

Cautiously Penny put her head around her own door. 'Have we got visitors?' she asked. 'Because I've only got this on . . .'

'No, no, you're all right,' said Maureen, picking up a big bag. 'Look, here's your stuff. All clean and sweet-smelling. The rucksack's still being worked on but the rest of your things are here.'

'God, how late have I slept?' asked Penny in a panic. 'How did that all get done so fast? Have I missed a day?'

'Stop it, not so fast,' laughed Maureen. 'You're up in time for a late breakfast or early lunch, depends how you look at it. Fancy some toast?' She led the way into the tiny kitchen area, and caught Penny looking round. 'Yes, I know, not much of a kitchen but then I don't do much cooking. You don't need to round here, with so many places to go out all hours of the day and night. You can if you want to, but you might need to buy a few things. Marmalade?' She spread the toast and passed it across.

'Mmm,' smiled Penny. 'But did you get up at dawn? I know you don't like to.'

'Well, only briefly,' Maureen admitted. 'Mark came round and took it all. He really does know a lot of people to call on for favours and he reckoned you'd hate to wake up with no clean clothes. So he sorted it out.'

Penny shook her head in disbelief. 'But he only just met me, and how would he know that?'

'Well, who would?' asked Maureen reasonably. 'First day in new flat, new city, new people to meet, and you've got no proper clothes – nightmare! Told you, he's got a heart of gold. And . . .' She stopped and started again, with a very small tremor in her voice. 'We both heard the news on the radio. More details about what happened last night. People died. So I suppose it's our way of saying thank God you weren't one of them.' She cleared her throat. 'Anyway, make the most of it, get yerself dressed, and then we've got things to do. You got to see where you'll be practising, because it'll take a while before you can go on stage, even though you're good. Then we're going to the Paradise Club. So look sharp.'

Penny looked away, all the memories of what had happened underground threatening to swamp her. 'It was terrible,' she said. 'How did I get out and others didn't? What if some of the people on my train died? I don't understand . . .'

'You can't go round thinking like that,' said Maureen. 'Way I look at it, when your number's up, it's up. Yours wasn't yesterday. Sorry if it sounds harsh. But you was put on this earth to dance and live another day, so get your arse in that bedroom and stick on some clothes, and make sure you can move in them. You got any high heels yet?'

Penny struggled to get a grip on her emotions and smiled weakly. 'No, I thought I'd be able to get better ones up here.'

'Damn right you will,' beamed Maureen. 'That'll be the first part of your job. Shopping for shoes. See, isn't life looking better already?'

Chapter Twenty-Four

By the time they reached the dance studio Penny was worn out. She'd never encountered such a welter of sights and sounds as when Maureen led her through the door onto the street where she lived. It had been too dark and she'd been too much in shock to notice much the night before, but now she could see that the little flat was bang in the heart of the action, with shops crowded in every-where, neon and painted signs competing for space, and people everywhere – on the narrow pavements, in the roads, coming in and out of shops and offices, going about their business at high speed, or hanging around the café doors gossiping at leisure.

Turning the nearest corner, Penny had been surprised to find a bustling street market, with colourful stalls of fruit and veg piled high, flowers, bread, oddments of hardware and items she simply didn't recognise. 'What's this?' she asked.

'Berwick Street,' said Maureen, waving to one of the traders. 'Now if you was to be interested in cooking, here's where you should get your ingredients. There's a supermarket over there' – she pointed to a brightly lit doorway – 'but generally you're better off getting stuff here, 'specially if you get to know the stall holders. Morning, Jimmy!'

'Morning? Might be for some of us,' huffed the man behind one of the fruit and veg stalls, 'but the rest of us been up since three. Don't you want your dose of sunshine today, then?' He held up a plastic bowl full of oranges.

'Maybe later,' Maureen shouted and made to head off.

Penny was brought to a standstill by something she'd never seen before, a rounded green shape covered in spiral patterns made up of little points. 'What's one of those?'

Maureen misunderstood and thought she was looking at the woman standing in the doorway behind, who promptly turned and made an ugly face at them. 'That's the competition,' Maureen said, tossing her hair, 'and you don't want to take no notice of the likes of her. She'd love to work for a high-class act like we do but she got no chance.'

Penny glanced up and saw the doorway was surrounded by painted boards showing silhouettes of very curvy female figures. Abruptly she realised what was on sale there. 'Oh, right,' she said, embarrassed, 'but I meant that vegetable.'

Jimmy, watching all this, laughed and picked up the strange object. 'It's what we call a romane,' he said. 'Half broccoli, half cauliflower. You cook it like either. Do it with a bit of cheese sauce for your lunch.'

'Not today, Jimmy, we ain't got time,' said Maureen, trying to move on. 'Shoes to buy, people to see.'

'Don't let me hold you up then,' he said, putting the vegetable back and shoving his hands into his overall pockets, 'but if you want to try it, young lady, you come and see me another day.'

'Thanks, I will,' beamed Penny.

From there Maureen had dragged her off to Oxford Street, assuring her that it wasn't very busy as it was only a Thursday morning. Penny struggled to believe that as the crowds were almost impossible to get through, but she allowed herself to be guided into various enormous department stores and shoe shops until she had what Maureen regarded as acceptable footwear: three pairs of towering high heels. Now all she had to do was stay upright in them when she learned her new moves.

Finally they arrived at the dance studio, as Maureen called it, a large room surrounded with mirrors that they got to by squeezing down a narrow alley and climbing up three flights of stairs which smelled of the rubbish she had seen being collected outside. Penny didn't have any great hopes of the place and privately wondered if she was doing the right thing. But when they stepped through the door the place was flooded with light, and there was a breathtaking view across the rooftops from the huge windows.

The music stopped, and everyone turned to look at them.

Penny took in a group of people mostly a little older than her, some tall, some not, some very curvaceous, but all seeming as if they exercised a lot. She could tell they were assessing her and hoped she looked the part and wouldn't let Maureen down.

'Right, everybody, this is Penny,' said Maureen, 'and she's learning the moves so she can join some of us at the club. So, I want you to come and stand between two of the current dancers who can show you what you'll have to do when I'm not around. Okay, Michelle, Juliet, you make a space and Penny will go there. Good. We'll start with another warm-up routine and go from there.'

Penny cast a swift glance to either side to check who these dancers were. To her left stood a young woman with abundant long blonde hair, almost as tall as her even though her heels were shorter, and with a figure that Penny imagined Maureen couldn't complain about. The woman looked back at her quickly, with a kind but rather distant gaze. Penny, who had developed a nose for such things at school, suspected the woman's clothes were of a very high quality, certainly better than the ripped T-shirts some of the others were wearing.

To the other side was a shorter girl, with a tumble of brown curls and again a very curvy shape. She grinned broadly, which made her nose crinkle, drawing attention to its smattering of freckles. Penny grinned back, but she began to see why Maureen had said she was too thin. If firm flesh was what was needed on stage, there was a lot of it here. Well, if she wasn't going to be the star of the show yet, she'd better make sure she was a brilliant dancer to make up for it and earn her space. She looked up, ready to learn the routine.

Ten minutes later, and Penny thought she was going to die. She'd happily assumed that because she could dance non-stop to her records at home she was fit and wouldn't have to try hard to keep up. Now she knew better. Her feet hurt, her knees hurt, her lungs felt as if they would burst. She could tell her face had gone bright red and that she was pouring with sweat, although she wasn't the only one. So that's why so many dancers wore bands or scarves around their foreheads. She'd always thought it was for show but now she realised she'd have to get one or she wouldn't actually be able to see what was going on as her hair was plastered to her face. Not a good look, she thought.

'Water's over there,' said the blonde woman, nodding to a basin in the corner. 'Looks like you could do with some.'

'It's the heels,' said Penny, which was partly true, 'I always had lower ones before.'

'If you can dance in those ones, you can dance in anything,' said the woman. 'So it's good to practise. Grab your drink as we only get two minutes' break, but I'll explain after if you like. I'm Juliet.'

Penny nodded gratefully and grabbed a glass of water, gulping it down before pouring another and holding it to her hot face.

A strenuous routine followed, but at least everyone else was learning it from scratch as well and she didn't feel too out of place. In fact, as they went through it for the third time, she realised she'd picked it up faster than many of the dancers around her. So that was something. Maybe this was going to be all right after all.

'Okay, that's it for this session,' called Maureen from the front of the studio. 'Afternoon class starts at three for those who signed up for it.'

People began to break apart, grabbing their bags and running, or forming small groups in corners, slowly changing into street clothes. Penny looked around, wondering what had happened to Juliet. She saw her blonde hair emerging from a side door and headed towards her. 'Can't bear not to have a shower and brush my hair after a class,' she said. 'Through that door if you want to do the same. I'll wait for you – I know you've come with Maureen but she'll most likely be busy so I'll have a word then take you for a coffee.'

Perched on tall chrome stools with leather seats at a narrow Formica bar, the three young women sipped their espressos in the café. Michelle had joined them – the girl with the brown curls. 'So, what did you make of it?' she demanded. 'Bet you're so knackered you can hardly speak.'

'It got better as it went on,' said Penny, unwilling to admit how hard she'd found it. 'This stuff is gorgeous. I've never tasted anything like it. How do they do it?'

'You can ask them but they won't tell you,' Juliet replied, shaking her shiny blonde hair out to dazzle the waiter. 'They just claim it's a secret recipe. Don't you, Tony?'

'Ah, don't tease me,' protested the waiter, mockingly clasping his hands to his chest. 'You gonna break my heart one day and how you gonna get your coffee then?'

'He's got a point,' grinned Michelle. 'Don't hurt him, Jools, he's too cute.' She deliberately licked coffee off her top lip at which the waiter groaned extravagantly before disappearing to the kitchen.

'He is quite cute,' Penny said, as if she sat around flirting with waiters every day of the week. 'Good hair.'

'Bit like yours, it's so dark,' said Juliet. 'Are your parents Italian?'

'No,' Penny said, 'but they're both dead anyway. Dad

died when I was born and he was very English and proper, from what they all say. And my mother . . . my mother had dark hair but would have had a fit if anyone called her foreign. She lived in Spain for years and never spoke a word of the language. So, no. What about you? Where are you from?'

'Oh, I'm also very English and proper,' Juliet replied, exaggerating her accent. 'You couldn't get more proper than me. Proper school, proper parents, proper house in the country – you've no idea.'

'So why are you here?' asked Penny. 'I went to what you might call a proper school too but only because they couldn't think of what else to do with me. I can't imagine any of my classmates dancing on stage in Soho.'

'Well, maybe that's why I'm doing it,' Juliet said, drawing out a packet of cigarettes from the pocket of her beautifully cut jacket. 'Want one? Suit yourselves. My entire life was planned out for me before I was out of my nursery. And I didn't want any of it. Don't get me wrong, I love my mother, but I don't want to turn into a clone of any of her friends, some of whom are frankly ghastly. I'm good at dancing, I love the theatre, and I'd be lying if I didn't know the effect I have on men. So here I am.'

Penny turned on her stool, catching the edge of the bar to stop herself falling off. 'What about you, Michelle?'

'Complete opposite,' smiled Michelle. 'I've got such a big family that they haven't even noticed I'm not home of an evening. This is a good life, I like the work and if you've got it, flaunt it, is what I say. Get up late, maybe come to a class to keep in shape, see your friends then go on stage. Then I get the night bus back to Bow, or on a good night I grab a taxi.'

Penny raised her eyebrows. 'But isn't that really expensive?'

'That's what I mean by a good night,' Michelle said. 'I get tips.'

'I've got a tip for you, Michelle,' said Juliet. 'Don't keep going off with the punters. You know the management don't like it, and once you're off the premises they can't protect you.'

'Oh leave it out,' groaned Michelle, and Penny got the impression they'd had this conversation many times before. 'You're not my mum. I don't need protecting from a bit of fun, and who knows, I might meet a proper sugar daddy one day. It's all right for you, you don't need one, but I'm sick to death of sharing a room with my sisters. I'm not going to stop it, so sorry if you don't like it.'

'No, I don't like it,' said Juliet, blowing out a smoke ring. 'And you know why. We're artistes, not sleazy tarts. And we have to act as if we know the difference. And you give us a bad name, I'm sad to say.'

'Gets me a taxi home at night though,' said Michelle, curls bouncing. 'Better than the bus with all the drunks and gropers. You leave me to worry about my name. What about you, Penny, how you going to get back once you start performing?'

'I'm sharing a flat with Maureen and it's just around the corner from here,' Penny explained. 'So I won't need a taxi. Not sure when I'll be starting on stage, though.'

'It won't be long, judging from how fast you picked up that routine today,' Juliet predicted. 'Tall and graceful like you, they'll love you. Mind you, if you want to do solos, you'll have to . . .'

'Fill out a bit,' said Penny.

'Exactly,' said Juliet. 'That's the hard facts of the business. So how about I buy us some of those delicious Italian desserts to give us energy and fatten you up a little?'

Chapter Twenty-Five

'Isn't she with you?' asked Mark. He was sitting at a small table in a dark corner of the dressing room, stitching a bright feather boa to the neckline of a black satin waistcoat. 'Bit early to be letting her out on her own, isn't it?'

'She'll be fine, Juliet and Michelle are looking after her,' said Maureen, collapsing onto the chair opposite him. 'I don't know how you can see what you're doing in this light.'

'I can't,' said Mark. 'Can't you ask His Nibs to put in some proper spots? He wants the costumes to look sophisticated and not tacky and yet I have to make them half blind.'

'Not sure he'll listen to me any more,' sighed Maureen, flexing her ankles and wincing. 'My days of being able to wind him round my little finger are long gone. I'll try, but don't get your hopes up.'

'So you're not going to ask Penny to persuade him, then?'

'No,' said Maureen, suddenly serious, 'no, I'm not. And don't you put her up to it neither. She's too young and naïve for all that. She's going to dance in the background and that's it, I promised my cousin. God knows I don't want her to go through what I did, nobody back home speaking to me. Yes, I done all right out of it in the end but you got to be tough.' And I don't reckon the girl's tough enough, Maureen thought. Not yet, anyway. Aloud she went on: 'Lorna will kill me if anything happens to her, and I'd like to think that at least one of my relations doesn't hate me.'

'All right, calm down,' said Mark, holding up the waistcoat and inspecting it. 'Hmm, bit more on the left . . . no, I didn't mean it. I know she's almost like a niece to you. She must be okay if she can go through shit like last night and then straight into a class this morning. I got her rucksack back from Betty's by the way. It doesn't smell any more but it's wrecked – looks like someone's pulled half the buckles off. God knows what was going on down that tunnel.'

'I don't want to think about it,' Maureen told him, 'and she don't neither. We got to keep her mind off it. I'll bring her along this evening so she can meet everybody and see a bit of the show, that should cheer her up. Are you going to be here?'

'Where else would I be?' asked Mark. 'No, really, where else? Because that bastard has chucked me again and this time I've had enough. If he comes crawling round here saying it was all a mistake and begging forgiveness I'll tell him where he can shove it. He's done nothing but waste my time and I won't stand for it again.'

'Calm down yourself,' said Maureen. 'I'll happily tell him to piss off if he shows his face. A lovely looking face, I grant you, but a narrow little mind behind it, when

209

all's said and done. So that's good, you can look after Penny while I check on the new girls. I hear last night went off without any disasters – but best to be careful.'

'That suits me fine,' Mark agreed, biting off the thread with his teeth. 'There, isn't that better? That's turned out a treat.'

'It has,' said Maureen, waving as she made her way back to the stage door. She'd been unusually sharp with Mark but he hadn't seemed to mind, which was just as well, as she relied on him more than she cared to admit. But she didn't want him getting ideas about why Penny was there, or, more precisely, she didn't want him joking about it, then the rest of the cast and crew assuming that was the truth. Maureen realised that she'd taken on quite a lot, looking after Penny. True, the girl seemed far more interested in dressing up and dancing than getting off with men, but she knew what some of the other dancers were like and she hoped the girl wouldn't be swayed by them. Michelle was lovely, and not half the tough nut she made herself out to be, but she was heading for trouble if Maureen was any judge of the situation. And, having been perilously close to such situations herself, she could usually tell.

Last night had brought home to her how dangerous life in the capital could be if you didn't know your way around – or, in the case of some of the poor sods who had died, even if you did. Well, she was no mother hen like Lorna but she'd just have to do her best. She'd get back to the flat, grab a bite to eat, get Penny to phone home then take her to her first night at the club. And that was about the best she could manage.

* * *

210

'I saw Jimmy as he was packing up for the night,' said Penny as Maureen came through the door. 'He gave me these on the cheap. Do you want to try some?' She waved a bag of the strangely shaped green vegetables.

'Dunno,' said Maureen dubiously. 'I told you, I don't usually cook and them don't look like the sort of thing you can eat raw. What would you do with them?'

'Like he said, have them with cheese sauce,' Penny said, amused. Since she was a little kid she'd always thought that Maureen could do anything. Now it seemed she'd found something she couldn't.

'I don't have any of that in,' said Maureen, apologetically.

Penny laughed out loud. 'You don't get it in, you make it. Butter, flour, milk, cheese. No, don't worry, I got them at Gateway. Have you got salt and pepper?'

'What do you take me for?' Maureen asked. 'Course I have. I'm not a total savage, you know.' She paused. 'How come you know things like that?'

'Living with Lorna,' Penny said at once. 'And when I got a chance I cooked at school, as the muck they gave you made you want to spit it out. So I've had lots of practice. Shall I make a start while you get ready?'

Well, thought Maureen, there's an unexpected plus. I shan't have to run out for chips or a kebab if there's someone around who can actually cook a vegetable. Maybe she'll be looking after me, rather than the other way round. She shrugged out of her day clothes and pulled a face as she caught sight of herself in her bedroom mirror. All that famously firm flesh was beginning to go south, no matter how many killer workout routines she taught. Perhaps some good home cooking was what she needed.

Maureen brought out her evening outfit – nothing too special, as she never knew when she'd have to run to the rescue of one of the performers. But no harm in showing a bit of cleavage and wearing a bit of sparkle, which she could get away with when teamed with plain black trousers and only moderately high heels. She'd let the girl off the hook tonight and give her the choice of comfortable footwear, but she'd have to get back into the skyscrapers tomorrow.

The smell of cooking from the kitchen was mouthwatering. Following her nose, Maureen made her way into the small room and was astonished. Penny had unearthed the table – little more than an oversized dropdown shelf – and two stools, which Maureen had used to stack post or clothes on. The girl had also found a jam jar and filled it with flowers. 'I got them from one of the other stall holders,' she said. 'He told me the stems had broken and they wouldn't sell so I could have them. Brighten up the place, don't they?'

'Are you telling me my flat needs brightening, you cheeky mare?' grinned Maureen. 'It looks great, I must say. I forget what the place looks like when it's just me here. And it's very nice to be cooked for. I shall tell Lorna when we ring her later that you've paid close attention to all she's taught you.'

Penny could hardly contain her excitement when she finally stepped through the doors of the Paradise Club that she'd heard so much about. Even though the front of house was almost empty as yet, she was enchanted by the place – the little tables, the candles, the concealed lighting, the posters, the air of barely hidden risqué fun.

I'm on the set of *Cabaret*, she thought. Only it's real. She approached the stage, taking in the cleverly arranged spotlights and dazzling silver drapes. This was a million miles from Margate or stuffy school plays. Here was where she wanted to be.

'Here we go!' said Mark, emerging from the wings. 'Do you want to stand with me and watch the sound check and last-minute rehearsals for Fifi? She's one of the new ones and we aren't sure she's got it right yet.'

They stood to the side of the auditorium as a young woman in sequinned shorts and corset strode to the microphone and tapped it. 'One, two, one, two.' The music started and Fifi sang a little 1950s number, posing and pouting, managing to keep in tune and time. 'So far, so good,' hissed Mark. 'Better than last time anyway.'

Someone in the audience clapped and Fifi smiled and walked off, wiggling her hips as she left the stage. On came another girl, apparently covered in fans.

'Now watch this,' said Mark. 'This is harder than it looks. You need really strong wrists for those things, they're heavier than you think, and you don't want to be poking yourself in the eye with the end of one when you're doing your dance.'

The girl pirouetted to the music, twirling and re-arranging her fans, throwing aside her glittery top and yet managing to keep herself covered with a combination of the fans and a gigantic paste-jewellery necklace. As the music finished she turned her back saucily to the audience and raised her fans in the air. 'Now that's well judged,' said Mark solemnly. 'See, even though we were at the side, we couldn't see much really, but she made us think we were going to? That's clever. The really good ones could be wearing anything behind those fans and we wouldn't know. I tell you, some nights in here they could do with thermals on, even under those spotlights. The manager is dead stingy about the heating. Sorry, shouldn't be telling you that, it'll put you off.'

'Put off?' said Penny in astonishment. 'No, never. This is magic. I'll never get tired of it. What happens now?'

'The show itself won't start for another hour or so,' Mark said, 'so we'll make our way backstage and meet some of the others. Did you like Fifi's outfit? I made that. I'll show you my work area. By rights I should have my own room but no, the manager's too mean and I have to make do with a dark corner. Still, it's my dark corner and I shall show you where it all happens.' He led the way to a small red door marked ARTISTS ONLY and pushed his way through. Penny followed, thinking that she was getting used to his ways – although he was nothing like anyone she'd ever known in Margate.

At once he was mobbed. 'Mark, look, the hook's come off this thing, will you fix it?' 'Help, Mark, my gloves don't match, someone's had one of mine and I need another long scarlet one.' 'Mark, these shorts don't fit, they've split up the back.'

'Should have stayed off the cake then, shouldn't you, darling?' Mark said, leading Penny away from the crowd. 'They drive me mad, always panicking, never able to lift a needle for themselves. And that last one, she keeps insisting I give her size eights when anyone can see she needs twelves. And who wants to see a size eight arse up there? Not most of the punters we get in here, that's for

214

certain.' He stopped by a clothes rail full of silk, satin and feathered creations. 'These are mine. Well, the girls wear them, obviously, I'd look a bit odd, but I designed them.'

'They're lovely,' said Penny, meaning it, holding up a fitted basque in black and silver. 'How do you breathe in this though?'

'It doesn't stay on for long, dear,' said Mark archly. 'It's very much for show. Now this,' he held up a black lycra halterneck with diamanté edging, 'this, you can move in and yet look completely enticing. We'll get one made for you. This would be for someone shorter.'

'I would absolutely love one of those,' breathed Penny, thinking that Madonna herself wouldn't turn down something like that.

'And you shall have one, just as soon as you get good enough to dance with confidence in five-inch heels,' promised Mark. 'Now, let me introduce you to the manager. He knows you're joining us, so you don't have to say anything. In fact, the less the better.'

'Why?' demanded Penny, but Mark shook his head.

'Here he comes now. Mr Prescott! I'd like you to meet Penny, who's going to be joining the dancers soon.'

'Penny,' said the rather florid-faced middle-aged man. 'Yes, I've heard about you. Welcome. Maureen's friend aren't you – no, niece, is it?'

'Almost,' said Penny, but before she could explain further the man had smiled vaguely and moved off.

'Was that it?' she asked Mark.

'That's all you want to have to do with him,' Mark said. 'He hasn't got where he is today by being nice to people. A word of warning. He really, really doesn't like dancers going out with punters. Yes, I know some of them do it, but take it from me, he doesn't approve at all, and you don't want him to catch you out. Promise me?'

'I'm not interested,' Penny replied at once. 'I've got a career to make. There's no time for any of that.'

Chapter Twenty-Six

Gradually Penny got into a routine; going to dance classes in the morning, meeting Michelle, Juliet or Mark afterwards, getting to know the market and the stall holders, exploring the rest of Soho with its cafés, delicatessens and odd shops that seemed to be found nowhere else. 'There's even one for left-handed people,' she told Lorna, in one of her regular calls to Margate.

'Not sure that's of much use to you,' Lorna said doubtfully. 'What have you been eating? Have you been feeding yourself properly?'

'Feeding myself *and* Maureen,' Penny assured her. 'Honestly, Lorna, she's been great but she can't cook at all. She'd have takeaways all the time if I didn't stop her. But there's a gorgeous shop just round the corner run by an Italian family and they do all sorts of things you'd approve of. Fresh pasta! With pumpkin in it! I nearly died the first time I had it, it was so good. I've missed the real pumpkin season so I can't really try to make it myself, but maybe next year.'

'You are taking the cooking seriously, then,' said Lorna, secretly delighted. 'But isn't your kitchen the size of a postage stamp?'

'It's not so bad when you get used to it,' Penny said. 'I got Mark to put up some more shelves and sorted out loads of stuff that really belongs in the bathroom or bedrooms, and it turns out it's fine if you keep tidying up after yourself.'

'Now I am impressed,' laughed Lorna. 'When did you start being so tidy? Not that I'm complaining,' she added hastily. 'Just surprised, that's all.'

Michelle was carefully painting her nails in the dressing room, matching the colour to the exact shade of her costume. 'What do you think?' she asked as Juliet pulled up a chair. 'Will this do?'

'Weren't you wearing long gloves?' Juliet asked. 'Won't this be a waste of time?'

'Yes, but they're fingerless,' Michelle told her, blowing on the nails to help them dry. 'Anyway I want to look good for later. I'm seeing Rudolfo.'

Juliet looked up in disgust. 'Not again. He's really sleazy. Honestly, I don't know how you put up with him. What do you find to talk about?'

'We don't exactly bother with much talking,' Michelle grinned. 'Though he has told me about all the businesses he owns back in Italy. Or at least I think that's what he was saying. He's loaded, and he treats me to all sorts. You may mock, but I'm having a good time.'

'And that's all that matters?' asked Juliet, getting out her make-up bag.

'No, silly,' said Michelle. 'It's having a good time with someone who's *loaded* that counts. You could have a plain old good time with Tony and Angelo from the café but what would be the point?'

'At least you'd know who they were and that they have jobs,' Juliet pointed out. 'You don't know anything about Rudolfo except for what he tells you, and even then you aren't sure. He could be an axe-wielding maniac for all you know.'

'Rich axe-wielding maniac though,' Michelle shot back. Then she relented. 'Look, I can take care of myself. Don't you worry about me. You don't last long in Bow if you're wet behind the ears.' She paused, then changed the subject. 'Did Penny ask you round for a meal at Maureen's place? She spoke to me earlier. She's taken to this Soho life like a duck to water and wants to show off all these new ingredients she's come across. So I don't think it'll be chicken and chips. I'm definitely going.'

'Yes,' said Juliet, delicately applying mascara to make her already stunning eyes look enormous. 'It sounds like fun. I'm desperate to see Maureen's flat because as long as I've known her she's never mentioned anything except takeaways – that's when she wasn't being wined and dined by her latest admirer. So it should be a very interesting evening. God, I wish they'd put in some decent lights. How am I expected to look right when everything's fifteen watt? Cheapskates.'

Penny was anxiously studying the makeshift table in the kitchen. She'd dragged the small table from the hall to add on to the end of the tiny wall-mounted one, and brought through the chairs from her bedroom and Maureen's. She wasn't convinced everyone would fit, but perhaps she could eat from a tray on her knees, perched on the nearby sofa. Maybe she shouldn't have asked Mark along as well, but he'd been so kind to her ever since she'd come to London, and besides, he was so thin, it made her want to feed him. Penny had got over her shock at first meeting him and now she felt she could tell him anything.

Maureen had turned down the invitation to join them. 'Thanks but no,' she'd said. 'You young people don't want me breathing down your necks. And besides, I've had another offer.' She winked. 'We'll see how it goes but it won't be a dull evening, that's for sure. Just be sure to leave me some milk for the morning – that's if I make it home.'

So Penny was left alone to arrange the flat as she wanted to, adding candles and the odd sprig of holly to make it more seasonal. Now all she had to do was toss the salad, boil the water for the pasta and reheat the sauce she'd made earlier. As long as nobody turned around too quickly, there should just about be room.

Gazing out of the window, she could see the street below in full flow. It was never quiet, no matter what time it was. Even though it was dark, the bright lights from the bars, cafés and clubs lit up the pavements, and taxis hooted as heedless pedestrians stepped out in front of them. One particularly loud hoot caught her attention and she wasn't surprised to see the cause of it was Michelle, sashaying along in the road, waving cheerfully at the furious cabbie. She was followed by the stick-thin figure of Mark, recognisable even from here by his haircut, and finally by Juliet, the only one to look as she crossed the road. Penny grinned to herself as she headed down to the front door to let them in.

'So this is where you've landed,' cried Michelle. 'Very

nice, very close to everywhere. Up how many flights? No, that's fine. Look, if I can dance night after night in those shoes and then climb up to the studio, this is a piece of cake. Here, have this. Rudolfo says it's wonderful.'

'Oh Rudolfo says, Rudolfo says,' chorused Mark as he followed them up and into the flat. 'It must be right if Rudolfo says so.'

'Let me see what he's recommended,' commanded Juliet, as Penny took their coats and ushered them through. 'Oh, I take it back, actually that is rather good. Give me the corkscrew and we'll let it breathe. Meanwhile, let's have some of this.' She brought out a bottle of sparkling wine from her bag. 'At least on a night like this you don't have to worry about it getting warm on the way here. Have you any glasses, Penny?'

Penny passed her the corkscrew. 'Not matching ones, no, but these'll do.' There were no more than two matching items of anything in the flat, as if Maureen had never bothered entertaining more than one person at a time.

'Cheers,' said Michelle, clinking her glass to the others in turn. 'Happy days, my lovelies. You've done this place up real nice, Penny, or was it like this before?'

'Well, some of it was me,' said Penny, going back to the cooker and igniting the two rings.

'Most of it was you,' said Mark. 'Let's face it, Maureen's not one for staying in. Her priorities lie elsewhere. You've done wonders.'

'I like doing it,' said Penny, stirring the sauce.

'You're going to make some man a proper little wife,' Mark teased. 'When you give up the stage and all that malarkey, you'll be a right little homemaker.'

'Don't be daft,' said Juliet. 'It's perfectly possible to have a decent flat and carry on a career. You won't catch me living in squalor while I rise to stardom. Just you watch.'

'Hark at you,' said Michelle. 'Well, I'll happily give it up if the right man makes me a decent offer. Or an indecent one, I don't really care. It's all right for you, you wouldn't know squalor if it bit you.'

'So how was Rudolfo?' asked Penny. 'Come over to the table, it's nearly ready.'

'He was as generous as always,' Michelle told them as they took their seats, squashing in so they could all fit. 'We went to that new place just off Soho Square where all the actors go after their shows. He knows how to give a girl a good time.'

'As long as you give him a good time in return,' snapped Juliet.

'And what man wouldn't want to be seen out with me?' asked Michelle. 'It works both ways. Though we didn't go on anywhere special last night as his friend joined us. Silvio. Actually I got the idea that he'd like me to bring a friend along next time. Any takers? Penny?'

'No, no and no,' said Juliet. 'If you want to date these dodgy men we can't stop you but don't try and drag any of us into it.'

'Nice restaurants, though,' Michelle reminded her.

'Thanks but no thanks,' said Penny, handing round the food. 'Can you fit all the plates in all right? No, I'm not interested in men. If I want good food I'll learn to cook it. This okay for everyone?'

'It's bloody lovely,' said Michelle. 'Good as that place we went last night. Did you do it all?'

'I got the fresh pumpkin pasta from that little place round the corner. You know, Lina Stores,' said Penny, 'but I did the sauce myself with stuff from the market. Jimmy who does the vegetable stall advised me. He's brilliant, he tells you what you need and how to cook it and what goes with what.'

'There you go, Michelle,' grinned Mark. 'You can get top-class food right on your doorstep and no need to go out with sleazeballs.'

'Talking of sleazeballs,' said Michelle, who was tired of being picked on, 'how's your latest? The charming Brian, wasn't it?'

'Don't talk to me about him,' groaned Mark. 'He was a disaster. Couldn't understand why I had to work evenings, jealous if I so much as said hello to another man. So that's over before it really started. It's so unfair, he seemed so fun on the first date, but it didn't last five minutes after that.' He shrugged. 'You women have it easy.'

'Hardly,' said Juliet.

'Well, *you* have it easy,' Michelle went on. 'You get hard up, you can always call on Daddy's money.'

'Actually,' said Juliet, putting down her fork, 'I don't take a penny from him. Nor do I intend to. I earn my own keep. Obviously he doesn't like what I do but I'm proud of it, and I pay my own way. So less of this having a go at me for being rich, please.'

'I'm not blaming you,' said Michelle. 'You can't help what family you're born into. I'd love to have a rich father. But since mine isn't, I'll settle for a rich sugar daddy or even better, a rich husband, to keep me in style. This paying your own way is overrated. It's bloody hard work for a start.'

'You can say that again,' sighed Mark. 'There's no chance of my family helping me out. There's not much chance of them even talking to me, or at least not until I find a nice girl to bring home to them. And that's not going to happen.'

'Let me take your plates,' offered Penny, reaching across to start stacking them. It was strange. Here were her friends, all with parents still alive, and yet they all had unhappy families in their own way. She wondered what life would have been like if her father had lived, if her mother would have been more loving and less obsessed with money. Or would they have turned against her, like Juliet's seemed to have done? Penny had always thought that life would have been easier with a different mother, but maybe it wasn't that simple.

'Snap out of it, Penny!' called Mark, and she realised she'd been staring at the plates. 'You sit back and relax now, I'll put the coffee on, I know where everything is. You've done us proud.'

'Yes, you come over here,' said Juliet, patting the worn old sofa. 'If you're not interested in dating the men, thank God, what do you want to do? What's the new year going to bring?'

'I'm going to be dancing on stage from January,' said Penny, with a mixture of excitement and relief. 'Maureen says I'm good enough now and Mr Prescott has agreed. So I'll need that black and silver top, Mark, and those Liza Minnelli shorts. I can't wait.'

'You're going to look wonderful,' said Mark, reaching for the mugs. 'I wonder what routine they'll put you in. I bet they have you opposite Juliet here, as you're the two tallest. I can see it now. I'm going to design you a fabulous pair of outfits. It'll be my job over Christmas – I can't think of anything better to do while everyone else is stuffing their face with turkey.'

Chapter Twenty-Seven

Maureen found the flat quiet after Penny left for a few days to go to Margate for Christmas. She'd been asked to go as well but family Christmases had never been her thing, even when her family had been speaking to her.

Stuart, Maureen's new admirer, had apologised for not inviting her to spend the day with him, saying he had unavoidable commitments, from which she assumed he was married. She didn't care. She didn't want a husband and she didn't want to sit down at a big table laden with food she didn't particularly like. Instead, Mark was coming round and they were going to treat themselves to a big Indian takeaway. She knew Penny would be cross that as soon as her back was turned the takeaways had started again, but what she didn't know wouldn't hurt her.

Penny didn't know about the conversation Maureen had had with Mr Prescott either, when he'd called her into his office before the club shut down for a couple of days.

'So you're bringing in that niece of yours,' he'd said. 'Are you sure she's ready?'

'For God's sake, Dave, do you think I'd let her on stage

if she wasn't?' she'd snapped back. 'This is my reputation at stake as well as yours, you know. She's a natural talent and now she's been trained she's as good as any of them.'

'Bit thin,' he observed. 'She'll have to stay in the chorus line, no one'll pay to see her out front.'

'That's the idea,' she'd said, biting back her irritation. Dave Prescott had always had a foul temper but she used to be able to cheer him up. It was years since they'd had their brief affair but she'd remained one of his favourites and had assumed he still trusted her judgement. Now it seemed she was out of favour.

'Bit young as well,' he'd continued. 'Is she going to stay the course? Not going to go running after the clients and bringing us into disrepute? I won't have that, niece or no niece.'

Maureen looked at him, with his red face and growing paunch, and wondered what she'd ever seen in him. If he carried on like this it would be him not lasting the course. She wondered when he'd last seen daylight.

'She's not in the slightest bit interested in any of that,' she assured him. 'All she wants to do is dance, and she's bloody good at that.'

'Well, see it stays that way,' he'd said, pouring himself a double whisky. 'No one's indispensable, you know.'

She was pretty certain it wasn't his first drink of the day even though it was not yet lunchtime. 'That's what you've always said, Dave,' she replied, trying to keep it light. 'You'll have a lovely addition to your chorus line and you'll have made their dance teacher very happy. So it's win-win.'

Now Maureen hoped that would be true. She could teach anywhere, of course, and not all her students worked

227

at the Paradise Club, but it was that connection which brought her most business. She didn't like the veiled threat behind the whisky-fuelled words and wondered what had brought that on. Maybe he'd got wind of what Michelle had been up to, silly little cow. She'd have to keep an eye on her – but that was easier said than done.

Still, Maureen thought as the doorbell rang, not a lot she could do about it now. She ran down the stairs to let Mark in with his bags of steaming takeaway, and sighed in anticipation.

Penny had been oddly apprehensive about going back to Margate, wondering if it would feel even stuffier after all her new experiences in Soho, but she needn't have worried. Lorna and Robert had pulled out all the stops for Christmas, putting up the biggest tree she could ever remember, and surrounding it with presents ready for the big day itself. Penny had made up her mind to contribute as well, not just sit around to be waited on as she had when she'd come back from school. Now she arrived laden with goodies from the market and the Italian deli, which Lorna had exclaimed over.

'These look wonderful!' she'd breathed. 'I remember these little almond biscuits – you can soak them in alcohol and have them with cream.'

'Did we have them in Spain?' Penny asked, not sure if she'd tasted them before. The young man behind the counter had assured her this was the right thing to buy for the festivities but she hadn't sampled them in the store, which had been packed with everyone doing last-minute shopping.

'No, but we did have all kinds of other things with almonds,' Lorna replied. 'Clever of you to think of that. You've really taken to this cooking business, haven't you?'

'I love it,' Penny admitted. 'You can't imagine, it's like being surrounded by every sort of food that exists. It'd be criminal not to try everything.'

'Well, if you ever want to make a career of it, you have only to say,' beamed Robert, coming through the door with a big bag of wood for the fire. 'And meanwhile you can practise on us as much as you like.'

So that's what she'd done, and she could tell Lorna was delighted by how much she'd improved her skills in the kitchen. She didn't feel inclined to throw away her dream of being a dancer but she couldn't deny their support had boosted her confidence in cooking enormously. Still, she couldn't wait to get back to London. I'll have to do more classes to dance off these extra pounds, she thought grimly as the train made its chilly way back to Victoria.

Penny's first evening on stage went by in a blur. She'd been so nervous that she could hardly remember the first part of the night, and then when the time came to take her place before the curtain went up, everything went so fast that she didn't have time to think of anything. But her body seemed to move of its own accord when the music began, going through the well-rehearsed routines, and she knew she'd done all right when Maureen stepped out to greet her as they filed into the wings.

'You'll do,' she'd said. 'Carry on like that and you'll be a star.'

Now she sat on Mark's worktable, gulping from a bottle

of water, wrapped in an old sweatshirt. She felt far from glamorous but was as happy as she could ever remember. She'd done it, she'd appeared on stage. So there, Mum, Penny thought, I'm a real dancer, not a common stripper like you were, and a liar on top of it all. I'm the real thing.

'Well done, you survived,' said Mark. 'I watched you from the bar and you were fine. Did you see me?'

'Couldn't see anything except the spotlights,' she confessed. 'I tried to look up and make eye contact but I had to imagine where the audience were sitting, as you can't make anything out.'

'You did that all right,' Mark told her. 'I wouldn't have guessed. You've got that knack of making everyone feel you've noticed them specially and are dancing just for them. That's a real art. Keep it up.'

Michelle came over, beaming. 'Congratulations, that was really good. Bet you feel better now, don't you? Trust me, first time is the worst and you'll never feel that shaky again.'

'How did you know I felt shaky?' Penny wanted to know.

'Everyone does,' said Michelle. 'Stands to reason. It didn't show though, and tomorrow you'll be even better.'

'Fancy coming out to celebrate?' asked Mark.

'I'd love to,' said Michelle, 'but Rudolfo's back from Italy and he's taking me to the Gay Hussar. He wants to make up for being away.'

'Back home to his wife, was he?' sniped Mark.

'Don't be so sour, it doesn't suit you,' said Michelle, not in the least upset. 'He's here now, isn't he? A bird in the hand and all that. Have fun.' And she sashayed off.

'Bar Italia, then?' said Mark. 'Not quite the Gay Hussar but I'll treat you to a coffee.'

'I'd like that much better anyway,' said Penny loyally, although she couldn't help thinking that one of these days she might like to try one of the famous restaurants they passed so often.

Juliet had returned from a brief break with her family but didn't want to talk about it. 'I'm going to see them as little as possible,' she told Penny as they stood in the theatre bar after they'd finished their performance one night. 'They simply don't understand I'm serious about dancing. Let's not let that get in our way though. What are you drinking?'

'Water,' said Penny. 'They won't serve me because they know my age. Anyway I don't care. You get something, I'll stay here.'

'In that case, I will,' said Juliet in relief. 'I tell you, I need something. That last row before I left was too much. I deserve a little something.'

As her friend waved to her favourite barman, Penny was aware of a group of dark-haired men around a tall table, drinking spirits. One was particularly good-looking and seemed to be watching her. As she caught his eye he raised his glass and gave a small smile.

She smiled back but then turned as Juliet returned, large glass of wine in hand. 'Let's go backstage,' she suggested. 'I need one of my seams fixed before tomorrow's show.'

'Okay,' said Penny, taking her water from the table she'd been leaning against, 'but you know Mark hates doing basic mending. He'll only tell you to do it yourself.'

'You can't blame me for trying,' said Juliet. 'He does it so much better than me. Let's see how busy he is.'

As they made to walk away, Penny noticed that the dark-haired man was still watching her.

'Michelle, can I have a word?' asked Maureen, catching the younger woman as she was putting on her coat.

'Yeah, of course,' said Michelle, 'but I can't stay long.'

'It won't take long,' Maureen assured her. 'Keeping someone waiting, are we?'

'What if we are?' demanded Michelle. 'It's not a crime.'

Maureen sighed. This had started badly already. 'No, I know it isn't strictly a crime,' she said carefully, 'but the someone we're keeping waiting is a punter, isn't he? And you know Prescott don't like that.'

'Well he can lump it then,' said Michelle heatedly. 'I'm over age and free to do as I please. It's not as if I'm the only one doing it. You know damn well loads of the girls do it. How else are we meant to meet anyone, working nights like we do? So of course we do it.'

'That might well be,' said Maureen, determined not to lose her temper, but irritated with the girl's stubbornness. 'But you're the most obvious one. You make no attempt to hide it, you're out there cavorting at the stage door nine nights out of ten. Prescott might well turn a blind eye now and again but this is right in his face. He can't ignore it.'

'Filthy old sod he is, then,' blazed Michelle. 'And why should I hide it? How come you're telling me this anyway? Don't tell me you never done it. Hey, weren't you and Prescott an item once? Getting you to do his dirty work for him now, is he?'

'Listen to me, you stupid mare,' hissed Maureen. 'Don't you insult me, I've outlasted more chorus girls than you've had hot dinners, whether you paid for them yourself or not. If you bring the club into disrepute, then everyone's affected. You, me, all the dancers, all the backstage lot. So think whose jobs you're putting at risk. Is it worth it? Promised you the earth, has he?'

'None of your business what he's promised me,' shouted Michelle, fastening her coat and turning up the collar. 'I'm not standing around here for all this. I've got better things to do. At least I'm young enough to have fun.' She spun around and almost crashed into Penny and Juliet, spilling some of her wine as she did so.

'Hey, watch it, Michelle,' protested Juliet. 'Where are you off to in such a hurry?'

'Did you put her up to this?' Michelle yelled at Penny. 'Because you can piss off if you did. You all can.' She pushed her way past a rail full of costumes and was gone.

'Bleedin' hell,' said Maureen, shaking her head. 'Sorry you had to see that, girls. It's not your fault. Our Michelle has ruffled a few feathers high up and by the looks of it she's going to ruffle some more. I just hope we don't all take the rap for her. But I'm sure it won't come to that.'

She tried to put on a brave face, but she was seriously worried. Michelle was right, of course – lots of the dancers did see punters outside the club, and it wasn't always easy for them to meet anyone else because of the long hours. God knows, Maureen was aware of that better than anyone. But to do so blatantly, flying in the face of a direct warning, was asking for trouble. And Dave was on the case, for whatever reason. She'd heard rumours of a rival club starting up on the other side of Soho

Square, so maybe that was it. But whether that was it or not, Dave on the warpath was not something to be encouraged, as he wouldn't care who got in his way. And that meant any, or all of them.

Chapter Twenty-Eight

A couple of nights later, Penny was in the bar once more with Juliet, one drinking water and one drinking wine. 'I'm still not sure about these shorts,' muttered Juliet. 'It was kind of Mark to sew them up but do you think he could have done it too loosely on purpose, to make me do it myself next time?'

'No, he wouldn't do that,' Penny replied. She knew by now Mark was far too good-hearted to do such a sneaky thing. She looked critically at her friend. 'Do you think you've just lost a bit of weight? Have you had them long?'

'Not very likely over Christmas and New Year, is it?' Juliet asked. 'Suppose it's possible. I've had them for a few months. I really hope I haven't lost much – no disrespect, but we can't have too many thin dancers.'

'No, you don't want to reduce your assets, as Michelle would say,' grinned Penny, then she pulled a face. 'Or maybe she wouldn't say. She's hardly talking to me, as she thinks I grassed her up to Maureen – when anyone can see what she's up to. And she's getting worse. She sat on Rudolfo's lap right here in the bar yesterday, in front of everybody. It's as if she wants to be sacked.'

'I hope she doesn't imagine that if she's sacked he's

going to step in and make an honest woman of her,' groaned Juliet, draining her glass. 'Right, if I'm to put some weight on, I'll have another glass of this.' She disappeared to the bar.

Penny felt slightly worried by her friend. Juliet was always the sensible one, never shy of speaking her mind; always in control, always knowing what to do, and Penny had come to rely on her steady advice and years of experience in the business, but something wasn't right. She didn't usually have more than one glass if she had to go to a morning class the next day, for a start. And yet here she was, ordering another large one, taking a big sip, chatting to the barman and getting topped up.

'Hello, you're one of the dancers, aren't you?' said a voice at her side. Turning, she realised it was the dark-haired man. 'And so is your friend.'

Just talking to him couldn't hurt, Penny reasoned. 'Yes, that's right. Did you see all of the show?'

'We didn't get here in time for the beginning,' he said apologetically, nodding towards the group of men he'd been with before. 'Did we miss much?'

'Only Fifi and her singing, which you either like or you don't.' She couldn't quite place his accent. 'You aren't from London, are you?'

'No,' the man laughed. 'No, we definitely aren't from London. We are from very far away. Mexico, in fact.'

'Really?' Penny said, about to mention that she spoke Spanish, but then she noticed Juliet coming towards them, with a face like thunder. The man noticed as well.

'Don't let me interrupt your conversation with your friend,' he said. 'Nice to meet you.' And he was gone.

'What was that about?' Juliet demanded, gripping her

wine glass so hard her knuckles turned white. 'What does he want, chatting you up like that?'

'He only wanted to say hello,' Penny protested, annoyed now. It wasn't as if they'd even exchanged names.

'That's how they all start,' said Juliet grimly. 'Not you as well, Penny. Haven't we got enough trouble with Michelle and her carryings-on?'

'Actually, he was very polite,' she said. 'He didn't want anything, he didn't ask me anything much. There were no carryings-on. I thought he was nice.'

'Nice?' echoed Juliet. 'Nice? Have you noticed the one thing about the punters in here? Very, very few of them are nice. God, the sooner I get out and into proper theatre the better.'

'Juliet!' cried Penny, alarmed now. 'You love what you do, you've always said so. You never mentioned moving on before. What's wrong? What's happened? What's changed?'

'Absolutely nothing has changed,' said Juliet, speaking very slowly, emphasising every word. 'That's the bloody problem. Same old men trying to take advantage, same silly young girls encouraging them. Well, maybe I'm sick of babysitting you all. Maybe I've had enough.' Juliet made to turn away, ever so slightly unsteady on her high heels.

'Don't be like that, Juliet,' said Penny, realising her friend was slightly drunk. 'Come on, we'll go together, how about Bar Italia . . .' It was too late, the other young woman strode off, pushing back her wonderful blonde hair and causing all the men to look her way. Except for one, Penny noticed. The good-looking Mexican had his eyes on her, ignoring Juliet's dramatic exit. Should she go over and continue their conversation? It was tempting – he had been charming and not at all pushy, so that had to be a good thing. But she couldn't face losing another friend so soon after Michelle. I do fancy Bar Italia, though, she thought. I'll go and find Mark and see if he'll come along. At least he's still speaking to me.

Next morning, Juliet turned up for the dance class on time, looking very slightly the worse for wear, and immediately apologised. Penny was relieved. She'd replayed the scene in the bar over and over, and couldn't see how she'd done anything wrong. Mark had agreed with her, pointing out that it would have been very rude not to have answered a civil question, and it didn't do to annoy the punters, particularly when there was a group of them who made a point of coming back. 'You have to be friendly to them to keep in business,' he told her. 'Prescott would want that. It's what goes on beyond the club he objects to. You have to know the difference and not overstep the line. But I can't see how you did that.'

'Do you think there's something wrong with Juliet?' she'd asked, unable to let go of that worried feeling. 'Is she ill or something?'

'Can't say as I've noticed,' Mark had said, 'but I'll keep an eye on her. She won't want anyone sticking their nose in, so don't say anything about it, or not just yet.'

Now here was Juliet, saying how sorry she was for flying off the handle. 'I shouldn't have jumped to conclusions but I'm so fed up about Michelle, I couldn't bear the thought of you doing the same thing.'

'Well, you know I wasn't,' smiled Penny, more than

happy to bury the hatchet. 'I had to say hello back, didn't I, or I'd have been in trouble that way too.'

'Damned if you do, damned if you don't.' Juliet searched through her bag. 'Shit, I've finished my water bottle already. Can I have a gulp of yours? I'll replace it later.'

'Help yourself,' Penny said, bringing out her own bottle, which she'd never forgotten since that first exhausting day. 'Let's line up. Don't do anything to set Maureen off, she's been in a right state since that row with Michelle.'

'Tell me about it,' said Juliet, moving into her place.

Maureen didn't know how she'd managed to get through the morning, she was so wound up. Bloody Dave had called her into his office the day before and had another go. He'd heard about the row and wanted to know why, after such a straightforward warning, the girl had then turned up in the bar sitting on the knee of the very man she'd been told not to be seen with.

'From what I heard, Maureen, you didn't mince your words,' said Prescott, 'so what I want to know is, how can she have misunderstood? What is she thinking of?'

'You know as well as I do there's no misunderstanding,' said Maureen. 'She just doesn't like to be told. She's taking the piss.'

'Then stop her,' said Prescott.

'Stop her?' cried Maureen. 'I'm not her boss. You are.'

'She'll take it better from another woman,' Prescott said, glass of whisky in his hand. 'I don't need this shit. Bloody bastards have got planning permission to turn the old Ashdown studios into a club and guess what, they're going to have a burlesque show. They never should have got it, God knows I wined and dined the right people to stop it going through but they must have nobbled someone higher up. Our reputation is on the line and that little tart can either stop it or sling her hook, it's all one to me. She's pretty enough but there are others. Got any likely replacements in your class?'

'Why would I do you any favours?' Maureen had demanded. 'You're dropping me right in the middle of this mess and it's not even my responsibility.'

'For old times' sake,' he leered. 'And because you want your skinny niece to keep her job. And, as I said before, because no one is indispensable.'

So there it was. Sort out that daft cow Michelle or watch Penny lose the job she loved, and maybe lose her own position as well. Bloody marvellous. 'Okay, take a break,' Maureen shouted over the booming music, and searched the group of dancers for the trademark bouncy brown curls. But Michelle wasn't there. Probably sleeping off another five-course meal, she thought bitterly, wondering how someone who claimed to be so streetwise could actually be so pig-ignorant.

Chapter Twenty-Nine

Penny had now taken to going to the bar every night after the show, mainly to check that Juliet was all right and didn't get too sloshed. They'd had no more rows but she was still concerned for her friend, who in her eyes was still acting out of character. Mark had said he couldn't see it but Penny was sure there was something up.

But tonight there was no sign of her friend and so she stood at one of the tall tables, nursing her glass of water, to which Frankie the barman had added some ice cubes and a slice of lime out of pity.

'Hello again,' said a familiar voice. 'On your own this time?'

She turned and found herself face to face with the good-looking Mexican. 'I'm just waiting for my friend,' she said.

'May I join you until she turns up?' he asked, smiling irresistibly.

Well, why not? Penny thought. As Mark said, mustn't annoy the punters.

'All right,' she said, and smiled back.

'What's that you're drinking?' he asked. 'I'll get you another. A gin and tonic?'

'Oh no, no,' she said, but he misunderstood.

'Vodka, my mistake,' he said and called over to one of his group who had reached the front of the queue at the bar. Penny heard what he said quite distinctly even over the general noise: 'A vodka and tonic for the most beautiful dancer.' Part of her was smug that she'd understood his Spanish. She was even more delighted with what he'd said, but then instantly grew suspicious. Did he realise she'd understand? But how could he? Relax, she thought. You've been listening to Juliet too much, it's just a nice man offering to buy you a drink. A very good-looking, Spanish-speaking, nice man.

While she'd never taken much direct interest so far in men, it hit her that the one in front of her was exactly right in so many ways. Of course they all talked about their ideal man being good-looking, nice-mannered, charming, well-dressed – but the fact that he spoke Spanish cut right through her defences.

'Eduardo,' he said, passing her the drink and clinking the glass with his own. 'Delighted to meet you.'

'Penny,' she said, trying not to giggle. She suddenly felt very self-conscious and exposed. 'And what do you do, Eduardo? All the way from Mexico?'

She noticed that when he smiled his eyes crinkled at the corners, which she found she liked. So it meant he was quite a bit older than her – but it didn't matter. She hadn't thought much of the few boys of her own age she knew, as they were too childish and most of them obsessed with football. No, this one was a real man.

'I can't tell you exactly,' he said. 'It's difficult to explain. But I am attached to the Mexican embassy.'

'Oh,' she said, impressed despite herself. Surely even Juliet couldn't object to that. She'd mention that detail as soon as she could. 'That sounds very interesting. You must be busy.'

'Of course,' he laughed. 'They wouldn't bring me to London and then give me nothing to do. That would be crazy.' He paused and smiled again. 'But I'm not so busy that I don't have some free time. I wonder if you'd like to have dinner with me one night? We could go to somewhere near here – what is that place everyone talks about? L'Escargot.'

Oh God, Penny thought, he speaks Spanish and he loves good restaurants. Even Michelle hadn't been taken there. How could she say no? She'd wanted to go ever since she'd heard about it. But a little voice urged caution.

'We're not supposed to date audience members,' she said honestly.

'But who said anything about a date?' protested Eduardo. 'This would just be two friends, sharing a love of good food. You love good food, I can tell.'

He can read my mind, she thought. This was meant to be.

'In that case, it would be lovely,' she beamed.

'Wonderful!' he exclaimed. 'Would it be too much to ask if you are free tomorrow? Yes? Then I will make a reservation and meet you here. Will that be all right?'

It would be so much more than all right, she thought, her head spinning. 'Y— yes,' she managed to say.

'I shall see you here, then, after the show,' he said. 'Now my friends are telling me that I must go. Until tomorrow.' Eduardo leant forward, held her hand to his lips and kissed it.

243

God, she thought, do people still do that? Maybe they did in Mexico. How charming. She followed him with her eyes as he made his way through the busy bar to the exit with his friends. Her first date, even if they weren't calling it that, and it was with a gorgeous older man from the Mexican embassy. Well, that wouldn't have happened in Margate.

'Oooh, who was that?' said Mark, emerging from the door to the auditorium. 'Very tasty.'

'Hands off,' she grinned. 'He might be mine.'

'And what's that you've got there?' he went on, sniffing her glass. 'Tonic and . . . not vodka? Yes? A proper drink. Naughty. You'll get Frankie into trouble.'

'Well, I didn't buy it,' she said. 'My new friend did.'

'New friend, is it now?' he teased. 'I don't know, we leave you alone for one hour and you get some hunk to buy you a drink and you're not even embarrassed.'

'He did more than that,' she admitted. 'He asked me to go to L'Escargot with him and I said yes.'

'Oh my God!' cried Mark. 'You jammy cow. You never. Oh, we'll have to find you something to wear. No, hang on.' He calmed down. 'Look, I know he's gorgeous-looking but what do you know about him? He's not another Rudolfo under those lovely looks, is he?'

'No, no,' she said, 'he works for the Mexican embassy.'

'Gorgeous and connected,' Mark sighed. 'I can't pretend I'm not jealous. Still, we must be practical. You can't tell Maureen, not when she's just had to threaten Michelle with the sack.'

'I know,' she said, beginning to feel a stab of guilt. 'I didn't really think about that. I just saw how handsome he was and then he said he'd take me to this place I've wanted to go to for ages – and so what was I meant to do?'

'Hold your horses,' Mark said. 'You can still go, but be careful. Don't tell Maureen – or at least not until afterwards. Don't tell Juliet, she'll go spare. Let me know your arrangements and I can chaperone you from a distance. Make sure he doesn't try any funny business. Just because he's good-looking doesn't mean he won't try it on. I usually walk you most of the way home anyway, so just regard it as an extension of my services.'

'Mark, you're lovely and I don't deserve you,' Penny said, hugging him fiercely.

'That's my trouble,' he sighed. 'I'm so good nobody does deserve me and nobody comes near, except the miserable little heartbreakers. Still,' he brightened up, 'we'll get you all dolled-up tomorrow and you'll have the best evening ever.'

Penny could hardly sleep that night, her emotions were in such turmoil. Would this be the beginning of a big romance? Would she end up as an embassy wife, dining at wonderful restaurants all around the world? Maybe she'd have to organise big parties. Maybe she'd cook amazing dinners for important visitors and everyone would compliment her. Maybe he'd be posted to Madrid and she could impress them with her fluent Spanish . . .

As dawn began to break she finally drifted off, and when she woke up found it was so late she'd missed the dance class. Maureen had let her sleep in. Well, Penny thought, she could miss the occasional day. It wasn't compulsory to attend every one and she was much fitter now. She'd have a leisurely bath and take her time getting dressed, then she'd go and find Mark to see what he could come up with for her to wear tonight.

Chapter Thirty

'For God's sake,' hissed Michelle as they made their way off through the wings after their first routine. 'Can you concentrate, please? You stood on my foot twice. What's wrong with you this evening?'

'Sorry,' said Penny. 'Didn't mean to.' She had no idea how she'd got through the dance as her mind was anywhere but on what she was doing. She'd tried to scan the audience to see if Eduardo was already there but the glare of the lights made it impossible. Now she had to sit tight and wait until they'd done their last routine before she could go and join him in the bar. Usually she liked sitting through the other acts but this evening they seemed to go on for ever. She realised she was grinding her teeth during one of Fifi's slower numbers.

Mark had picked out a gorgeous cocktail dress which appeared silver in some lights, pearly grey in others. 'Perfect for you,' he'd said, holding it up against her. 'Not everyone could get away with this as it's basically a straight line of fabric but on you it's just right.'

'You mean I still haven't got any curves,' groaned Penny. 'What if I stay this shape for ever? What if he doesn't like me?'

'Face it, darling, he's seen you in your tiny shorts and halterneck so he isn't under any illusions,' Mark pointed out. 'Not much room left for surprises there. You'll look divine, so just believe it.'

Now she sat with the other dancers, counting the endless minutes before they went on again, still worried that she'd say the wrong thing or look out of place somehow. Michelle threw her a filthy look.

'I can't sit next to you no longer, you're all fidgety and it's driving me mad,' she complained. 'I'm off to get some water.'

Michelle made her way past the racks of discarded clothing to the tiny kitchenette and found a glass. She turned on the cold tap, filled the glass and held it against her hot forehead. She was as nervous as Penny plainly was, she just didn't intend to show it.

She hadn't set out to get into trouble over Rudolfo. He'd been the latest in a whole string of clients she'd gone out with and she hadn't foreseen that there would be any more fuss than before. But when the storm had broken, a rebellious streak in her objected to being told what to do. She wasn't a kid any more and she should be able to see who she liked. She'd also rather enjoyed the very public shouting match with Maureen. It was better than taking a cold shower, really refreshing. Although she knew it would be wiser not to repeat it, a devilish voice inside Michelle whispered that it might be fun.

She wasn't too sorry that Rudolfo hadn't returned from Italy after Christmas. She gathered that his businesses had been affected by the downturn and it didn't seem likely he'd have been able to entertain her as lavishly as before. So now she was about to embark on a date with another client, one she knew much less well, but he seemed to offer all that Rudolfo had and more. A pity he was so old, but that had never bothered her in the past. In fact it might be an advantage, as he'd probably tire more easily . . . She jumped when Mark came round the corner and put a hand on her shoulder.

'What are you doing here? Aren't you on again in a minute?' he hissed.

'Taking a little break,' she said. 'Just collecting my thoughts together before going out later with you know who.'

Mark rolled his eyes. 'You're going ahead with it, then? Do you really think it's a good idea?'

'Why not? He seemed like the perfect gentleman and I can tell he likes me. As he damn well should.'

'Look, I know you're an old hand at this but please be careful,' Mark said earnestly. 'You've only just avoided getting the sack. Don't go looking for trouble. You don't need it, we don't need it.'

Michelle sighed and folded her arms across her tight sparkly top. 'I know you mean well. I appreciate it. But I've got to cast my net wide while I'm young. And I'm damned if they're going to stop me.' She glanced up at the clock above the ancient steel sink. 'Shit. Gotta go, we're on any minute. See ya later.'

'See ya later,' echoed Mark, watching her run along the corridor. 'Hope he's worth it.'

Penny wasn't sure how she managed to walk calmly across the bar, her legs were shaking so much. She could see the group of friends that Eduardo usually came in with over in one corner, though she couldn't see if he was with them or not. She decided to risk it and get herself a drink for Dutch courage. Penny slipped to the side of the long bar, where the staff collected the glasses, and where she could see the rest of the bar but they couldn't see her. It was a good vantage point. 'Go on, just a vodka and tonic,' she begged Frankie. 'No one'll know.'

'You'll get me sacked,' he hissed. 'All right, just one, or you'll put the punters off with your sad face. What's up?'

'Nothing,' said Penny. 'Bit tired, that's all.' She didn't want the entire staff to find out what she was doing – though Frankie generally knew everyone's secrets, as he saw all the dramas playing out before his eyes. Still, there was no sense in inviting trouble.

Sipping her drink, Penny forced herself to breathe deeply and calm down. It seemed to work. Over the hum of voices she gradually began to pick out the Spanish sounds from the group of men not far away, hidden from view around the corner.

They seemed to be talking about importing something. That must be the sort of thing embassy staff had to deal with all the time. She listened more closely.

The next big consignment was due tomorrow. There had to be complete secrecy about it. It was top quality and so they could all expect to make a lot from this, provided the authorities didn't get wind of it.

'You've made the necessary payments?' asked one.

'Of course. What do you take me for, an amateur? They'll look the other way when it comes through and if not, I have taken the precaution of finding out where their children go to school,' said another voice, as calmly as if he was discussing the weather. 'If there's any trouble

250

we step in and remove the kids one by one, and then they'll get the message.'

Penny's blood ran cold. Were they saying what she thought they were saying? Had she heard it wrong, or mistranslated it in her nervousness?

'You'd better have this all confirmed by tomorrow or Eduardo will see that you end up like the last one who messed up,' the first voice warned. 'And there wasn't much left of him. Tonight he told me he's planning a little recreation. Then from tomorrow he's going to be checking every detail of this. If we can set this up we'll be the prime importers of cocaine for all of Western Europe. Think what that will mean. So there's absolutely no room for mistakes.'

'Recreation, isn't that we're all about?' said the other voice, and there was a round of laughter.

So there was no misunderstanding. This wasn't some embassy trade delegation, these were hardcore cocaine smugglers and Eduardo appeared to be their boss. And if anyone slipped up, then their families were hurt. Penny thought she was going to be sick. The smell of the tonic and lime made her gag.

'You all right?' asked Frankie. 'If you're going to throw up then don't do it here. I'm not clearing up after you, I've done enough of that already.' He dashed off to mix another cocktail.

Penny shook her head, unable to speak, and tears came to her eyes – of disappointment, but mostly of terror. What should she do? Eduardo still wasn't here – she could just leave now, slip through the side hatch to the bar and out that way. But then would he seek her out for the punishment the others talked about so casually?

Her lovely, kind, charming Eduardo oversaw the kidnapping of children and the routine punishment of anyone who crossed him. Would he do the same to her if she let him down? Think, think, she told herself. His friends hadn't seen her yet. They wouldn't know she'd overheard them. Had she told him she spoke Spanish? No, she didn't think so. So they wouldn't know that she'd worked out what they were doing. But how could she get away without making him angry or suspicious?

'Ah, there you are!'

Before she could make a decision, there was Eduardo, even better-looking in a blue shirt open at the neck, his curly dark hair swept back, smiling his heartbreaking smile. Penny tried to imagine that beautiful mouth giving the order to get rid of children and gagged again, trying to hide it by covering her mouth.

'What is the matter?' he asked, all concern. 'You are so pale this evening.'

She couldn't speak, just swallowed hard.

'You're looking very special in that dress,' he went on. 'I am a lucky man. Everyone will be looking at us.'

That was worse than ever. She couldn't be seen with him now she knew what he'd done, what he was planning to do. She managed to find her voice.

'I'm . . . I'm so sorry,' she whispered. 'I'm really not very well. I don't think I can eat anything. I . . . I feel terrible.'

Was that her imagination or did his eyes narrow in disbelief? Had he taken one look at her and realised that she knew everything? Was he going to force her to come with him?

'What are you still doing here?' said Frankie in

exasperation as he came to collect the tray of glasses. 'Pardon me for interrupting a private conversation, but the sooner you go home the better. Nobody will thank you for spreading a bug around the place. I certainly don't want to catch it.' He was off again, all smiles at the new customers.

She shrugged. 'I only came here so you wouldn't think I'd stood you up. But I'm really not up to going anywhere. I'd better go straight home. Or,' she tried to laugh, 'the barman will kill me.'

'Oh, that's so sad!' said Eduardo, and he really did seem to care. 'Of course you mustn't force yourself if you don't feel well. I am dreadfully, dreadfully disappointed, but maybe another time, when you are better, yes?'

'Maybe,' she gulped.

'Shall I walk you home? Do you live far away?'

No, no, he mustn't find out where she lived. She'd be an easy target and then Maureen would be in danger as well. If they could kidnap children she dreaded to think what they'd do to a grown woman.

'I . . . I couldn't let you do that. You might catch what I've got,' she improvised. 'I'd never forgive myself if you did that. Really, I'll be fine but I have to go now.' Now, before I'm actually sick in front of everybody, she thought.

'If you insist,' he said, his eyes all kindness. He kissed her hand again. 'Until the next time, then.'

'Yes, until the next time,' she said, and turned and almost ran through the door. Her only thought was to find Mark, but first she hurried to the toilets and shut herself in the stall. The coldness of the tiles sent a wave of shock through her and she was violently sick, even though she'd hardly eaten all day in anticipation of the meal to come. Ugh, she thought, that's disgusting. I'm never going to be able to even look at a vodka and tonic again, let alone drink one.

Penny crouched on the floor until the nausea passed and gradually the line of tiles grew steadier. Eventually she pulled herself to her feet, at first holding on to the wall for support. This is no good, she thought, I've got to get out of here. Mark will be looking for me. What if he finds Eduardo and asks where I am? Will that make him a target as well?

That idea was so frightening that she forced herself to go back into the corridor and along to the worktable. To her huge relief he was still there, doing a last-minute repair to Fifi's headdress, all red feathers and gold sequins.

'You still here?' he asked. 'Not meeting up with lover boy after all? Got cold feet? Because it's a shame for such a good-looking fellow to be lonely, so maybe I'll . . .'

'Mark, shut up,' she hissed urgently. 'I have to talk to you but not here. Can you leave that?'

'Blimey, what's rattled your cage?' he demanded. 'Yes, all right, this is finished anyway. I'm sick of the sight of it.' He tucked the pile of feathers under the table, grabbed his coat from the back of a chair and stood up. 'Shall we try Bar Italia?'

'No, someone might see,' Penny whispered. 'We've got to get out of here and back to the flat without anyone seeing us and I'll tell you then. It's not safe before that.'

Mark rolled his eyes, clearly thinking she was crazy, but he went along with it. 'Must be something important then. You'd better not disappoint me. If we go out of the fire exit we'll end up in the side alley, so no one coming from the main or stage door will know we've left.'

'That should be okay,' she said, taking his arm to hurry him along. 'Quick as you can, without drawing attention.'

They made their way to the fire exit and into the alley, which smelled of rubbish, discarded takeaways and worse. From there they could slip into a side street that led away from the club, and work their way around to the entrance to the flat.

Penny just about managed to get up the stairs and then collapsed on the sofa. The tears which she'd somehow held back since overhearing the group of men's conversation now gushed out and she buried her face in a cushion as the sobs shook her body. Mark fetched a glass of water and waited.

At last she calmed down and sat upright, gratefully reaching for the glass. 'I'm sorry. I couldn't help it. I was so terrified, you wouldn't believe.'

'For God's sake, what is it?' he asked, seriously worried now. 'Are you ill or something?'

'No, it's worse,' said Penny, and she told him what had happened in the bar less than an hour before.

For once Mark was speechless. He just stared at her, as if he couldn't believe it. 'You sure?' he finally asked. 'Sorry, stupid question. But it's incredible. Hey,' he said, attempting a smile, 'most girls find their first date is married, or something boring like that. It's not everyone who can say he was a homicidal cocaine smuggler.' Penny didn't laugh. 'Sorry, bad taste. But you'll be okay, because he doesn't know that you know, and you were clever, pretending to be ill.'

'I didn't exactly have to pretend,' she said.

'Well, he won't be suspicious. You did the right thing. God, I was completely taken in, I thought he looked like a total sweetie.' Mark shook his head. 'Just goes to show. Oh, you poor thing, all got up in your beautiful dress, and you didn't even get your lovely meal. I wish I had the money to take you there. I would if I could, you know.'

'I know,' she said, managing a smile, 'and I'd love that. But what do we do now? Do we tell someone? Do we call the police?'

'I don't know if Prescott would like it,' said Mark. 'He gets all sorts through those doors and plenty of them wouldn't welcome a visit from the police. Anyway, what can you say? A group of men whose names you don't know said something you can't prove. And you don't even know if Eduardo is his real name. You don't know if he really has any connection to the embassy. Hell, you don't even know if he's Mexican.'

'But they might harm the children!' she wailed. 'How can we stop that? Should we tell Maureen?'

'But then won't you have to say that you were going to go out with a punter?' Mark pointed out. 'Have you thought about that? So, do you still want to tell Maureen?'

'Tell Maureen what?' asked Maureen, who'd come in without either of them hearing. She wanted nothing more than to slump into a comfy chair and take off her shoes that pinched, but clearly there was a crisis. 'What's the big secret?'

Penny glanced at Mark but she didn't have any energy left to pretend any more. So she confessed everything – being asked out, the idea of the date, and what had happened earlier that night.

Maureen sat and nodded and acted as if she'd heard it all before, even if this was one step beyond anything even she had experienced. Penny had feared she'd do her

nut when she learnt about the date but it seemed as if
Maureen took it in her stride, almost as if she'd expected
nothing else. When she'd taken it all in, she straightened
her shoulders.

'Right,' she said. 'It's not up to us. We tell Dave. It's his
club, so it's his decision. We don't tell him why you were
hanging around the bar, just that you happened to overhear what was said and thank God you knew Spanish.
I'll do it right away. You stay here. We don't know where
Eduardo and his mates are so you wait until morning
before going out. Mark, you okay to stay here?'

'Of course,' said Mark, offended, 'where else would I
be?'

'Good,' said Maureen, not even stopping to take off
her coat, 'and have lots of hot sugary tea, that's good for
shocks.' She went across to Penny and hugged her. 'It'll
be all right. We'll talk properly tomorrow, but you get
that lovely frock off and get into bed and let Mark look
after you. I'll see you in the morning.'

It had started to rain, and all the streets of Soho were
shining and reflecting the coloured shop signs, the drains
blocking up with wet cardboard, newspapers and all the
dropped wrappers and beer cans of the day. Maureen
picked her way through them, cursing her uncomfortable
shoes. They'd seemed like a good idea at the beginning
of the evening but now they were agony. Maybe she was
reaching the age where she'd have to choose her footwear
for comfort, not fashion. She shuddered. No, that was
never going to happen.

Maureen turned over in her mind the best way to
proceed. Part of her was mortified that the girl had had

such a shock, and she knew that if anything had happened to her then Lorna would have had her guts for garters. But had she really been in danger? Could she have been exaggerating? No, Maureen thought, she wasn't the sort to do that. If it had been any of the others – Michelle, say – she'd have wondered if she was lying to get attention or show off, but Penny wasn't like that. All right, she shouldn't have agreed to date a customer but the temptation of a meal at L'Escargot would have been hard for anyone to resist, let alone in the company of an interesting and attractive man. Still, they could talk about that tomorrow and she was willing to bet this would put the girl off men for a long while to come.

So how best to speak to Dave? He could hardly be surprised that criminals had been visiting his club – everyone and anyone passed through Soho and not all of them were going to be legit. So what would he want to do?

He'll want to gain something from this, Maureen thought, use it to pay off a favour or make sure someone owed him one in the future. And if that was the way he'd approach it, then that was what she'd do as well. He'd thought he could threaten her with losing her position or sacking Penny. Here was her chance to show him just how indispensable some people could be. Right, Dave, you miserable drunken bastard, she thought. We'll see how much you need us after this.

She paused at the corner of the street, pretending that she had to adjust her collar, checking the club's main entrance and stage door for any signs of Eduardo and his friends, but the coast was clear. It was late and the bar would have shut a while ago, so presumably they'd gone off to somewhere that opened later or to get a good night's sleep before the consignment arrived. The light in Dave's office was still on, though, which was good, as long as he hadn't had so much whisky that he'd fallen into a stupor at his desk. But that was unlikely. He seemed to be able to put it away steadily all day and keep functioning, God alone knew how.

Maureen opened the stage door and made her way to the office to confront him.

'Let me get this right,' said Dave after he'd heard what she had to say. 'Our youngest, most wet-behind-the-ears dancer has uncovered an international drug-smuggling ring right under our noses? Do you really expect me to believe that?' He'd definitely been drinking but still seemed able to think. 'She's not trying it on, is she?'

'Give me some credit,' snorted Maureen. 'I know the girl and she's no liar. Naïve, yes, but she wouldn't make it up. She's terrified. But you should be glad we got someone like her on board. Who else would have understood? Not only understood, but had the nous to know what it could mean and then tell me all about it? That took some nerve. And she hasn't gone running off, she wants to be back in here tomorrow.' She thought there was no harm in laying it on thick, even if the girl had said no such thing.

'Hang on, let me work that one through,' said Dave, rubbing his sweating forehead. 'No, she is not coming in here tomorrow. If what you tell me is true and that's when it all kicks off, it only takes one of them to think back and she becomes a target. *We* become a target. I'm not having anything disrupting the show. She can work behind the scenes if you like, have her help that poofter who does the costumes that she's so friendly with. You think I don't know nothing about what goes on but I know they're thick as thieves. Or have her work in the office. She can translate this stuff' – he picked up a handful of flyers – 'into Spanish. Pull in some different tourists for a change. Yes, in fact that's not such a bad idea. Let me sleep on that and we can sort something in the morning. Meanwhile, I've got some calls to make.'

He paused and moved around to sit on his desk, which groaned under his weight. 'We can make this work for us, Maureen.' Oh, so it was 'we' now, she thought. But she said nothing. 'Yes, it's occurring to me that this is a very useful piece of information. A word in the ear of the right authorities could be very handy. Oh, they'll love us. We'll be slap bang in their good books. A reputable business, eager to work with the law. Unlike that bunch of shysters doing the Ashdown development.' He smiled, showing brown stained teeth, and Maureen thought she preferred him when he was angry. 'Yes, we can turn this to our advantage and get one up on that sorry load of bastards. You know what? I love it! I absolutely love it! I knew you'd see me right!' He smiled even more repulsively. 'Don't suppose you'd like to make a night of it and celebrate properly?'

Maureen felt her stomach heave at the very idea but kept her revulsion from her face. No point in getting back in his favour and then blowing it after two minutes.

'Afraid I'm completely bushed, Dave,' she said, which happened to be true. 'Me feet are killing me. I got to get back and check that Penny's okay, if you don't mind.'

'Shame, Maureen, we was good together, wasn't we?'

he said, attempting to put an arm round her. But before she could give him what for there was a piercing scream from the direction of the stage door.

'Help! Let me in! Let me in!'

Chapter Thirty-One

'What the bleedin' hell is it now?' growled Dave, making no move to help whichever woman was shouting. 'Leave it, Maureen, come on, we was just getting interesting.'

But Maureen couldn't ignore a woman shouting for help, and ran out of the office and towards the stage door. Flinging it open, she was greeted with the almost unrecognisable sight of Michelle. Her clothes were torn, her face was beaten and there was blood pouring from her mouth. If it wasn't for her curly brown hair Maureen would have struggled to know who she was. She had never seen a woman so badly battered.

'What the hell has been going on?' she demanded, as if she didn't know. With a sinking feeling, Maureen guessed that what everyone had warned Michelle about had just happened.

'Oh Maureen, thank God it's you,' cried the girl. 'Help me, get me inside, get me away from that maniac. He's after me, I can't take no more.' She collapsed onto the pavement, while the rain continued to fall.

'Get up, get up,' Maureen urged her. 'I can't help you if you sit there. Come on. Give me your hand. Shit, look at your nails, you poor cow. Look, I'll lift you by your arms if that hurts too much. Okay? That better? God, didn't realise you was so heavy, you have been at the pies, haven't you?' Despite her best efforts Maureen was beginning to recognise that she couldn't actually lift the girl. She was just contemplating taking off her high shoes and standing barefoot in the rain to have another go when there came the sound of running footsteps. Alarmed, she looked up, prepared for the girl's attacker, but it was a female shape hurrying towards them.

As the woman got closer Maureen was able to make out that it was a familiar figure – Juliet.

'I don't know what you're doing here but help me, quick,' gasped Maureen. 'We got to get her inside. I can't lift her on my own, she's a dead weight.'

Juliet didn't seem to need to ask who it was, but just got on with the task in hand. 'Okay, on the count of three. One, two, three. Up we go. Come on, Michelle, you're safe now, we've got you. In we go.'

With some difficulty they half-lifted, half-dragged the young woman into the club and sat her on the nearest chair.

'Let's get her cleaned up a bit,' said Juliet. 'All right, Michelle? We're just going to wipe your face so you can see us better. Maureen, you stay with her while I get some towels and cotton wool from the make-up box.'

Michelle made no attempt to reply as her friend hared down the corridor. Maureen was impressed despite herself – Juliet seemed to know exactly what to do.

'You want to talk about it?' she asked. 'Up to you. I won't blame you for nothing.'

Michelle groaned, leant over and was violently sick all over Maureen's shoes.

'S— sorry,' she moaned.

'Don't you worry about them,' said Maureen gamely, 'they was ruined anyway, what with all the rain tonight. I've been running round in them for hours and they hurt like the devil so they can go. You tell me what's wrong if you like then we can work out how to help you.'

'It . . . it was that bastard Silvio,' wept Michelle. 'You don't know him but he was one of Rudolfo's friends. I don't know what he'd heard but he said . . . he said that he knew what I did with Rudolfo and he was going to have some of the same. And some more. When I said no, I didn't like it, he raped me anyway. Then said there was no point in me complaining because I'm a dancer and everyone knew that was as bad as being a prostitute, so who was going to believe me? I started to scream and then he hit me, jeez, Maureen, I thought he was a little old chap but he was so strong and I couldn't fight him off. Then I finally got away and come here. Ugh, I'm going to be sick again.' Maureen hurriedly stepped back until the girl had finished. 'You do believe me, don't you?' she asked pathetically, glancing up through one half-closed eye. 'I didn't want that. I thought it would be fun and he'd treat me like a princess, like what Rudolfo did, but he didn't even pretend to be nice to begin with. He was a beast and I couldn't do nothing. You do believe me?'

'Yes,' said Juliet, who'd returned with a tray of useful items. 'Of course. Why would you make this up? Stay still, I'm going to wash your face.' She began to dip cotton wool in a jug of warm water.

'I'm so sorry,' wept Michelle. 'I'm keeping you both up. But I didn't know where else to go. I couldn't go home looking like this and I was afraid he'd follow me. I couldn't have my parents seeing me like this. Oh God, it's all my own fault.'

Juliet stopped what she was doing. 'Look at me,' she demanded. 'Listen to me, Michelle, and listen well. Never, ever, ever say that. Never even think it. It is not, I repeat, is not, your fault. It is *his* fault. Nobody else's. Get that in your head right now.'

'But . . . but . . . he said I was asking for it,' sobbed Michelle.

'They always say that,' snapped Juliet. 'It's utter crap. Asking to be raped? Asking to be beaten? Forget it. They'd love you to think that because it gets them off the hook. Well, you remember this: it is not your fault, it is his. Say it over and over until you get it into your head. Anything else is total bullshit.'

Maureen had never seen Juliet so angry. In fact she'd never seen her anything other than cool and collected, no matter what was going on. But she had to admit she was glad the golden girl was there, as she seemed to be getting through to Michelle at last.

'That's right,' Maureen agreed. 'No such thing as asking for it. Yes, they'll tell you that. But it's not true. I know I've given you a hard time lately, Michelle, but you don't deserve this – nobody does. Look, tell you what, we'll make up a bed for you on the dressing room couch and you can kip there. Then you don't have to go back out. We'll stay here, won't we, Juliet?'

'Of course,' said Juliet, resuming her careful wiping of her friend's face. 'Just get you cleaned up a bit more and then we'll help you walk over there. It isn't far. And then do you want us to call the police?'

'Nooooooooooo,' moaned Michelle. 'No, for God's sake, don't do that. I couldn't stand it. They'll say I was asking for it, no matter what you say, and then they'll poke and pry and I'll feel even more shit. I can't go through with it. Don't make me.'

Juliet stepped back and sighed. 'Nobody's making you do anything. It's up to you. You don't have to decide now. Let's get you over to the couch and make you comfy. Do you want to go to the bathroom? Shall I take you?'

'Yes please,' said Michelle and started to cry again.

Maureen watched as they staggered to the bathroom, and then she began to clear up, using the rest of the warm water to wipe away the mess of sick and blood Michelle had left behind. She couldn't say anything but was relieved they were out of sight, because what if Dave had called in the police about Eduardo and his gang? They wouldn't be able to turn a blind eye if they saw the state of the girl and then the shit would well and truly hit the fan. So she wiped and scrubbed as fast as possible, trying not to gag on the smell. She'd have to say one of the punters must have been backstage and got out of hand if anyone asked.

Satisfied that she'd done as much as she could, she walked barefoot over to the couch and hunted around for some drapes to serve as blankets. Luckily there were plenty, and lots of cushions were strewn about. At least Michelle could make herself comfortable and get a good night's sleep, if she wasn't too agitated. A nightcap would help – would help them all. She went over to a filing cabinet where Dave kept what he thought was a secret stash of whisky, and then rinsed out three glasses from the kitchen. When she returned to the makeshift bed, the young women were back and Michelle seemed a little calmer.

'Thanks,' she sniffed when Maureen poured her a generous double. 'Don't mind if I do.' She tossed it back. 'Oh that's good. Can I have another?'

'You sure?' asked Maureen dubiously. 'Didn't have you down as much of a spirit drinker.'

'I don't care,' said Michelle. 'If it'll help wipe out the memories I'll have the lot. That's better. Shit, my head hurts. Think I'll lie down. Do you mind? I think I'll try to get some kip.'

'We'll leave you to it,' said Maureen. 'We'll go and make ourselves comfortable in Mark's corner. He's got all the mod cons hidden around his table – kettle and everything, the sneaky bugger. You just give us a shout if you want anything.'

She and Juliet crept away as Michelle snuggled down. They paused at the door of the dressing room for a moment and there came a little snore.

'So tell me,' said Maureen, lighting up and leaning on Mark's worktable, 'you were pretty good out there. I can't think of anyone else who'd have taken charge like you did. You've done this before, haven't you?'

Juliet looked away, her heavy blonde hair swishing like a curtain. She tipped her whisky back in one.

Finally she nodded. 'This goes no further, all right? I'm not very proud of what I'm going to tell you. But yes, I've been cleaning up after battered women for years, since I was a child, really. Or rather, not women. Just one woman.' She swallowed hard. 'My mother.'

'Your mother?' Maureen realised her mouth was

hanging open. 'What, wait a minute, how is that? That doesn't make any sense?'

'Sense?' repeated Juliet. 'Why does it have to make sense?'

'But . . . but look at you, listen to you,' said Maureen, trying to get her head around the revelation. 'I've never met anyone as posh as you. Met plenty who've pretended to be, but you're the real thing. I thought you was just a little rich girl running away from home, because that's what they tease you about, isn't it? Are you telling me that your mum gets beaten up? Is that what you're running from?'

'Sort of,' snorted Juliet. She reached across and helped herself to one of Maureen's cigarettes. 'Do you mind? I've just managed to give up but under the circum-stances . . .' She lit up and sucked at the filter. 'Took me ages to kick the habit and here I go, falling at the first fence. Never mind.' She exhaled. 'So, yes, my mother is a battered housewife. My father beats her – and has done for as long as I can remember. So when I had the choice I got out. Don't get me wrong, I love dancing here, but I'd have had to have got out one way or another and I was damned if it was going to be the only way they approve of, which is marrying someone who might turn out to be every bit as violent as my dad. I couldn't stand it any more. I couldn't protect her, only patch her up, as you saw for yourself. I've had lots of practice at that. And she won't go for help, she can't bear to admit it. He's cleverer than Michelle's attacker, he only ever hits her where it won't show. If she can't walk properly she says she's got arthritis. Which, given the amount of broken bones he's given her, she probably has. The stupid thing is, I still love him, even though he's a bastard. I love them both.' Juliet stopped and Maureen could see her eyes were filled with tears. 'Everyone thinks it doesn't happen among the rich. But it does. They just have more money to cover it up.' She smiled bitterly.

'So how come you turned up tonight?' demanded Maureen. 'You been following Michelle or something? Did you know she was meeting this sick bastard?'

'No, it was complete coincidence,' admitted Juliet. 'I was in Bar Italia, having a coffee. I can't sleep much at the moment because it's been getting much worse at home and I'm worried sick. So I go there once the bar at the club has closed and just try to get a bit of peace and quiet.'

'In one of the busiest late-night spots in Soho?' said Maureen, raising her eyebrows.

'I know, I know, it sounds stupid, but it does the trick,' said Juliet. 'Anyway, there I was, watching the rain, when I saw Michelle stumbling by. I caught a glimpse of her face and saw she'd been hit, though I didn't realise it was as bad as it was. She was going so fast it took me until she got here to catch her up. You know the rest.'

'Lucky you was there,' said Maureen. 'Don't think I could have managed her alone. Couldn't even lift the poor sod. At least we got her comfortable for now. We'll tackle the rest in the morning. Don't suppose she'll feel much like dancing tomorrow.'

'Don't suppose anyone will feel like paying to see her,' Juliet replied brutally. 'That's the truth of it. Funny old business, isn't it?'

'I don't even want to think about it,' sighed Maureen. 'I reckon I'll just try to kip down here and let it all wait until the morning.'

'What about Penny?' asked Juliet. 'Is she all right in the flat by herself?'

'Mark's there,' Maureen told her, and then it all came rushing back to her. 'Oh God, that's another story. You'd better hear all about it. But that can definitely wait until tomorrow.'

Chapter Thirty-Two

By the next morning the rain had stopped and Juliet found herself despatched on a series of errands for Maureen. 'I can't go nowhere in me bare feet,' she'd pointed out. 'Can you go round to the flat and pick up some shoes for me? Get the blue ones, Penny or Mark will know which they are. And then we'd better get some clothes for that poor cow asleep on the couch. Mine won't fit her and Penny's definitely won't so you better get her something down the market.' She fished in her bag for some money. 'Here you are, don't get her none of that cheap nylon shit or she'll feel we're punishing her. Find her something that is easy to put on so she won't have to use her arms too much, they're that bruised.'

Juliet wandered around the stalls, surprised that the hard-faced Maureen had put so much thought into what she was to get. Everyone now thought that Maureen and Michelle were sworn enemies, but last night had shown that wasn't so. Juliet wondered about the woman's reaction; she'd immediately recognised that Juliet had seen this sort of thing before. Was Maureen familiar with it too? Maybe it was better not to ask.

Maureen had also filled her in about Penny's narrow

escape. 'Don't tell her you know unless she mentions it first,' the woman had said. 'She'll be upset and thinks you'll blame her for promising to date a punter.'

Well, she wasn't far wrong, thought Juliet. She'd wanted to believe the girl when she'd protested that she had no interest in men, but it just went to show, along comes a good-looking charmer and all the promises go out of the window. She mustn't say I told you so, though that was exactly what she felt like doing.

'You all right, love?' shouted the man behind a vegetable stall – the one who was friendly with Penny and Maureen. What was his name? Jimmy, that was it. She'd better snap out of it, things were coming to something when stall holders noticed how distracted she was.

'Yes, thanks,' Juliet called back. 'Just daydreaming. Now I think about it, maybe you can help me.' She walked over to the brightly coloured stall, laden as always with a huge variety of fruit and veg. 'My friend Penny isn't feeling too great. What can I take her to cheer her up?'

'That lovely Penny, the tall one?' asked Jimmy. 'I'm sorry to hear that. She's one of my best customers, she is. Can't resist buying something new when she sees it. She'll try and cook anything, that one.'

'Don't think she'll feel much like anything new today,' said Juliet.

'She's always on about Spain, ain't she?' said Jimmy. 'I know, I got just the thing. Give her some of these oranges.' He picked up a plastic bowl full of them. 'She'll like these, I know it.'

'She will,' said Juliet, reaching for the fruit which Jimmy had tipped into a bag. 'How much?'

'No, these are on me,' he insisted. 'Lovely oranges from

Seville, full of flavour and goodness. That'll see her right. I don't want no payment for that. You just tell her to get better.'

'That's really kind of you,' beamed Juliet. 'She'll be delighted.' Making her way along to the clothing stalls she thought about the irony of it. Penny had made a big enough impression on the tough-sounding stall holder that he knew her likes and dislikes and was prepared to give her a present, but when it came to choosing a boyfriend she'd ended up with a lying criminal. Life wasn't fair.

'Do you give presents to all the girls?' asked a dark-haired man who'd been looking at Jimmy's stall. 'You'll never earn your fortune that way.'

'Nah, just to the special ones,' sighed Jimmy. 'That young lady needs looking after. And don't you go telling your dad what I did or word'll get round the markets and they'll think I've gone soft. Can't be having that.'

Maureen stuck her head round the door of the dressing room but Michelle was fast asleep and snoring loudly. Good, she thought. Let her sleep in, best thing she could do. It was still early enough that nobody else would be in for some while. Once Juliet returned with her shoes, she could go back to the flat and maybe ask Mark to come and stand guard so that the girl had a few more hours undisturbed. But even before that, there was one person who'd have to be told, or at least given an edited version, and she might as well do it in her bare feet. It wouldn't go down well, however she was dressed.

'Bleedin' hell, Maureen, no sooner do you solve one

of my problems than you bring me another,' shouted Dave, foul-tempered as always in the morning. He wasn't so keen on making up to her now, she noticed. Things were back to normal. 'So you mean to tell me we're now two dancers down? What's that going to look like?'

'You're all heart, that's your trouble,' Maureen shouted back. 'She hasn't done a runner, she hasn't flouted herself with one of the punters in front of the whole bar; the poor kid's been beaten up through no fault of her own. So you can try looking sympathetic for once, if you can remember how.'

'Sympathy won't get me a replacement dancer,' he snarled. 'But you will, won't you? From that little stable of yours down the back alley?'

'Look on the bright side,' she said. 'With two down we can still do the same routines because it'll be symmetrical.' She was disgusted to see he did indeed brighten up at this thought. 'And then I can look at finding you two more to go in the line.' She sighed. She still had to break it to Penny that she wouldn't be dancing again in the near future. 'So, tell me, how did it go when you had a word with the authorities? Did they do what you wanted?'

'Nothing's definite but I got a shedload of brownie points,' beamed Dave, showing his tobacco-stained teeth. 'That turned out to be the best piece of news in a long time.'

'Maybe we should advertise for more criminals,' suggested Maureen. 'Get them to pass the word round Parkhurst and Pentonville. They can come here on the day of their release, we'll do them a special deal.'

'Oh no, Maureen, I don't think that'd work,' said Dave,

not getting the joke. 'If that's the best you can do you'd better piss off and let me up the ante on those Ashdown conmen.'

'Happily, Dave, happily,' said Maureen, and headed back to check on Michelle.

Penny threw one of the oranges across the room in frustration. 'Do you mean he never wants me back?' she demanded. 'After all that work I've done, and all the time you spent training me? And all the costumes Mark made? But I love dancing and I'm good at it. I really am. What's he playing at?'

'You are good, no one's saying you aren't,' Maureen soothed her. 'But you must see it'll be less risky if you aren't up on stage at the moment. I'm sure everything will be fine but we ought to be as careful as we can. He still wants you to work for him, you won't be out of pocket. You can still earn your keep. You'll just be behind the scenes, that's all.'

Penny slumped back in her chair. 'I don't know what to do. I can't think straight, I hardly slept, even with Mark here. I'm frightened. I know I'm being silly and they probably won't trace anything back to me but what if they do? But if they don't, then I'll have stopped dancing for nothing. Oh God, why did he have to lie to me? Why wasn't he from the Mexican embassy? It was going to be perfect and now it's all spoilt.'

Maureen let her rant, knowing there wasn't much choice. Even if Dave hadn't forbidden the girl to go on tonight, she herself would have put a stop to it. 'Look, it needn't be for ever,' she said. 'Give it a while. See what working in the office is like. You might like translating

275

the tourist leaflets. Test out your skills. Bet they never gave you anything like that to write about at school.'

Penny managed a small smile. 'You're right, they didn't. I'm sorry, I don't know what to say. Okay, I'll try it. But I don't want Prescott to think I've given up.'

'He won't,' Maureen assured her. 'He owes us big time. He knows how lucky it was that it was you who overheard, not one of the others. And that you were quick-witted enough to get out of it. Trust me, you've gone up in his estimation, and that's a bloody hard thing to do.'

Penny pulled a face. It didn't seem like much of a consolation. 'I'm going to wander down to say thanks to Jimmy. Juliet said he wouldn't take any money for these and they're gorgeous. Try one.'

She passed Maureen an orange as she went out of the room, grabbed her coat and went downstairs.

Jimmy was beginning to pack away his stall for the evening, tipping the fruit out of the bowls and into crates before loading them on a big metal trolley. 'Hello, my lovely,' he said, smiling broadly. 'Feeling better? Out for a little fresh air?'

'Call this fresh?' she said, pretending to sniff. 'In Margate we have proper fresh air, and it comes at you at high speed all the way from France. Not this polluted muck.'

'Mind who you're calling muck,' said Jimmy. 'Those oranges did the trick, did they?'

'Yes, that's why I came down,' she said, serious now. 'I wanted to thank you. Made me feel better at once. That was really kind.'

Jimmy smiled from ear to ear. 'Then that's all the

276

payment I need. See this young lady here, John? The one her friend said was at death's door? She's a testament to the power of good fruit. She's right as rain now.'

'Oh, you're the one who loves Spain,' said the dark-haired man. Penny couldn't help but notice how handsome he was. Just what she didn't want right now. 'Pleased to meet you. I'm John, and Jimmy here knows my dad. I went to Spain for work a few months ago and had a great time.'

'Oh,' she said. Wonderful, she thought. A few days ago I'd have been really excited to be talking to a good-looking man who had an interest in Spain. Now that's the last thing I need. 'I'm Penny,' she muttered.

'John's dad was on the market down in Battersea for years,' Jimmy went on, apparently not noticing she wasn't very interested. 'A diamond, he was. Semi-retired now. That's what I ought to be thinking of doing, but I'm too dedicated to the job.' He winked at her. 'See, you need somebody to keep an eye on you, feed you up a bit.'

'You're too good to me, Jimmy,' she said, attempting a laugh. 'I've got to go, I've left Maureen upstairs and she's got to tell me about my new job.'

'Anything exciting?' asked Jimmy, picking up another bowl.

'Using my Spanish,' she said, turning to go. The two men exchanged approving looks. 'Thanks again, Jimmy. See ya.'

Chapter Thirty-Three

Penny found she didn't mind working in the office. The hours were more regular and it was less hard on the feet. She hadn't wanted to admit it at the time but they had begun to hurt towards the end of the final routine. The job itself wasn't difficult. She was more fluent than she'd thought and finding the right words to describe what went on at the Paradise Club made her brain work for the first time in ages.

The worst bit was everyone asking why. Maureen put it about that she was too young to be on stage and someone had reported her. Several dancers knew that she was only sixteen and had been seen drinking alcohol in the bar, so that made some kind of sense. Frankie backed this up and said he didn't want to be in trouble but how could he turn down a pretty dancer in front of the punters? So having her behind the scenes was accepted by everyone for the time being.

Michelle's absence was harder to explain, as she'd had to disappear completely until her bruises and cuts healed. Again, Maureen tried to cover for her by saying her mother was ill and she'd gone back to the East End to look after her. Quite a few of the cast and crew commented that the girl had never shown much interest in her family's welfare before and didn't she have loads of sisters who could do the job equally well, if not better? Juliet stood up for her, saying that they didn't know Michelle like she did and she was actually devoted to her family underneath her good-time exterior.

Juliet's own secret remained unspoken after that fateful night. Maureen kept her confidence and while Penny and Mark still wondered about their friend's change of attitude, they couldn't pin it on anything. In fact it was Juliet who suffered from the new arrangements the most.

'It's a bloody bore actually,' she complained to Penny and Mark early one evening as she was getting ready to start and Penny was finishing her own day's work. 'Without you two in the line I've no one to talk to. They're completely empty-headed, especially the replacements. God, I hope they're temporary. Heaven only knows where Maureen found them.'

'One's Fifi's cousin,' Mark said, straightening a silk top on its hanger, 'the redhead, that is. She told me when I had her in for a fitting.'

'Thanks, well, I'll try not to be rude about her in front of Fifi as God knows she's touchy enough already,' groaned Juliet, 'but it'll be hard. The sooner Michelle gets back the better.'

'Maybe she's enjoying spending some time with her family,' suggested Penny. 'Having a bit of a rest, getting looked after.'

'From what she always said about them, it didn't sound very restful,' sighed Juliet. 'She'll probably be driving them mad, complaining about how bored she is. Okay, I'd better start make-up and doing something about this hair. Mark, are you owed any favours with that stylist friend of yours at the moment? I could do with a cut soon.'

She and Mark wandered off, earnestly discussing whether she should try a different style, leaving Penny to pack her bag and leave the club while it was still daylight.

Penny was in no hurry to get back to the flat and wandered aimlessly along, staring in the windows, waving at the shopkeepers she knew. They were all much livelier than Mrs Manning, who would have thrown up her hands in horror at some of the customers around here. She realised how much she had changed in her months in Soho, and how sheltered she'd been in Margate, even though she'd thought she knew it all. There had been the close escape of the fire, the sheer exhaustion of getting fit and good enough to appear on stage, learning to look after herself, putting on a smiling face and dancing, even if she felt off-colour. There had been the mixing with people from all walks of life. And of course there had been Eduardo. Penny no longer walked around glancing over her shoulder, checking in shopfront reflections, wondering if he or one of his friends was going to come for her. Dave had hinted that matters had been taken care of and that none of them were likely to show their faces in central London again.

She told herself not to be so childish and to get over it, but she had felt terribly let down. He had seemed so lovely. How could she have been fooled so completely? She didn't like to talk about it because she felt rather stupid for falling for him, but he'd appreciated her in a way nobody else had. He'd made her feel like a woman, not a naïve, gawky girl. But he had been a criminal. It was too much to take in. When she thought of all the hopes she'd had that evening, she cringed in embarrassment. Well, she wouldn't be fooled that way again.

She made her way to the Italian deli that sold its own fresh pasta, and decided to cook herself a decent meal that evening. She bought extra so that she could make some for Maureen to eat when she got in, whenever that might be. She saw less of her now she wasn't going to dance classes in the daytime and Maureen was out most evenings, either at the club or with Stuart. But the woman would still appreciate a plate of home-cooked food to heat up.

She might just have time to find one or two of the veg stalls open, so she turned the corner into Berwick Street. Jimmy had packed up for the evening but one of the others hadn't finished serving, so she hurried to buy some tomatoes and peppers. That'll do, she thought.

'Deserting Jimmy's stall?' asked a voice at her shoulder, and she turned to find the dark-haired man she'd met when she'd gone to thank Jimmy for the oranges. He was grinning broadly, which annoyed her.

'Not a bit,' she said. 'But some of us have to work all day and then buy our veg when we can. I can't be leaving my desk to go out shopping, my boss would go spare.'

'Quite right,' he said. 'Do you remember me? I'm John.'

'And your dad is one of Jimmy's mates from Battersea,' she said. 'Yes, I remember.' All she really wanted to do was to get home and start cooking, but she forced herself to be civil. No sense in offending one of Jimmy's friends, as the stall holder had been so kind to her. She registered again that he was very good-looking, even though that was of no interest to her any more.

'What brings you here, as he's already packed up?' she asked.

'Oh, I wasn't here to see him,' said John, pushing his hair out of his eyes. 'I'm here for work. I had a meeting nearby and walked this way on the off-chance he'd be here, but I've missed him. But I'll be up this way again so maybe I'll catch him then.'

'Right,' Penny said, casting around for something to say. 'What do you do, then?'

'I'm a photographer,' he said, and she noticed the camera bag swinging from his shoulder. 'As you can see, I take this everywhere. I specialise in wildlife photography, especially birds, and one of the magazines based around the corner wanted to use some of my pictures, so I had to come in.'

'Right,' she said again. Apart from the ever-present pigeons, her only dealings with birds had been the seagulls in Margate, and they were total pests, stealing your sandwich if you weren't careful. Penny didn't think he'd be very impressed if she told him that. Not that she wanted to impress him, she reminded herself.

'That's why I was in Spain last autumn,' he went on, as if she was interested. 'You get all these migrating birds, some that are hard to find anywhere else. There's nothing like it. I got some great shots. It's particularly good down on the south coast – do you know it?'

'I lived on the Costa Blanca till I was seven,' she said, wondering why she was bothering to tell him. 'I can't remember anything about the birds though. I can't remember much at all, except for the weather and the food. And my nanny, who taught me Spanish. I've never forgotten that.'

'Didn't you tell Jimmy you were starting a new job using Spanish?' he asked.

Damn, he had a good memory. Was that good or was it creepy?

'Yes, that's right,' she said, growing enthusiastic, despite herself. 'I translate publicity leaflets into Spanish, to try to get the tourists in. In fact, I might be doing more than that. My boss wants me to approach travel companies and see if we can arrange to be included in guided tours or stuff like that. So I might have to go to a lot of meetings soon.'

'Sounds as if you enjoy your job,' he said.

'I do,' she admitted. 'There's always something different going on. I worked in a shop before I came to London and it was awful. Whenever I begin to feel I'm getting bored here, I remind myself what that was like and count my blessings.' She grinned. 'Sounds stupid, doesn't it? But it's true.' She smiled, and got the strong sense that he was going to ask her to spend more time with him – and she'd had enough of that. What bad timing. If only she'd met him a few weeks ago, she'd have loved to hear more about what he did. 'I'd better go. Got to cook these.' She tapped her bag of veg. 'Maybe see you around.'

'Maybe,' he said, and smiled again.

A few weeks later, and spring was on the way. Even in built-up Soho, windowboxes began to come back to life and people started to wear brighter clothes. The most noticeable change at the Paradise Club was the return of Michelle.

'You keep an eye on her,' Dave muttered to Maureen as the girl flung open the door to the dressing room and started hugging her fellow dancers. 'I'm thinking she's bound to have learnt her lesson but I don't want no more trouble from her.'

And he didn't know the half of it, Maureen thought grimly. But who was she to deny the girl her moment of welcome? She'd been missed, there was no doubt about it, and it would do her good to see just how glad her friends were to see her. She couldn't imagine the girl would court danger as she had before and she'd give her the benefit of the doubt.

Meanwhile, Maureen had other things on her mind. Stuart had given her a present, but not the sort of thing she'd expected from him. Jewellery, yes, that was always nice to have, a ticket to a show, an invitation to a new bar or bistro, always acceptable. But this latest gift had arrived in a big box at the club. She'd opened it when she was on her own in Dave's office and had groaned.

It was a microwave oven. What the hell was he thinking of? Yes, it would have been expensive and most people she knew still didn't have one. But she'd never discussed her domestic arrangements with him and couldn't imagine what had possessed him to get her such a homely thing. Was that how he really thought of her – as someone who should do the cooking? Or was he saying she was too scrawny, that she should eat more? Whatever way she looked at it, she was offended.

She was still staring at it in horror when Penny came into the room.

'Sorry, have you seen the . . .' She came to a halt. 'What's that for?'

'It's a microwave oven,' said Maureen with a deadpan face. 'You heat food with it.'

'I know that,' said Penny. 'Lorna's had one for ages. But what's this one for? Is it for the cast here?'

'No,' said Maureen, shaking her head in disbelief still, 'it's a present. For me. Stuart had it sent here, as I won't let him near the flat. He seems to think it's the sort of thing I'd like. Not sure why.'

'It'll be really useful!' exclaimed Penny. 'When I make dinner and leave you some, you won't have to put the big oven on. Or eat it cold straight out of the fridge – and don't say you don't because I know you do.'

Maureen shrugged, not prepared to be told off by her young flatmate yet again about her eating habits. 'I'll kill him. It's an insult, that's what it is. He's telling me I need fattening up, the bloody cheek of it.'

'You and me both,' said Penny cheerfully. Since deciding she wasn't interested in men she had stopped worrying about her lack of curves and had begun to come round to the idea that she might never have any. 'It'll be brilliant. Don't look so miserable. If you don't want it I'll have it.'

'Bloody marvellous,' muttered Maureen. 'He's got a wife at home to fuss over and talk kitchens with, why does he want to do the same with me? He's never even seen my kitchen. If he did he'd know there's no bleedin' room for this – this monstrosity. Don't they say they give you cancer and make you infertile? It's a liability, that's what it is.'

'Oh stop moaning,' Penny told her. 'You're spouting a load of old wives' tales. We'll make space. Let's get it back to the flat while Prescott is out. Do you know where he's gone?'

'He's seeing someone from the council about planning permission for the Ashdown development,' said Maureen. 'Now he's got a bit of leverage, thanks to you and your smuggler friends, he's got a much better chance of over-turning their decision to let it go ahead. So he's in a good mood, which I don't trust a bit.' She sighed. 'All right, then, let's try to get it back. Can't we borrow something with wheels?'

'What, like one of the costume racks?' asked Penny dubiously. 'Can't see Mark being happy with that. It'll be simpler for both of us to lift it. Come on, I'll take this end.'

It was easier said than done. The box was bulky and heavy and by the time they got it to the street door of the flat they were exhausted. It didn't help that Maureen was back in her high heels, which made it almost impossible for her to balance the weight.

'Leave it here for a bit,' she gasped. 'I need a breather. Let this be a lesson to you, young Penny, and don't take up smoking. Bleedin' hell, I can hardly get my breath. What a stupid idea this was. Just wait till I see Stuart next, he won't know what's hit him.'

'Maybe we could borrow a trolley from Jimmy to get it up the stairs,' Penny suggested.

'Nah, they're too narrow. We'd never manage it. We could just stand here and try to sell it,' Maureen groaned. 'Some other daft mug might actually want it.' She collapsed and sat on the box, reaching into her bag for a cigarette.

Penny tried not to show her irritation. Maureen was a wonderful landlady, kind, tolerant, fun to be with – but her attitude to everything to do with the kitchen drove her mad. Somehow she had to get the present into the flat before Maureen lost it completely and gave it away to the next passer-by.

On the other side of the street she spotted a familiar figure and was suddenly really glad to see him. 'Hi there!' she called, waving, not trusting Maureen to be left alone with the box. 'Lovely day, isn't it?' Well, Penny thought, the sun's almost shining, so that's not a total lie.

'Out enjoying the fine weather?' asked John, making his way to their front door. 'How are you? Hello, I'm John,' he went on, turning to Maureen, who was standing up, grinding out her stub under her shiny stiletto. 'Are you a friend of Penny's?'

'Yes, and I'm her landlady,' said Maureen, smiling and smoothing down her jacket, reacting as she always did to an attractive man. 'Pleased to meet you. How very fortunate. I don't suppose we could ask you for some help?'

'Maureen!' exclaimed Penny. Honestly, the woman was too much, she'd only known him for thirty seconds and she was asking for favours already.

John didn't seem to mind. 'Having trouble with the box?' he said. 'What's inside? Oh, I see what you mean, they're heavy. Nothing I can't manage though.'

'Do you get to do much lifting out taking photographs?' Penny asked, not convinced he'd be able to lift it on his own. She thought he'd seemed genuinely kind before, and now she realised she was right.

'I haven't spent my whole life taking pictures,' he grinned. 'Remember my old man worked on a stall? I often helped him out. He sold china, huge tea sets sometimes, and you had to be able to lift those and yet not break anything. I tell you, if you can do that, then you can lift just about anything. This'll be a doddle. Leave it to me.'

'You're a knight in shining armour and no mistake,' beamed Maureen, opening the door and hurrying up the stairs to undo the top lock. John followed with the box, not even out of breath. 'In here, stick it on the table; that'll do until we work out where to put it. Penny, you never said you had a friend like this. Can we get you a cup of tea?'

Tea, thought Penny, she doesn't even know if we've got any milk left. She is the limit.

'Better not,' said John, patting his camera case. 'I've got to be off, got an assignment to hand in. I shan't even have time to speak to Jimmy beforehand. Nice to meet you,' and he shook Maureen's hand, while she batted her eyelashes, 'and good to see you again, Penny.' He smiled broadly. 'Now I know where you live, maybe I'll knock on your door next time I'm in town.'

'Maybe,' said Penny, seeing him out, getting him safely away from Maureen as fast as she could.

'Oooh, you dark horse!' exclaimed Maureen as soon as she came back into the kitchen. 'Who was that? What a very nice young man. You kept him quiet.'

'Nothing to keep quiet about,' said Penny shortly. 'He's a friend of Jimmy's. I met him that day he gave us the oranges. Good of him to help us when he hardly knows me.'

'Extremely good timing,' Maureen agreed. 'Don't suppose we have time for a cuppa, come to think of it. We'd best get back. But he reminds me of someone. Who can it be? Someone off the telly?'

'No idea,' said Penny, locking the door behind them, already with half a mind on what she could do with the new gadget.

'How does Jimmy know him?' Maureen persisted. God, she was impossible when a new man came on the scene.

Why don't you bloody ask him yourself, Penny wanted to snap but didn't. 'From the market down in Battersea, I think,' she said. 'Or something like that.'

'Hmm,' said Maureen. 'Would I have known him from there? I grew up round there, you know. But no,' she shook her head, 'got to be honest, he's much younger than me. He'd have been a kid when I left to pursue my career in entertainment. And, as you know, they won't have me back, so that can't be it. Still,' she went on, leading the way out into the weak sunshine, 'he can drop round any time he likes. You make sure to tell him so.'

'Fine,' said Penny, thinking that even though he was so striking-looking and interesting, she'd do no such thing.

'So what's it like to be back?' Mark asked Michelle. 'Are you glad to see us? How are you finding the dancing after taking a break?'

'Left me breathless the first couple of nights,' she admitted as they made their way towards Bar Italia. 'You forget what hard work it is, and having to smile all the time. Makes your face ache. Especially after being bashed in the face.' She grinned up at him, showing her slightly crooked front teeth. 'But of course I'm glad to be back. I missed you all. My sisters were fine about me being home for a bit and they looked after me brilliantly but we got nothing in common. One's just got a job down a bookies on the Roman Road and you'd think she'd won on the Premium Bonds. I tried to be excited for her but it don't compare. Give me the bright lights any time.'

'This is where you belong,' Mark agreed, holding open the door for her. 'Bet they don't serve coffee like this either.'

'This is the best,' Michelle agreed, squeezing in behind a table. 'This is the life. Now all I need is an invitation or two to the latest restaurants and I shall be as good as new. Have any good ones opened since I was away?'

Mark raised his eyebrows. 'And how are you going to pay for those? No, don't say it. Michelle, I don't want to sound like your granny but please, watch out. Have a care for yourself. I don't know about you but I found the whole thing totally harrowing and I don't want to go through it again. You wouldn't do that to me, would you? Not to your old friend?'

'I was joking,' she protested, waving happily at a waiter. 'The usual, please. No, of course I'll be careful. I know how you all looked after me and covered for me and I'm truly grateful. So of course I was only joking.'

Mark looked at her and had a horrible suspicion that she wasn't.

Chapter Thirty-Four

Juliet caught up with Maureen at the end of a morning dance class. For once she hadn't rushed off to shower as soon as the routines had finished, and her famous blonde hair was plastered to her forehead. 'Can I have a word?' she asked quietly.

'Of course,' said Maureen, gathering her things together – sweatshirt, cassettes, water bottle. 'Spit it out.'

'Could we speak in private?' Juliet asked, and Maureen looked up sharply. 'I wouldn't ask but it's important.'

'Come with me, then,' said Maureen, and led the way out of the studio, down the stairs and along the dank alley, which smelled even worse now that the weather was turning warmer. Juliet followed, trying to avoid brushing her big bag against the crumbling walls. When they reached the street they stopped.

'I need to make a phone call,' said Juliet. 'I don't want to use the pay phone at the club because you might as well shout your business from Speaker's Corner. And if I try to use a phone box round here I get pestered by every pervert in the area. I was wondering if I could use yours. I'll pay you.'

'You don't have to do that,' protested Maureen. 'I trust

you. Not planning on an hour to New Zealand, are you? Then it'll be fine.' She noted the girl hadn't said what it was about but if it was what she thought it was, then Maureen wasn't going to pry. 'Shall I give you my keys? You can lock up after you've done and then give them me back this evening. I'm off to Oxford Street to treat meself to some more leotards. This one's gone all stretchy.'

'Oh, I know, what did we do before Lycra?' Juliet smiled, but it didn't reach her eyes. 'That's great, I really appreciate it. I won't take long.' She took the keys and headed off, and Maureen thought the girl's usually immaculate posture had collapsed. In fact, she looked like she had the weight of the world on her shoulders. Perhaps she did.

Maureen wondered for the hundredth time which was worse: for your family to throw you out and cut all contact, or to be stuck in one that was nothing but trouble, as Juliet seemed to be. True, she'd been lucky with Lorna who, though quiet, didn't let anyone tell her what to think, and there was the occasional call or letter from Pete back in Battersea. As for the rest, she considered the club her family now. It worked both ways. They'd cut her off and she didn't intend to go crawling back. Funny, she thought, as she threaded her way along the side roads to Carnaby Street towards Oxford Circus. Here am I, a successful businesswoman, running my own dance school. Right little entrepreneur, I am. Just what they want in Thatcher's Britain. You'd have thought they'd be proud. Well, sod them. My family look down at the people at the club for having loose morals and yet they've all got more kindness in their little fingers than my lot put together. That's if you take Prescott out of the equation, anyway.

Maureen did a double-take as she approached the junction with Carnaby Street. There in the window of a small wine bar was a very familiar head of curls. How could that be? The girl had only just been in her class and would have had to sprint to get here, let alone get changed. Surely it couldn't be her.

Then the figure in the window turned slightly, saying something to her companion and laughing, tossing her head and raising her full wine glass. It was her all right. And that didn't look like fruit juice in the glass either.

Michelle, Michelle, what are you doing? she thought. The girl was meant to be performing tonight and the number one rule, even above not dating punters, was that you never drank beforehand. The dancers could drink what they liked afterwards, as long as they were all right the next day, but never, ever beforehand. Yet here she was, bold as brass, knocking back the wine and it was barely midday. And it looked as if they'd got a bottle in.

After what had happened, after all the warnings and the consequences of ignoring them, Maureen was flabbergasted. Had the girl no sense of self-preservation? Was she completely stupid? Then she realised that she'd come to a dead halt in the middle of the pavement and that she was causing an obstruction. 'Mind what you're bleedin' doing,' somebody muttered as they pushed past.

'Mind yourself,' Maureen snapped back, but moved so she was leaning against the wall of the nearest building. What was she to do? She couldn't exactly barge into the bar and march the girl out. Michelle was over eighteen and legally entitled to drink and meet who she liked. She wasn't her mother. She just didn't want the girl to mess up royally, and so soon.

Sighing, she decided there wasn't much she could do short of catching her quietly later and checking that she was all right and at least safe to go on stage without falling flat on her face. Meanwhile, she had to get those leotards. Even if Stuart had said she was too scrawny she could at least look her best in front of her students.

'Stupid bleedin' fool,' Maureen muttered, and realised she'd said it aloud when several office girls, all bouffant hair and shoulder pads, turned to glare.

Michelle was wandering along in a hazy glow, still a little merry from the lunchtime wine. She'd known it was a bad idea to have that second bottle but somehow she felt powerless to resist. It had led to a lovely afternoon, tucked away in a little hotel room off Regent Street. Now she could barely be bothered to put one foot in front of the other, but was confident that she'd snap out of it once she'd changed into her costume. It would all come back to her. Dancing the routines was like riding a bike.

'Oh no you don't,' said Maureen, and grabbed her as she walked past the office door. 'Dave's out on business, which you should be bloody glad about, so just you come in here, young lady.'

Stumbling a bit, Michelle did as she was told, perching stubbornly on the arm of the one comfy chair. 'I haven't done . . .' she began, but it was pointless.

'I saw you,' said Maureen. 'I was there, this lunchtime. You must be the fastest dancer on two legs, I don't know how you got to that bar so quick after class, but it was 'definitely you and you were drinking wine. Not that anyone would have to be Sherlock Holmes to tell that,' she added, as the girl swayed a little.

'So what if I was?' demanded Michelle, all her old attitude back now. 'It's a free country. And, before you ask, no, I wasn't meeting a punter. So there's no problem.'

'There's a problem if you go on stage pissed,' said Maureen. 'Look at you, you can barely sit up straight. How the hell are you going to dance? You'll be falling over your own feet. You'll be lucky if you don't take the others down with you. You can't go on like that.'

'I'll be fine!' Michelle assured her, waving her arm and knocking a pile of papers off the desk. 'Whoops. Sorry.'

'Give me strength.' Maureen closed her eyes. 'I'm going to have to call back Fifi's idiot of a cousin. She's daft as a brush but at least she never fell over. I wonder if I can get hold of her for tonight.'

'Really?' asked Michelle. 'I heard about her. The rest of them can't stand her. Don't do that. I'll be fine. It's ages away yet.'

'Michelle, listen to me,' said Maureen with exaggerated patience. 'You are pissed out of your tiny brain. And it must be very, very tiny because only a few months ago we sat in this very building and you were warned about how you were carrying on. Now I know you didn't deserve what happened after that but at least I thought you'd take the time to come to your senses. What's gone wrong? And so soon?'

Michelle looked up, still swaying slightly, and her defiance melted away. 'I met this lovely man,' she said.

Maureen groaned.

'No, no,' the girl went on. 'He really is. And he's not

even that old. Well, much older than me, obviously, but not like those Italian bastards. He treats me very, very nicely. Now I know it's not for ever but really, you got to take your chances when you're young. He might be just a little bit married . . .'

'You don't say,' said Maureen.

'. . . but it doesn't matter, as he's only here for a short while. In the meantime we are going to have ever such a lot of fun.' Michelle beamed. 'He's just the nicest person. You'd love him, yes, you would.'

'Does he know you were meant to be dancing tonight?' Maureen asked. 'And he still let you get pissed and then come here? Because if he did, no, I don't think I would love him. I would have his guts for garters.'

'I might not have told him,' admitted Michelle. 'I might have said I wasn't on until tomorrow. But I'll be fine. Seriously, I will.' She fell off the arm of the chair and landed on the floor.

'Get up, go home, get out of my sight,' sighed Maureen, hauling the girl to her unsteady feet. 'Come back sober tomorrow and we'll say no more about it. Do this again and you're out, end of. Do you get it?'

'I will,' said Michelle solemnly. 'Thank you, Maureen. You're a star.'

'I'm too good to you, that's for certain,' said Maureen, guiding her towards the door. 'On your way.' As Michelle was on her way out, Juliet hurried in, looking from right to left, clearly relieved to see Maureen.

'Here are your keys,' she said. 'I can't thank you enough.'

'Juliet, you look like shit,' said Maureen, shutting the door of the office once more. 'Are you sure you want to go on tonight? I'll be honest, it'll be simpler if you don't, as Michelle won't be back until tomorrow and that leaves us with an uneven number. So you'd be doing me a favour if you was to pull out.'

'Would I really?' Juliet asked, clearly tempted. 'Don't suppose I could bum a cigarette before deciding?'

'No problem,' said Maureen, throwing her bag across the room. 'Help yourself. You can pay me back when you owe me a full packet – and the way you're going that won't be long. Want to talk about it?'

Juliet lit up and sighed with pleasure. 'That's the best thing all day. Looks like I'm back on the tobacco again. Thanks but no thanks, Maureen, because if I start talking I won't be able to stop and somehow I've got to keep it together a while longer.' She looked up. 'What was up with Michelle?'

'You don't want to know,' said Maureen. 'Take it up with her tomorrow. You won't get no sense out of her this evening. She's back on the path to self-destruction and loving every minute of it.'

'You know what,' said Juliet, 'I really don't want to know. Not right now. I've got enough to cope with, I can't take her on as well. She'll have to manage by herself for a bit. Sorry if that dumps you in it. But there it is.'

Chapter Thirty-Five

Penny assumed when the doorbell rang that it was Maureen forgetting her keys. She often wondered how her landlady had managed before she'd arrived, as it happened pretty often. So she was prepared to have a bit of a go as she opened the door. Then she looked up into the warm eyes of John and found herself at a loss for words.

'Thought I'd drop by to see how your new microwave's working,' he said. 'Didn't damage it getting it upstairs, did I?' He was clearly waiting for an invitation.

Penny decided she might as well ask him in. 'Come on up and I'll make you a cup of tea in it,' she said.

'Really?' He didn't look too happy.

She shook her head. 'You're all right, that was a joke. Well, we can if you like. But I can also do you the normal sort.'

'Normal, please,' he said, following her as she led the way upstairs to the flat.

Penny wasn't sure what to make of this, being alone in the flat with John. She made herself look busy, boiling the kettle and finding the clean mugs – why did one seem to have what looked like Juliet's lipstick on it? – and quickly checking that there was milk and Maureen hadn't used it all on the sly.

'Are you in London about another assignment?' she said. 'More bird pictures?'

'That's right,' he said. 'I'm going to be sent up to Scotland for the spring migration. At least I can speak the language there – well, almost.' He grinned. 'It's all right, you don't have to pretend to be interested. I love it but I know not everybody does.'

'I suppose it's the sort of thing you have to love to be able to do it,' she said, pouring the boiling water. 'Do you have to be out in all weather?'

'That's part of the fun,' John said instantly. 'If you have the right gear you can stay out in anything, then you don't miss a thing. I've been out in the driving rain all day, lying on my stomach, waiting for a chick to hatch, and it's the best feeling in the world when you capture the moment.' He checked himself. 'One of the best feelings, anyway.'

'If you say so,' she said, passing him his mug. 'Give me the warm and dry any time. I love the heat.'

'You need the right gear for that too,' he said. 'Once you're protected from the sun you just sit it out. You have to make sure the camera and film are okay, that they don't overheat.'

'You won't have that problem in Scotland,' she predicted, beginning to relax. John was very easy to be with, not like some of the men at the club. He seemed to be comfortable in his own skin and she found she liked that.

'All sorts of other problems, though,' he said. 'Midges, mainly. You wouldn't believe it, and the springtime is the worst. I've been on assignments to Africa and come back with fewer bites. I tell you, it's unbelievable.'

'Africa? Really?' she said, interested now. She might not be particularly keen on wildlife but she'd always had a hankering to travel, to see what the rest of the world was like. 'How was that? Where did you go? Were you there for long?'

'One at a time,' he laughed. 'I've been several times. Usually to South Africa, so I can do wildlife and garden shots at the same time. They have amazing plants. It's okay, you don't have to be interested in that either.'

'Not much call for plants here,' Penny said. 'Some people opposite have windowboxes but Maureen's never bothered. We'd probably forget to water them.' She thought of Lorna's garden, which had been carefully tended and had always looked lovely, but she'd never bothered to find out how to do it – it seemed like hard work. 'She gets given flowers sometimes but they usually end up in the bin as they make her sneeze.' She looked at him and pulled a face. 'That sounds awful, doesn't it?'

He shrugged. 'No, why should it? Some people like them, some don't. I'd rather see plants in the wild than all tidy inside.'

John was good at making awkward moments pass quickly. She suddenly felt that she'd known him for ages. How had that happened?

'When are you off, then?' she asked. 'Will it be right in the middle of the midge season?'

'Next week,' he replied, 'and yes, that'll be prime time for them. I'll be bitten to bits the next time you see me.' He looked up at her directly. 'Did that sound out of turn? If there is a next time. I'd like there to be.'

Penny realised she very much hoped so too. 'Of course.' She wasn't sure what to say next that wouldn't sound forward but she wanted nothing more than to talk to this fascinating man.

'I'll come round and show you my pictures,' he grinned, 'and then you can see how bad the bites are. You can tell me if you think it's worth it or not.'

'All right.' She broke into a big smile. 'I'll look forward to that. And you can tell me more about your travels. Who knows, I might have worked out how to do more than just heat things up in the microwave by then.'

'I didn't carry it all the way up these stairs just so you could make tea in it,' he pointed out. 'It's a deal. Look, I'd better be going, I have to be back in South London. And I don't want to hold you up from whatever you had planned. I hope you didn't mind me just dropping in like that.'

'No, I'm glad you did,' she said truthfully. 'Make sure you do it again once you're back. Tell you what, take the phone number then you can let me know when you're coming and I'll cook you something properly, if you'd like that. Jimmy can tell you I'm not bad.'

'Good idea,' he said, as she scribbled down the number. 'And he's already told me about you buying all his most unusual stuff. So I know I'm in good hands.'

Penny smiled and gave him the slip of paper then followed him to the door. 'Good luck in Scotland,' she said. She smiled up at him for what seemed like a long time. For a moment she thought he was going to lean forward to kiss her, but he didn't, he just went down the stairs and waved to her from the bottom. 'See you soon.'

Well, she thought as she closed the door to the flat.

Who'd have thought it? Don't go getting ideas, she warned herself. You've been there before. It's only a conversation, don't go building your whole future life upon it.

But this felt different. Eduardo had been exciting and charming, exotic even. That had been part of the attraction. John was so easy to be with and equally good-looking, though in a different way. He felt familiar. He felt safe. Penny was seized with an urge to get to know him better, and hoped she hadn't been too eager in giving him the phone number. Maybe he only wanted to be friends – he was older than her, after all. But even though she was inexperienced she was sure there had been that little buzz when he almost kissed her.

Either way is fine, she assured herself. There's no hurry. Let's just see how it goes. She tried to imagine how sensible Juliet would think about it, never rushing into things, never panicking. But in spite of herself Penny couldn't help but wish he'd be back soon.

'Do you want to go for a coffee after the class?' Juliet asked Michelle the next day. She'd forced herself to come in, to act normally, to look good. She tried not to think about the way her leggings and leotard felt too baggy, and knew she'd lost even more weight. Maybe she'd have a huge slice of cake with her coffee.

'Sorry, can't,' said Michelle. 'I've got prior commitments.'

Something about the way the girl said it made Juliet look at her friend sharply. 'What are you up to? Is it anything to do with what happened yesterday?'

'Don't get your knickers in a twist,' said Michelle, tossing her curls. 'I'm not going to turn up pissed again.

302

That would be really stupid and I'm not that daft, whatever Maureen might have told you. I'm just going for a walk with someone.'

Warning bells sounded in Juliet's head. 'Are you sure?' she said. 'Do you know what you're getting yourself into this time?'

'Look, I know you all mean well,' said Michelle, 'and don't think I'm not grateful. You saved my skin before, and I'll always remember that. But I'm okay again now and I know what I'm doing. This guy is safe, he's a poppet, he won't harm a hair of my head. You can all relax, I'm going to be fine.'

Maybe Michelle was right. Maybe it would be all right this time and Juliet was just overreacting because she was so on edge. Not every man was a violent abuser, and she shouldn't assume the worst every time. She should stand back and let Michelle have her fun. She closed her eyes briefly.

'Okay, good luck,' she said tiredly. 'But I want to go on stage tonight so you'd better be all right to go on. Despite what you all think, I can't miss too many shows in a row, I need the cash.' That was true too, not that she expected anyone to believe it.

'I'll be there, don't you worry,' said Michelle blithely, as if she had no trace of a hangover. 'Did you hear me? I said, don't you worry. Look at you, you mustn't get into a state about me. We'll show 'em this evening, we'll dance our socks off.' She ran off to take her place in the line.

God, if only her friend were her only problem, Juliet thought. If only she knew she was the tip of the iceberg. But it wouldn't help to tell her. It wasn't as if anyone could do anything, she just had to wait it out. But the waiting was killing her inside.

Mark had been growing steadily more uneasy and finally decided to speak to Penny. He picked a moment when he knew Dave was out of the office and slipped in to find her slipping two pieces of paper separated by a sheet of carbon into the typewriter.

'I don't know how you do it,' he said. 'Doesn't this drive you mad? Don't you get bored?'

'Don't touch,' she said, slapping his hand away from the paper. 'I've only just got this lined up. And you'll get ink on your hands and then it'll get on the costumes.' She looked up at him properly. 'Oooh, nice haircut. Your mate back, is he? That's really good. Maybe he could take a look at mine?'

'Juliet's first in the queue,' he said. 'I promised her ages ago, but he's been off all that time. And talking about being off, did you hear what happened earlier in the week? Did Maureen say – Michelle got pissed and couldn't go on. It was just luck that Juliet was sick that night and Maureen didn't have to get the ghastly redhead back in.'

'She mentioned something about it,' Penny said, 'but I haven't seen either of them since. I've been really busy. It's all right for Dave, he phones up these travel companies, tells me this, that and the other has been agreed and then sends me in to meet them. Then it's up to me to type it all up and make sure that they actually did agree what he says they did.' She pointed to a big file. 'I've done all that. So when I'm in the club I'm in here typing and when that's done I'm out doing more

304

meetings, which then means more typing. So I've hardly seen anybody. By the time everyone comes in I'm worn out and just want to go home.'

'You are bored, then,' he said, flicking his stunning new fringe.

'Well, the funny thing is, no, I'm not,' Penny admitted. 'Okay, the typing bit I could do without. But the going out and meeting people, speaking Spanish some of the time, trying to work out what Dave has said without landing him in it – that's all good fun. I'm getting the hang of it. And he hasn't shouted at me for ages, which must be a good thing.'

'Just as well he wasn't here the other night,' Mark replied. 'He'd have had good cause to shout then.'

'Maureen covered it up though, didn't she?' she said. 'And Michelle's been all right since, or she'd have come home and given me an earful.'

Mark sat back in the tattered comfy chair and raised his arms behind his head. 'It's not her I'm worried about. Well, either she'll be all right or she won't, doesn't seem there's much anyone can do about it. No, it's Juliet.' He stretched. 'You thought something was up ages ago, didn't you? I didn't believe you at the time, but I've changed my mind. She's definitely lost weight, and I'm not just saying that because she's needed alterations. Happens all the time to you lot, you go on diets, you have a binge, whatever. This is different. She's almost haggard. God knows we'd all love sculpted cheekbones but she's more like a skull. That's not good. She wants to be careful or Prescott will haul her in. Punters don't like to think a dancer is sickening for something.'

'I know, I know,' Penny said, realising this was exactly

what she'd feared. 'I convinced myself I was imagining things but I wasn't, was I?'

'No, I think you were right all along,' Mark replied. 'I feel a fool for not seeing it when you did. I'm just so used to her sorting everything out, being in control, I didn't imagine anything could be wrong. Some friend I've been.'

'But what do we do, then?' she demanded. 'Do we ask her outright? She doesn't really like that, does she? She's great at handing out straightforward advice but doesn't say much about herself. I'm not even sure where she lives.'

'She's a dark horse, all right,' agreed Mark. 'She's never asked me to her flat. I know Michelle's way out east and your place is like a second home to me but Juliet keeps herself to herself.'

'Should we speak to Maureen?' she wondered. 'She'll know what to do.'

'Don't you think she's got enough on her plate?' Mark asked. 'She'll be keeping an eye on Michelle, and then there's Prescott still fussing about the Ashdown development. He thought he had it sorted but it's not that simple and she gets the brunt of it.'

'And she's not getting on so well with Stuart,' Penny added. 'Well, you probably knew that.'

'Yeah, I don't give it long,' said Mark gloomily. 'If he will get her stupid presents what does he expect? He's got her totally wrong, that's the trouble.'

'All right, we don't ask her,' said Penny. 'We'll have to try to get it out of Juliet somehow. I agree, if we're her friends we can't let her go on like this. Tomorrow. Let's do it then.'

'Deal,' said Mark, getting up and sweeping back his fringe. 'Tomorrow it is.'

Chapter Thirty-Six

Penny arrived at the club the next day determined to confront Juliet and find out what was going on. This time she wasn't going to take no for an answer. Nobody was around when she got in, but this wasn't unusual as the dancers were often at their various classes and the crew wouldn't strictly be needed until later. So she thought nothing of it, just went through the diary to see if Prescott had arranged any meetings for her or if he'd decided to go to any himself. It looked as if she had a day at the desk, typing up notes before starting on another round of travel companies next week.

She began to plough her way through the pages, cursing every time she made a mistake. It was simple enough to Tippex out anything on the top sheet but it didn't work on the carbon copies. Concentrate, she thought. What's wrong with you today?

Just as she was wondering when to break for lunch, Mark appeared, waving an envelope.

'Hi . . . what's up?' she asked, at the sight of his stricken face.

'Did you know about this?' he demanded.

'About what? What are you talking about?'

'This,' he repeated. 'This message. It was left on my worktable. She'd weighed it down with my scissors so it wouldn't get knocked off.'

'Who had?' Penny asked, confused.

'Juliet,' said Mark. 'Look at this. She's done a runner.'

'Juliet has?' she asked. It didn't seem right. That was totally out of character.

'Read it for yourself,' he said, dropping the envelope on her desk.

Nervously, Penny smoothed out the piece of paper inside.

Dear Mark,

Sorry to leave this with you but it seemed the simplest thing to do. I have to go away for a while. I'm fine so please don't worry about me but there's something I have to do and I can't carry on performing at the same time. Please do not attempt to find me. I'll be back in contact when everything is sorted out.

Please also tell Maureen how very sorry I am that I've let her down and perhaps she will understand.

I'll be thinking of you all, my very dear friends.

Juliet.

Penny reread it very slowly to see if it made more sense the second time around but it didn't. There was nothing to give them any clue what this was about.

She looked up at Mark. 'What do we do? She can't expect us not to do something?'

'No idea,' he said. 'Well, it proves one thing, we were

right and there's something really serious going on. We'd better tell Maureen at least.'

'It'll have to wait,' said Penny. 'She went to teach her first class and then was going straight to the dentist. She couldn't get an appointment at such short notice but they told her to come in and wait. She could be there all day, and she's got such bad toothache she can't think straight. So there's no point in saying anything till she's been treated.'

'God, what timing,' groaned Mark. 'I'm sorry for her but really, we need her here. She'll have to know.'

Penny frowned. 'Look, we don't have to do what Juliet asks. We could try to find her. Do you have her phone number?'

'I've got it in my address book at home,' he said. 'Won't it be in the office somewhere? Bet they have contact numbers for everyone in here. And addresses, they'll need them for the payslips.'

He was right. They found the number and tried it from the office phone but it rang and rang before finally cutting out. 'Might not mean anything,' suggested Mark. 'She might not be answering or there might be a fault on the line. Let's take the address and go round. Too bad if she's angry, I'd rather know she was okay.'

Penny knew they were clutching at straws but agreed anyway. It was something to do, and at least then they could tell Maureen that they'd tried to find her.

'Okay, why not?' she said. 'Get that A to Z and see where it is.'

It turned out not to be too far – a side street between Covent Garden and Holborn. 'We can walk that, easy,' said Mark. 'You haven't got those high heels on, have you?'

'Thank God, no,' said Penny, pointing to her pixie boots. 'I was glad to have a rest from them to tell you the truth. These are much better.'

Zigzagging through the back streets Penny tried to put from her mind all the images of what they might find at the flat. She couldn't believe Juliet had done anything stupid or tried to harm herself in any way, but then until recently she wouldn't have believed that Juliet's life was anything but easy and under her complete control.

Mark led the way, taking her down shortcuts and what she thought were blind alleys until they found themselves in the small street of redbrick buildings. None looked in good repair. 'Blimey, I always assumed she lived in somewhere upmarket paid for by her parents,' he muttered. 'This is a bit of a dive, isn't it?'

'I don't know what I expected,' admitted Penny, 'but it wasn't quite this.' She stepped sideways to avoid a suspicious pile on the pavement. 'God, it smells worse than the lane to the dance studio.'

'It's rank, that's what it is,' said Mark, wrinkling his nose. 'Let's see if it's any better inside.' He counted the doors until they were at the right one. It was in need of a lick of paint, and the ground-floor windows were filthy. There were several doorbells and he squinted until he found Flat F. When he rang it there was no response.

'Damn,' said Penny. 'What do we do now?' They stood around trying to make up their minds and before they'd reached a decision, the door opened and a man rushed out, carrying a motorcycle helmet. He held the door for them without waiting for an explanation. They hurried in and began climbing the stairs.

'No wonder she doesn't complain about the way up

to ours,' groaned Penny. 'This is far worse. Is she really this far up?'

'It's this one,' called Mark, who had reached the top. 'Come on, you're meant to be fit.' He started hammering on the door. 'Juliet, come on out if you're in there. We're dying of thirst, come on, you owe us a cuppa at least.'

There was no reply.

Penny pushed past him and looked through the letterbox. It was hard to see much as the corridor was dark but she could make out a small pile of post on the doormat. 'Juliet!' she called, but she was sure now that their friend wasn't there. The flat was empty. 'Shit,' she said, squatting to sit on the doorstep. 'It's no good, Mark. Wherever she is, it isn't here.'

'What the hell is going on?' he groaned. 'She really doesn't want us to know, does she?' He bent down to join her.

'This is getting us nowhere,' she said after a while. 'We'd better get back. Someone's going to have to tell Prescott if Maureen doesn't make it in before long.'

There was no sign of Maureen for the rest of the day and by late afternoon Penny could put it off no longer. 'Juliet's gone off sick,' she told Prescott, not sure if this was a lie or not. 'She won't be able to dance tonight.'

'Just what I need,' fumed Dave, crashing his hand against the desk. 'What is it with you girls? First she's ill, then she's back, then she's off again. She shows her face round here again and she's on a warning. You can tell her that from me. So can you get someone else in for this evening?'

'Me?' said Penny. 'I don't keep the other dancers' details. Maureen does and she's still at the dentist.'

'Bleedin' marvellous,' Dave exclaimed. 'Well, you'll have to go on. You're here, so you might as well. Don't worry, I've got it on good authority your dodgy Mexicans won't be anywhere in town for a very, very long time to come, so there's no excuse there,' as he saw her face fall. 'Get that poofter to sort your costume and on you go.'

Penny knew this was a way of taking the pressure off both Juliet and Maureen but found that she really didn't want to dance. At first she'd missed it, even while she'd dreaded being spotted by Eduardo or any of his friends, but now she was reluctant to tread the boards again. She felt uneasy about being watched by all those men, when the bright lights prevented her from seeing them. She couldn't explain what it was, but the excitement wasn't there. Still, now was not the time to cause a fuss. 'Mark,' she called from the office door, 'have you got my outfit there? I'm just going to run home for my shoes after all.'

The evening passed without incident, other than some of the dancers making sharp remarks about her sudden return, but they shut up when she said Juliet had a bug and there hadn't been time to find another replacement. Tomorrow Maureen could get somebody else in. There was no denying it. Penny could go through the motions but the magic had gone.

The days passed and there was no word from Juliet. Maureen, still puffy-faced from having a tooth removed and short-tempered because of the pain, promoted one of the new dancers from her class, much to Fifi's annoyance but to everyone else's delight. Penny sighed with relief. She couldn't explain her change of heart but the thought of dragging herself up onto the stage every night was unbearable. Maybe, she reasoned, it was because she was already working a full day in the office and had no time to recover. That was partly it. But, if she was honest with herself, it wasn't the only thing. The incident with Eduardo had changed something deep down and she didn't want to put herself in that position again if she could help it.

She wished John was around to talk to. Even though she'd never told him about being a dancer, she felt as though he would listen to anything and not judge her for it. He'd be in Scotland by now though. She kicked herself when she realised she didn't know for how long he'd be away for. She couldn't bring herself to ask Jimmy. She couldn't talk to Maureen – she could barely say hello without having her head bitten off. Mark was worried enough about Juliet without burdening him with her sudden change of heart. And as for Michelle, she was hardly around these days, turning up at the last possible moment to dance and then dashing off to meet her new man, seemingly with no time to spare for anyone else.

She tried to raise it in one of her regular phone calls to Lorna but found she couldn't find the words to describe how she felt. It all came out wrong, as she began by saying a friend of hers was losing weight. Lorna immediately demanded to know if she was eating properly, which brought them on to the comforting subject of cookery, and for a while Penny forgot her troubles as she described the early summer fruit and veg she'd been experimenting with. But when she put the phone down she realised nothing had been solved.

Penny took to wandering the streets of Soho on her own once more, as she had done when she'd first moved into Maureen's flat, not sure how to snap out of her low mood. The shops were the same, the shopkeepers friendly, the market as busy and colourful. But something was missing. She couldn't put her finger on what, but she was restless, edgy, and longing to talk to the one person she felt would understand.

Maureen's temper finally erupted one evening when Stuart suggested he take her to a steakhouse after the show. Mark overheard the row and tried to block his ears as it got so personal but the shouting was just too loud.

'How do you bleedin' think I can eat a steak when half of my own mouth is like a load of raw meat?' she'd thundered. 'How can you even suggest such a thing? Oh I'd love to, I would bloody love a decent meal, I've had nothing but piddly soup for a week and I'm sick of it but I can't. And why's that? Because I've had a tooth out as an emergency. Did I mention that? Did I mention I've been driven half mad by the pain all week? Did I? THEN WHY DID YOU JUST ASK ME TO GO OUT TO A STEAKHOUSE, YOU BLEEDIN' IDIOT?'

After that there was nowhere for the man to go but home to his gullible wife. Maureen sighed with relief as she shut herself away in the office, only for Mark to tap on the door a couple of minutes later.

'So that's that, then?' he asked, eyebrows raised.

'That's that.' She raised a glass she'd found behind the desk, and which she'd filled with Dave's not-very-secret stash of single malt. 'And good riddance. Why do I bother, why do I bother?'

'At least he was worth the bother for a while,' Mark

pointed out. 'You had some good times. You went places. You had fun.'

'But he was an idiot,' Maureen sighed. 'I always knew it deep down. This was just the final straw. I kept thinking he'd improve, he'd see I wasn't going to change, that he'd misunderstood me. But the opposite happened. He started buying me things and taking me places his wife would have liked.' She shuddered in revulsion. 'Can you imagine? Why would I waste my time on a fool like that? I'm better off without him.'

'You're better off without him,' Mark echoed, taking a sip from her glass and shutting his eyes. 'Hell, that's strong. Works like medicine, does it?'

'Better than medicine,' Maureen assured him. 'Only thing that does bloody work and all. Seriously I thought I was going to go mad this week. The last thing I need is that idiot and his idiot questions. At least I won't have to put up with that again.' She sighed. 'Just you and me again, Mark, you and me against the world. And what do we say?'

'We say, sod the lot of them,' Mark told her solemnly.

'Damn right,' said Maureen, letting her head fall back. 'Boyfriends, bosses, lovers, idiots. Sod the bleedin' lot of them.'

Chapter Thirty-Seven

They knew something was up when Michelle started turning up well before the show started and wanting to go for coffee with them again.

'Let me guess, Michelle,' said Mark, as they sat in their usual spot in Bar Italia, him with a large espresso and Penny and Michelle with cappuccinos. 'Someone who usually requires all of your time and attention is out of town again and so you've fallen back on us as stopgaps.'

'Never!' cried Michelle, brown curls bouncing. 'I'm sorry if I've been neglecting you. It wasn't that I'd forgotten you or got the hump. It's just that I knew he wouldn't be around for long so I wanted to make the most of it. He'll probably be back next week but after that he just doesn't know. So of course I spent a lot of time with him. Didn't let the club down though, did I? Give me credit where it's due, I never got pissed before a show again.'

'True,' said Mark, 'though only you would think that's something worthy of praise. Most of us don't even think of turning up for work after knocking back a bottle of wine. That's your speciality, that is.'

'Nonsense,' said Michelle, not offended in the slightest.

'I take my dancing very seriously. Where would I be without you all? It's just that there are so many temptations to give in to.' Her eyes lit up. 'And don't tell me you always resist temptation, Mark, 'cos I know very well you don't.'

'Chance would be a fine thing,' he moaned. 'I haven't had much opportunity to practise my resistance recently. I'd welcome the practice, really I would. But I've hit a bit of a dry spell. Oh well, no sense complaining. Back to the grindstone.'

A week or so later it was a different story.

Michelle was throwing things into the dressing room waste bin with force, scowling, as Maureen walked in, Penny on her heels with a notebook, trying to work out something Dave had written down. 'But you know his handwriting better than me,' she was saying, 'just take a minute to see if you can tell what this is meant to say ... Michelle, what's the matter?'

Michelle looked up at them and they could tell she'd been crying. Her eyes were red and her face was swollen, and as she began to speak her lip trembled. 'Bloody left town for good, hasn't he,' she said. 'I know, I know, I shouldn't be surprised. I'm not surprised at all really. But I kidded myself he'd be around a bit longer. Now he won't be back and I'm back at square one.'

'You and me both, love,' said Maureen, without much sadness. 'At least we know where we are with that, eh? You better put that bin down before you break it.'

'Suppose so,' said Michelle, but she sounded so down that they had to stop what they were doing.

'Come on,' said Penny, giving her a hug. 'You'll be okay. You always are.'

317

'Yeah, I'm the expert,' sighed the girl, wiping her eyes, staring at the floor. 'Bounce right back, that's what I'll do. Just give me time, that's all.'

'It does help, love. I know you think it's a cliché but it really does,' Maureen assured her. 'This time next month you'll be laughing at this. Think of that.'

'Yeah, maybe.' Michelle wouldn't meet her eyes any more.

Penny tried a different tack. 'Do you know where he's gone?' she asked. 'Perhaps you could write to him. Perhaps it's not the end.'

Michelle shook her head. 'Nah, thanks for the idea but it won't work. I can't contact him, that was always the understanding. Remember, he's a little bit married.' She almost smiled. 'Gets in the way, that does. He won't want letters from another woman falling on his doorstep.'

'Oh get away, Michelle,' laughed Maureen, 'you can't be a little bit married. That's like being a little bit pregnant.'

Silence fell. Michelle didn't react, refusing to look up. Maureen and Penny exchanged a glance.

Maureen spoke first. 'You're not, are you?' There was no answer. She waited. Still no answer. 'Oh. You are.'

Finally Michelle replied. 'Okay. So there it is. It wasn't planned and we'd been so careful but one night the condom split. I thought we'd get away with it, but no. And before you ask, no, I'm not going to tell him. This is my mess and I'll sort it out.'

'How?' asked Penny, reaching to rub the girl's shoulders.

'I have absolutely no idea,' confessed Michelle. 'But I know one thing. I'm not getting rid of it.' She shuddered. 'Never again. Once was bad enough.'

'What?' exclaimed Penny, unsure if she'd heard right. 'You went through this before?'

'Sure did,' said Michelle, tossing her hair back and squaring her shoulders, forcing Penny to back off. 'A couple of years ago, before I worked here. I wasn't much older than you. Bastard didn't want to know, said he'd tell my parents, and I thought my dad would kill me. Left me with nowhere to turn and frightened as hell. I went and got rid of it, and it was disgusting. Hurt a lot and I had to pretend I had flu when I got home, trying to sleep it off while I was sharing the room with my sisters. Like I still do. Then I've blamed myself ever since.' She paused. 'So I won't be doing that again. Trouble is, I don't know what I will do.'

'You poor mare,' said Maureen. 'I don't know what to suggest. If you was to change your mind I could help you, put you in touch with someone. It's all legit, no backstreet business, I wouldn't do that. It's all hygienic and everything.'

'Thanks but no thanks,' said Michelle with determination. 'I might not know much but I know I won't change my mind on this one. It's not that I want to be a mother or anything, I just don't want the guilt of knowing there was a life in me and then the next minute there isn't.'

Penny gasped. 'But if you don't want to be a mother then how can you go ahead and have the baby?' she cried. 'You can't keep it and not want it. That's not fair on the child, it really isn't. Believe me.' She was nearly in tears herself. 'It's no fun being an unwanted child. It's the worst feeling in the world. I should know.'

'Oh come off it,' Michelle began. 'There's a lot worse.

From where I'm standing now it seems as if there are plenty of worse things. Kids manage. Was your mum so bad?'

'Yes, she absolutely was,' spat Penny, unable to restrain herself though she knew her friend wanted comfort and advice, not to be burdened by her own sorrows. 'She was awful. She didn't give a shit about me. She should never have had me: I spent half my childhood wishing I'd never been born. She didn't know how to love anyone except herself and the terrible thing was that when she died part of me was glad, because we wouldn't have to pretend any more. I'm not making it up. Am I, Maureen?'

Maureen sighed bitterly. 'No, I can't say you are,' she said. 'That woman was something else. I'm sorry you ended up with her, but we can't choose our family. At least you always had Lorna.'

Penny was crying now, which strangely made Michelle buck up and take notice. 'So how come you've turned out as normal as you have?' she asked. 'If you didn't get loved when you were little?'

'That would be down to Lorna,' Maureen explained. 'For some reason she put up with Penny's mum as a friend and then a boss, before she finally had the sense to tell her to stick it. But she knew Penny from when she was a toddler and always looked after her. She does still. She's my cousin and she's pretty well looked after me too, plenty of times when I was in hot water, even though she's not much older than me. Sometimes I think it's Fate's way of balancing things out.' She stopped to think it through. 'You get given a shit deal, like having Ruth for a mother. But then along comes someone who just loves you anyway. That Lorna knows how to love. She

320

got a raw deal too, she couldn't have children, but then she got Penny. That's just how it was.'

Michelle gave a wan smile. 'Then maybe you were lucky after all, Penny. Pity my kid won't have a Lorna to look after it. Suppose I'll have to think of something else.' She almost laughed. 'Maybe one of my fairy godmother friends will step in. Talking of them, where's Juliet? She always sorts things out.'

Maureen managed to stop herself from commenting that Michelle had finally noticed. She took a deep breath, wondering how much she should reveal. 'She's not here at the moment, love,' she said. 'She had stuff to do and has gone away for a bit.'

'What?' Michelle's face fell. 'What, she's done that now? Shit. I . . . I . . . kind of counted on having her around. I know that's selfish but she always knows what to do, and I thought . . .'

'You'll have to make do with us,' said Maureen. 'Will that be so bad?'

'No, no, I didn't mean that,' Michelle said hurriedly. 'You won't tell anyone, will you? Well, Mark will have to know, I realise that. But otherwise? I'll need to keep working until the last possible moment.'

'He'd better start thinking of something else for you to wear then,' said Maureen matter-of-factly. 'As there's not much to hide behind in your costume at the moment.'

Michelle groaned. 'Oh no, everyone'll see my stretch marks. They'll never pay to see me again.'

'You can put concealer on them,' Maureen told her. 'You won't be the first. What, you think no girl in our line of business ever had a baby? I know all the tricks, I've seen it all. So if I can't help you get rid of it I'll help you hide it as long as you can. But then, after that, it'll be up to you.'

It wasn't until some weeks later that the phone finally rang in the small flat. Penny went to answer it as Maureen was not yet back. She'd all but given up hope of John ever calling and expected it to be Lorna, with more news of what was going on in Margate – which never seemed to be very much. She didn't know whether to tell her about Michelle's pregnancy, realising that it might make her worry, fearing the same could happen to Penny. Yet it seemed strange not to talk about something that was affecting all of their lives.

When a male voice spoke she almost dropped the receiver.

'Hello? Hello? Penny, is that you?'

'Yes, it's me.' There was no mistaking who it was at the other end. A thrill shot through her. 'How are you? Where are you?'

'I'm back in South London,' he said. 'Thank God. As for how I am, I'm being driven half mad by the midge bites. They were worse than ever this time. I can't describe how glad I am to be away from them.'

'How . . . how was the rest of your trip?' She was almost shaking with delight and relief. 'Did you get the pictures you wanted?'

'Think so – I haven't had them all developed yet but I saw some amazing stuff and hope I caught it all on film.' John paused. 'I'll tell you all about it when we meet, shall I?'

'I'd love that,' said Penny, wondering if he could hear the smile in her voice. She took her courage in both hands. 'Would you still like to come round here and I'll cook you something?'

'Yes please,' he said at once.

'Brilliant. When can you come?'

'Give me time to get some decent pictures done. Let me see . . . next Tuesday? How would that be?'

'Perfect,' said Penny, already planning on getting Maureen out of the flat that evening. 'Is there anything you don't like to eat?'

'Any instant or tinned soup,' he said. 'Anything deep-fried. Or fish and chips. I usually love it but I'm sick to death of it as where I was for ages only had one hot takeaway and that was the chippy. I've had enough to last for years.'

'Okay, I won't do that then,' she said happily. 'You'll get something special from Jimmy's stall. How does that sound?'

'Perfect,' he said. 'Shall I come round at about seven? I can drop round to the office and then come to you from there.'

'Sounds good,' Penny said, hugging herself. 'I'll see you then.'

She almost burst out singing as she put down the receiver.

Chapter Thirty-Eight

Maureen told herself that it was a crazy idea and to forget about it, but somehow it wouldn't go away. It had lodged in her mind the day Michelle had broken her news and now it was fixed there, demanding that she do something about it.

She didn't even know if it was possible. It might be out of the question. She also didn't know if anybody else involved would be happy about it or not. She might be living in a fantasy world but the idea kept insisting that it was the perfect solution to everyone's problems.

The one thing she did know was that she couldn't mention it without checking out some details first. She didn't want to raise false hopes or, if it went down badly, give massive offence for no good reason. She debated with herself the best thing to do and faced the fact that it would all take ages.

Well, isn't as if you haven't got time on your hands, Maureen told herself sternly. Now that you've given Stuart the boot, look at all those empty hours in the evenings. And you wake up fresher and raring to go, not knackered or hung over. So jump to it and stop putting it off. Do something for someone else for a change.

She paid for her groceries at the local supermarket and wandered back out into the sunshine, waving at some of the market traders as she went. She was tempted to stop for a natter or to see if there were any bargains to be had, but knew she was just putting off the moment when she had to act. Right, she thought. Do it now. Get yourself up those stairs and open the Yellow Pages. Because if it does take a long time, any delays now might mean it's all too late.

Penny was also walking through the market, pausing at each stall, wondering what to cook that would demonstrate how good she was in the kitchen without taking up too much time while her guest was there.

'I hear you're going to have company,' shouted Jimmy. 'Word travels fast around here you know.'

'It's no secret,' Penny said, thinking it was a good job it wasn't, as several of the other stall holders were nodding their heads as if they knew exactly what Jimmy was on about. 'It's only a meal for a friend. What have you got for me, then? If I do chicken and pasta, what would go with that?'

'I got you just the thing,' Jimmy told her, turning for a bowl. 'Here, you have these lovely tasty red onions, and some red peppers as well, and seeing as it's you I'll put these in on top. How about that? Can't say fairer than that.'

'They look lovely,' she said, tipping them into her bag. 'Here you go. I'll bring you any leftovers if you like.'

'Don't expect there'll be much in the way of those,' Jimmy replied. 'I hear your friend has arrived back starved of good food. Says he'll never eat another chip again. So you better do him a huge portion.'

Penny waved at him and made her way to the flat, hurrying up the stairs, throwing the vegetables into their rack. Maureen was putting down the phone as she did so.

'Who was that?' Penny asked idly, picking up an onion that had fallen from the bag.

'Never you mind,' said Maureen shortly. 'Got something to sort out, that's all. None of your business.'

Penny pulled a face behind her back, thinking she didn't have to be so sharp. Maybe her landlady was missing Stuart after all. Best let her get on with it. 'I'll be off again then,' she said hurriedly.

Maureen sighed. 'No need. I got to go out, got to see some people down the council. They don't tell you nothing down the phone. I got to show my face and persuade them in person.' She nodded decisively. 'And no time like the present to do it, so I'll catch you later.'

'Not too much later,' Penny said in alarm. 'You did say you'll be out this evening, didn't you?'

'Keep your hair on, yes, I haven't forgotten,' said Maureen. 'You want the place to yourself so you can reward the Microwave Man. I'll be nowhere to be seen. Just make sure you give him my very best regards.' She winked as she left the flat.

What was Maureen up to, Penny wondered, it wasn't like her to react like that. Well, she didn't have time to worry about that now. She had a meal to plan and an evening to prepare for.

Michelle struggled grimly with her sequinned top, finding that she couldn't get the hooks to fasten and the spaghetti straps dug painfully into the flesh of her shoulders.

Glancing in the dressing room mirror, she shook her head. It was as if she had been squeezed into a strange new shape. It was not a good look. Nobody was going to pay to see that.

'Mark!' she called. She could see him on the other side of the room behind a clothes rail. 'Can you give me a hand?'

'Think you're going to need more than a hand, dear,' he said, coming over and eyeing her critically. 'Crowbar more like. Ugh, look at those red marks. Do they hurt?'

'Of course they bloody hurt,' she scowled. Was he winding her up deliberately? 'You got to get me something else to wear or else make this thing bigger. My boobs are swelling and they won't fit in this no more. I can't go on in this.'

'Hmmm, maybe a strip of extra material here . . .' He pulled at the hooks and Michelle let out a little scream. 'Okay, maybe not, as that won't help the straps and they're too thin to let out. We'd better get you something different. You need reinforcing, darling.'

'Bloody marvellous,' muttered Michelle. But she didn't have the energy to argue. She didn't have the energy to do anything. It took all her will power to get out of bed in the morning and drag herself over here, and not to be sick while she did so.

Mark wandered off and then returned with a similar top but with thicker straps. 'Here, try this. It's one size bigger and you can adjust it here, and here. That'll give you room to manoeuvre.' He helped her into it, trying to avoid the painful red welts from the first straps. 'How are you feeling, then? You seem to be managing all right in the evenings, getting out there and keeping up with the rest.'

'Sort of.' Michelle pulled at the hem and looked at herself in the mirror, smoothing out the creases. 'Yes, this is much better, thanks. Well, I'm glad you think I'm managing. It doesn't always feel like that.' She sank into a chair. 'Tell you the truth, I don't know how I'm going to cope. I'm just about keeping going for now but not knowing what's going to happen is doing my head in.'

'Must be difficult,' agreed Mark, sitting down beside her. 'What about your parents? Have you told them yet?'

'Had to, when I was sick one morning and they could hear me,' she admitted. 'That wasn't much fun. They're very disappointed in me. They didn't get angry but I just knew.' She shook her head. 'It's not that they don't want to help, but there's so many of us already. The house is bursting at the seams.'

'Bit like you, dear,' said Mark.

'Stop it. It's not funny. I can't stay there with a baby and I can't really go anywhere else. I wouldn't want to be on my own with it, I wouldn't know what to do. To be honest, I don't want to be with it at all.'

Mark looked directly at her. 'So what do you want, then? Stop for a minute and just imagine what you'd like if it was an ideal world. Other than to put the clock back and the condom not to split.'

Michelle twisted her hands, trying to find an answer. Eventually she said, 'I don't think I'm the right person to bring up this baby. I'm not saying that I'm bad or what I did was wrong, I just don't think I'm old enough. Not in my head.'

'So . . .' said Mark, encouraging her.

'If my fairy godmother was to show up right now, and it would be spot-on timing if she did, I'd say find this baby a lovely family. One that had a bit of money to give it a good life, one that had space for it, one that would love it and know how to look after it as I would like to but just can't.' Michelle burst into tears.

'There, there,' said Mark anxiously. 'Don't cry. Don't whatever you do drip your mascara on this nice new top. No, no, don't take on.' He gave her a hug. 'Who's to say we can't find your baby a family?'

'How?' demanded Michelle. 'Do you think I haven't thought about that? How?'

'Don't know,' said Mark, 'but watch me try.'

'Mark, I know you're owed favours by all sorts of people all over London,' said Michelle, wiping her smudged eyes, 'but this might be beyond even you. Because for the life of me I don't see how you can manage this one.'

It was just after seven when John rang the bell to the flat. Penny had been watching from upstairs while trying not to make it obvious she was doing so, dodging behind the windowframe when she saw him approaching. She felt like one of the curtain twitchers back in Margate, old busy-bodies who used to cluck with disapproval when she walked down the street in her Madonna gear. God, how long ago all that seemed. She'd done a lot of growing up since then.

The sun was shining and it was hard not to feel opti-mistic. Even here in the heart of the city signs that spring had well and truly arrived were everywhere. The neigh-bours opposite had replanted their windowboxes with bright geraniums, and she wondered what it had been like in Scotland, if there had been lots of colour in the sweeping countryside. She'd never had much time for the countryside. She'd been surrounded with it at her boarding school but as she had hated it there, it wasn't much use. It had been one more thing to emphasise how far she was from her mother and how her mother didn't care.

Well, maybe John was going to change all that. She wouldn't mind. Penny was willing for him to change all sorts of things about her. Tingling with excitement, she went to answer the door.

He looked up at her as she stood on the bottom stair above him and his eyes crinkled with pleasure. 'Good to see you,' he smiled.

'It's been ages!' she exclaimed, beckoning him in. 'Come on up.'

Once inside the flat, she could see he had caught the sun, though his hair was as thick and dark as ever.

He laughed when she pointed it out.

'No one ever expects Scotland to be that fine in spring,' he told her. 'I was lucky, we got great conditions and I took all the shots I needed. I'll show you later.' He tapped a wide, flat bag he had tucked under his arm. 'Here, I brought something to drink.' He handed her a bottle. 'What's it been like here?'

'The weather?' she asked. God, he'd been away all this time and they were talking about the weather? 'All right, I think. I haven't really noticed.' She shrugged. 'I'm not out in it much. Too much else going on. Things at work, things going on with my friends.'

'Ah yes, how's the world of translation?' he asked, and she remembered she hadn't actually told him what it was she translated.

'Busy,' she said shortly. 'No, it's fine, most of it is fun. It's just . . . nothing. Are you hungry? Come over to the table and we can eat.'

The smell of freshly made chicken pasta filled the room and they ate swiftly, exchanging smiles and small talk. She was reminded of how comfortable she was around John, how there were no awkward moments or gaping silences. He was the best listener she could think of. She hadn't imagined it. She'd worried that she had, that she'd missed him so much that she'd created a perfect image of someone who didn't exist, but it turned out he was even better company this time.

They made their way over to the sofa after they'd finished, and John poured them some wine. Penny found it went to her head fast – she hadn't had much to drink since that terrible evening when she'd had the vodka and tonic, when she'd learned the truth about Eduardo. This tasted completely different and made her feel very relaxed, so relaxed that she found herself leaning up against him. He didn't pull away.

'So tell me what's been happening to keep you so busy,' he suggested, and before she could stop herself, it all came out – about the club, how Juliet had disappeared, how Michelle had ended up pregnant, how she now no longer felt the same about dancing.

'Sounds like you're pretty much alone,' he said seriously.

'Well, not alone exactly. I've got Maureen, you've met her. And my friend Mark. But they're always busy too.'

'Maybe it's better to call it lonely, then. Is that it? You're feeling lonely?'

'Yes,' Penny said, and stopped. That was exactly it, and she hadn't wanted to put a name to it. She'd been so determined to make it in London, not to call on anyone for help, to set out independently. But the result was that now she was lonely. 'Yes, I suppose I am.'

Gently John stroked her face. 'I don't like to think of you as lonely,' he said. 'You're far too lovely to be lonely for long.'

She smiled uncertainly, not wanting to seem weak. But she was sure he was genuine, not one of these men waiting to take advantage of vulnerable young women. She wasn't so naïve now, she could tell the difference.

'Sounds like you need a special friend,' he went on, gazing into her eyes. 'Is that what you'd like?'

'Yes,' she said, and knew she trusted him completely. And then suddenly they were kissing, and she could feel all her doubts and fears fading away. She had no idea how long it lasted but time seemed to stand still as she floated, her worries and pains disappearing as she held him and felt him hold her, and thought she had never been so safe.

Slowly they pulled apart and he swept her hair away from her eyes.

'You aren't shocked?' she asked, suddenly afraid again. 'About the club, I mean. It's not just any old office job. I know some people don't approve.'

'Don't be silly, Jimmy's always known what Maureen did for a living,' he said. 'It's up to you how you pay your way.'

'That's good,' she laughed. 'Yes, of course, he'd have known for ages. But I know she's had a bad time from her family, nearly all of them won't talk to her.'

'That's unfair,' John said soberly. 'She seems nice.'

'She is,' she said. 'Anyway, it's not as bad as my mother, who was really two-faced. All the time I was growing up she was this heartless businesswoman, really worried about what people thought of her. But Maureen knew her years ago and she was a stripper. Not even a burlesque dancer, just a plain old stripper. She even had a silly stage name, Adrianna.'

'Did you say Adrianna?' asked John, taking a quick gulp of his drink.

'Yes, why?'

'It's a very unusual name,' he said, pulling away. 'Don't think I've come across many of those. I hope you don't mind me asking, but how old are you?'

'Does it make a difference?' she asked, her old fears returning in a rush. 'You must have known I was much younger than you. I'll be seventeen in July.'

'Don't worry,' he said, stroking her hair. 'I just felt I should check. I know you're younger than me, just didn't realise by how much. But it doesn't feel as if we're different ages. You'll think this is silly but I feel as if I've known you for ever.'

Penny sat back as well, but this time in pleasure. 'Really?' she exclaimed. 'That's exactly what I thought when you came round last time. I can't describe why. I told myself it was stupid to feel that way when I'd hardly met you before but those were the very words I used. It's like we're connected somehow, deep down.' She wanted to kiss him again but wasn't sure how to draw him closer. It wouldn't be right to grab him. Yet now John seemed to be moving further away.

'Look,' he said, 'I'm going to leave these pictures with you. I know you're not as obsessed with wildlife as I am and I don't want to bore you. You'll probably think I'm very rude but I need to get back to South London. My . . . my mother hasn't been well and I should drop in on her before it's too late.'

'Oh,' Penny said, disappointed. He hadn't mentioned this before. She was surprised. He'd given no hint that he'd have to leave so soon. But it showed he cared for his family. Maybe it was her talking about her own mother that had reminded him. 'Oh, okay. Pity you can't stay longer.' She smiled invitingly at him. 'You'll be back, won't you?' She tried not to sound too desperate.

'Of course,' he smiled. 'I've left you my pictures, haven't I? I trust you with them. Look after them, won't you?'

'Yes, definitely,' she said, confused now, as he rose to go. She followed him to the door of the flat. 'Well, you have my number, give me a call.'

'I will,' he said, and hugged her. 'Look, here's mine.' He kissed her cheek, but only briefly. How strange, Penny thought. Only minutes ago they'd been kissing properly and now they seemed to be back to being friends. Maybe he didn't like to be rushed?

'Hurry back,' she said. 'I missed you when you were away.'

'And I missed you,' he said. 'I thought about you a lot. Believe me. Thank you for the food, thank you for everything. I'll see you soon.'

And he was gone.

Penny stood there in the middle of the kitchen, not sure what to feel. She'd wanted him to stay much longer, she wanted to be kissed again – she wanted more. Unfamiliar feelings surged through her, quite unlike anything she'd experienced with Eduardo. This felt profound. She couldn't be mistaken. This wasn't an infatuation. This was the real thing. And he'd felt it too – that they'd known each other for ever, that they were connected. So why had he run off?

That's what John had done. He'd escaped, but why? Try as she might she couldn't make sense of it. Picking up the photos, she carried them through to her room and laid them out on the bed, her bedside light shining dimly on them.

Even in those conditions she could tell they were outstanding. Penny didn't know much about photography, but he seemed to have captured the essence of the creatures – birds, hares, deer. It was as if he was in sympathy with them, somehow he understood them.

How could he take pictures like this but let her down? She couldn't have got it wrong. John was a good man through and through. She just didn't understand him. Yet.

Chapter Thirty-Nine

John almost ran down the stairs and only the thought that Penny might be able to see him stopped him from flying down the street outside as fast as he could go. He couldn't believe what he had just heard. Surely there was a mistake. He tried to think clearly but all he could hear was the name Adrianna over and over in his head.

There had to be other women by that name, he told himself. It was unusual but not completely unheard of. And yet that hair, the shape of her face . . . was he imagining it or was there a resemblance? And the fact that she was only sixteen – that was surprising enough on its own, he'd thought she was older, but if she really was that young then did that fit with what had happened in the past?

There was a pub coming up on the corner and he went in and ordered a beer to give himself a chance to calm down. This wasn't how the evening was supposed to go. He couldn't believe it when he'd arrived. Penny was even more beautiful than he'd remembered her, and she was so interesting to talk to, so lovely in every way. He'd hoped against hope she'd feel the same and when she'd held him and kissed him he had had the overwhelming sensation that somehow he'd come home. Now he feared something unspeakable had very nearly happened.

John cast his mind back to the strange events when he was a schoolboy. He'd always known that the man he called Dad wasn't his real father. Everyone had been open about that, but it didn't matter as Derek was the man who'd raised him and looked after him as well as anyone could have done. But when he was about thirteen he'd been told that his real father, Kevin, was going to be released from prison. They hadn't wanted him to hear the full extent of Kevin Dolby's crimes but he'd found out anyway and they sickened him. Dolby had pretended to repent and to find religion but it had all been a ruse to con his own parents out of their money.

Even though John's mother, Pearl, had wanted nothing more to do with her first husband, she'd been happy for her son to continue to see his grandparents. John had loved his grandfather, who'd encouraged his love of birds and nature and praised him for his skill at drawing. His grandmother had been a difficult character, but he knew she'd loved him, in her own way. It was while he'd been staying with her that he'd encountered Adrianna.

Kevin had turned up at the little bungalow with a very glamorous woman in tow, and there had been a right to-do, as there hadn't been room for everyone to fit in the place. Adrianna hadn't exactly helped, seeming to think she was above it all, looking down her nose at them. But even then John had been able to tell there was something very special about her. He'd been too young to have had anything to do with girls and had barely begun to think of them in that way, but this woman had made a deep impression on him. It was only when he grew older that he'd put a name to her star quality: sex appeal.

Could this woman have been Penny's mother?

Sickened to his stomach, John began to count back the years. Was it possible? If Adrianna was her mother, could it be that Kevin Dolby – his own father – was her father too? Was the young woman he'd been kissing so ardently just an hour ago in fact his own half-sister?

Mark was watching the dancers anxiously from the wings when he sensed Maureen coming up behind him. He nodded towards Michelle.

'Doing all right, isn't she?'

Maureen watched for a while and then nodded. 'Not bad at all. You wouldn't know. But it's early days yet.'

Mark turned and whispered, 'Let's go where we can talk properly.' He knew the dancers hated anyone having even a muttered conversation anywhere near them. Although the audience couldn't hear it, they claimed it put them off.

Leading the way to the small kitchen area, where he automatically put on the kettle, Mark wondered how to put what he wanted to say. 'I was talking to her earlier,' he began.

Maureen waited, not sure where this was going to go. She opened the biscuit tin to see if anyone had brought in something interesting but there were just the remains of some old Rich Tea. She didn't fancy those.

'She looks okay but underneath she's a mess,' he said. 'She told me what she'd really like, in an ideal world.'

'And what's that?' Maureen asked sceptically. 'Not to be pregnant in the first place?'

'Well, apart from that,' he said, pouring two cups of tea.

'No, as that isn't possible, and she's still clear about that, then what she'd want is a family she knew was suitable to raise the baby. She knows she can't do it herself. So I said I'd help find her one.'

She raised her eyebrows. 'You did, did you? And how are you going to do that, then?'

'Not the foggiest,' he said. 'That's why I thought I'd ask you. You know everybody.'

'Thanks a lot,' Maureen said. 'Well, now, as it happens I've been putting out some feelers. I haven't got very far yet. But maybe her and me have been thinking along the same lines. If she wants to have it but not keep it, it's the obvious thing. It's just a case of how to manage it.'

'You make it sound easy,' he said, stirring his tea.

'No, it won't be that,' she said, knowing she was understating it. 'It's going to be bloody complicated. And that's if everyone agrees. I haven't asked people yet. But it helps to know that's what she'd like. I didn't want to suggest it in case I said the wrong thing again.' She sighed and ran her free hand through her hair. 'Penny was right, it can't be no fun being an unwanted child. Funny, I knew she'd had a bad time when she was younger but I'd never heard her put it like that before. Makes you think, don't it?'

'Sounded grim,' Mark agreed. 'She didn't have a father around, then?'

'I think Lorna said he died around the time she was born,' she said. 'Couldn't stand the thought of a lifetime with that bitch Adrianna, or should I say Ruth, I would imagine. Can't say I blame him.'

'She was that bad?' asked Mark.

'Oh yes,' she said. 'She was that bad.'

* * *

John got on the tube at Oxford Circus and was lucky to find a seat. The journey back down to his mother's in Battersea always took ages and he wanted to think. Maybe the beer hadn't helped after all, and on top of the wine as well, but it had given him space to go over what had happened. He'd come to the conclusion that he'd have to talk to his mother about it. She wasn't exactly ill – he'd exaggerated to make his escape – but she wasn't getting any younger and he knew she'd missed him while he'd been away.

The more he thought about it, the more the dates added up. He could remember very clearly that fateful visit to his grandmother. He knew what year at school he'd been in as he could recall his form teacher; it had been not long after they'd moved from Winchester back to his parents' home turf of Battersea, and this teacher had been good to him and helped him settle in what was to him a strange city. Counting forward from then, he could see that what he most feared was only too possible. Adrianna would have been with his own father at exactly the time Penny was conceived. But he couldn't have any way of knowing if she'd been faithful to him or whether he was just one of many boyfriends. Kevin had died not long after, and so there was no way of checking with him – even if his word could have been trusted. Somehow John thought that even if his biological father had lived to a ripe old age, he still wouldn't have believed a word he'd said.

As he changed from the tube to the mainline train he realised he was in shock. While he'd been round the block a few times he still hadn't met the one soul mate who was right for him and he'd begun to nurse the hope that

340

it might be Penny. Now if what he suspected was true that was out of the question. Thank God they'd only kissed. That was bad enough. He paused as the mixture of beer, wine and chicken pasta threatened to come back up again.

If it was true he'd have to break it to her somehow and he didn't think he could bear it. His own disappointment was bad enough; he couldn't stand the thought of witnessing hers. She was blameless in this whole thing. All she'd done was offer him love and kindness and he was going to have to turn her down flat as the consequences didn't bear thinking about.

He strode along the road to his mother's house, the one they'd moved to all those years ago when they'd left Winchester. On the ground floor was the shop she still ran, selling art supplies and crafts. She'd built it up practically from nothing, and he was very proud of her. It cut him to the quick to think he was going to bring the pain of the past back into her life but there was no way round it.

Shutting his eyes, he rang the bell.

Penny was finishing the last of the washing up, a distracted look on her face, when Maureen got back to the flat.

'Not too early, am I?' she grinned. 'Didn't want to interrupt anything but I'd been at that club quite long enough and if I'd stayed any longer Dave would've got me working on something else. He's up to something with the planners again, have you noticed?'

'Mmmmmm,' said Penny, not really listening. 'Sorry, what? No, no, it's fine, he left a while ago.'

'Did you have a good time?' Maureen asked, thinking

that the girl seemed a bit out of sorts. 'Did he like your cooking? Didn't have a row, did you?' She threw her coat on the sofa.

'Of course not,' said Penny, her expression wary. 'Why'd you say that?'

'Because you don't look like someone who's had a wild evening of passion with a wonderful man,' she said frankly. 'Or even a wonderful evening with a lovely, interesting man. You seem a bit . . . I don't know, a bit down.'

Penny deliberately hung up the tea towel as slowly as she could and then turned to face her.

'It was wonderful to start with,' she said. 'We got on better than I could have imagined and everything seemed to be going really well but then he had to leave early. It all happened very suddenly. I don't know, maybe he'd forgotten to tell me when he'd have to go, or he felt . . . he felt I was rushing him. But he'd seemed so happy.' Penny stopped and Maureen thought for a moment she was going to cry. Then she recovered and went on. 'Maybe I was imagining it.'

'Maybe,' Maureen said doubtfully. 'Did he say anything about coming back? You are seeing him again, aren't you? Did you say anything in particular to drive him away?'

Penny shook her head in anguish. 'I don't think so. He said he'd come back – he's left me his new collection of photos and he'll need them. We were just talking about our backgrounds and I mentioned my mother. I was worried he'd be shocked when I told him what she used to do for a living but that didn't seem to be it. And he knew all about the club. So it wasn't as if he was put off by that. So I don't really know.'

Maureen shook her head and tried to think what to

say. She hadn't come across this situation before, in all her vast experience of men. Still, the one thing she did know was that the better you thought you knew them, the less true that proved to be. Maybe this John was more complicated than he'd seemed.

'Not to worry then,' she said as brightly as she could. 'If he's left his stuff here he'll be back. Who knows what the rest of it was about? If it's important he'll tell you. It's good he doesn't mind about the club because, no getting away from it, some folk do. Still, Jimmy would no doubt have told him anyway. So that won't matter. It could be anything and nothing to do with you at all.' She walked across to the little kitchen and hugged the girl, who even in her flat shoes towered above her now. 'You really like him, don't you?'

Penny nodded, and her chin banged against Maureen's shoulder. 'I've never met anyone like him. We feel right together. He thinks so too.'

'There you are, then,' said Maureen, rubbing her back, even while she wondered what all this was about.

'So that's what I'm worried about,' John finished, staring at his mother's kitchen table as he slumped in a chair. 'Am I going mad? Please tell me I'm going mad.'

Pearl shook her head, finding it all too much to take in. It was late, she'd had a tiring day, and now this story of John's seemed almost too impossible to be true. But her heart ached for her son. He was so distressed and she had no way of knowing if he was right or not. She reached out and took his hand across the table.

'You aren't mad,' she reassured him. 'What you say makes some kind of sense. The dates are right. I'll never forget that time, what with your gran ending up in hospital and then Kevin dying. But that doesn't mean this girl's your sister. I never met this Adrianna, neither did Derek, so that doesn't help. But all we knew from what happened after was that she was a stripper, had worked for Vincent Chase the local heavy, and had disappeared around the time his house caught fire. Which was just after Kevin came out of prison. So it could be right.'

John sighed deeply. 'I'll have to ask her if she knows anything. It's not fair on her to keep her in the dark. It's not fair on us, full stop. I thought we . . . I hoped we . . .' He couldn't go on.

Pearl continued to hold his hand, realising how much this young woman must mean to her son. It was strange. She'd often wondered what she would do when he finally met somebody he was serious about; Derek often teased her about still being over-protective of John even though it had been a very long time since he'd needed that protection. But never in a million years had she imagined something like this.

'You'll sleep here tonight,' she told him. 'No sense in going back to your flat this late. We'll think about it in the morning. We'll ask your dad.'

'He won't tell anyone, will he?' asked John, alarmed. 'It mustn't get back to Jimmy. I can't have them all looking at Penny and wondering. That would kill her.'

'No, of course not, you know you can trust him with your life,' said Pearl instantly. 'Now I'm going to make us some cocoa. What we need is a good sleep. Everything might look different in the morning.'

Chapter Forty

Maureen decided to stop by Dave's office early in the morning to see if she could pick his brains before they were too addled with whisky. It was a close-run thing whether it was better to tackle him hung over or drunk, but she needed names and she needed them to be accurate – she didn't need him to be good-tempered.

Just as well, she thought as she pushed open the outer door. She could hear him swearing from the other end of the corridor. 'Bleedin' jobsworths!' he was shouting.

Hurrying down the corridor, Maureen knew all she had to do was get the information and get out, not stick around to be yelled at, blamed or drawn into whatever he was up to this morning.

'Hiya!' she called breezily as she went into his office. 'What's gone on here? Hurricane hit it, has it?'

'Don't be so bleedin' smug,' growled Dave, wiping his already sweaty forehead. 'You have no idea what I go through for this place, no idea. I try to expand it, set up new lines of business, keep your pet niece in work, and then the council try to stop me. One step forward, two steps back. Every bleedin' time.'

'I thought you were all square with them now?'

Maureen asked innocently, beginning to stack the papers that had fallen off the desk. Dave didn't look as if he was in any state to bend down to pick them up.

'Oh we're all right with the Ashdown stuff now,' he said grandly. 'It's a miracle what the right word in the right ear can do. They won't get any further forward with their cockeyed plan. I've cooked their goose good and proper. No, it's the other lot now. All I wanted to do was make one small change to the opening hours and they're on my back soon as you can say knife. You'd think I was a criminal. You'd think I was a Central American cocaine smuggler.' He leered. 'But we sorted them out, didn't we?'

'And I'm sure you'll sort these out as well,' said Maureen, neatly avoiding his attempt to grab hold of her. 'Leave it out, Dave, it's early. I got work to do and so have you. No, I just wondered, with all that hobnobbing you did with the council, if you had any contacts in other departments.'

He looked at her suspiciously. 'Might have, what's it to you? What other departments?'

'Social services,' she said. 'Children's social services.'

'What? You gone soft? You suddenly care about kiddies?'

'Give it a rest, Dave,' she protested. 'You know me better than that. It's not for me, it's for a friend. She's got all tied up in red tape and I said I'd try to find her a short-cut through. You know how it is.'

'I do indeed,' sighed Dave. 'Well, I suppose I owe you a favour. Where's the book?' He hunted through his desk drawer and pulled out a small blue address book she'd never seen before, and flicked through it until he found the page he wanted. 'Here you go. Try either of these but don't say I told you. And I want that book back soon as you've called them, that's my insurance.'

'Thanks, Dave,' she beamed. Maureen took the book and ran out before he could change his mind.

John put down the phone, not knowing whether to be upset or relieved. Penny wasn't in. He had known there was a chance she'd already have left for work but had wanted to try her anyway, after the conversation he'd had with his parents over breakfast. No matter how they tried to reason it away, they'd come to the conclusion they were most likely all talking about the same Adrianna. If that was the case then they had to face the fact that Penny had in all probability been conceived at the time Adrianna was having the affair with Kevin. It didn't prove anything but the possibility was there: they could be half-brother and -sister.

Derek had voiced the other thing that had been worrying him: Penny might have to be told what sort of person Kevin was. Even if she got the watered-down version, it was difficult to make him sound anything other than deeply unpleasant. John didn't want to add to her sorrow, especially as she had such difficult memories of her mother. If these people really had been her parents, how had she turned out as lovely as she had? The three of them had agreed they would face that if they had to, but in the meantime he owed it to her to explain why he'd left in such a hurry and to ask if she knew anything about her father. He'd chance it and drop by her flat again, although he didn't feel happy about spending time alone with her now. But she had to know. Then he could take it from there.

All of this did little to heal the ache inside. Whatever happened John knew he could never look at Penny the same way again, suspecting what they did, even if it could never be proved. He felt they'd been cheated of their chance of love, of happiness. He didn't know what could possibly make up for that.

Maureen almost ran up the stairs to the flat. Now that she knew what she had to do she didn't want to waste a minute. She'd caught up with Michelle when the girl had managed to complete the late-morning dance class, despite looking white as a sheet for most of it. They'd gone to Bar Italia, although Michelle had only had a mineral water, explaining that coffee now made her gag. She was struggling with the journey into town and back as her sense of smell had become extremely sensitive and all those bodies crushed together on the tube made her sicker than ever. Drinking coffee would be the final straw.

Maureen had wanted to check that she'd got the right end of the stick and that what Mark had reported was right. Michelle had laughed and said yes, that if her fairy godmother flew through the door of the coffee bar then that would be what she'd ask for: a sensible, solvent, loving family for her child.

'And you don't trust the authorities to find one?' Maureen said.

'You hear all these horror stories,' Michelle shuddered. 'I wouldn't want to interfere but I'd be happier if I knew for sure the family was the right one. I don't know how the hell that would work but that's what I'd want. Mark said he'd try to find a way.'

'Well, Mark has worked all sorts of miracles,' said Maureen noncommittally. 'Let's see how he does with this one.'

Now she burst through the door of her flat, only to find Penny standing in the middle of the living room, her face stricken.

'Oh my good God, what has happened?' demanded Maureen, all other thoughts driven from her head. 'Why aren't you at work? What's going on?'

Penny was shaking as she went across to the sofa and slowly lowered herself on it. 'It can't be true,' she said. 'This is the craziest thing I've ever heard.'

'For God's sake, what is it?'

'It's . . . I can't believe it. I only popped back to change my shirt as I got tea all over the other one. The phone went when I got here and it was John. He got me to meet him outside, wouldn't come up here. He told me the most unbelievable thing.' She was trembling as she spoke.

'Go on,' said Maureen, with no idea of what this could be about.

'You know I told him about my mother. Well, he thinks he knew her. He said I looked like her. I do, don't I?'

'Yes,' Maureen replied. 'You do. The hair, the shape of your face. There's a definite resemblance. That's no bad thing, she was a real looker, as you know.'

'There's more,' said Penny. 'It turns out Mum used to go out with John's father – his real father, not his step-father who's Jimmy's friend. He went to see his family last night and they worked it out. I might be their child. He might be my brother.'

'Hang on,' said Maureen. 'That can't be right. Your dad

died in Spain, and he was much older than your mum. Don't you have any pictures of him anywhere?'

'Mum did,' said Penny, 'but I didn't bring them with me. What's the point? I never knew him. And I didn't want a picture of her, you'd have to pay me good money to have her face staring down at me. I left one at Lorna's.'

'Then that's simple,' said Maureen decisively. 'We'll go down to Margate, find the picture, see how much you look like him and ask Lorna what she knows at the same time. How's that? That mean old sod Dave owes you time off and I could do with a day or two away from his moaning. You should have heard him this morning. So let's give her a ring. I miss Margate, and it'll be lovely now, while the sun's out but the crowds haven't arrived yet. We'll soon put this stupid idea to rest. How does that sound?'

'Okay, yes, that'd be good,' said Penny, and yet she couldn't shake the feeling that it wouldn't be that easy.

'Guess what,' said Lorna as Robert put down his briefcase in the hall. He'd been working late again – she'd tried to tell him to stop but business was booming once more and he was making up for all the time they'd lost waiting for the insurance after the big storm. She could see how tired he was by the skin around his eyes but he tried to hide it.

'What?' he demanded, giving her a hug. 'Must be something important for you to meet me on the doorstep. Good or bad?'

'Good, I think,' said Lorna. 'Well, yes, definitely good. Penny and Maureen are coming down tomorrow for a couple of days. But Maureen sounded a bit odd, so there might be more to it than a last-minute break.'

'You have to admit it, Maureen often sounds odd,' Robert pointed out. 'That's just how she is. Nothing unusual there.'

'That's not what I meant,' insisted Lorna, following him through to the kitchen. 'We'll eat in about twenty minutes, is that all right? No, she sounded odd for her.'

'Well, we'll find out tomorrow,' remarked Robert, who plainly wasn't in the mood to speculate what her cousin might be leading up to. 'It'll be nice to see Penny. She hasn't been down since Christmas and I keep missing her when she phones.'

'Shouldn't work late so often then,' said Lorna before she could stop herself. 'Well, don't look like that, you know it's true. Yes, that was one of the strange things. Maureen asked if I could dig out that old photo of Penny's father. I don't know if you've ever even seen it. He's about seventy and wearing a navy jacket.'

Robert shook his head. 'Doesn't ring any bells. But no harm in you having a look for it. That girl's had no luck, has she? First a father who dies before she's born and then a stepfather who doesn't want to know. I haven't bumped into Adam for ages but to be honest I'm happy to keep it that way. She's better off without him.'

'I couldn't agree more,' said Lorna. Even thinking about that man made her furious all over again on Penny's behalf. How could he treat that lovely girl so badly? He didn't deserve a stepdaughter. He'd been given a gift and he'd thrown it away. 'If I saw him again I'd want to slap him. Still, she does have one good father figure in her life. You've been wonderful with her for all these years, you've just never got the credit from him.' She shut her eyes. That made her angry too. Robert had had no reason to take Penny in, and, given the way Adam and Ruth had treated him, in fact had every reason not to. But he'd never objected and had welcomed her, even with her stroppy teenage attitude and taste for loud music and weird clothes.

Robert smiled and almost blushed – a rare outward display of emotion. 'I'd like to think so,' he said. 'Because when it comes down to it, we are her family, aren't we? I know it's not official. But in every way that counts, we are.'

Chapter Forty-One

Penny found herself looking forward to the trip back to Margate. It felt like ages since she'd been back. Although she regularly talked to Lorna on the phone and sometimes to Robert, it wasn't the same. After everything that had happened she found she missed them more than she wanted to admit. She was also looking forward to Lorna's home cooking. It was the most comforting food in the world.

The sun was out and the seagulls were crying as they arrived. 'Should have brought our swimming costumes,' she grinned at Maureen as they made their way along the platform. 'We could have gone to the lido.'

'No thank you very much,' Maureen shuddered. 'It'll still be freezing. And I haven't had time to perfect my body for the beach yet. I'll stay under wraps if it's all the same to you.'

Lorna was waving excitedly at them from the car park. She ran towards them as they approached, and gave them each a big hug. 'About time too,' she exclaimed. 'Do you want to go straight back to the house or along the front for a bit?'

'Along the front,' said Penny instantly. Now they were

here, she wanted to make the most of it and to put off the moment of truth for as long as possible. 'You don't realise how much you'll miss the sea until you're away from it.'

So they drove back the long way round, going past the few early holidaymakers clutching their hats in the breeze, stopping for ice cream, pointing out their old haunts. It was over an hour later before they pulled into the neat drive, and Penny could see that the garden was as immaculate as ever.

It was strange to step back into her old room. When she'd been down for Christmas she'd been taken up with all the rituals of the season and hadn't really had time to think then. Now Penny was struck again by all that had happened since she had lived here. She could have stayed here and been safe from it all. But then I'd have been stuck with Mrs Manning, she thought. That was like a living death. Despite it all I did the right thing in leaving. I just hope Lorna and Robert agree.

It wasn't until that evening that they got down to business.

'Did you manage to find that old photo I asked you about?' Maureen began.

Lorna went to a box on the sideboard and took one out. 'Is this it? It had got stuck between a couple of books we moved from your room, Penny.'

Penny took the photo which showed a good-looking man in a smart navy jacket, who was maybe in his early seventies. 'That's my father,' she said. 'It's Laurence Hamilton-Smyth. I think that's the only picture of him that's left.' She looked up at Lorna. 'Unless you have any?'

'No, I'm afraid not,' said Lorna. 'He had already died by the time I moved to Spain and met your mother. She used to have other pictures of him around your house, I remember that, but I don't know what happened to them. He always looked the same – well turned out, quite formal. If he looked like that at his age, he must have been quite something when he was young.'

'Can I have that?' Maureen asked, taking the photo from Penny and holding it up. She looked at it critically. 'Hard to say, really.'

'What's hard to say?' demanded Lorna. 'What are you doing?'

'Trying to see if there's a resemblance,' her cousin explained, turning the picture at an angle. 'We wanted to see if Penny looked like her father in any way.'

'Why?' Lorna asked.

Maureen and Penny looked at each other. Finally Maureen said, 'You'd better tell them what this is about. Are you okay to do that?'

Penny nodded and then, with a sensation of diving in at the deep end, she started the story.

Lorna grew increasingly uneasy as the tale unfolded, shifting in her seat and looking at the floor.

'So,' Maureen said when Penny came to a stop. 'Can you tell us anything? I know you weren't there when Ruth moved to Spain or when her husband died, but was there anything you remember that might help? I don't see how we can tell from one old photograph.'

'Penny, you poor thing,' Lorna gasped. 'I'd no idea you were having such a terrible time. You hide it so well over the phone. I wish I'd been there to give you a big hug.'

Penny smiled, grateful for the way Lorna always loved

her and wasn't afraid to show it, but impatient now to see if there was anything new to learn. 'It's hard enough to talk about it face to face,' she said. 'There was no way I could do it when I rang. So that's why we wanted to come here, or one of the reasons anyway.' She tried to look positive but was afraid her lip was trembling again.

'I see,' said Lorna. She took a deep breath. 'I'm not sure how much help I can be. As you know, I only met your mother when you were a toddler, and Laurence was long dead by then. As far as I knew, she was a respectable widow, whose much-older husband had left her comfortably off. From the pictures of him around the place I assumed she'd loved him and there was no more to it.'

'But?' said Maureen, sensing that wasn't the whole story.

'Well, for a start you came out on your visit,' said Lorna. 'When you said you recognised her and where from, that rather destroyed the respectable bit. She didn't like that at all. She hid it well but I think she was furious. She was also short of money by then so, as you know, we both sold up and came back.'

'Yes, we know that,' said Maureen, growing irritated, 'but what else? Come on, I know when you're not saying something.'

Lorna twisted her hands together and wouldn't meet their eyes. 'It might be nothing,' she said. 'It's hardly definitive proof either way. But yes, she did say something. We used to drink at lunchtimes over there quite a bit – well, you know that too, we did that when you came over.' She grinned briefly at her cousin then looked away again. 'One day we'd been to the bar together and had some wine with our salads. It was when my marriage was breaking up and I was pretty upset, so I said to her

356

that I was sorry, as it must bring back what it was like to lose Laurence and even worse not to have him round when Penny was little.' She sighed. 'It was hard, as I was falling apart really, so what she said was a shock and that's why I never forgot it. She said, not really. He'd been a means to an end. He'd been nice enough and she'd been lucky to meet him when she did but she wasn't particularly sorry he was dead. She even laughed about it. She said he'd looked the part but hadn't been up to much otherwise, which she was glad of, as she'd had quite enough of all that. As for fathering a child, that had been nothing to do with him.'

Penny gave a gasp. 'So we're wasting our time trying to see if I look like the photo.'

Lorna shrugged. 'Well, she might have been saying it to make me angry, or rub in the fact she'd had lots of men and I'd lost the only one I'd ever loved – sorry, Penny, but it was exactly the sort of thing she'd do. Or she might have been carried away with the drink and made up any old thing.'

Maureen looked sceptical. 'Always possible, I suppose, but that's not how I remember her. She could always handle her drink. Vince would have killed her if she couldn't, she knew too much and could have dropped him in it if she was loose-lipped. Even when she'd had a few, she never got carried away.'

'Oh no.' Another thought struck Penny. 'You don't think that thug could be my father, do you?'

'Hang on, you counted the months,' said Maureen. 'Nobody who had anything to do with Battersea in those days would have forgotten the night Chase's house caught fire. I remember the uproar at the club at the time – we all thought we'd be out of a job. No, unless you were an unusually late baby, I can't see it. And, to be frank, you look absolutely nothing like him. Which you should be heartily glad about.'

'Would that be worse than finding that my real father is also John's real dad?' demanded Penny. 'I don't know what to believe. She didn't tell you who it was by any chance? But in any case I'm not who I thought any more. I thought my dad was this nice rich old chap who died seventeen years ago. Now I find he's probably someone my mother had a fling with before fleeing the country. I don't know if I look like him, if I have any of his habits or if my character is like his. And I've got no way of knowing. So who am I?'

'You're who you've always been,' Lorna assured her, going across and hugging her. 'You are your own person, you've always known your own mind, and just because you have someone's genes it doesn't mean you have to be like them. I mean, you look like your mother but you're nothing like her in many ways.'

'Thank God,' muttered Maureen.

'That's not what I meant,' said Lorna hastily. 'Well, she was very determined and you have some of that. And also she was very bright, which you are. But you know how to love, Penny, and that's a wonderful thing. She never had that, I think it was because she'd had an awful childhood and nobody showed her any affection. I used to feel sorry for her.'

'Sorry!' exclaimed Penny. 'I never felt sorry for her. She knew how to love herself all right. And her bank balance. And that selfish bastard Adam. Just not me. It's too much. I want to be by myself.'

She ran out of the room, her eyes brimming over with tears.

Lorna made to follow her.

'No, let her go,' said Robert, who'd been listening to it all without commenting. 'She's got a lot to take in. We can't do it for her. It's bad enough for us to try to understand, heaven only knows how she feels. Thank God they found out now is all I can say.'

'I thought John was such a nice man,' groaned Maureen. 'Well he was, he is. I encouraged them. This is unbelievable. If it was anyone else telling me this I'd wonder if they'd made it up but as it's you there's no doubt. That sodding Adrianna is having the last laugh from beyond the grave again.'

Lorna half-smiled. 'Don't. The more I think about that day, the more certain I am that she was telling the truth. She'd no reason to make it up and had every reason to keep it quiet. She'd just had one glass too many. She never referred to it again. But looking back it all makes sense. She never showed any signs of wanting Penny around.'

'Must be strange, being a mother but wishing your child was elsewhere,' Maureen said slowly.

'I can't begin to imagine what that feels like,' said Lorna hotly. 'I think it's beyond understanding. I've never got over not being able to have children. I don't feel like a freak any more' – she glanced gratefully at Robert – 'but knowing your body has let you down like that is hard to bear. I feel for Penny as if she was my own child. We both do. It's hard to accept that she's growing up now and having to face problems like this.'

Maureen sat back in her chair and exhaled slowly.

'While it's just us,' she began, 'there's something else I want to talk to you about.'

Penny felt lethargic as they travelled back on the train. She didn't have the energy to talk and wouldn't have known what to say anyway. It was still sinking in: the man she had had such high hopes for was probably her brother. Her mother had lied to her all her life about who her father was. She was left with nothing.

Everyone had been very kind and had crept around her as if she was ill, but she'd barely noticed them. It was as if she was sensing the world from beyond a wall of glass. Lorna had made her favourite meals and Robert had talked about teaching her to drive after the summer, and half-joked about her making a career from her skills in the kitchen, but there seemed no point to any of it.

As they pulled into Victoria Station she made up her mind to act. As soon as they reached the flat she dropped her bag by her bedroom door and went straight to the phone.

Fingers trembling, she dialled the number on the scrap of paper.

'John?' she said, as her call was answered. 'It's Penny. I've been asking around and it's awful. I think you were right. I think your father was my father.' She waited while he had a chance to take that in and respond.

'No, I know. I thought they were going to say I was talking rubbish but they didn't. Look, you'd better come round and collect those pictures. I can't keep them here, there's no room. Whenever you like. All right, Monday after work.'

She put down the phone and looked up at Maureen,

who was watching her with concern. 'So, I'll tell him what I know and then we can call it a day,' she said quietly. 'That'll be that. I'll never see him again. It's for the best, isn't it?' Penny stared at Maureen as if there might be some last-minute way out of it.

'Afraid so, love,' said Maureen. 'I'm afraid so.'

Chapter Forty-Two

Waiting until Monday evening was agony. Penny was dreading seeing John again, knowing that this must be their final meeting, and yet she longed for him to be there, she missed him so much. She dragged herself to work and went through the motions but hardly heard anything anyone said to her. Dave tried to get her interested in some new clients but didn't get very far. She even found it hard to talk to Mark.

'What's up with you today, then?' he demanded. 'Cat got your tongue? You've just had a couple of days at the seaside, you lucky cow. You should be full of the joys of spring.'

She smiled at him but her heart wasn't in it. 'I'll tell you about it later,' she promised. 'Just not now.'

Finally it was time to go back to the flat and face what was coming.

John arrived just after seven and she didn't know how to greet him. Every fibre in her body wanted to hug him and draw him close but she didn't dare. She waved him into the flat, keeping her distance, unsure what to say. There was nothing to say that would make things any better.

'Do you want something to drink?' Penny asked. At least if she was making tea she wouldn't have to look at him.

He shook his head. 'Better not,' he said. 'I think we should just get this over with, don't you?'

Part of her wanted to agree and part of her wanted to make him stay as long as possible. 'Okay,' she said. 'You're probably right.'

'It's not what I would have wanted,' he said hastily. 'You know that, don't you?'

She couldn't bear to look at him. 'Of course,' she said. 'Me neither. I wish . . . I wish . . . it was anything but this. I'll go and get those pictures.' Penny almost ran out of the room as she was sure she was going to cry and couldn't stand the idea of breaking down in front of John. She shut her bedroom door and took some deep breaths, struggling to control herself. Get a grip, she thought. You can't just leave him out there. Like he said, get it over with.

Picking up the photos, she forced herself to go back into the living room. 'Here you are,' she said. 'They're really good. I hope you do well with them.'

'Thanks,' he said. 'Glad you liked them.'

Oh God, she thought, is this it? What must we sound like? She couldn't think of a way of saying what she really felt but luckily he must have thought the same.

'Penny, this is the hardest thing I've ever done,' he said suddenly. 'We can't see each other again, it's too much. I'd hoped for so much more. I've never met anyone like you. But we can't go on, not now we know we're related. And I can't bear to see you. I want to comfort you but I can't. So I'm going to go.'

She gave a big sob, she couldn't help it.

'You've got my number,' he said. 'The one thing is, if you ever decide you want to know more about our family, then ring me. It's only right. You probably don't feel much like it at the moment but the offer's there if you ever want it.'

She nodded, trying not to give way completely. 'Thanks,' she managed to say.

'I'll go,' he said hastily. He came across to her and pecked her very quickly on the cheek. Then he turned towards the stairs.

'Bye,' she said, frozen to the spot.

He was gone. All Penny's hope, excitement and plans for future happiness went with him. She stared at the door, not wanting to believe it was true. Any minute now she'd wake up and they'd be back at the beginning of the evening when she'd cooked for him, when things had gone so well to start with. Only this time there'd be no mention of her mother, no recognition of her stupid name. They'd be able to love each other freely, just as they both wanted so desperately.

It was too much. She threw herself on the sofa and cried as if her heart would break, for all the things she thought she was going to do and to have and now were forever beyond her reach. Penny couldn't imagine feeling that deep sense of connection with anyone else again and now it had been ripped from her. How was she to go on, knowing that everything that really mattered was over before it had had a chance to begin? She cried until she could cry no more and finally, totally exhausted, she fell asleep.

Somehow Penny got through the next few days. She had no idea what she did or who she talked to but mechanically went through the hours, speaking very little and avoiding Mark and Michelle. She did her work, she came home, she ate whatever was in the cupboard without tasting anything, then she went to sleep. Then she did the same thing over again the next day. And the next. All the while she felt as if she was one big gaping wound, the hurt so intense she thought she would die of it. It was strange, but most people didn't even notice. If Dave saw something was different he didn't show it, just deluged her with piles of paperwork, which in a strange way she was grateful for, as it meant she didn't have time to think. She typed up notes and filed them away, sorted out his diary and typed some more. It filled the time and that was all that mattered.

Maureen mostly left her alone and for that Penny was thankful. She wasn't interested in her pity as it wouldn't solve anything. Nothing could ever put this right and yet somehow she had to learn to live with it. It felt like an impossible task.

Slowly the weeks dragged by, then a month, then another. Spring turned into summer and people were out on the streets, sitting in the pavement cafés and bars until late at night, taking more time at the market, making the most of the sunshine. Penny wasn't one of them. She rarely went to the market now as she couldn't face Jimmy; she had stopped shopping at the Italian deli as she couldn't pretend to be friendly and interested in the food. She went to the supermarket now, bought as little as possible to get by, and cooked only if she had to. Maureen had gone back to takeaways and sometimes she joined her. Everything tasted the same so it barely mattered.

* * *

It wasn't until they were well into July that something changed.

Penny had at least stopped avoiding Mark, which was just as well as it was hard when they both worked at the same place. They were sitting in their favourite café one lunchtime, watching the crowds flow by outside, when a familiar figure came into view.

'Bloody hell!' exclaimed Mark. 'I don't believe it. Look over there!'

Pushing her way through to the door of the café, long golden hair swinging, was Juliet: Juliet as she used to be, skin glowing, beautiful as ever, no sign of the haggard features of some months ago. She waved in delight.

'Thought I might find you here!' she called. 'Room for another?'

Penny gasped in surprise. 'Is it really you? Where have you been? What's been going on?'

Mark reached across and hugged her. 'You're looking marvellous again, darling. We should hate you for that really. Come and sit down on this stool and tell us all about it.'

Juliet squeezed into the corner and waved at a waiter, miming for a coffee. 'It's so good to see you both,' she smiled. 'I don't know where to begin, it's been one hell of a year so far, but yes, thank you Mark, I do feel better now. I know you're trying to tell me I looked like shit before.'

He shrugged but couldn't deny it.

'I've just been to see Maureen,' Juliet went on. 'She deserved an explanation. She was the only one who knew what had happened at home and even she didn't learn the full picture. And she hasn't breathed a word to you, has she? I'm so relieved. I couldn't have managed if you'd all been looking at me knowing what was going on.'

'Why, what on earth was going on?' demanded Mark, passing the sugar. 'All we knew was you were getting thinner and thinner and then you did your disappearing act. We thought you were ill. We were really worried.'

'I'm sorry about that,' said Juliet, slowly stirring her drink. 'I didn't mean to cause a fuss. I wasn't exactly ill. Just sick with anxiety, really. It was to do with my family.' She paused. 'Look, I know you all think I'm a spoilt bitch with no problems in the world but that's not quite true. I ran away from home because I couldn't stand it any more. My father was a wife beater and I couldn't take being there in the middle of it all, seeing my mother pretend nothing was wrong. I'd always wanted to go on the stage so I did this, partly because I knew it would annoy him the most. It did and he cut off my allowance. So I really did need the money.'

'We kind of guessed,' confessed Penny. 'We saw your flat.'

'Hardly a palace, was it?' Juliet said grimly. 'But it served a purpose. I could get by and keep in touch with my mother, and even visit occasionally after a while. But then when I went back over Christmas I could see something had changed, things had got worse. It turned out my father was very ill and they reckoned he hadn't got long. You'd think that would make someone weaker, wouldn't you? Well, it didn't. He got far worse, quite manic for a lot of the time, and my mother was in fear of her life. I didn't know what to do. Then one time I rang and she couldn't speak properly. She couldn't get her words out right, and at last she said he'd hit her round the head so hard she'd

367

lost some teeth and her mouth was too swollen to talk. So I decided enough was enough. She was still trying to nurse him. She didn't want anyone else in the house as they'd see what was going on. So I didn't really have a choice. I went straight home.' Juliet sighed and moved her spoon across the little table, making a small heap of sugar.

'So what happened?' Mark asked.

'It was awful,' she said. 'I don't want to describe it. I never want to see anything like it again. It was like a war zone. When he saw me, he went completely crazy and destroyed half the house, breaking things, throwing stuff, either at my mother or at me. I had to get the doctor in, who finally managed to sedate him. Then we got a rota of nurses to help. He didn't dare turn on them. I kept my mother out of the way. This went on for months. Finally he died. And I can only say I'm glad. Isn't that terrible?'

'No,' said Mark slowly. 'Well, it must have been terrible for you. But you couldn't have gone on like that. It sounds like, I don't know, a siege or something.'

'That's pretty well what it felt like,' Juliet admitted. 'Like we were shut off from everything, just waiting for the end. But when it did come my mother was heartbroken. It didn't matter how badly he'd treated her, she loved him. So I felt like a hypocrite. All a dreadful mess, really.'

'And what are you doing now?' Penny asked. 'Are you coming back to join us?'

Juliet shook her head. 'I don't think so. I used to love it but I was getting fed up even before all this happened. No, I'm going to go to drama school.' Suddenly her eyes lit up. 'I've been thinking about it for ages. It wouldn't have worked if I'd still been dancing and paying for that dosshouse but now I can look after Mum and we can

368

get somewhere together up in town. We're staying at Brown's at the moment.'

'Oooh, fancy,' said Mark. 'That's Mayfair, isn't it?'

'It is,' said Juliet, 'and you needn't look at me like that. Mum's hidden away enough. Now she can come back and see her friends from the old days and to be frank that's exactly the sort of place they'll expect her to stay at. She's having all her remaining teeth fixed and for the first time in ages feels like showing her face. So as far as I'm concerned she can do whatever she likes.'

'Yes, yes, of course,' said Penny. 'We're jealous, that's all. I'm glad you're doing that. But you will come to see us at the club, won't you? There are some new faces but you'll know most of them. They'll all want to see you.'

'I'd love to,' said Juliet. 'Not a word of this, all right? We'll say I've been looking after my sick father, which is true enough in its way. They'll understand that. And I've got to see Michelle. How's she?'

Penny and Mark exchanged glances.

'She'll tell you herself,' he said cryptically. 'Things have changed a bit for her too, since you've been away.'

Michelle was slowly coming to terms with the idea that her dancing days were numbered. She'd been lucky so far. Thanks to Mark's clever changes to her costumes she hadn't really begun to show, but this couldn't go on much longer. Dave would have kittens when he found out and would throw her out of the lineup. There was no way his punters would want to pay to see a pregnant dancer.

She sat in the dressing room, sipping a cup of tea and unwrapping a sandwich.

'Better lay off too many of those,' snapped Fifi as she wandered past. 'You'll be getting all lardy.'

'Shut it, you're just jealous of me curves,' Michelle hit back, but her heart wasn't in it. It was good that people assumed she'd been overeating but it wouldn't last. Then she'd have to face them all. There would be plenty who'd say I told you so. She'd definitely made some enemies among the other dancers and now they'd be circling to take her down. Well, she'd made her decision and she'd live with it. She'd known it wouldn't be easy and she'd just have to deal with it.

Michelle was shaken out of her thoughts by the noise of several people coming through the door and at first she couldn't believe her eyes. 'Juliet!' she called. 'Oh my God! You're back!' She ran across the room and hugged her friend hard.

Juliet hugged her back and then held her at arm's length. 'You're looking well,' she said. 'Sorry to have disappeared like that. I'll tell you all about it later but I've had to explain it twice already today and I'm sick of the whole bloody story. So tell me what you've been up to since we last met. Oh . . . maybe I can guess. Have I got this wrong or are you . . .'

'Shhh,' Michelle said, scanning the room. Mark and Penny had come in but Fifi had disappeared. 'Yes, you got it. Well done. I've been hiding it from everyone apart from these two and Maureen, but you've gone and found out my little secret.'

Juliet raised her eyebrows. 'Well, it's probably easier to hide it from people who see you every day. I haven't seen you for a long time and remember I've danced alongside you in the shows and in class for ages so I know your shape as well as my own. It's . . . rounder.'

'Thanks,' groaned Michelle. 'And it's going to get a whole lot rounder than this. I won't be able to shake it all about on stage when it gets to that point.'

'What are you going to do?' Juliet asked with concern.

'Have it then give it up,' said Michelle bluntly. 'Then maybe come back here, if Dave hasn't tried to kill me by then.'

'God, that's brave,' exclaimed Juliet. 'That's going to be difficult, isn't it? Do you think you'll be okay to go through with it?'

Michelle was about to give one of her usual wisecracks but something stopped her. Suddenly her eyes filled with tears. 'I have to,' she said. 'I know it's for the best and I'm not ready to be a mum. But I'm terrified. Absolutely bloody terrified. I know it's going to hurt like crazy and everyone's going to have a go at me.' She sniffed loudly. 'God, am I glad to see you. I don't care why you went away, you'll have had your reasons and you can tell me all about it another day. But I'm so glad you're back. I need you. You won't call me names or blame me. I need you because you're a real friend.'

For a moment Juliet said nothing then she reached across and grabbed Michelle's hand. 'I am,' she said. 'And don't you forget it. You won't be alone, I promise you. We'll help you get through this. Looks like I got back just in time.'

'You did,' said Michelle, smiling through her tears, and for the first time in a very long while she felt the heavy burden lift a little from her shoulders.

Chapter Forty-Three

Maureen put down the office phone and drummed her fingers against the desk. Almost there. It was all about contacts and she'd called on everyone she'd ever met who could be useful, and some of Dave's names as well. Finally someone had put her on the right track and now everything was nearly ready. She silently congratulated herself. It was all going to be legit and above board. While she had no objection to doing things otherwise now and again, this wasn't about her.

A burst of shouting outside was enough to tell her that Dave was back in the building and as she listened to whatever words she could make out, it sounded as if he'd realised the truth about Michelle at last. Men were so dense. Half the cast and crew had worked it out weeks ago, and the girl had been at the sharp end of their comments ever since. It was a good job that Juliet was back – ever since her return she'd been to the club nearly every day and had rounded on anyone who said anything in her presence. Most people didn't dare but it didn't stop them having a go once she'd left for the night to go back to her mother. Then Michelle was fair game for all the snide remarks and outright insults. She was more than paying the price for all her previous behaviour, Maureen knew. The others had resented her, and now they were taking full advantage, some of them secretly glad that it hadn't happened to them.

Well, now it was time to play her ace. Juliet had told her something very interesting when she'd first got back and Maureen had been waiting for the right moment to pass on the news. This looked like it.

The door crashed open and almost fell off its hinges.

'Do you know about this?' Dave shouted, face even redder than usual. 'I suppose you've all been laughing at me behind my back. That little tart has gone too far this time. I'll kill her for making a laughing stock of me. And she's been on stage! A wonder I haven't had complaints. What if they want their money back? She can pay that out of her own pocket, the lying little cow.'

'Relax, Dave, I'm taking care of it,' Maureen said, wondering how much he'd put away today already.

'What do you mean?' he demanded. 'How can you take care of it? You aren't a doctor, you have no idea . . .'

'No, not like that,' she said, yet again wondering what she'd ever seen in him. 'I mean I'm going to look after her when the time comes and sort things out. So there's nothing to bother you. Punters have had so much to drink half the time they can't see the girls properly anyway so if you haven't had any complaints yet then there probably won't be any. Besides, I've got some news you'll want to hear.'

'Not about any other girls getting into trouble, is it?' he thundered. 'I won't have it, this is a respectable establishment, not a bleedin' nursery.'

'Sit down a moment,' she said, not wanting him to get

so worked up he would forget what she was going to tell him. 'Take the weight off your feet, calm down and listen to me. You know the Ashdown development?'

'What, are you winding me up?' he snarled. 'That's dead and buried. Don't try and change the subject with that old crap.'

Maureen stopped herself from groaning out loud. She walked around the desk so she could face him head on. 'It is dead and buried. All very neatly squared with the planning department and no more said. But you did worry that they'd just try and get another site to turn into a club, one that would be easier to sort out.'

Dave looked at her in horror. 'They'd better not. Is that what you've heard? You ask me to calm down and then you come out with that? Are you mad? Don't you know what that will mean for the Paradise Club?'

'That's not what I was going to say,' she protested. 'The very opposite, in fact. I found out who one of the major investors in the project was. You won't have met him, he was very much behind the scenes, didn't want to get his hands dirty. Well, he's just died. The wife and daughter want nothing to do with the Ashdown group so they are well and truly done for. Isn't that good news?'

'How do you know all this?' Dave demanded, his face full of suspicion. 'Are you having me on?'

'Oh for Christ's sake, give me some bleedin' credit!' she shouted. 'Turns out the daughter is a friend of mine. Actually you know her too.'

'Don't talk soft, how am I going to know someone like that?'

'But you do, Dave. Remember Juliet, the blonde dancer who had to go and look after her sick father? That was him. He's now died and Juliet and her mother get all the money. They don't give a toss for the Ashdown lot, so you're safe. We're all safe.'

'Really?' It sounded as if he was still having a hard job believing it. 'That posh bird with the long hair? Didn't she drop us in it when she ran off?'

Maureen forced herself to speak calmly and not scream at him for being so ungrateful. 'It was fine. I sorted it, remember? She didn't have much choice. God, you should be thankful. If she hadn't gone back to look after him, he might have disinherited her and given the money to someone else, someone from Ashdown even.'

Dave nodded. 'Suppose so. Suppose that makes sense. Good.' He rubbed his hands. 'So there's no trouble brewing there, then?'

'None at all,' Maureen assured him with a big smile. 'Right, must be off. But I wanted to stick around to tell you the good news.' She moved towards the door.

'Excellent!'

She could see he was back in a good mood again and the danger of him punishing Michelle had passed, or at least for the time being. So she'd better act sharpish, find the girl and tell her the latest, before he changed his mind.

Summer turned into autumn and Michelle gave up any pretence of hiding her bump. She came into Soho less and less often as she grew more ungainly, but every week or so would turn up to see what everyone was doing. Juliet would usually join them in Bar Italia even though she had now started at drama school.

'Blimey, never thought I'd know anyone who went

there,' Michelle grinned. 'I must be going up in the world. Did you have to do an exam to get in or anything?'

Juliet shook her head. 'Not exactly. You have to do an audition.'

'You must be really good,' said Penny. 'Aren't they meant to be very difficult?'

'Depends,' said Juliet, pushing back her hair. 'I've spent most of my life pretending that everything was absolutely fine at home, acting my socks off day in, day out, so you could say it comes naturally.' She smiled. 'Silver lining or what?'

'That's one way of looking at it,' Penny agreed.

'Not bad for a dancer from the Paradise Club,' Michelle said. 'Ooof, I feel like a beached whale. Not sure how long I'll be able to keep on coming in to see you lot. This bump is doing my back in, even sitting here. I'll come next week but that might be it. I'm all set to have it in the Homerton hospital so I don't want to come too far west when I'm near my time.'

'You aren't due yet, are you?' asked Penny. 'Still a little while to go?'

'It feels like it could come any minute,' Michelle groaned, shifting uncomfortably in her seat. 'Suppose this is how it's meant to be but I can't wait to get it over with now. When I think of all the effort I used to go to to keep my figure.' She met their glances. 'I know, I know, this was my choice. I don't regret it. I'm just saying.' She shifted herself again, pulling a face. 'Anyway, how's the world of Dave's dodgy deals? Who's he putting the frighteners on now?'

'The really weird thing is, he seems to have calmed down,' Penny told her. 'I don't know if that's good or bad. It's so unlike him I don't want to say anything in case it sets him off again. I don't understand it at all.'

'Better make the most of it then,' smiled Juliet, keeping what she knew to herself. 'He's bound to be back to his old ways soon enough. Then you'll be longing for a bit of peace and quiet.'

'You got to admit it's odd though,' said Michelle. 'Wish I was there to see it. I'd say to give him my best but I don't suppose he'll want to know.'

'No, better not push things too far,' agreed Juliet. 'Right, time I was off. I know everyone thinks drama school is a doss but they actually work you bloody hard. So I'm off to put some hours in.' She leant across the table to hug Michelle. 'Look after yourself and see you next week. Ring me if you need me.'

'Oh, everything will be fine,' Michelle assured her. 'I was just having a whinge. See you next week, same time, same place.'

By the next week Michelle was feeling heavier than ever. She wondered if she'd be better off ringing her friends to say she couldn't come. Then she decided that it would probably be her last chance to see everyone before the birth and she didn't want to miss that. So she dragged herself onto the Central Line, glad it was at least cooler now. Somebody even gave up their seat for her and she smiled at them weakly. Be grateful for small mercies, she thought. You don't get that every day, even at eight months pregnant.

She got off at Tottenham Court Road and cursed every set of steps as she made her way up to street level. When she reached the ticket hall she had to stop to catch her breath. She was exhausted already. Glancing at her watch she forced herself to start walking, heading down Oxford

Street then cutting down a side road to Soho Square. There were some benches free and she sank onto one, just as she felt a strong cramp in her stomach. Must be something I ate for breakfast, she thought. I knew that new cereal Dad got in was dodgy. Serves me right.

There it was again. Was it really indigestion? It felt different somehow. She began to feel anxious. Was she going to be taken ill? Another cramp. It couldn't be. Not the baby. It wasn't due for another month. It was going to be born in the East End, not in Soho Square in front of all the winos. Better get to the café, she thought. Juliet will know what to do, she always does. She got to her feet and began to make her way to their meeting point, heading towards Berwick Street. At least nobody would expect her to pick up any bargains today.

Just as she reached the first of the market stalls, Michelle felt a wetness between her legs and suddenly liquid gushed out of her. She was standing in a pool of it and people were staring. But her stomach hurt too much for her to be embarrassed. Another even stronger cramp hit her and she grabbed hold of a lamppost for support. 'Nooooooooo,' she moaned. She couldn't think what to do any more. It was all too quick. She wasn't even going to make it to the café. This baby was deter-mined to arrive right now, in the middle of the street.

One of the stall holders nudged a man beside him, who came running over. She registered that he was dark-haired and very good-looking but she didn't care. 'Can I help?' he asked. 'Do you need a hand?'

Breathlessly she nodded.

'Can I get you to a hospital? We're not far from UCH . . .'

'No, wrong one,' she said. 'Need to get to the Homerton. No time. Aaargh.' Another contraction stopped her saying any more.

'What about anywhere round here? Is there somewhere you could go?'

Somehow, amid the pain and fear, Michelle remembered where Maureen lived. That would be worth a try. Penny wouldn't be there but there was every chance Maureen would be at this time of day. At least they had a phone. She gritted her teeth through the next contraction and then told him the address.

He looked a little surprised but all he said was, 'All right, I know where that is. Lean on me and we'll get you there.' Miraculously it seemed to work. He wasn't what she'd call a bundle of muscle but he half-carried her along the pavement to the familiar street door to the flat, and rang the bell.

'Who the hell is it?' came Maureen's shrill voice from the floor above. 'Hold your horses, I'm on my way down . . . oh my good God.'

Michelle looked up and attempted a smile. 'Baby's on its way already,' she said. 'Didn't have time to . . .' She didn't need to explain any more, even if she could have done. Maureen took a moment to absorb what was going on and who was on her doorstep and then said, 'Right, let's get you upstairs. We'll worry about anything else once we're there.'

Slowly she and the young man helped Michelle up to the flat, where she could do nothing more than collapse on the living-room floor, holding her stomach and groaning.

'Okay, let's make you comfortable,' Maureen said,

turning to the man. 'You know which is my room, don't you? Go and grab all the pillows from there and then some towels from the bathroom. I'll boil some water and then I'm phoning 999. They can tell us what to do down the phone while they send someone who knows what's meant to happen.'

Michelle almost fainted with relief when she realised that someone was taking charge and seemed to be doing all the right things. She sank back against the pillows and gave in to an overwhelming urge to push. She was aware of phone calls going on, and people arriving, but none of that seemed important. She just needed to push. She lost all sense of time as her body took over, seeming to know what it had to do to get this baby out. She dimly registered that a paramedic had come into the room and was getting everyone else out of the way. 'Good girl,' he was saying. 'You're doing really well. One more big push. There you go, that's baby's head out. And another, breathe, breathe, breathe . . . and there you go. Here she is.'

There was a pause and then a small cry that soon grew to a loud wail.

'Oh, she's a beauty,' said the paramedic, wrapping the bundle in a towel and handing it to her. Michelle looked down and saw a tiny face, with what looked like brown hair very like her own. 'Did they say she was early? Well, she's a very healthy early, that's for sure. Nothing wrong with those lungs.'

'Blimey, do they do this all the time?' she managed to say after catching her breath.

'For quite a lot of it,' he said. 'Now I need to tidy you up. If you'd like to hand her over to your friend . . .'

Juliet and Penny stepped in and between them took the baby girl. Michelle looked around for Maureen.

'Did you ring them?' she asked anxiously. 'Could you get hold of them?'

'Of course,' said Maureen. 'They're on their way. They've been ready for weeks, even if this one caught us all by surprise. So don't you worry.'

'Who?' asked Juliet. 'Do you mean Michelle's parents? What's going on?'

Penny looked at her friend and smiled. Once the paper-work had been sorted out Maureen had let her in on the plan and she knew that it was exactly the right solution to everyone's problems. But she'd been under strictest orders not to tell anyone else just in case anything went wrong.

'You'll see soon enough,' said Maureen. 'Why don't you let Penny take the baby and you ring the club to see if Mark's there. He'll want to know. Then we'll all wait here to see who turns up.'

Michelle had been led to Maureen's bedroom to rest after being examined by the doctor who'd finally turned up. Juliet and Mark were fussing over the baby, who had stopped crying and seemed content to sleep. Maureen was going through some files, apparently looking for something urgent that had gone missing. Which left Penny to face John.

'I don't understand it,' she said falteringly. 'Why are you here? I didn't realise you even knew Michelle.'

'I didn't,' he said. 'Not before today. It was a complete coincidence. I saw her nearly collapse in the street, as I was coming back from the magazine. She was on her own and crying out in pain. I couldn't just leave her there, could I? Then when I asked her if she knew anyone round here, she gave the address of Maureen's flat. So I couldn't exactly say no. I brought her here. I hope you don't mind. I didn't try to break our promise. You do believe me, don't you?'

Penny nodded. 'Of course. You couldn't exactly plan something like that, could you? That was an amazing thing to do, just step in and help a stranger like that. Heaven knows what would have happened if you hadn't. She might have died, or the baby might have, or both. It doesn't bear thinking about.'

'Oh, it's not as bad as all that,' John said, embarrassed. 'Someone else would have done what I did, I just happened to be right there. Now I think about it, it was frightening. I don't know anything about babies arriving. Hatching chicks are more my thing.'

'Good job you didn't think, then,' Penny said. She looked at him and smiled. Something felt different. She still had that sense of being closely connected to him and what had just happened made it even stronger, but she didn't feel as if her heart was breaking any more. She was just unbelievably glad to see him, and glad that he'd been the one to help in a crisis. How typical of him.

'Do you think,' she began hesitantly, 'do you think we might start again? As friends this time? I've missed you so much. There still isn't anyone like you. I don't want to make things awkward, but if you wanted to . . .'

'I'd love that,' John said, interrupting eagerly. 'If you think we can do it. I'd love to try. We've got something special together, it just isn't what we thought it was to start with. We almost got it very wrong. But it's been

382

months and I've missed you too. I feel different about you seeing you now but there's no getting away from the fact that you're my sister and we share something nobody else can. So yes, I'd really, really want to try.'

She didn't know whether to laugh or cry, and ended up doing a bit of both. 'It's all this,' she said, waving her hands towards the baby. 'A bit much, isn't it?' She gave a gasp and he hugged her.

'We'll be fine,' he said. 'And they'll be fine too.'

'Hope so,' Penny said, remembering. 'Michelle isn't going to keep her. She's on her own, her parents have masses of other kids, there's no room. And she can't go back to work until she's fit enough which might be ages. So I don't know . . .'

She was interrupted by the ringing of the doorbell.

'More people?' exclaimed Mark from the sofa. 'Where are you going to put them, dear?'

'It'll be them!' Maureen was delighted. 'And I just found that final sodding form.' She ran for the stairs and they could hear the door opening and excited whispering.

Then Lorna and Robert walked in.

'Meet the parents,' said Maureen simply. Her face glowed.

'Don't worry,' said Lorna, looking happier than Penny had ever seen her. 'It's all right. We've been planning this for months. It's perfect. Michelle didn't want to raise a child. Robert and I want a child more than anything else in the world. What could be better?'

'But can you do that?' Mark asked, astounded. 'Just take someone else's child like that?'

'Well, not just take them, no,' said Robert. 'That would be kidnapping. No, this is a private adoption. Michelle has agreed to it and we've got all the paperwork sorted out, largely down to Maureen here, who turned out to have friends in the most surprising places.'

Maureen raised an eyebrow.

'And before you ask, yes, it is all legal and above board,' she said. 'So let's introduce baby to her proud parents. Mark, bring her over here. Give her to me a minute.' She took the bundle and gazed at it. 'Right, I'm your Aunty Maureen. I warn you, I'll take no nonsense from you, as your birth mother drove me to distraction, and there's only so much of that one person can take. So you see to it that you're well behaved. But I reckon your parents will sort that out.' She grinned at her cousin. 'Here you go. Here's your daughter.'

Lorna stepped forward and held the baby, knowing at once how to support her tiny head. 'Oh, we'll sort you out all right,' she said, her voice full of love. 'We've had plenty of practice with that Penny. We've seen it all. So you'll never be able to shock us. We'll be there, whatever happens. Won't we, Robert?'

He came to stand behind her and put his arm round her. 'Whatever happens,' he said. 'That's a promise.'

Chapter Forty-Four

Penny grew more and more nervous the closer the bus got to the stop where John had told her she should get off. As they rounded the corner, she could see him waiting, looking up as he heard the bus approaching. He waved as he caught sight of her.

'You made it, then,' he said as she got off.

'I nearly chickened out. Will it be okay? Won't she think it's strange, me turning up like this?'

'I told you, she really wants to see you,' John said. 'It's hardly as if you've barged your way in without an invitation. Of course she wants to meet you, after all that's happened. Come on, this way. She isn't going to bite your head off, you know.'

Penny laughed but couldn't get rid of the feeling of butterflies in her stomach. She wasn't sure what to expect, even after John's reassurances. Gazing around she took in all the shops and restaurants, many of them looking new and smart. 'Nice round here, isn't it?'

John nodded but had a slight frown as he said, 'It's changing fast. Lots of new people moving in, mostly young professionals, and plenty of the old families are selling up. Sometimes I hardly recognise it.'

'Must be weird,' she said.

'It's not so bad for me as I didn't move here till I was about thirteen,' he said, 'but Mum and Dad really notice it. Still, it's not all bad. Mum sells all sorts of crafts in her shop and the new people love it. They buy that kind of thing when they're doing up their houses.' He turned off the main road. 'Down here.'

John led her towards a row of three-storey buildings and came to a halt outside a brightly lit shop. In the window was a range of colourful cushions and rugs, and a collection of artists' paint and brushes. 'This is it – Mum's shop.'

He pushed open the door and pointed her towards the back. 'That's the way up to the flat.' They went through, John nodding to the woman behind the counter and calling out, 'Hello, Lucy.'

The woman with the curly blonde hair smiled as she looked up. 'Nice to see you,' she said. 'They're up there waiting.'

'Better not keep them then,' he grinned, and pushed open the door, which gave onto a bright corridor. After a flight of stairs they reached another door. 'Here we are. You all right?'

Penny nodded. 'I'll be fine.' She hoped this was true as John knocked quickly and then turned the door handle. She knew it was too late to back out now but wondered what sort of welcome would await her.

Standing in the doorway to what looked like a living room were two figures.

'Mum, Dad, this is Penny,' John was saying, and she found herself face to face with a slight woman of about fifty, whose elfin features were breaking into a warm smile.

'Hello,' the woman said. 'It's lovely to meet you at last. John's told us so much about you. Come on in, sit down and we'll have some tea.'

The man stood back to let them through and Penny noticed he had a kind face but his nose was misshapen. He gave a short laugh as he saw her glance.

'So you're Jimmy's young friend,' he said. 'Don't worry about my nose, that was from years ago. My misspent youth in the boxing ring.'

She was briefly embarrassed that he'd caught her staring but then she realised he didn't mind. His pale blue eyes were twinkling.

'Just you come in here, and have that seat. I expect you'd like a bite to eat, wouldn't you, after coming all that way? Pearl, where's that cake gone?'

'Right there where you saw me put it,' said the woman, putting a slice on a plate and passing it to Penny. 'Try that. I'd love to say it was home made but to tell you the truth I'm so busy with the shop I don't often get the time these days, so Lucy made it.'

'We saw her downstairs,' said John. 'She's got a real name for her baking these days so we're in for a treat.'

Penny took a bite and understood what he meant. For a moment she was tempted just to sit and eat cake all afternoon, avoiding all the difficult things she wanted to ask. But that wouldn't do. She steeled herself to begin.

'Thank you so much for seeing me,' she began shakily. 'I realise it must seem a bit odd. I almost didn't come. But I did want to find out more about the man I believe to be my real father.'

The woman nodded. 'Of course you did. We understand. We thought you might want to do that and we're very happy to have you here.' She was studying Penny carefully as she spoke and nodded decisively. 'Derek, what do you think? I'd say there was no doubt at all. You look like Kevin Dolby's daughter to me.'

Derek looked at her for a moment without saying anything and then he too nodded. 'I'd say you're right. I know that might not be what you want to hear but you do look like him in lots of ways.'

'No, it's all right,' Penny said, tucking back her hair self-consciously. 'I'd much rather you said that than you weren't sure. At least I know now. It was the uncertainty that was so hard. Even when we added up the dates and worked it all out there was still a bit of me that couldn't believe it.'

'Stand up a moment,' said Pearl. 'You too, John. Come over here.' She pointed to the rug in front of the fireplace. A mirror hung above the mantelpiece. 'Now stand side by side. Penny, keep your hair like that. Do you see the resemblance now? And look at your ears. They're almost identical.'

They gazed at their reflections. Then John laughed. 'You're absolutely right, Mum.' He turned to Penny. 'How funny I never noticed. Come to think of it, I don't remember seeing your ears before.'

She shook her head. 'That's because I've always worn my hair down, apart from when I went to dance classes and you never saw me then. Even when I was going through my Madonna phase, I covered them up with headbands or scarves. So it's no wonder.' She laughed, overcome with relief. 'So it is true and we look alike. And I look like my real father. So I suppose you do too.'

'He's the spitting image of him,' said Pearl ruefully. 'He

was a good-looking man, was Kevin Dolby. I'll say that much for him.'

Penny took her seat once more and plucked up courage to ask the question that had been on her mind ever since the weekend in Margate. 'So . . . what was he like? My father – what sort of man was he?'

She felt a chill go through her as the other three exchanged glances. Then Pearl turned to face her directly.

'There's no point in lying to you,' she said. 'So I won't pretend he was a saint. He did some very bad things: he let me down and he let John down. You might as well know that he spent time in prison for burglary and worse. But over the years I've come to understand that there were reasons why he was the way he was. His mother spoilt him rotten when he was younger and he never had a sense of what was right and what was wrong. She made him think he could do anything and get away with it. By the time he found out he couldn't it was too late.' She sighed. 'Then he mixed with some very dodgy people, so there wasn't much hope for him.'

'I sort of guessed that bit,' said Penny, gazing at the carpet. 'Maureen let slip what sort of woman my mother was, before she reinvented herself in Spain, and I figured out she must have known some pretty dodgy people herself.'

'Well, we never met her so we couldn't say,' Derek pointed out. 'Pearl's right, though, your dad didn't have much of a chance with a mother like his. His dad was lovely but he was completely under her thumb. Kevin thought the world owed him a living and never understood the value of hard work. So he missed out on a lot. Bringing John up, for one thing.'

'I can't complain,' said John. 'I've got the best parents in the world. I used to wonder what my real dad was like when I was little and when he got out of prison I wanted to get to know him, but that didn't last for long when I realised what kind of person he was. He couldn't be straight with anybody – he was so used to lying to get his way that he just couldn't stop, even with his own son. So that made me understand that even though he was my biological father, Derek here was my dad in every way that really counted. He raised me, he taught me everything that was important about life, he and Mum made me the person I am today. So don't feel that you'll turn out like him. Just because you've got his ears doesn't mean you've got his character.'

Penny nodded slowly. 'It's hard to take in but I know what you mean. I've spent my life hating my mother and blaming her for everything. Now I'm beginning to see that a lot of who I am is down to Lorna – well, and Robert, but he didn't come along until a bit later. She was always there, from as far back as I can remember, and she doesn't have a bad bone in her body. Now she's finally got a baby she's going to be a fantastic mother.'

'Yes, but don't forget what they said,' John reminded her. 'They think of you as their daughter in all but name. So for everything that really matters, they're your family.'

Penny nodded again and felt tears gathering as she recognised that it was true.

'You can't choose your birth parents,' said Pearl slowly. 'I never knew my own mother until I was grown up. But you can choose who is important to you as you get older, whose beliefs you share, whose values are true ones. It sounds as if you have a lovely family, just not related to you.'

'And now I've got a brother.' Penny smiled even as a tear fell down her face. 'I can't tell you how much that means to me. One who's going to be a close friend as well. So I must be lucky after all.' She couldn't go on.

'And I hope you'll come to regard us as family too,' said Pearl seriously. 'I mean it. After all, I'm . . . what am I? Your stepmother? Something like that. You must feel you can always talk to us. Just pick up the phone. Or come here whenever you need to. The door will always be open for you.'

'Really?'

'Of course,' said Derek steadily. 'We've never had a girl to spoil in the family. We'd love one. I've got no brothers and sisters, neither has Pearl, so we haven't even got nieces or young cousins. It would be good for John to have some competition for our attention, wouldn't it, John?'

John nodded. 'I can recommend them, even though I'm biased. As families go, they're the best. What do you say?'

'I grew up thinking I had no one,' said Penny, smiling through her tears, 'and now I've got two sets of parents and a brother. I couldn't ask for more.' She stood and went to give Pearl a big hug. 'I'm so glad I came. I nearly didn't. But I feel I could belong here. It's the best feeling in the world.'

'So you won't be interested in John's latest news then,' said Derek with a wink.

'What's that? John, what's this about?'

'I was going to tell you,' John said, with a broad grin

391

on his face. 'Remember that magazine that sent me to Scotland? They want me to do another special for them, and guess where?'

She shrugged.

'They want me to go to Spain. Even better, they've found money in the budget for an interpreter and told me to choose my own. So how would you like a trip with me?'

'No, you can't mean it!' Penny cried. 'Back to Spain? With you? I'd love it, I can't believe it. Yes, of course I'll come with you.' She turned to him. 'Thank you. Thank you for everything. I could pick up some recipes, the stuff I remember from when I was little. Robert's always saying I should run a café or something and he'd help. Maybe I could have one that specialises in Spanish and Italian things. If my mother and my new stepmother can run their own businesses, why shouldn't I?"

'That's the spirit. And then you can come back here,' said Pearl, hugging her fiercely even though they were so different in height. 'You can come home.'